RIDE TO GLENCOE

Ride to Glencoe

JULIET DYMOKE

KIMBER FICTION

First published in 1989

William Kimber & Co Ltd is part of the
Thorsons Publishing Group,
Wellingborough, Northamptonshire,
NN8 2RQ, England.

Brith Library Cataloguing in Publication Data

Dymoke, Juliet. *1919-*
Ride to Glencoe.
I. Title
823′.914 [F]

ISBN 0-7183-0708-9

Photoset in North Wales by
Derek Doyle & Associates Mold, Clwyd
and Printed in Great Britain by
Billing & Sons Limited, Worcester

1 3 5 7 9 10 8 6 4 2

For Jane Aiken Hodge, née MacDonald.

The Massacre of Glencoe

The hand that mingled in the meal
At midnight drew the felon's steel
And gave the host's kind breast to feel
Meed for his hospitality.

The winter wind that whistled shrill,
The snows that night that cloked the hill
Though wild and pitiless had still
Far more than Southron clemency.

Sir Walter Scott

Chapter 1

'To Scotland? I'd rather you went back to Flanders than to that God-forsaken place.' Lady Standen regarded the upright and unbending figure of her son. 'There's naught but trouble up there and always has been.'

Richard Lincourt listened to this indignant speech in some exasperation. 'My dear Mother, I have to go where I am sent.'

'But Scotland! What possible reason can his Majesty have for sending you there?'

Richard hesitated before he answered. 'I'm to raise a regiment. I received the order from the King himself this morning to present myself to the Commander-in-Chief in Edinburgh.'

The news caused a sudden silence at the supper table and Richard was aware of his family's curiosity, for his orders were surprising to say the least. Outside in the Strand the noise of London was dying down though horsemen and carriages still passed by on their way to an evening engagement. The well-furnished parlour ran from back to front of the house and at the opposite end the garden sloped down to the river.

'Well, it is the most extraordinary thing I ever heard,' his mother said. 'I was sure you would be leaving with the King for the summer campaign in Flanders any day now. And I should have thought,' she added, 'that he had need of all officers as experienced as you. Why, you've been his friend for years as well as serving in his army.'

'I'm not indispensable.'

Lady Standen gave a petulant shrug. She had been a beautiful woman and now, in her late fifties, she still

7

retained her fair skin and delicate colouring, keeping about her that air of gaiety that had given her half a dozen suitors even during her widowhood in the difficult days of the Commonwealth that had followed the Civil War between King Charles I and his Parliament. She had married, at the instigation of her family, a certain Colonel Robert Lincourt of Heronslea hall in Gloucestershire and had found the years of marriage to that good and worthy man unbearably dull. With the birth of a son in 1659 and a daughter two years later she felt condemned to a quiet life in the country with a rather staid visit to London perhaps once a year. By the time he died, Charles II had staged a triumphant return and despite her loss she at once took herself off to London, leaving the children with their nurse, and under the patronage of her uncle, the Marquis of Winchester, went to court.

She was soon accounted one of its beauties, and with that indefinable attraction of a young widow had several offers of marriage. She chose Sir Walter Standen with whom she genuinely, as far as her rather shallow nature would allow, fell in love. He held a post in the Lord Chamberlain's office and her marriage was a happy one. She moved in London society like a slightly ageing butterfly and at the moment was concerned with finding a suitable husband for her only child of this second marriage, Nell. For her son Richard she had affection but no understanding whatsoever. That he should choose to join the army at the age of seventeen when he might have found a place at the lively and licentious court of King Charles was beyond her comprehension and that he should prefer four years later to transfer his service to the English regiment serving under the Prince of Orange in Holland simply exasperated her. The fact that the Prince was now King of England had, she was forced to admit, enhanced his career, and, to look at him now, he was at thirty-two in many ways a son to be proud of.

He had come straight from the Royal Mews and was still in uniform, scarlet coat with yellow facings, the large cuffs turned well back, long waistcoat and loose black breeches, a yellow sash across his breast, white silk stockings and black buckled shoes. He wore his own thick brown hair, cut short over his forehead and falling on either side of his shoulders, disdaining the fashionable periwig which he only adopted for very formal occasions and she couldn't blame him for King William had chosen for his most recent portrait to be painted wearing his own hair.

She didn't think Richard handsome but he had a pleasing face with dark brows set over dark grey eyes and a straight nose that widened at the tip. His mouth was well shaped but not full, only she wished he would smile more often for only then did the habitual serious expression lift. To him life was a serious business and to her it seemed he had little thought for anything but soldiering. This latest news seemed inexplicable to her while her husband was also puzzled, but he had never had any kind of a relationship with his stepson and sat at the other end of the table watching him with only a bored curiosity. Sir Walter was something of a fop in dress and manners and he and Richard had little to agree upon.

The table was laid with glittering glass and silver for he was a wealthy man, but the people gathered round were family and close friends and there was none of the formality reserved for outsiders.

Sir Walter said, 'I hope it will be to your advantage, Richard, but it seems extremely odd. Why should the King send you from him when you've been constantly at his side these ten years? Have you quarelled?'

'Certainly not,' Richard said sharply, but the question of the commission had been worrying him since the interview this morning. He had served under William of Orange both as officer and friend – an odd friendship and cool perhaps, for William was a cold man but Richard was as reserved as a man could be and they understood each other. It suited William to have Richard Lincourt's companionship on the hunting field and in the perpetual campaigns against the French; now he was sending him to Scotland, ostensibly to raise a regiment and though Richard would, as he had said, go where he was sent he both resented and disliked the order, his first feeling, justifiably, that a lesser man might go as profitably as he.

But there was more to it than that, which he was not permitted to reveal to anyone.

Eventually he said, 'If the King thinks the task suited to me, then I must go.'

'But I don't see the need to send you.' Judith Wilmington wrinkled her straight fair brows. 'Oh, I know you raised a regiment two years ago with Colonel van Wyngarde, but surely someone who is not in the King's immediate circle could go?'

'Perhaps Scotland needs his particular talents?' Sir Walter drawled and Richard disdained to answer this remark.

'Well, I think it is horrid for you,' Richard's young half-sister said. 'Why, Queen Mary told me that she and the King didn't wish to even when they were accepted by the Scottish people. She thought the cold up there would not suit the King's asthma.' Nell was lady-in-waiting to Queen Mary and at eighteen somewhat in awe of her much older brother, though she was at the same time devoted to him. 'Richard, pray do tell us more.'

He made an impatient gesture. 'There's nothing more to tell, Mischief,' he answered giving her the family nickname.

Judith's father, Lord Wilmington, elderly and in poor health, said, 'Perhaps it is indeed a task for a senior man.' He paused as a footman brought him a silver platter and helped himself to one slice of meat. He had been a close friend of Richard's father and the two families had been intimate for many years. 'I know little of Scotland, but it is undoubtedly a hotbed for the Jacobites, as King James's followers call themselves now. They are puffed up by their victory over government troops last year at Killiecrankie and though they lost their leader in Viscount Dundee their cause is far from dead. Is it perhaps that the King wishes to unite old foes under one banner and spend their energies fighting the French instead?'

'Exactly,' Richard said, hoping that would put an end to the subject. He fell silent, his eyes on his plate of excellent beef.

'Really, Richard,' his mother said, 'you can be very

tiresome. Can't you tell us more? Whatever you have said so far gives us no real reason why you of all men should be sent away from the King's side. And God knows if such dreary folk, from what I know of the Scots, should have any good society or dancing or anything delightful.'

'I don't imagine I am being sent there to dance,' he said drily and allowed himself a faint smile.

'Of course not, but you know what I mean. They say at court that the people in the north are all savages and Catholics and Jacobites into the bargain, and in the south of the country you will find no one but Psalm-singing Presbyterians.'

'Gossip,' Richard said, 'which may or may not be true. I'm surprised you are so knowledgeable about Scotland.'

'Oh, I listen to talk and that tiresome Sir John Dalrymple is always at court.'

At the mention of that name Richard's mouth tightened but he made no comment other than to remark that he supposed Ediburgh to be a civilized city to which his mother shook her head unbelievingly.

'What does Colonel van Wyngarde have to say to your going?' Lord Wilmington asked. 'I can't imagine he is pleased to lose his lieutenant-colonel.'

Richard shrugged. 'I would be having my own regiment soon in any case. And van Wyngarde has to accept the King's wishes, as I do.'

'How long will you be gone?' Judith asked and her father hazarded a guess that the business might take the whole summer.

Richard said he could not imagine that it would take less. He was aware that his inability to satisfy their quite reasonable curiosity had caused a tension at the dinner table and as a sop added that he was to go as a full colonel.

Judith said, 'Well, that's good news indeed. It will be a new experience for you, Richard, and I'm sure Edinburgh will prove interesting.'

'I believe it's dank and foggy,' Lord Wilmington said gloomily. 'No good for a man with the ague, but that's nothing to you, my boy.'

'I'd as lief be in the Hague.'

Richard's mother gave a studied sigh. 'Oh, we all know you think Holland the finest place in Europe.' Being a cantankerous woman, having wished he was going there, she now taxed him with not being enough at home. 'But it is time and more that you should pay some attention to your duties here. Why, Heronslea has been yours ever since you came of age and you show so little interest in it that I shouldn't wonder if it falls into ruins. You should marry and make a home of it again.'

He laid down his knife and fork and wiped his mouth with his napkin before he answered. He thought of his father's house with its memories, that mellow red brick mansion and its echoing emptiness and the silent rooms that he had once loved so much, hallowed for him by the memories of his father. His eyes were shadowed as he answered. 'I've no desire to bury myself in the wilds of Gloucester and I can trust our steward. As for my marriage – my affair, I think.'

'Your mother only wishes your welfare,' Sir Walter said languidly, and Richard inclined his head.

'I'm aware of that, but it's not a subject I wish to discuss at the moment. If I marry it will be in my own time.'

Nell said teasingly, 'Perhaps you'll fall in love with a Scottish lady and surprise us all.'

He gave her a brief glance. 'Mind your tongue, miss.'

'I'm sorry.'

She looked so confused that he relented and smiled across at her. 'I think it is your marriage we shall be looking to soon.'

She blushed and laughed and said, 'Well, at least our sister gives me encouragement for she is so happy with Frederick.'

'And expecting another little one,' Lady Standen added.

'Good God,' Richard said, 'how many does she have now?' He seldom saw Dorothy for she lived near the Wilmingtons outside Oxford, but he was fond of her, for they shared childhood memories.

'Five, as you know very well,' his mother answered, 'but with your being the only Lincourt left I'm sure your father would wish to see an heir for Heronslea.'

His face closed up and for once she refrained from pursuing the subject. But if only he would marry and fill a nursery! He must marry some time and surely what more suitable bride could there be than Judith who would, Lady Standen was certain, be willing enough? But Richard treated her as a sister. Once, long ago, when he was nineteen, Richard had seemed to look at Judith with more than brotherly affection, but he was always off soldiering and it had come to nothing. She sighed and decided to try once more to give him an opportunity to be alone with Judith.

Knowing her, he changed the subject by asking if she had been to the theatre lately, always a safe conversational topic.

'Oh yes, indeed. We took Judith and my lord here to see Killiegrew's *The Parson's Wife* at the Duke of York's, a naughty piece but it made us laugh a great deal.'

She chatted on and Richard was free to withdraw into his own thoughts, his mind being full of the unwelcome interview of this morning. Apart from the King and himself there had been only two other people present, the King's great friend and Richard's own colonel, Kit van Wyngarde, and Sir John Dalrymple, the Master of Stair and Secretary of State for Scotland.

The project was outlined to him by Stair, a devious man and brilliantly clever, whom Richard disliked as he had disliked few men. The Master was always at William's elbow, even travelling with him to Holland during the summer campaign, and Richard recalled the King's uncle, King Charles II, saying once that there was never trouble in Scotland but a Dalrymple or a Campbell caused it.

'You must understand,' the King had said, 'that Scotland is a thorn in my flesh, a backdoor to my kingdom where the French may land troops at any moment, to reinforce the Jacobite army, disintegrated as it is. Isn't that so, Master?'

'Aye,' Dalrymple agreed. 'With James in exile and plotting with the French King we must be constantly on the alert and to my mind the only way is to send more troops to Scotland and settle the Jacobite cause once and for all. The Highlands are a hotbed of unrest.'

'I am well aware of it,' William said tartly. 'There are seven troops of Horse and many more companies of Foot engaged along the Highland line as they call it. Why, it is being said, that I – *I*, who have held off the might of France from my Dutch borders, can't reduce a few savages to obedience.'

'If they're taken from the border there might be more trouble,' van Wyngarde suggested. He was a tall fair man with a quiet manner and he had known William all his life.

'Getting more of them into our uniform is one way to mend the matter and I want it tried. There is another way to be explored, however. My lord of Breadalbane, who is a Highlander himself, is to meet with the clan chiefs next month in an endeavour to bring them to terms with my government and if necessary to buy them off for I've heard the chiefs are avaricious people. Isn't that so, Master?'

'Aye,' Dalrymple said again, 'a man minds his bawbees in my country, but the Highlanders are more inclined to steal what they don't own. Siller will mebbe bring them to heel, but I doubt it.'

After a few more moments of discussion the Master departed to prepare Richard's letters of introduction, and when the door closed behind him, William turned to Richard.

'Now that we are alone, there is more I want to say to you. Sir John is all very well, but he is a Scot for all he appears to hate every Scot north of his own lands. I have a further commission for you. What I want is an agent, a man I can trust, on the spot to inform me of any movements, of men to be watched, of undercurrents of treachery.'

'A spy, sir,' Richard had asked harshly, in a tone he seldom employed to his King.

'An agent,' William repeated. 'I want you to keep your eyes and ears open. Report everything to me, every conversation that may be relevant. I cannot trust anyone there to be unbiased, but you will see that I hear the truth. I trust you, Lincourt, as I would trust few men. And no one is to know of this but myself and Colonel van Wyngarde. Direct your letters to my secretary Huygens.'

Richard glanced at his erstwhile colonel and van

Wyngarde smiled. 'I shall be sorry to lose you, Richard, but in any case you must have been having your own regiment soon.'

The fact that the two of them seemed to think it a reasonable mission to be sent on, offered some sort of encouragement, but to Richard it was spying and he bitterly resented being sent on such a mission when all he wanted was to return to Holland and live the life of a plain honest soldier. He knew nothing of Scotland and had no desire to learn more, nothing of the north-western area called the Highlands and he had a black feeling about the whole affair. What use would wild tribesmen who apparently robbed and pillaged and burned for a living be to him, and the Lowlanders were probably not much better? But such was his commission and he felt nothing but loathing for it. He had protested, made his feelings clear but it was to no avail, and where William commanded him to go, he would go.

Before he left he had a brief interview with Stair.

'You're an odd choice for the post,' Sir John had said bluntly, 'seeing you know naught of my country, but we must abide by the King's order.'

'He thinks I shall be impartial,' Richard answered rather tartly, 'which I shall.'

'No doubt, no doubt. Well, when you visit the Highlands with your drum ride west and acquaint yourself with Colonel Hill at the fort at Inverlochy, named Fort William for the King since it was rebuilt last year. He knows the Highland men better than many Englishmen and he will give you good advice. But keep away from the MacDonalds, you'll do no good there, particularly the Glencoe men. They are the worst of a rotten breed, a gallows herd who will rob you as soon as look at you or put one of their murderous black knives in your back. One of these fine days I trust we shall find a way of ridding the world of them once and for all.' His mouth had twisted in hatred and for a moment there was black passion in his eyes, but almost at once it was veiled.

With these ominous words ringing in his head Richard took his leave with a sheaf of letters tucked into his wide cuff.

He wondered whether he should go to the King, make one last appeal, but he knew William and the stubborn set of his mind once he had decided upon a course. It was the unpleasant secret part of the business that galled him and he looked forward to the next few months with nothing but gloomy foreboding. To most of his acquaintances the assumption would be that he had fallen out with the King and was being sent to do a job any colonel of the line could handle and though he cared nothing for mess-room gossip he jealously guarded his high standing in the army. It was all damned unpleasant and for the first time in his life his anger turned against the King. But there was no solution and he gave a heavy resigned sigh.

He became aware that supper was ending, napkins being discarded and his mother suggesting that Lord Wilmington and Sir Walter might enjoy their usual game of chess, their evening occupation whenever the Wilmingtons came to stay at Standen House.

'I must send Nell back to the palace in the carriage,' she went on, 'and as it's such a beautiful evening, Richard, why don't you escort Judith into the garden and take a stroll by the river?'

A flicker of a smile crossed his lips. She was so obvious. However he rose, kissed Nell on the cheek and then held out his arm to Judith.

Outside the lawns sloped down to the Thames and in the flower beds the tulips he had brought home from Holland two years ago made a fine display in the twilight of this early summer evening. For a few moments they walked in silence and he thought that one of the qualities he liked best about Judith was her restfulness. She was looking calmly at the river, watching the hoys and ferries moving on the water, her fair hair stirred by the light breeze and she had gathered up a shawl for her shoulders.

'This is a strange turn for you,' she said at last. 'You've not been from the King's side these many years. But perhaps you've had enough of discussing it. It can't be very pleasing to you.'

'No,' he said gratefully. 'Tell me about yourself, Judith. How have things been with you?'

'Oh, we had a quiet winter at Oxford, our main excitement being to entertain some of the Fellows to dinner. We
kept indoors during the very cold weather we had in
February. I never wanted the spring to come so much.'

'You saw something of Dorothy?'

'Yes indeed. There were one of two visits to the
playhouse and a very fine concert in January, but as you
know my father doesn't like going out at night and I only
went when Dorothy and Frederick made up a party.'

'Poor Judith, it sounds very dull.'

'Oh no, not dull – just as life usually is at home. Your
sister is a very good friend to me and her children are
charming.'

'I presume they thrive. They're always extremely noisy
when I'm there.'

'That's because the visit of a soldier uncle in a red coat
excites them. Little Jack is growing into big Jack, a stalwart
ten-year-old now, and your namesake whom we call Dick is
an imp of mischief.'

He wondered briefly how Judith felt when she visited
them, comparing Dorothy's state with her own. 'I half
expected,' he said abruptly, 'having been from home for a
year to hear perhaps of your betrothal.'

'But you have not,' she said lightly, her eyes on a barge
making its way down river. 'And you know very well my
father would be shattered if I left him, or brought some
stranger into the house.'

He paused before he answered. It seemed obvious what
she was implying, for he had a shrewd idea that Lord
Wilmington would indeed be pleased to accept him as a
son-in-law. Rather abruptly he said, 'Has there been no
one?' and then stopped, surprised at himself for even
asking such a question.

Not in the least embarrassed, Judith shook her heard,
but there was more colour in her cheeks. 'Richard, be
honest. I'm sure your mother sent you out here with me in
the hopes that we would reach an understanding but we
decided long ago that we had a firm friendship and no
more, didn't we?'

'Yes,' he said in answer to both questions. 'She can't bear

it that I should have reached my age with no attachment, but the circumstances of my life have been such – ' He broke off. 'But I wonder why you've not wed, Judith. I can't think so little of my sex that there haven't been a few who have aspired to your hand. You're a fine-looking woman.'

She gave a deep chuckle. 'You make me sound like a dowager. But I've had my reasons for refusing my suitors – oh yes, there have been a few – which, if you're not about to ask for my hand, and I'm sure you're not, I don't propose to tell you.'

'I'm sorry,' he said. 'I don't mean to pry. As for me, my heart belongs to no one, and I doubt I'm the marrying sort. I prefer a camp bed in a tent.'

She laughed outright. 'My dear, you need make no excuses. I understand very well that you are content as you are. As for me I'm independent enough not to marry when it is arranged for me but when I wish to do so. Scandalous, I know! In the meantime I'm very well as I am.'

'You've more sense than any woman I know,' he said.

'Thank you for that compliment, sir!' Then, more seriously, she added. 'But perhaps your mother was right about Heronslea. It is a shame that it is empty year after year. I've such memories of visiting there in my childhood.'

Richard stared at the water, watching a swan glide slowly past. 'After my mother married Sir Walter we only ever went there when there was plague in London. The place is a weight about my neck.'

'And yet I always thought you loved it.'

'I did – once.'

She looked at his face but could read nothing there. 'Don't you care for it now, even for your father's sake.'

At once she saw she had trodden on dangerous ground and she said quietly, 'Forgive me, but – Richard, why do you never want to speak of him.'

'I can't,' he answered, 'not even to you, Judith, though I can say more to you than to most people. But it's an old wound I don't care to re-open.'

'Very well,' she said gently. 'I think perhaps I understand.' But it was a very tenuous understanding. She had no memory of Colonel Lincourt and it was only a guess that his widow's flighty behaviour and lack of grief had somehow deeply offended and hurt the young Richard, child though he was, for that he had been devoted to his father, Lord Wilmington had told her. She judged it time to change the subject and asked for news of a friend of hers who had married a Dutchman, and their talk turned into less personal channels.

He followed her lead gratefully and as they began to stroll back to the house in companionable silence it occurred to him that if he must marry Judith would be by far the best choice. He thought, despite what she said, that she might be agreeable, for Lord Wilmington would undoubtedly accept him. And she would not ask too much of him. But it need not be yet and he closed his mind to the necessity.

He said, 'I've few close friends, Judith – you and Otwell Skinner perhaps, and the King I suppose,' he added as an afterthought.

She wanted to say that it was partly his own fault because of that deep reserve and cool manner, but it was more than apparent he was happiest in the company of soldiers. She doubted if Richard had so much as cast an eye on any of the Queen's ladies – he had told her William called them the 'beggarly bitches' which scandalized the court – though no doubt some of them had cast their eyes on Richard.

'How is Captain Skinner?' she asked.

'Well, as far as I know from his last letter. It is fortunate for me that after he was wounded at the Boyne, he should go home to Edinburgh. I've every hope of seeing him soon.'

'I'm glad he will be there to be at least one welcoming face,' she said. They had reached the house and as he held the door open for her she paused for one last look at the river over his scarlet shoulder. The peace of the night was settling on it, a few swifts diving over the slowly moving water, but she did not at the moment share that peace. She would never divulge her true feelings until and if an opportunity came and now yet another had gone. But she would wait, as she had waited since she was a girl, for Richard to see what they might have together. Patience was so much part of her nature that she was prepared to continue to exercise it, sure deep down that one day he would come to her.

In a rare impulsive moment she said, 'I must own I wish you weren't going to Scotland.'

'So do I,' he said.

Chapter 2

His first sight of Edinburgh was on a bright June morning. He had landed at Leith with his servant John Robb, his horses and baggage, an ensign and an escort of six men, and was now riding at their head towards the great mass of rock on which Edinburgh Castle stood, outlined against the blue of a summer sky. Below it was the Nor' Loch, the water sparkling in the sun and on the slopes of a high ridge the town itself, a tight huddle of houses leading down to the palace of Holyroodhouse, and he paused for a moment, taking in the outline of the place.

'A fine position to set a castle, eh, Fuller?' he said.

The ensign riding beside him was very young and very much in awe of his colonel. 'Aye, sir. The Scots chose well to build there. I'd not like to try an assault on that rock.'

They followed the road that led upwards and eventually came to the cross roads where the gate to the town divided the long road downwards. Being mid-day it was open and they passed under it into the High street. Richard drew rein for a moment. He thought London busy but this place must surely equal it for so much was crowded into a small space. The houses were packed together, some low and of wood and plaster and thatch, but others were stone tenements built tall to house Edinburgh's growing population, all living higgledy-piggledy, some of the tenements with six, seven, or even eight floors. At ground level many had shop fronts with shelves put up by day to display their goods and apprentices bawling at passers-by, extolling their masters' wares, goldsmiths, silversmiths, grocers and vinters, and here and there alleyways for the sale of fish or meat.

There were better houses belonging to the gentry, some riding out on their day's business, carts and carriers jostling the horses, busy housewives and men of trade all intent on their own affairs while beggars roamed and children whined for pennies. Occasionally a kilted figure passed, brown knees bare, scarlet and white check stockings on the legs, giving Richard a first sight of the tartan and John Robb gaped at what seemed to him outlandish dress. All this robust humming life was packed into the street and Richard and his escort had some difficulty in threading their way through.

On his left he passed a great church and there the road divided, a mass of building in the centre and narrow ways to each side of it. Stalls laden with goods attracted women with baskets on their arms while young men with empty pockets stared longingly at leather gloves, waistcoats and stockings.

Skirting the church Richard rode up into the Lawnmarket where clothiers and makers of all kinds of linen goods earned their living, and though as he went up he found much to admire in the buildings the filth underfoot seemed to him far worse than in London, the ground a morass of mud and unsavoury rubbish, the kennel running down the middle almost blocked by waste of all kinds.

John Robb, a phlegmatic man from the West Country, looked about him in some amazement. 'A man need lack for nothing in this town but being clean,' he observed, thinking of the Hague, and Richard nodded. Robb had been his servant for more than ten years and had acquired a certain respectful familiarity. Richard was vaguely fond of him as he was of his horse Juno or his favourite hound. Their conversation was always brief and to the point and the relationship suited them both.

At the Castle Richard presented his credentials, a deferential guard admitted him and he led his escort under the gate and up the slope, beneath several more defensive entrances following the man's direction to the Governor's house. Lord Leven was not there it seemed, but Sir Thomas Livingstone, the Commander-in-Chief for Scotland, would be pleased to receive Colonel Lincourt.

Richard was shown into a small stone-built room, cool

even on this warm day and a man rose from behind a table littered with papers. He was handsome, though his features were not strong, and he came forward with a smile.

'Colonel Lincourt, I received a letter from Sir John Dalrymple a few days sin' and you come hard upon it. I bid ye welcome, sir.'

Richard bowed. 'Thank you, Sir Thomas. I'm afraid I come as one very ignorant of Scotland and I'd grateful for any help you can give me in my task.'

'Of filching some of our young men, eh?' Livingstone asked in a jocular tone and Richard answered sharply, 'Not of my wishing, sir, believe me. I come at his Majesty's express order.'

'Lands sakes, man, I'm no questioning that. 'Tis just my bit o' fun,' Sir Thomas said easily. 'But pray be seated. You'll take some wine after your ride? 'Tis a warm day.' He had a decanter and glasses on a small table and poured the wine himself. 'Did you have a good journey?'

'A calm sea all the way.' Richard accepted the glass.

'I'm not much of a sailor myself,' Livingstone grimaced. 'I prefer to ride to London, far though it is, but I've not, thank God, been there more than twice. Have you brought any men with you?'

'A small escort, my horses and my servant. My captain and twenty men with an excellent sergeant are following to provide a knot of experience for my regiment.'

The commander nodded. 'Your men can be quartered at Leith and no doubt you'll want ground for training when you bring in your recruits – that can be arranged – but as for yourself I can offer you comfortable quarters here and my table for your dinner.'

Richard bowed, 'I don't wish to put you to any inconvenience.'

'Nonsense, we shall have some interesting talks, I'm thinking. No doubt you heard the news that Mons fell to the French and the King was forced to retreat. He had heavy losses, it seems.'

'I heard that the day before I left London. My men will be needed all the more.'

'Well, I'll give you all the help I can,' Sir Thomas said amiably. 'What do you know of Edinburgh?'

'Nothing, sir, but what I've seen as I came in.'

'A busy, bonny town, eh?'

'Certainly busy,' Richard agreed.

'But not bonny?' Sir Thomas laughed outright.

'As to that, sir, some of the buildings seem very fine but I've seen little yet.'

'Well, you've time to spare to find your way about.' Sir Thomas rang a handbell and a soldier appeared. 'Pray show Colonel Lincourt to his lodgings in the Queen's house.' And as Richard rose he added, 'I'll look forward to your company at dinner.'

Richard followed the soldier, collecting John Robb who, having found the stables, was now waiting outside the Governor's house with their baggage. They were conducted to a house on the far side of the upper courtyard and up the stair to a room on the first floor. It was small and panelled and sparsely furnished with a bed, a table and one chair with a few hooks on the wall for hanging cloak and hat and sword. A small chest stood by the far wall. The soldier saluted and withdrew and Richard went to the narrow window and looked out. On this side of the castle the rock fell sheer away to a lane below and beyond that to the chimney-pots of houses round an elongated square that he was later to learn was the Grassmarket. An impregnable fortress indeed, he thought.

Robb set about unpacking his gear and he stayed by the window trying to sort out the geography of the place. Robb had laid out his writing equipment, travelling inkpot and quills and paper on the table, and he sat down to record his impressions so far.

Dinner with the Commander-in-Chief was an easy-going affair, and he found Sir Thomas had with his pleasant manner an overt sense of humour that tended to pick up some of his remarks and make them an object of mirth. His host talked, however, in his strong Scots accent, a great deal that was of interest about the military situation in Scotland, about the recent fighting, of the patrolling by that bad-tempered but efficient man, General Mackay, about the Highland Line that separated north from south, behind which the clans lived their feudal and undisciplined lives, acknowledging no authority but that of their chiefs.

'But some of the chiefs are mighty civilized these days,' Sir Thomas conceded, 'Sir Ewen Cameron of Lochiel being a fine gentleman though in his past he's been as fierce as the rest. Why, he boasted to me once that he bit the throat from a soldier in a fight when he was young! Wild they are, all of them, for all their panelled houses and fine silver to eat from. But we must come to terms with them, by fair words or the sword, I care not which. The French have been seen off the coast of Skye this spring.'

Sir Thomas refilled Richard's glass with fine claret. 'Glengarry, sleekit fellow, has been occupying himself in rebuilding his defences – he lives in wild mountainous country west of the Great Glen, but you'll not know where that is. I'll find some maps to show you later. Colonel Hill, who's Governor of Fort William, seems to think the chiefs will stay quiet and give no trouble if they are persuaded with siller, but I think they will not. My Lord Breadalbane may bring them to heel, but myself I'd rather take an army into the Highlands to deal them a blow they'll not forget and I've written to the Master of Stair to tell him so, but he's away to Flanders now and God knows when I'll get a reply.' He laughed, rubbing his hands together. 'Who knows but I may have first need of your soldiers, Colonel.'

Richard listened, somewhat taken aback. Considering how badly the English soldiers fared at Killiecrankie, he thought this no way for a responsible general to talk of his command, and he said nothing.

Livingstone went on, waxing confidential and refilling his own glass again, for Richard's was untouched. 'Breadalbane was away to his castle at Achallader on Tayside last week and I believe he has a purse of twenty thousand pounds to try to pacify the chiefs who ever look to how much siller they've got. A Scot is awful careful of his siller, you ken.'

Richard sat taking in everything Sir Thomas had said and by the end of the meal had summed him up as a light man, overfond of jokes and puns and not of the discipline and gravity required by a Commander-in-Chief. Still, for good or ill he had to work under his auspices, nominally at any rate, and he asked a great many questions to fill up his ignorance of all things Scots.

'You'll soon learn our ways,' Sir Thomas said comfortably, 'aye, and I'm sure you'll raise a fine regiment. My letter from the Master speaks highly of your services in the Low Countries. Send your officer and recruiting sergeant into the countryside between here and Stirling to begin with. There's no doubt a few lads who can be persuaded by the sight of a uniform and the sound of the pipes and drums. Do you have a piper?'

'They're not easily found in London,' Richard answered with a faint smile.

'No, I'm sure of that. Well, my piper Jock MacPhail has a laddie who's a fair hand at the drones. He's no more than seventeen but a braw willing fellow and I'm thinking he'll serve you well.'

'Then I'll take him, sir, and thank you. He can come out with me for I intend to ride out myself most of the time.'

'Oh aye, if you take it as your duty, but if your captain's a good hand he'll do the work for you. When you've got your men 'tis time for you to make them into a fighting troop.'

'Which I mean to do,' Richard said, nevertheless intending to follow William's dictum that if a man wanted a job done to his liking he'd best see to it himself. He had no doubt of Captain Ripley's qualities; officers who had served under him knew the high standards he expected. Now he asked Livingstone to excuse him as he meant to get down to some paper work, asking for the proffered map. Sir Thomas looked surprised at this eagerness on his first afternoon, but he rang for an orderly and produced the map and also a survey of the Lowlands made by a zealous previous commander. Armed with these Richard retired to his room and burned his candle late studying them.

In the morning at breakfast he met other officers of the garrison, among them Lieutenant-Colonel Hamilton, a man with a hard face and a manner to which Richard took an instant dislike. Hamilton greeted him in a cool tone and made no secret of his surprise that an Englishman should come recruiting in Scotland when a Scot might do the work better.

Richard answered in the same manner that he imagined his Majesty knew what he wanted done, and the fact that his commission came from so high a source momentarily silenced Hamilton, but he subjected Richard to a long and penetrating stare while spooning porridge into his mouth.

A Captain Fletcher, lounging in his chair, said lazily, 'London's a far cry from here, Colonel. You'll find things very different.'

'I expected to,' Richard answered. As always he was more at ease among fellow officers.

'Your first command, sir?' a young lieutenant asked and Richard nodded, adding:

'I built up a new regiment under my last commanding officer and have some experience of the business.'

Hamilton shrugged. 'But then you don't know our Scots fellows.'

'We've had some in Flanders,' Richard retorted. 'Put a uniform on them and they fight as well as anyone. And,' he added, 'from what I heard they love to fight. Were any of you gentlemen at Killiecrankie fight?'

'Oh aye,' Fletcher told him. 'I was serving under General Mackay then and a drubbing Dundee gave us. You'd never ken the sight of Highlanders charging. They throw off their philabegs which are mighty heavy and tie their shirt-tails between their legs and they carry great targes, shield with metal spikes that can spear a man to death, as well as claymore swords and murderous dirks in their belts. Oh, they look mighty fearsome and waste their breath yelling their clan battle cries; they're braw, Colonel, mighty braw. God knows what would have happened if Dundee had not been shot. Maybe we'd be having King Jamie back in Scotland by now.'

'Nonsense,' Hamilton said sharply. 'Our forces soon

rallied, and half naked wild savages have no discipline. As soon as they have a victory they march off home with all the plunder they can carry.'

'They've better generals now,' Livingstone said, 'and chiefs like Lochiel have learned something of strategy. And they'll follow their chiefs to hell and back. I doubt you'll get men in the Highlands, Colonel.'

'It's scarcely worth the trying,' Hamilton put in. 'Stealing is the only thing they understand, and I shall urge Colonel Hill to be more stern with them.' He paused and added, 'I'm to be deputy governor at Fort William shortly.'

'I see,' Richard finished his coffee, 'but I mean to carry out the commission that has been given to me in the best way I can.'

'Without the benefit of experience from those that know the Highlands I may say a great deal better?'

'As to that,' Richard said coldly, 'I have no doubt Sir Thomas will support me in my efforts, and Colonel Hill too when I ride west.'

'Of course.' Sir Thomas hastily smoothed out the awkward moment. 'If the King wants Colonel Lincourt to try the matter my only advice is that he wait until after my lord of Breadalbane's meeting with the chiefs. If he brings them to heel there may be many a braw lad eager to fight overseas. In the meantime, Colonel, may I suggest Lieutenant Johnstone acts as your guide to Edinburgh today – that is, if you wish it?'

Richard would have preferred to go alone but it would have been churlish to refuse the offer and the young lieutenant blushed with pleasure. He was Edinburgh-born himself and eager to show off his town to the new arrival. He spoke such broad Scots that Richard found many of his words hard to understand, but he liked the lad's enthusiasm. They set off together on foot and his guide took him first down a set of steps to a wide street. This was the Grassmarket that he had observed from his window, and there was in fact a market in progress, stalls set up all through the open space, carts from the country trundling in with fresh milk and eggs and butter, chickens and ducks. Some of the houses here were fine stone buildings and seemed to echo back the din of the market, while round the White Hart Inn were groups of men doing business over drams of whisky.

Richard learned that the alleys leading from one street to another, from the Lawnmarket to the Upper Bow, from the High Street, to the Cowgate, were called wynds, that the courtyards through archways behind the main buildings were closes and that a property was called a land. Lieutenant Johnstone conducted him to St Giles 'kirk' as he called it, the fine church in the High street which Richard had passed yesterday and which was Edinburgh's chief place of worship. Inside he saw the tomb of the great Marquis of Montrose who had fought so brilliantly for the Royalist cause in the Civil War and he thought of the monument to his father in the church at home, a soldier of the opposite cause.

'Have you seen any action?' he asked abruptly and the lieutenant answered eagerly:

'Yes, sir, at the rout of Cromdale last year when we caught the Highlanders unaware. They'd raised the standard for the Stuart, you understand, but they hadn't posted proper sentries and we soon had them on the run. Sir Thomas led us at a gallop out of the mist and I never enjoyed anything so much in my life, only it was over too soon.'

Richard smiled at this youthful enthusiasm. 'No doubt you'll see more action in due course. If my Lord Breadalbane makes peace in the Highlands perhaps you'll come to the Low Countries. In fact, I wonder if Sir Thomas could spare you to me? Would you care for that?'

The young man's face was creased with pleasure. 'I'd like it fine, sir.'

'Well, I've no lieutenants yet, so I'll speak to him about it.'

Gradually they make their way down the hill, pausing at the Royal Coffee house for some refreshment. Through the crowded Netherbow Port they came out into the Canongate and went down past the Royal Mews to the Palace of Holyroodhouse. It had been an abbey, Johnstone explained, and was now the King's residence in Scotland

and the place where a great deal of the nation's business was done. There was open parkland to the right of it – 'a pleasant place to ride' the lieutenant said and added shyly, 'perhaps I might accompany you there some time, sir, if you would like to ride.'

Richard agreed, liking the young man, and suggested that Johnstone might show him a good inn to take their dinner, insisting on paying the reckoning afterwards. Learning he had been in Flanders for many years the lieutenant asked eager questions about the campaigns while they ate a dish of haddock followed by mince collops, simple food but to Richard's taste, and as they walked up the hill afterwards Richard surmised that Johnstone had the right attitude and the physique to make a good officer. Strolling past the Mercat Cross and the stinking entry to the fish market, he paused at the Luckenbooths to buy himself a new pair of Spanish leather gloves. Again the noise and the dirt of the place made him think longingly of the Hague where the people and their work places were clean and the streets properly swept every night. He was jostled by a small ragged urchin and had to remove his silk handkerchief from the boy's clutches, administering a smart box on the ear with his other hand. The boy ran off, howling, and Lieutenant Johnstone grinned and said, 'The place is full of thieves, even wee bit laddies like that.'

'It's the same in London.' Richard replaced his handkerchief and kept his purse out of reach.

'This is the Tolbooth.' Johnstone reached to the large building set in front of St Giles which Richard had seen yesterday.

' 'Tis part meeting place, but mostly serves as a prison now.' He led Richard round to where a portion of the first floor jutted out, the roof flat and railed. 'You see that? 'Tis where they execute traitors. I saw the Earl of Argyll, father to our present earl, beheaded there and a fine brave show he made of dying.'

Richard glanced up at the grim place. It put him in mind of Newgate in London though it was much smaller.

He had seen executions in his time, one or two among his own men hanged for plundering or rape, but it was not a spectacle he enjoyed and he made no comment. At the castle gate he thanked the lieutenant for his offices as a guide and the lieutenant looked extremely gratified. He hoped the Colonel would not forget his offer to take him into his new regiment.

At supper that night Richard sat next to Lieutenant-Colonel Hamilton who asked him a great many probing questions about what service he had seen. Richard answered in monosyllables and in return pressed a few of his own. It seemed Hamilton had been in Ireland and Richard enquired in what regiment.

'Cunningham's,' was the answer. 'I'm here to await orders to proceed to Inverlochy. In the meantime I command troops to reinforce Colonel Hill's regiment. I gather they're much needed.'

Sir Thomas Livingstone overheard this remark. 'Colonel Hill has done well to make a force out of the remnants and riff-raff we spared him,' he said and the corners of his mouth turned up. 'I'm told he parades them in the glens to make some show of authority.'

'It's time and more to teach the Highlanders a lesson,' Hamilton said in a taut voice. 'Insolent, saucy fellows. I've no time for them and the sooner we root out the worst of them the better. If Colonel Hill thinks to win them with fair words, as I gather he does, then I hope to wean him away from such a course and show them cold steel. It's all they understand.'

Richard was listening to this exchange and searching in his mind for what Cunningham's regiment meant to him. He was sure there had been some scandal concerning it that had reached them in Flanders a few years back. He gave Hamilton a swift glance and at that moment Hamilton looked across at him. Their eyes met and held, both cool and appraising.

Then Captain Fletcher, who appeared to have drunk rather a lot, made a remark and both men turned away.

Later when they all rose to retire, Sir Thomas clapped a

friendly hand on Richard's shoulder. 'I hope you've begun to form a favourable view o' we Scots. We're no such a bad lot.'

He laughed and Richard had no idea what to reply to such a remark, so he merely said, 'I thank you for your welcome, Sir Thomas. And Lieutenant Johnstone was a most helpful guide. I must confess however, that I found the accent and some of the words used by the innkeeper and the sellers at the booths very difficult to understand. Which brings me, sir, to a request I'd like to make of you. I'd like to have Lieutenant Johnstone with me; he would be of the greatest assistance. Do you think Lord Leven could be persuaded to release him to me?'

'Well,' the Commander said, 'you don't waste time, I'll give you that. But I can't see any difficulty there and I'll certainly speak to his lordship when he returns. I'm sure he'll agree.'

'Thank you,' Richard said and retired to bed.

Captain Otwell Skinner and his wife lived in a close named for Lady Grey who had a house there, and Richard had no difficulty the next day in finding it, a man with a cart having directed him reasonably intelligibly. Entering through an archway from the High Street he found himself in an inner courtyard. The house that had belonged to Lady Grey was a fine stone building but crowded around it were tall tenements obviously packed with people, for washing hung from the windows, babies cried, children rushed in and out and women sallied forth with baskets on their arms. He stopped a man carrying a tray of bread and enquired for Captain Skinner. He was shown a door up two steps at the bottom of a circular stairway.

It was opened by a pretty woman with dark hair tucked under a neat white cap and with a baby cradled in one arm.

'Mistress Skinner?' Richard asked. 'We've not had the pleasure of meeting before but I'm Colonel Lincourt.'

He heard a shout from an inner room and the next minute Otwell Skinner swung himself into the entrance on a pair of crutches. 'Richard! I've been expecting you ever since your letter came. It's the most marvellous fortune that you should be sent here. This is Alison, my lady, and there's my fine son to greet you – and he bears your name.'

'Mistress,' Richard took Alison Skinner's free hand and put it to his lips, then he looked down at the baby, no more than a few weeks old with a puckered face and closed eyes, long dark lashes on pink cheeks. 'I'm flattered, Otwell. I must see about a gift for my namesake.'

Otwell's homely face was shining with pride. 'Come away in and have a dram. It's so good to see you, Richard. I'll not deny I miss the army days.'

He led the way in to a small room which served as a parlour and indicating a chair for Richard lowered himself into another, setting his crutches to one side. 'Alison, I'll hold the bairn while you find us some cups. Isn't he a fine young fellow, Richard?' He rocked his young son in his arms, smiling down at him with a look that despite his crutches and obvious lack of means suddenly caused a twinge of envy in Richard's mind. He had seen his sister with her children often enough and found their squawling tiresome but there was something in Otwell's face in this plain setting that seemed to him strangely appealing.

Alison brought the cups and took the baby away into a farther room. As he filled them Otwell said cheerfully, 'Usquebaugh! You'll have to take to whisky up here.'

Richard accepted the cup. He was not fond of whisky but allowed that it was an invigorating drink and found its way quickly to a man's head. A quick glance round had shown him that these lodgings were poor quarters and he said, 'How are you faring, Otwell? I hope – '

'Oh,' Otwell broke in, 'it's no so bad. Let's be honest, as we always have been. I've little money but we manage. I teach the sons of grand folk and Alison does fine embroidery to sell to a stall holder in the Lawnmarket. We are more than fortunate to have three rooms to ourselves. Above us there are twelve folk living in the same quarters.'

Richard thought of the huge empty rooms at Heronslea. 'I can see you're well contented and with such a wife and babe I'm not surprised.'

'It's time you took a wife,' Otwell said, and grinned at him, 'or are you wedded to the army, I wonder? You'll stay for your dinner?' And when Richard said he would like to do so if it was convenient, Otwell laughed again and said, 'When would it ever be inconvenient for you to be a guest in my house?' And he said it for all as if he lived in a mansion.

'Now tell me why you are here and allay my curiosity. Your letter was the greatest surprise. I made sure you'd be in Flanders by now.'

Richard told him what he could and wished he could reveal the further commission that troubled him so much.

'It's an odd thing to send you to do,' Otwell remarked. 'There must be plenty of officers who can go recruiting.'

Richard shrugged. 'The King seemed to think it needed my special talents, whatever they are.'

'But you're his friend, not just a senior officer.'

'I know that. But he wants me here to do what I can. He feels he's threatened by the unrest in the Highlands. Did you know the French have taken Mons and William's had to retreat? Any more setbacks and we'll be seeing French ships around the coast. He needs replacements urgently.'

Otwell said, 'It's still a damned odd thing. I suppose it may work, putting divided loyalties together, especially if the chiefs come to terms but from the talk I hear it's not all that likely. Major John Forbes from Fort William was here a while back – I've known him for some time – and he says that if Colonel Hill is left alone he can do the job better than anyone of keeping the Highlanders settled. What men are you getting to start with?'

'Captain Ripley and Sergeant Morrison, he has Scots blood, and a couple of dozen men. Some aren't here yet.'

'Well, I like Ripley, though he has little to say. I never knew such a clammed up fellow. Morrison is the best sergeant we had as far as I recall and he's recruited before.'

'Yes, more than once, but – ' Richard paused, leaning back in his chair, 'I can't hide from you that I mislike the job. I can't help wishing a Scot were doing it.'

Otwell gave him a wry smile. 'Maybe, but I can see the

King's thinking on this, though I detect the hand of the Master of Stair in it as well. Up here you can raise a Lowland regiment, or like Argyll a Highland one among your own people, but to mix the two! You don't know this country yet, Richard, and I tell you I'd not like the task. You'll get your Lowland men but if I were you I'd take my recruits solely from them. The Highlanders will give you nothing but trouble.'

'The King thinks,' Richard said slowly, 'that if Lord Breadalbane gets the chiefs' submission to the Government at this meeting with them, there'll be peace. They may be bought off, you know, and then I might get men from the west.'

'It's a big "if",' Otwell told him. 'I wish I could see what Dalrymple has to gain by this. He does nothing without a secret and devious reason, that man.'

'It's William's scheme. The Master only did what he was asked and I don't think he liked it much.'

'I'm not surprised. He hates the Highlanders.' Otwell leaned forward and refilled his guest's cup. 'And he is equally hated up here – by the Presbyterians for being King's Advocate under King James and by the Jacks, that's what we call the Jacobites, for turning his coat. A slippery one, that! More than one hothead has threatened to pistol him one day when he rides down the Canongate to Holyroodhouse. But he's seldom here now.'

'He stays by the King to advise him on Scotland,' Richard said. 'I've to see his father as a matter of courtesy and I also have a letter to Viscount Tarbat, though what good that will do me I don't know.'

'Nor I,' Otwell grinned, 'too exalted society for me, but people speak well of him. He's a MacKenzie,' he added, 'and may be will tell you more about the Highlands. I suppose you'll be meeting the Earl of Breadalbane some time. Nobody cares for him except his own Campbells.'

'Otwell, you're a mine of information. How do you know so much?'

Captain Skinner's smile widened. 'Why, I'm tutoring a couple of talkative Campbell lads, and I go nearly every day to one or other of the coffee houses – the Royal by

Parliament Close is the best. I like to talk to folks and if I can't be active any other way at least I can hear all the latest news.'

'Thank God you're here,' Richard said, 'You'll save my sanity.'

'It would take more than a few quarrelsome Scots to upset that, you old sobersides. Have your fellows arrived yet?'

'No, I don't expect them for another ten days or so.'

'Then spend some time with me,' Otwell said. 'It'll be like the old days. I'll take you to St Giles on Sunday to hear a good sermon – we've some hell fire preachers, I can tell you – and to coffee houses where you may get to know something of Edinburgh folk, one particularly that the Killiecrankies use, but you'll have to discard that uniform.'

'Who the devil are they?' Richard asked.

'Jacobites who call themselves so after their victory at that pass. Oh, they don't make a rumpus but they meet there all the same. You can see them whispering in corners or creeping up the stairs to a room they use. And more than one great lord who ought to know better has flirted with their cause. I've seen both Lord Crawford and Lord Murray there but I doubt they're involved too deep. Spying more like. And I heard one of them boast that he'd been talking with Lord Breadalbane, though *he's* always at odds with Lord Murray, some quarrel about land, I think.'

Richard gave one of his rare laughs. 'I can see you keep your eyes and ears open. Shall we go out tomorrow morning if you've no pupils? And I'll come soberly dressed.' He wondered how Otwell got himself about the town but he obviously did and Richard could not but admire the way he made light of his disability.

The dinner was a modest meal of boiled mutton with a spicy sauce but Richard enjoyed it far more than he would a more elaborate affair. Alison Skinner was a charming woman, her care of Otwell and her baby occupying her time. Together they bore the disappointment of his lost career and their reduced circumstances with no trace of self-pity and he felt warmed by their obvious pleasure in his arrival.

As he was about to leave he suddenly asked, 'Otwell, do you remember anything about Cunningham's regiment? There's an officer of his at the castle and I've been racking my brains as to what happened to Cunningham for I'm sure something did.'

'He was cashiered,' Otwell said. 'Don't you recall? It was two years ago, I think, in Ireland. Cunningham's was sent to relieve Londonderry and he landed his troops. Then he didn't think it could be done and despite messages from the townsfolk that they could hold if he assaulted the place he re-embarked his men and sailed back to Liverpool. He was court-martialled for that and his senior officers were tainted with the same charge of cowardice in everybody's thoughts even if they got off free.'

Richard walked back to the castle very thoughtfully. The rememberance of the incident did not make him like Hamilton any better.

Chapter 3

During the next week Richard began to grow accustomed
to his surroundings, and accustomed to being awakened
every morning by the sound of Reveille being played on
the bagpipes, a sound he at first found too like the
screeching of a barn owl, but he began to get used to it and
even to recognizing some of the tunes, for he had always
had an ear for a catchy song.

He went out to Leith on Sir Thomas's advice and
arranged quarters for his men; he also found a suitable
piece of open ground for the drilling of his recruits. From
a draper in the Lawnmarket he ordered his standard,
green with a white scroll and the words *Fidelitas et Fides*
embroidered on it, as well as other smaller standards in
green with white mullets on them numbered according to
seniority for his company officers.

The evenings he spent mostly with Otwell, astonished at
the way his friend swung himself along on his crutches,
and it relieved his sense of exile to have at least one old
acquaintance in this grey city.

He called one morning on Viscount Stair and found the
Lord President a dry old man, affable enough but politely
remarking that he did not see how he could be of service to
Colonel Lincourt, with which sentiment Richard privately
agreed.

Lord Stair had been the most brilliant lawyer Scotland
had ever produced and had written books on the law, but
their conversation was stilted and Richard was glad to
escape from the stuffy parlour. He found George
Mackenzie, Viscount Tarbat, a far more pleasing
acquaintance. Tarbat was tall and still at sixty an

exceptionally handsome man, cultured and aristocratic, witty and amusing. He was more foppish in dress and manner than Richard cared for but he couldn't help liking the man. He was presented to him one windy morning at the castle gate and when he explained his reason for being there and produced his letter of introduction Tarbat promptly invited him to supper that evening.

Richard accepted and dressed carefully, not in scarlet coat, but in his dark blue satin and on reaching the Viscount's fine house in the Cowgate he was glad he had taken trouble with his appearance for the evening had obviously been arranged before he had received his own invitation. Quite a large company of Edinburgh society was there. The first person to whom he was introduced was the Earl of Melville, a great contrast to their host, being short with a large head and ugly features, but they seemed to be good friends. It was here Richard also met Lord Leven, Melville's son and Governor of the Castle, returned from his visit to his estates at Lasswade on the Esk. Leven was a far more prepossessing man than his father and interested in military matters, having raised his own regiment and he and Richard talked on the subject for some time.

The quarrelsome Lord Murray was also there, professedly William's man and a Whig in opposition to the rest of his clan, but Richard summed him up as one person he would not be inclined to trust. There were no ladies present tonight and Richard sat listening to the talk with the uneasy thought that he must report to the King anything he heard that might be of interest. He did learn things about the men of this country, so unknown to him, but nothing of much moment until the talk turned on the meeting of the Chiefs at Achallader, Breadalbane's castle overlooking Glen Tulla.

'I've little hope of a good outcome there,' Lord Melville said cynically. 'What can bring men like Keppoch and Glengarry and MacIain to heel? Plunder and raiding and killing are their way of life.'

'Twenty thousand pounds sterling might do it.' Tarbat was leaning lazily back in his chair at the head of the table, and a glass of excellent red Bordeaux in his hand. ' 'Tis no small sum.'

'And my lord Breadalbane can pe persuasive. After all he's Highland like themselves,' Mr Crawfurd put in, but Murray pulled a grimace.

'Oh we all know Iain Glas – Grey John, Colonel Lincourt – he would be all things to all men.'

There was some knowing laughter at this and Tarbat added, 'Well, he knows his own people. Locheil has a great deal of sense and may well carry the rest.'

'It's an odd situation,' Leven remarked. 'The last time MacIain of Glencoe was on Tayside it was after they'd been sent running at Cromdale and his thieving MacDonalds stripped Campbell lands. Why, Campbell of Glenlyon had to earn his bread with a commission in the army for the wretches left him naught in his cupboard and no cattle in his fields – and Breadalbane is a cousin of his. No one can pretend there will be much goodwill at Achallader.'

Suddenly Melville banged his fist on the table. 'That sort of raiding must stop. We've been plagued for centuries by the wild men of the glens and it's time to put an end to it. Why, in a few years we shall be in the eighteenth century, not the fifteenth.'

There was a short silence. Tarbat being Highland himself might be supposed to understand the passionate nature of the Gael, his independence, his scorn for Lowland Governments, but it was he who passed the decanter round and said smoothly that a stop to hostilities had been ordered until after the meeting and that he imagined Lord Breadalbane able to achieve some sort of treaty with his old enemies who might well be bought for a scrap of paper. He changed the subject by asking Richard to tell them of last year's campaign against the French.

When the evening ended Richard walked back to the Castle with John Robb attending him and bearing a torch, his mind storing up all he had heard. They had left the Cowgate and emerged into the High Street by way of Blackfriars Wynd to find few people about, the place dark and noisome, the gutter swirling from the recent summer rain and carrying away cabbage stalks, eggshells, fish heads and discarded butchers' pieces, and the smell was singularly unpleasant.

Above Richard's head a woman yelled, 'Gardy loo' ' and threw out a bucket of most unsavoury slops. Richard dodged aside, cursing, and John Robb shouted back a pithy request to her to watch what she was doing. They had passed St Giles and the entrance to the Skinners' lodging when from an archway opposite they heard a sudden cry and the sound of a scuffle. Two figures emerged from the close and seeing Robb's torch ran off down the hill. It was too dark to see much, the torch not illuminating the entrance, but they heard a groan and Richard said, 'Come, Robb. There's someone in trouble.'

He crossed the road and in the archway of the close Robb held the torch high. A young man lay on the ground, clutching at his chest. He was trying to rise and gasping with pain as he did so.

'Let me help you,' Richard said and got an arm round his shoulders while Robb put out his free hand to steady the young man on the other side. Between them they got him up and Richard wondered whether he was hurt or drunk. Then he saw the blood trickling between his fingers.

'Those ruffians!' he exclaimed. 'What have they done to you?'

'One of them had a knife,' the young man said faintly and Richard could see now that he was very young, no more than eighteen or nineteen. He supported him as best he could and opening his coat he saw blood coming from a wound below the shoulder.

The lad was swaying dizzily. 'I – I think they took my purse, though little good they'll get from that – a few shillings was all I had.'

'I'm sorry we were not here in time to catch the fellows,' Richard said. With expert fingers he pulled the shirt apart and Robb held the torch closer. The wound was about an inch across and bleeding profusely, so Richard made a pad of his handkerchief and pulling off his neckcloth tied it into place. The young man leaned against him in the course of this difficult operation and appeared to be on the point of fainting.

'You must let us get you home.' Richard held him firmly. 'Tell me where you live.'

His words seemed to penetrate the mist in which the victim was rapidly being enveloped for he muttered, 'The – the Grassmarket – a land called Newsteads – '

'I'm not sure how to get there in the dark.' Richard slipped his hand into a pocket to find his flask of eau-de-vie which he always carried by a habit begun on campaign, and managed to hold it to the young man's lips, tipping some of the fiery liquid down his throat. He gave a gasp and Richard said urgently, 'Wake up, lad. Tell me how to find it and your name if you can.'

The wounded man opened his eyes and seemed to be making an effort. The light of the torch showed him to be very dark with regular features, clean shaven and with a small youthful mouth. He was having difficulty in getting the words out but he managed to say, 'I am David – David Stewart, sir. I – I don't know who you are but – I thank you for – your help. I'm afraid I feel – very dizzy and sick.'

'Come along,' Richard said. 'You need your bed and a surgeon. Now if I can get my arm about you, lean on me and we'll do very well. Do we go up the hill?' He eased him along and after a few minutes the lad said, 'Here, turn left – through to the – West Bow.'

Richard followed his directions and coming out into the curve of the West Bow reached the Grassmarket. 'Where is your house?' he asked but by this time the wounded man had become inert between him and Robb, unable to put one foot before the other.

'I'll have to carry him,' Richard said and getting his shoulder under an armpit got him up and into his arms, Robb holding the torch high to light their way. Having no idea how to find the house he accosted two men who were emerging from the White Hart tavern, asking if they knew the house. They looked at him curiously and assumed that the young man was as inebriated as they were. One of them nudged Richard knowingly and pointed out a tall building at the far corner.

'Forbye he hasna learned to tak' his drink,' the other said. 'His heid in a bucket o' watter is what he's after needing.'

Richard didn't answer but carried his burden across the open space, unsavoury with the refuse of the day's market, and when they reached the house John Robb lifted the torch, now spluttering and dying, to reveal a few steps. Richard went up them and knocked on the door. Nothing happened for a few moments and he banged again more loudly. At last he heard a bolt being drawn. The door was opened partially and a broad Scots voice said irritably, 'Dinna ding the door doon!' He pulled it wide and then exclaimed, 'Maister Davey! You've never been *there* again?'

Having no idea where 'there' might be, Richard said, 'He's not drunk, if that's what you think. He was set upon by a pair of thieves. I and my servant chanced to come by and they ran off, but not I fear before one of them had used a knife on him.'

'God ha' mercy,' the old man exclaimed and then shouted, 'Iain! Iain Dubh, come ye by this instant and help me wi' Maister Davey.'

Richard set his burden on his feet but David Stewart was unconscious, his head lolling against Richard's shoulders, his face white. From the nether regions of the house another man appeared, a dark, black-bearded, much younger man, wearing the kilted plaid and a fawn-coloured shirt.

'What iss it, Somerled? Dhé, iss that Master Davey?' He spoke with a soft lilt that Richard had not heard before and he came to take the weight of the unconscious man on to himself, lifting him easily into his arms.

'You'd better get him to his bed at once,' Richard said, 'and send for a surgeon. That wound will need proper care.'

'Aye, sir,' the man Somerled agreed. 'We'll be after tending him the noo. Thank ye for bringing him hame. His mither will be mighty obleeged to ye.'

'I'll bid you goodnight then.' Richard had no desire to be thanked by an emotional mother and adding that he hoped Mr Stewart would soon be recovered he left the house, pulling the door closed behind him.

Sir Thomas Livingstone was putting himself out to make the visitor welcome and he invited various Edinburgh dignitaries to dinner for his entertainment. Other invitations came from people he had met at Lord Tarbat's house and his first week passed busily. To his surprise Lord Tarbat seemed to be making a particular effort to be friendly. The Viscount was no fool and had surmised correctly from what the newly arrived colonel had said that he had come at the King's request and was furthermore a personal friend of his Majesty. George MacKenzie was nothing if not ready to cement any steps on the ladder. There was a further supper party and he took Richard riding and hunting in the woods about Linlithgow Palace. Apart from his first impression that Tarbat was foppish, Richard found him a different man on the hunting field, energetic for his sixty years and he introduced the Englishman to the game of golf. He was obviously a shrewd judge of men and regaled Richard with word pictures of his fellow countrymen that were neat and amusing. It was he who insisted on taking Richard to Holyroodhouse. They drove down together in his coach from his house in the Cowgate, turning into St Mary's Wynd and then right into the Canongate, past the Canongate Tolbooth where a poor fellow sat outside in the stocks while passers-by happily threw mud and filth of all sorts at him.

Reaching the royal palace Tarbat showed him the fine apartments, the magnificent ceiling in the throne room, made at the request of Charles II though he never went there to see it. Tarbat pointed out the room where Mary Queen of the Scots was supping with her secretary David Rizzio before he was dragged out and murdered more than a hundred years ago.

It was an absorbing visit and Richard met several lords of the Council there on business, Lord Aberuchill whom he found monsyllabic, Lord Southesk, a great-nephew of the famous Marquis of Montrose, the swarthy Lord Tweeddale and young Lord Lorne, Argyll's son.

Afterwards Tarbat took him to supper at the oyster house in the Fleshmarket, and Richard, who had a weakness for oysters, enjoyed his supper and the talk that went with it. The Viscount grew merry and his stories more racy, finishing with an account of the Earl of Argyll's passion for his mistress, Peggy Alison.

Richard listened to the spicy talk and when finally Tarbat insisted on sending him back to the castle in his own coach went to bed feeling he had learned more today than in all his visit so far. In the cold light of morning he sat down to pen a letter to Mynheer Huygens, recounting all that he had assimilated and felt a distaste in doing so. His comfort was that, at least to this present morning, he had gleaned nothing of a serious nature. Under cover to Mynheer Huygens, it was no more than a letter one might write to a friend.

He began to busy himself on the uniform he wanted, the standard red coat with, he thought, grey facings, white breeks and stockings, black hat. He went to a clothier in the Lawnmarket and to a tailor to set the work in progress, reflecting with some satisfaction that it was for 'Lincourt's regiment'. He had long ago learned that if a soldier was well turned out he would the better respect his profession.

A week after the incident with young Stewart it occurred to him to wonder if the boy had recovered and deciding he had been rather discourteous to David's mother he went down to the Grassmarket to enquire how he did.

The man Somerled opened the door and Richard explained his errand. Somerled gave him one astonished stare. 'Landsakes! So ye're a sodger. I dinner ken that when ye brought Maister Davey hame. Oh aye, he's going on weel now, but still abed. Come ye in-bye, sir. The mistress was wishing to ken who ye might be.'

Richard stepped inside and almost at once heard a voice say, 'Who is it, Somerled?'

'A sodger,' he said with scant ceremony, 'him what brocht Master Davey hame t'ither nicht.'

'Then bid him come in at once.'

A lady was coming down the stair and Richard looked up, expecting to see a grey-haired matron. Instead he saw the most beautiful young woman he had ever set eyes on and he stood rooted to the spot as she came down the stair. She was a little above average height with a perfectly proportioned figure. Dark hair curled freely about her face and was caught up behind to fall on her shoulders at the back. Her eyes were large and dark, her well-shaped brows arched, her features on lines that reminded him of a classical marble of a woman he had seen once in Rome. She was smiling, her face warm with welcome, her hand held out.

She could not be David's mother, he thought with astonishment for she could not be more than in her middle twenties, and he realized he was staring like a mannerless schoolboy. As she reached him, he took her hand and bowed over it.

'I've been wanting to meet you, sir,' she said in the same soft lilting accent as the younger servant. 'It was very good of you to bring David home.'

'I was glad to be on hand to render assistance,' he said rather formally. 'I'm afraid the ruffians who attacked him got clean away.'

'There are too many thieves and beggars lurking in the wynds,' she said. 'But pray come into the parlour. Somerled, some wine if you please.'

He accompanied her into a pleasant room, took the chair she offered and accepted the glass of claret served by the shuffling Somerled. Then she dismissed him and asked if she might know the name of David's rescuer.

He gave it and added, 'Your servant spoke of Mr Stewart's mother, but you surely can't be that. Perhaps you are his sister?'

She gave a low soft laugh, 'No indeed, Colonel Lincourt, I am his step-mother. My husband was married before.'

'Shall I have the pleasure of meeting him?'

She shook her head, grave for the moment. 'I am a widow, sir, and have been these two years. David is my one charge in life since his brother was killed a year ago at Cromdale.'

'I'm sorry,' he said. 'I understood from one of the officers at the castle that we lost so few men in that rout.'

And the moment he had said the words he regretted them for there was an instant change in her expression.

'I'm afraid you misunderstand, Colonel,' she said quietly. 'Obviously our allegiances are different from yours.'

'I beg your pardon,' he said. 'I should not have assumed – but tell me, how is Mr Stewart? I trust the wound was not serious.'

'Serious enough to be worrying and the first few days the surgeon was very anxious about him,' she said, 'but David is young and strong and he is mending fast now. If it had not been for you, Colonel, he might have bled to death in the dark. We do thank you.'

She gave him a charming smile and he was thankful she ignored his mistaken assumption. They must be Jacobites, or David's brother would not have been on the other side at Cromdale where Livingstone's men had fallen on the unprepared Jacobites in the dark and sent them packing in a total rout.

She had risen from her seat and opening a small cupboard took out his neckcloth and handerkchief, neatly laundered and folded. 'I believe these are yours, Colonel.' She handed them back to him and then added, 'But I have not introduced myself. I am Margaret Stewart.'

'I'm very glad to make your acquaintance,' Richard said, recalling with inward amusement his first desire not to be thanked by an over-effusive matron. 'But – pray forgive me – you are not from these parts surely? Your accent – '

She was smiling now. 'You are quite right, Colonel. I am from the Highlands. My parents live at Maryburgh near Fort William. My father is the doctor there.'

'I see,' he said, but that information only caused him to wonder how her marriage to an obviously much older widowed Edinburgh man came to take place. He might have also been of the Highlands, bearing the name Stewart, but as far as he remembered David Stewart did not have the same way of speaking that she had.

She was looking across at him with frank interest. 'And you, Colonel, you are certainly not a Scot. What brings you to our city?'

'I'm here to raise men for the King's war against the French,' he explained. 'I've quarters at the castle, at least until my captain and a few men arrive from England.'

'And the work pleases you?'

'It pleases me to have the chance of a command of my own,' he agreed and wondered if she was among the Scots who were looking to the French to aid their cause. If so, she must not regard him as a very welcome guest. Yet, she was being perfectly friendly — merely politeness, he supposed, and gratitude. Rather abruptly he asked if he might see the sick man before he left, yet he was aware he would be sorry to bring this interview to a close. It was a pleasure to sit here and look at her.

Regretfully she said she had just left David and he was asleep. 'Which is the best thing for him,' she added. 'But will you not call again, Colonel? Perhaps the day after tomorrow? He should be greatly improved by then and up to receiving visitors. I know you are one he will welcome for he is sensible of the debt he owes you.'

He brushed that aside, but said he would give himself the pleasure of calling. It was pointless, he thought and yet he did not refuse. As the conversation progressed he became more and more aware that with that incredible beauty she had a charm that was irresistible coupled with a warmth of nature that could not but communicate itself after that unfortunate start.

She came to the door of the hall with him where Somerled was waiting to hand him his hat and cane. Then, as if on an impulse, she said, 'Better still, will you not be taking your dinner with us?'

Startled, he found himself accepting and after a bow he walked away in the direction of Castle Wynd. The next day passed extraordinarily slowly. The muskets he had ordered from the arsenal in London arrived by cart from Leith and were stored away in the castle. He busied himself in writing further orders for back packs and belts and general equipment, including the necessary lash, and sent John Robb off with them. Robb came back with the report that apparently there was a Friday market for all kinds of military gear, proposing that he should visit it on the next Friday and bring a report of the prices in Edinburgh, as always making himself indispensable.

Richard wrote the briefest of notes to his mother and a letter to Judith in which he told her of his encounter with David Stewart. Then he went to spend an hour with the Skinners. He asked Otwell if he knew of the Stewarts of Newsteads, but Otwell shook his head. He listened to Richard's description of Lord Tarbat's supper and the subsequent invitations and said in some amusement that for one normally retiring Richard had not lost time in finding his way into Edinburgh society. Richard shrugged, saying it had nothing to do with him but was due to others, to which Otwell retorted that it was odd how without any exertion on his part it always seemed to be the same. Richard told him to hold his nonsense and they spent the evening enjoying each other's company in the manner of old friends.

In the morning he found himself impatient for the dinner hour. He was being ridiculous, he thought. He was merely accepting hospitality from people who felt themselves in debt to him and after ensuring that the young man was indeed on the mend he would probably not go there again. But he was curious, curious as to why they were settled so far from the Highlands, curious to know if her sympathies were with the Jacobites in any active way, wanting despite himself to know more of her, to look again on that rare beauty.

She intrigued him, and he castigated himself for being ridiculous, quite sure he had left romantic nonsense behind him, which never amounted to any great experience anyway. He considered such things best left to French poems and the theatre. Nevertheless at the right hour he set forth to walk the short distance to the Grassmarket with an odd sense of eagerness. The place was busy as always, a crowd from a horse sale milling round the White Hart.

The door of Newsteads was opened not by Somerled but by the younger servant whom Somerled called Iain something.

'Will you pe coming in-bye, sir,' he said and took

Richard's hat and cane. 'Mistress Marged iss after waiting for you in the parlour.'

She was there in a dress of grey silk with a white underskirt and grey velvet bows on the shoulders, sitting near a window open to a small garden at the rear, for here at the end of the Grassmarket houses dwindled away, open country beyond the gate of the West Port. It was a warm day, a breeze stirring those grey ribbons. A much older woman sat by her and Margaret Stewart presented her as her husband's aunt, Mistress Marie Robertson. They sat sedately at the table and made small talk and Richard wished Mistress Robertson elsewhere. After the meal she said she would see if David was ready for his visitor and disappeared. She was only gone a few moments before she returned to say that her great-nephew was sitting up in bed, eager to greet his rescuer.

Richard followed her upstairs. The Stewarts were in the fortunate position of owning the whole of their house, though as Miss Robertson told him on the way up an impoverished family were living on the top two floors.

'My niece has an o'er kind heart,' she said drily, 'but 'tis I who hear the bairns greeting for my chamber is below theirs. Still and all, they're decent enough folk. This is David's wee room.'

It was indeed a small room in the bend of the stair, but comfortably furnished and the wounded young man was sitting propped up by pillows, very pale, but otherwise himself.

He opened his mouth to speak, cast his eye over Richard's uniform and then said, 'My aunt tells me you are a colonel up at the castle. It was too dark to see the other night.'

'In any case I didn't happen to be in uniform,' Richard answered drily.

Miss Robertson gave her nephew's pillows a shake and reproved him in a low voice. 'David, where are you manners? You mebbe owe your life to this gentleman.'

David seemed to collect himself. 'I beg your pardon,' he said stiffly. 'I am indeed very grateful, sir.'

'There's no need for that. I trust you haven't been in too much pain.'

Young enough to have rather enjoyed all the attention, David said nonchalantly, 'Oh, not above what one would expect.' Then as Miss Robertson said she would leave them together and went out of the room, he added, 'The surgeon told me that it would have been a deal worse if you had not chanced upon me.' He looked again at the uniform. 'I suppose you were on your way back to the castle? I'm surprise you wasted your time on a brawl in an alley.'

Suddenly irritated Richard said, 'Would you rather not have been rescued by a redcoat?'

David flushed. 'I beg your pardon again, sir. I meant no disrespect. We are used to redcoats in Edinburgh. And I do thank you for what you did. Somerled said you carried me home.'

'You are not very heavy.' Richard sat down in a chair by the bed. The boy was obviously trying to make amends and he gave him a brief smile. He could be no more than twenty, if that, he reckoned, dark-haired and fresh-skinned and with wide grey eyes that held an ingenuous look. 'But what were you doing abroad alone at that time? It was hardly wise.' David began to fiddle with the sheet and he added, 'Not that it's any of my business.'

'But you are right, sir, indeed you are. It was foolish of me and I'll not do it again. I – I'd been to supper with my friends. Usually I take Iain Dubh with me – you may have seen him, he's my stepmother's gillie.'

'Gillie?' Richard had not heard the word before. 'You mean the black-bearded fellow.'

'Yes. He came with her from Maryburgh when she married my father. He's supposed to look after her horses, but he's a house servant as well – like most gillies, you know.'

'I see.' Richard's curiosity about this household increased. 'Well, tell me about yourself. What do you do with your days?'

'I'm studying to be a lawyer, as my father was. He had a partner in Skinner's close where Lord Leven has his house – of course you'll probably know that being from the Castle and Lord Leven being Governor there. Some day I'm to be a partner with Master Kirkaldy, I suppose.'

'You don't sound very enthusiastic,' Richard said.

David moved to another position, grimacing a little. 'I'm not – the law is so dull. At least, I find it so. I have been set to read a long dull book on jurisprudence by Sir James Dalrymple while I am recovering. Can you think of anything worse?'

Richard shook his head, a smile on his lips. 'Not I! But then I'm no hand at the law. Maybe you'll find it more to your taste as you progress.'

'I doubt it,' David said gloomily. 'My brother Alan wouldn't do it and now he's gone and I must.'

'You step-mother told me how you came to lose him,' Richard said more seriously. From what he had heard that whole Jacobite effort last year had been ill-considered and he wanted to say that the heir of this house would have done better to stay at home, but he did not voice this thought.

Looking at him, David's own curiosity got the better of his preoccupation. 'You're English, aren't you, sir?' he asked. 'I'm told you are up here to recruit soldiers for King William.'

'That's right. I've seen a good deal of service in the Low Countries and I am to raise my own regiment for the war against the French.'

'Oh,' Some animation came into the boy's face. 'I saw a sergeant recruiting once. It was very stirring. I was only about twelve but I remember listening to the pipes and drums and thinking how exciting it would be. I was staying with my uncle in Stirling at the time and I watched some fellows come forward and give their names to the sergeant. It was for Lord Leven's regiment, I remember.'

'Then they may be serving at the castle now.'

David sighed. 'And I'm to be a lawyer. I wish I were not. I hate it.'

Richard felt sorry for him, understanding his youthful desire for excitement only too well, for he had known it himself. In a genuine desire to help him, perhaps to wean him away from any idiotic notion of emulating his brother, Richard said, 'If you were not, would you want to try army life? I might be able – '

David's face turned crimson. 'Oh no, no – I didn't mean

'– it wouldn't be – ' He broke off in confusion. 'In any case I must do what my father wished.' He looked so unhappy that Richard got to his feet. 'I only wish to say, Mr Stewart, that if I can be of any service to you, pray let me know.'

David murmured, 'Thank you, sir,' and Richard left him lying back against the pillows and staring out of the window.

Downstairs he found Mistress Stewart alone in the parlour for which he was grateful. 'I hope my visit hasn't tired him,' he said. 'I think he will take a little while to get his strength back.'

'He's young and strong.' She smiled up at him. 'I don't doubt he will make good progress now. Do sit down, Colonel. I've ordered a tray of coffee. I'm afraid I've become very much attached to the coffee, is it very depraved of me?'

'If it is then I share your depravity,' he said. 'Thank you, I will stay.'

A maid came in bearing a tray which she set down in front of her mistress and Margaret Stewart poured two cups, handing one to Richard. He drank slowly and then said, 'Your step-son tells me he is to be a lawyer, but he doesn't seem to like the prospect.'

'No, he doesn't,' she said frankly, 'but he's not yet twenty and restless as the young often are. It was his father's wish, though sometimes I think – ' She paused. 'I don't know why I'm telling you all this, Colonel, it can't be of any interest to you.'

'But it is,' he said. 'I've taken a liking to the lad. He sounded more interested in soldiering when I talked about my mission here.'

She shook her head vehemently. 'I think not.'

'I would willingly do what I could for him. I hope the old troubles are over now and I shall need young keen men.'

The smile was gone from her face. 'You are very kind,' she said quietly, 'but I don't think that would really be what David wants, nor what I want for him.'

Richard was aware that he had said something to offend her. Perhaps he had been right in his surmise in the first place. 'I'm sorry,' he said. 'It was a mere suggestion, but not, I see, acceptable.'

'But you made it with the best of intentions. Pray let me fill your cup.'

He refused, thinking it was time he left. He would not come again and he was aware of a deep feeling of regret. When he rose she stood up at once and said, 'Thank you for your visit, Colonel. It was very kind of you and I'm sure it is entirely due to your quick action that he'll soon be up and about again. I miss our morning rides together.'

'You like to ride?'

'Yes, indeed. It's one of my great pleasures.'

'Then I wonder,' he said to his own utter astonishment, 'if you would take pity on a stranger to your town and allow me to ride with you one morning?'

She looked surprised and so hesitant for a moment that he almost wished he had not made the extraordinarily impulsive suggestion. She was looking directly into his face and after a moment inclined her head.

'That would be very pleasant, Colonel. Shall we say eight of the clock on Thursday? Have you been beyond the West Port yet? The countryside is very pretty.'

He took his leave and walked back to the castle deep in thought. From what had been said, and perhaps more from what had not been said, he now knew something of the leanings in that household for it was very clear that Mistress Stewart did not want to see her step-son in King William's army. He would do better to stay away from Newsteads – but he was outside the door at eight o'clock two days later.

Chapter 4

With the arrival of Captain Ripley and his men Richard's days became suddenly very full. He was entering a receipt for tents in his account book in his room in the castle when there was a knock on the door and the captain came in. He was a wiry young man with intense blue eyes and Richard already knew his worth as a soldier.

'Ripley! I'm glad to see you. Any difficulties on the journey?'

'None, sir.'

'Are the men in good shape?'

'Aye, sir.'

'Where have you left them?'

'Below, sir, awaiting your orders.'

Richard got up. 'Well, we've to march them back to Leith for their quarters are there, but I expect they'll be able to take their dinner here first. You'll dine with me at the officers' table?'

'Thank you, sir.'

'We've a great deal to discuss, Ripley, and the whole business to set in motion. I've had a list of officers from London who would be available. If you remember, quite a few have been on half pay since Rogers' was disbanded, and I propose to write asking for half a dozen. I've also written to request your commission as major.'

Ripley looked pleased but he said no more than a brief 'thank you'.

'And concerning officering our troops there's a young Lieutenant Johnstone, whom I think might be raised to captain and be useful to us. We should be able to recruit one or two ensigns. I've already taken on a piper. I can't

say I like the sounds he makes but I'm told I must have
him and I suppose it's stirring enough. Whom have you
brought as our drummer?'

'Jones, sir. You may not recall him.'

'Yes, I think I do – a big man who has a brother in the
regiment. Is he with us too?'

'Yes. He asked to come and Colonel van Wyngarde
raised no objections. He sent you this letter.'

Richard took it and laid it on the desk to read later.
Then he shepherded Ripley out of the room and at dinner
introduced him to the officers of Lord Leven's regiment.
Despite his brevity of speech Ripley acquitted himself well
at the dinner table and afterwards Richard rode with him
to Leith, his men marching behind in smart order. All of
them had served under their new colonel in the Low
Countries and were well aware of the high standards he
required. Sergeant Morrison gave him a swift salute and
on hearing the colonel express his pleasure in having him
here a broad grin spread over his face.

They began in Edinburgh itself by the Fountain Well,
with young Jock MacPhail playing his pipes and Jones
keeping time as best he could on the drums to this strange
instrument. Three young men came forward, a butcher's
son looking for a better life than that in the fleshers'
market, a fellow from Fife who had wandered aimlessly to
Edinburgh without any fixed idea of what he wanted, and
a pedlar who stepped forward. He had been robbed by
some broken men on the border and he laid down his
depleted tray with relief.

Richard took his little troop down to the Canongate and
added two more to their number, another two or three
joining them as they marched away towards the Leith
road. Over the next ten days the recruiting ranged the
countryside as far as Stirling and Perth, as well as south
into Peebles and Selkirk and Jedburgh.

Sergeant Morrison knew his job. 'Now come along, lads,'
he would bellow, 'here's a fine chance for you. Nine pence
a day and a fine uniform, good food and good company,
and you'll get to see action under his Majesty. What more

could a fellow want? You married men, you want a change from the wife's nagging tongue, eh? Come and see action with us and think o' the pay you can send home for your babes. And you lads who don't have wives, there are pretty girls abroad I can tell you – I've been there and I know!'

Richard rode with him, listening to his rough tones encouraging recruits to come in, and putting in an occasional word himself, promising them hard work and discipline but a good life. A motley collection were eventually assembled and listed, young men from all walks of life, many tousled and untidy, an unlikely looking bunch but he had seen worse. From among them he found two who had some knowledge of cooking and set them to work supervised by a corporal who had come north with Ripley. He began to know something of the countryside and the Lowland people who lived there. For the most part he found them reserved and unintelligible but with letters from Sir Thomas Livingstone he received hospitality from local gentry who lived, to him, rather rough and uncomfortable lives in their stone houses, many with pele towers attached, relics of the days of border raiding. His piper and his drummer attracted attention in the market places and usually gathered a crowd to listen to Sergeant Morrison's blandishments.

As the men came in Captain Ripley, aided by Lieutenant Johnstone and the sergeant, began the drilling in earnest. It seemed the word had gone round and on the next two market days more young men answered the call. A few Richard had to reject as unfit for one reason or another, but soon there were two hundred of them drilling in the field hard by Leith. He divided them into companies, taking the least promising himself with Lieutenant Johnstone as his captain-lieutenant. They began with simple marching and exercises and Richard had them leaping and running and playing games to toughen them up. Only two fell out, unable to keep up, and at the end of the first week he put them into uniform, working on the precept that the sooner a man had that to care for and wear with pride the more likely he was to turn into a good soldier. They learned to obey the drum call to Reveille and Tap-to and on a fine morning he had them all drawn up to take the soldiers' oath:

> I do sincerely promise and swear I will be faithful and bear allegiance to their Majesties King William and Queen Mary, and to be obedient in all things to the Commander-in-Chief appointed by their Majesties ...
> And I do further swear I will be a true, faithful and obedient soldier in every way ... So help me God.

He also had the rules of behavour and discipline read out to them, a practice which would be continued once every month. The men took the oath with reasonable enthusiasm and listened respectfully to the rules. Then he had muskets issued to them with the new plug bayonets fixed and the summer days echoed to the call of 'Pose your musket', 'Take forth your match', 'Prime your pan', 'Give fire!' as the recruits learned to handle their weapons. Neat rows of tents were set up and the men taught to care for their packs, belts, swords, powder and match and cartridges.

He promoted a man who had been a baker to be quartermaster, and so by dint of their colonel's organization the men found themselves well-equipped and fed. As recruiting went on further afield the numbers swelled until Richard looked out each morning with some satisfaction upon at least half the number he needed. He studied them carefully as they learned their business, wondering how many of them, when it came to it, would stand well in the face of an enemy and give fire. But his officers did their work well and his need now was for more officers. He approached Lord Leven who gave him Captain Fletcher on a temporary basis. He would rather have had any other for he suspected the captain of being addicted to drink, but he had to be grateful for what he could get. Half a dozen more officers arrived from London, bringing with them Ripley's commission as major and he donned the scarlet sash and shoulder knots of his new rank. The new arrivals however brought none of the requested funds and Richard paid the men out of his own pocket. He took on an earnest young divine as chaplain and had prayers read every morning; he also enlisted a surgeon from Perth who was not long from medical school and Richard hoped he would not be tested too far until he had learned his business.

From the start the main difficulty came in the situation between Major Ripley and Captain Fletcher. Obviously the captain held a grudge because he felt he should have had the majority being the older man, but from the first it became evident that they just did not like each other. Ripley was too self-contained to join in Fletcher's relaxed talk over the supper table; by nature he was abstemious and looked on with annoyance as Captain Fletcher reached constantly for the bottle. Richard frowned over it but managed to keep the peace.

Fletcher had a pretty wife, a naive girl many years his junior, and when Richard occasionally invited the officers' wives to the supper table, Fletcher seemed to enjoy making her feel small and ignorant. Ripley sat during these exchanges with a frown on his face, and Richard told his officers frankly that he wanted their wives kept in the background as far as possible. There were inevitably camp followers for some of the men arrived with wives and children, and it was so much the custom that Richard could do nothing about it but see that nothing got in the way of the serious business of making soldiers.

He discussed much of it with Otwell. 'Fletcher and Ripley don't sit well together,' he said one evening, 'but I hope they'll settle down and put the regiment first. I think I can begin to call it that now.'

'How many companies have you got now?'

'Nine. It's very gratifying how the men have come in, and to serve under an Englishman, perhaps it's because there's been no recruiting here since Lord Leven raised his regiment two years ago. So far, though I've got some ignorant numbskulls, I've only observed one trouble maker, a fellow named Sinclair who's inclined to be self-important and bully the others in his company, but I'm watching him.'

'And your other officers, apart from Ripley and Fletcher?'

'Satisfactory. I've promoted young Johnstone to be captain-lieutenant of my own company and it's working out well.'

'By God, I wish I could join you,' Otwell said. 'When I think of the times we've had together – '

'I know,' Richard agreed. 'It was the most damned ill luck. But it's good to have you to talk it over with, Otwell. There are problems, of course – it's inevitable – but will you come out if I hire a carriage and see the men drilling? I think you'll be impressed with our progress and you could dine with my officers afterwards.'

'Will I not?' Otwell's face lit up. 'As soon as you like, and I'd enjoy seeing Ripley again. In the meantime how about coming to the inn in Carrubber's Close this evening? I told you I'd take you to look at the Killiecrankies – but not in that uniform. Have you put your men into scarlet or blue?'

'Scarlet, with grey facings and grey knots of ribbon in their hats.' He picked up his own, cocked on one side with grey ribbons and decorated with a grey ostrich feather. 'I'll change and be back here by eight o'clock.'

The close was not far and they walked to it, Otwell managing his crutches without fuss. Apart from the loss of his leg he was strong and his other leg and his arms dealt easily with his disability. It was obvious he was known and liked in the town for many people greeted him warmly as he swung along.

The close was small and dark and surrounded by tall buildings, but lights hung outside the tavern and inside candles burned to give a yellow light. It was fairly full, maids and tap-boys hurrying to and fro with jugs of whisky, wine and beer. Richard and Otwell found a free table and sat down on stools, Otwell taking a dram.

'I don't recommend Scots ale,' he said with a grin. 'Most Englishmen complain it's so thick it can be eaten with a spoon.'

Richard ordered wine, which he thought of poor quality, and for a while they talked of military matters. Then, rather abruptly, he changed the subject.

'Otwell, I want to ask you a favour.'

'Anything you like,' Otwell said promptly.

'Do you recall I asked you once if you knew the Stewarts of Newsteads in the Grassmarket?'

'Aye, and I didn't.'

'No, but I'd like to mend that. The matter is that I've come to take my supper there often on a Sunday night. I'm in no position to return such hospitality and I wondered if I might bring Mistress Stewart to supper with you one evening?'

'Of course,' Otwell said. He gave Richard a curious look. 'Is there a husband?'

'No. A step-son and an aunt, but I don't think it necessary to invite them.' He didn't add it, but he had no desire to stretch Otwell's limited resources, intending in any case to send John Robb with a basket of provisions.

His friendship with the inmates of Newsteads had increased over the last weeks. He rode with Mistress Stewart once or twice a week and when David was sufficiently recovered he joined them. He was back at his work, studying the law, and any remarks about it were accompanied by a grimace or a deep sigh. As he got to know Miss Robertson Richard found her a well-read and intelligent woman whose conversation was always stimulating, but it was Margaret Stewart, whom he discovered the family called Marged, who fascinated him. He watched her mobile face as she talked, seeing her beauty lit up by her lively speech and her professed interest in Richard's project. She seemed to him to have all the qualities a woman should have and it was a desire to deepen that friendship that made him put the request to Otwell.

'Alison and I would be pleased to do it,' Otwell was saying, 'if you think our modest lodging suitable.'

Richard gave him a quick smile. 'She is not the woman to weigh people by anything but what they are,' and he wondered how he knew that.

'Then Alison shall write a note for you to take to Mistress Stewart.' He waited for Richard to say more but Richard merely thanked him and turned the talk aside by asking if there were any here with known Jacobite sympathies.

'The man in the black coat over there,' Otwell said. 'I don't know his full name, but he's a Cameron and always here. The man with him is John Graham, a cousin of Dundee's I think.' He watched as two men rose and went up the narrow stair at the far end. 'Ah, there's a meeting of some sort tonight. And there's another gone to join them,' as a cloaked and muffled figure hurried to the room above.

'Don't the authorities know about this?' Richard asked. 'It ought to be stopped.'

'Oh, I imagine the Council know – I've seen a Bailie-councillor here before now – but I reckon they think that if the Jacks do no more than talk over their cups of usquebaugh there's no harm done. I wouldn't be surprised if there was a similar place in London.'

'There is, the White Cock off Fleet street,' Richard said. 'There's precious little chance of more than hot air coming out of such a place in London but up here it must be a different matter.'

'Oh aye,' Otwell agreed, 'as you'll find if you ride west.'

Richard nodded. 'I shall go as soon as my companies are settled enough to leave in Ripley's charge. I wish the Treasury in London would move themselves to send me a chest of coin to pay my men.'

'We had the same trouble in the Low Countries, don't you remember? But it usually came in the end.'

'In the meantime my pockets are not bottomless.' He paused, watching as three men came in and went up the stair. Then, to his astonishment, he saw in the dull yellow light, that one of them was David Stewart. He had a sheaf of papers under his arm and he was talking volubly to one of his companions, not so much as glancing towards the other end of the room, for which Richard was profoundly thankful. He had no desire to have his presence here discussed at Newsteads. Probably this was the 'there' the servant Somerled had spoken of on the night when he had carried David home and his being here might look like spying.

After David had disappeared he said to Otwell, 'I've had enough of this place. The wine is execrable. Shall we go?'

'Willingly,' Otwell said in mild surprise. 'Alison is expecting you for supper.'

Thinking it over later Richard came to the conclusion that he ought perhaps to apprise Mistress Stewart of what he had seen and beg her to tell the boy to keep away from the Killiecrankies. For all the authorities winked at 'the Club', outright flaunting of their allegiance might bring individual members into trouble and he had seen eager excitement on David's face, rather more than might be put there by mere talk.

He felt uneasy about the whole situation and knew himself to be unusually silent on his ride with Marged Stewart on the following morning. He had been surprised by how easy he had found it to talk to her. He thought perhaps the fact that she was a widow and no inexperienced girl made him feel at ease, as if she expected nothing from him but friendship, whereas in society he tended to keep clear of girls with match-making mothers.

When they returned past St Cuthbert's church and entered the West Port he said, 'I wonder if I might come in for a few moments of your time?'

Usually he left her at the door where Iain Dubh would be waiting to take her horse to the stables, and she said, smiling, 'I thought you had something on your mind this morning. Come you in, Colonel, I hope it is not so grave a matter as it is seeming.'

He followed her in and in the parlour, with the door closed, he did not take the chair she indicated but stood with his hands clasped behind his back. She sat down, arranging the skirts of her green riding habit and laying her large black hat with its green plume on the table beside her. He thought how green became her, that she looked like a Diana cantering on horseback this morning, her eyes sparkling and a flush on her cheeks. Now she was looking up at him expectantly.

'I wondered if you knew,' he said bluntly, 'that David goes to a tavern in Carrubber's Close where a club called the Killiecrankies meets?'

'Yes I knew,' she said gravely, 'but I wonder that you do, Colonel.'

'I was taken there by a friend who thought I might be interested to see it, which I was, and I'm told the authorities are well aware of it. I saw David there.'

'Did he see you?'

'No, or I imagine he would've told you about it. He went up the stairs where I understand the Jacobites have a private meeting place.'

She sat very still, her eyes on her hands folded in her lap. 'You must know, Colonel, that we are Jacobites. I believe I told you my elder stepson was killed fighting for that cause.'

'Yes, I know,' he said, 'and you did make your sentiments plain but I thought that here in Edinburgh they could be no more than that. David may be playing with fire and I believed it only right to inform you.'

She looked troubled and paused before she answered. 'I accept that that is what you meant – a warning, no more.' She was silent again and then said, 'Please sit down. I think we must discuss this.' He obeyed, taking a chair opposite her and she went on, 'Yes, I know that David considers himself a Killiecrankie – he is always having the memory of his brother on him – and being young he must find some outlet for his feelings, though I wish it were not in Carrubbers Close. Alan meant a great deal to him and all he thinks of is some way of avenging him. It is understandable, but not what I am wishing for him.'

'Understandable, but foolish,' Richard said in answer to her comment. 'It might land him in serious trouble even here in Edinburgh. Surely you must see that the King and Queen are not going to be upset by a few hotheads who will quickly find themselves behind bars if they stir up any commotion.'

She gave a little laugh. 'Colonel, if I didn't know you better I would say you are being naive, or perhaps it is that you have not yet come to know our country. You may think the Jacobites are no more than a few hotheads, but you are wrong. Many people feel indignant at the way the English foisted their decisions on us, many didn't wish for the Dutch Prince and Princess Mary to reign over us and we are disgusted at the way our leaders here in Edinburgh mismanaged our affairs. We have had our own Stuart princes for centuries.'

'The Queen is a Stuart,' he pointed out.

'Yes, but she has taken what is her father's by right. Oh, I see there's little to be done at the moment but who knows what the future may bring. I believe the whole matter is far from being settled.'

Uneasily aware she was near to talking treason, yet respecting honest discussion, he said, 'I pray you are wrong.' He leaned forward and added earnestly, 'King James did too much to offend for the English ever to accept him again. We don't want a papist on our throne – that was ended a hundred and fifty years ago, and nothing can change that.'

She sat very still. 'We are papists, as you call them.'

He was taken aback. 'I beg your pardon. Should I have known?'

'How should you? 'Tis not a subject we have touched on and not all Jacobites are Catholics.'

'I wondered that I had never seen you at the Kirk of a Sunday morning,' he said. 'I have for years worshipped in the Calvinist persuasion and I find the Presbyterian way to my taste, but of course there was no reason why you should go to St Giles above the other churches in this town.'

She gave him a rather sad look. 'We are reduced to hearing Mass in Blackfriar's Wynd in an old house where a top room has been turned into a chapel.'

'I see.'

'Does it make so much difference? Would you rather not come here any more?'

He recovered himself. 'No indeed. I've always held that conscience is a personal affair. King Charles always believed that and did much to ease the life of Catholics, but his brother was a different matter. He went too far.' He paused and then added, 'Mistress Stewart, I wish all of your allegiance would understand that the changes that have taken place are for the best, and if there is rebellion in King James's name it will mean bloodshed, civil war, and that is a terrible thing. My father and many men alive today fought in one and we don't want another.'

She gave a sigh, leaning back in her chair. 'You are right, of course, but in the Highlands we are seeing things differently. Loyalties bind us and our men aren't afraid of war.'

'If you think – ' he began in astonishment, but at once she sat upright, a flush in her cheeks.

'Forgive me, I never meant any such slur. Only that the character of the Highlander, the Gael, is very different from that of the Lowlander, and certainly from the Sas – ' she broke off.

'I wonder,' he said in some amusement, 'what you were about to call my race.'

'I beg your pardon again,' she could not keep back a smile. 'That was very wrong of me. *Sasunnach* is our word for an Englishman.'

'And not a very complimentary one?'

'Perhaps,' she agreed. 'But I'd like you to be knowing more of us, so that you will understand us a little better. Perhaps one day you will be riding to the Highlands and seeing for yourself.'

'I mean to,' he said and was aware of a small glow of warmth that she did indeed want him to know more. He added, 'Won't you tell me something of your life there before you came to this city? Where do the Stewarts come from?'

'They hold Appin.' She seemed glad to divert from the painful subject of loyalties. 'But I am only a Stewart by marriage. My father is a Beaton, and there have been Beatons as physicians to the MacDonalds in Glencoe for many generations.'

He stirred in his chair, remembering the biting words the Master of Stair had used about that clan. What was it he had called them? 'The worst of a rotten breed, a gallows herd'? But how could he believe that, looking at this woman who sat opposite him?

Shrewdly she said, 'Oh yes, we have a bad reputation and I'm sure you've heard many tales of us, mostly true I expect. There has been murder and fighting and cattle thieving down the centuries and we are no worse than the MacLeans or the Grants or the MacKenzies, and the

Campbells have long been our worst enemies, but some things are changing now. Many of the clans want to live in peace and there is much good among us as well as the wildness you have heard of. MacIain, the Chief of Clan Iain Abrach, was my grandfather's cousin and when my grandfather died he took my father under his roof and then sent him to study in Edinburgh. It was here that he met Alexander Stewart. Then he went back to the glens and married my mother who was also a MacDonald, from the Keppoch line. They live in Maryburgh near Fort William where he practises medicine both at the fort and in the glens. He is much loved there, Colonel.'

'I'm sure of it,' he said.

'And I had a happy childhood, although being an only child, for I spent much of every summer in Glencoe. Oh, it is wild and beautiful there, the mountains are high and shelter the glen, the Great and Little Herdsman protect the pass from Rannoch Moor where you go down between steep crags and the waterfalls to Achtriachton and the lochan, to Achnacon and Inverrigan, and there are fields there with good corn land and grazing for our black cattle. The chief has a fine house among the fir trees where the glen opens out by Loch Linnhe. In the summer it is all purple with heather, our clan badge, and our people go up to the shielings on the high ground. You would think them no more than crude huts but one can live snug in them in good weather. The young men tend the cattle and hunt and enjoy games in the long evenings, the women spin our tartan cloth and sing the old songs while the children run wild and go barefoot in the burns. Our poets and bards sing of the beauty and of the old heroes of our race, of Deirdre and Angus Og and Colla the prince.'

She stopped and laughed. 'You must forgive me, Colonel, I'm afraid that sometimes in Edinburgh I am very homesick.'

He listened, captivated by the warmth of her feeling and the light in her face as much by her lilting speech which conjured up a distant and unknown place. 'I understand,' he said with rare gentleness. 'You have made me see your home very differently from what I have been told.'

'Oh, I am hoping you will see it in reality some day. I love it so dearly.'

'Then how did it come about that you wed an Edinburgh man?' he asked and wondered that she did so when surely a girl with such looks and charm could have found a younger mate among her own people.

She did not seem in the least offended by his question. 'I was very young, no more than seventeen, when my father's old friend from university days came to visit us. He was a widower with two young sons and when he wanted to wed me my father was overjoyed. He felt there was little for me in Maryburgh and the chance of a fine house in Edinburgh and a good marriage settlement seemed very appealing to him, and to my mother.'

'And you?' he asked involuntarily, yet aware he should not have done so.

'Oh, although Alexander was so much older than me, he was kind and attentive and I loved the boys from the start. At the time,' she paused, 'it seemed the right thing to do.'

'I'm sorry you should have lost him,' Richard said formally and tried to ignore an odd inner satisfaction that she was a widow.

'Yes,' she said and rose to ring the bell. 'You will stay for breakfast, Colonel?'

'I wish I could,' he answered, 'but I must get out to Leith. However, before I go, I would like to ask you if you would care to come with me one evening to take supper with a friend of mine and his wife who live in Lady Grey's Close. I've told them that we ride together.'

She looked surprised but she said at once that she would enjoy it and would await Mistress Skinner's invitation. Nothing more was said of David and the Killiecrankies.

The supper with Otwell and Alison was a great success. Careful not to tread on the Skinners' Scots pride Richard nevertheless managed to send a small basket containing three bottles of wine and a loin of beef as a gift for the supper and he told Otwell roundly that as the whole idea was his it would be his pride that would be offended if it wasn't accepted.

From the first the Skinners obviously liked their guest

and such was their easy manner that she seemed to feel quite at home. The talk was general and no dangerous ground trodden on. After the meal Alison took her to see the young hopeful of the house and Otwell gave Richard a sideways look.

'You sly fellow, where did you come across such a beauty? And she is charming as well. Come, tell me about her.'

Richard complied, recounting the rescue of David and the subsequent friendship, but he said nothing of the MacDonald connection – he was not quite sure why – and before there was time for Otwell to ask any further questions the two women returned.

In the hired coach, driving back to Newsteads, Marged said, 'I am always liking to see people happy and living simply. I learned to love simple ways and I don't care for grand society. I hope I may see them again. I shall be after asking Mistress Skinner to bring her baby to see me one day.'

'Thank you,' Richard said. 'I thought you couldn't help but like them.' At the door he put her hand to his lips, holding her fingers firmly. 'I can't tell you what a difference your friendship is making to my time here.'

'I'm glad,' she said. 'It can be very lonely in a strange town.'

He set her down at her door and ordering the coachman to drive him back to the castle reflected on how much more so it would have been if he had not found David Stewart wounded in an alleyway.

Chapter 5

Viscount Tarbat had himself driven out to see the progress of Lincourt's regiment and ordering his coachman to pull up by the field at Leith sat for a while watching the drilling. There was a great change in the men now. From being a disorderly mob they had emerged into smart companies, mastering the control of their muskets. They comported themselves well and Richard found himself growing proud of 'Lincourt's'. He walked over to the coach and greeted his visitor.

'Well, my lord, what do you think? Promising, eh?'

'Very,' Tarbat said. 'How are your numbers?'

'Four hundred and ninety-eight. I've been surprised how the men have come in, two more yesterday who came off a ship. They are Protestant refugees from France and they joined us at once, I suspect because they arrived with empty purses, but they're not ignorant of musket drill.'

Tarbat surveyed him for a moment. 'And your young minister, is he Presbyterian? Yes, I thought it would be so. You must realize that the Covenanting spirit never has spread very strongly north of the Tay. In the Highlands you'll find Episcopalians – I'm of that persuasion myself – and Catholics, and you may well be rejected upon those grounds by some.'

'I see,' Richard said thoughtfully, 'but I must make the attempt and I think that now I may leave matters here to Major Ripley and go west and north to try to complete my numbers.'

Tarbat gave him a wry smile. 'You may well go but whether you'll bring back more than the number you take is another thing altogether. But I congratulate you on

what you've achieved here with these fellows. Will you
dine with me tomorrow?'

Richard thanked him and Tarbet signalled the
coachman to take him back to Edinburgh. Accepted now
in Edinburgh society Richard was frequently out to dinner
or to supper and he listened to the topical conversation,
especially when the occasions did not include wives, and
faithfully set down his opinions and reported verbatim
various conversations in his letters to the King. He didn't
like doing it and sometimes wished he had tried more
strenuously to refuse the commission, but then he thought
of the other side of the coin, the house in the Grassmarket,
the evenings with Otwell and some of his friends, and
those companies of Scottish lads that were now under his
care.

There was, however, that very afternoon, an unpleasant
incident. He was in the room in the cottage he used as his
headquarters, though he still slept at the castle, when
Captain Johnstone came in, his open face bearing an
anxious expression.

'I'm sorry to disturb you, sir, but there's been some
trouble.'

Richard laid down his pen. 'What is it?'

'Sinclair, sir. He's just come on duty without his bayonet.
He says he's mislaid it but he's been drinking and I suspect
he sold it to buy whisky.'

'If he has he'll rue it,' Richard said. 'Send Morrison to
bring him to me.' In due course the sergeant marched the
man Sinclair in. He was a burly fellow with thick red hair
and he gave his commanding officer a truculent stare.
'Well?' Richard said. 'What have you to say, Sinclair?
Where is your bayonet?'

'Ah canna tell, sir. Mebbe some glaikit mon ha' tak't it.'

'Nonsense. Each man has been issued with his own. And
I can smell the whisky on you. Did you sell it for that?'

'That's a wheen o' blethers, sir, beggin' your pardon.'
Sinclair spoke in so strong an accent that Richard found it
hard to understand him. ' 'Tis no but a wee knife on the
end o' ma musket. Mebbe you could be after findin' me
anither?'

'Don't be impertinent.' Richard leaned back in his chair. 'I've neither muskets nor bayonets to spare and you're mighty lucky to be given this new bayonet. The men under my command, Sinclair, must learn that I'll not tolerate this sort of thing. I will have no man drunk on duty. What do you think might happen at musket drill if a man was drunk, eh?'

'Ah'm no drunk,' Sinclair protested. 'Ah was a wee bit drouthy, that's a'.'

'I'll not have any man with so much as one dram on him at drill. You shall have twenty lashes for that and twenty more if you don't get your bayonet back by morning.'

Sinclair opened his mouth to speak, swallowed, and then said, ' 'Tis a wee bit hard, sir. Ah've nae siller and ye'll no ha' me rieve it?'

'I don't care what you do,' Richard said pithily, 'but if you're not on duty tomorrow morning, sober and with your bayonet fixed, you will be dismissed. Sergeant, have the whole company assembled. The punishment will be carried out immediately.'

Sinclair, seeing there was no way out of it, put on a stoical air and was marched out. A post was driven into the ground, the men drawn up to witness the punishment. Sinclair's shirt was removed and his hands tied above his head to the post. Morrison found a strong fellow and handed him the whip.

Richard stood in front of the ranks and read them a stern lecture on the care of their issued clothing and weapons and on the taking of whisky other than at specified times. He had wondered how they had accepted him, an Englishman, as their colonel and knew well enough their way of whispering amongst themselves, but what they thought of him he didn't know. Now they would find out what he would and would not tolerate. They listened respectfully enough and looked askance at the man tied to the post.

The punishment began, the lash whistling in the air. Purple weals appeared on Sinclair's back but apart from a sharp gasp as the lash descended, he bore it well. The flesh broke and blood began to trickle down before the last stroke. When it was over he stood quivering, his knees threatening to give way but he stayed on his feet.

Richard nodded to the sergeant to have him released and addressed himself to the assembled men. 'I don't like the lash,' he said in a ringing tone, 'but I will use it if I have to. Learn this, all of you. When we take Lincourt's to Flanders it will be a regiment the King may be proud of and any of you who won't abide my rules may leave now and none the worse for it. Well?'

No one moved. The ranks stood still, watching, as Sinclair brushed off a helping hand and walked unsteadily away to the tents.

'Very well,' Richard said. 'Carry on with the drill, sergeant.' And send the surgeon to see to the man's back.'

He strode away and an hour later sought out the tent Sinclair shared with five others. He lay on a blanket, his face wet with sweat, flies buzzing about his bloodied back. When he saw the black boots standing beside him he struggled on to his elbow.

'Stay still,' Richard said. 'You've had your punishment, now answer me this. Do you wish to leave my regiment or will you stay and keep to my orders?'

Sinclair got himself painfully on to his feet. 'Ah'll bide, sir, and Ah'll get ma wee knife thing back afore the morn. I g'ie ye ma word.'

Richard left him and went back to this headquarters. His judgement of the man was not proved wrong for Sinclair kept his word and after that there seemed to be a new spirit amongst the men. They looked at their commanding officer with new respect and the flogged man, far from bearing resentment, appeared to be using his influence, which Richard had not underrated, and his bulk, to keep some of the more unruly element in order. Richard promptly made him a corporal and in doing so sparked off an argument at the dinner table between his two senior officers, which he overheard as he came in late.

'He's a trouble-maker,' Captain Fletcher was saying. 'I'd be damned if I'd have kept the fellow.'

'Then you would have been wrong,' Ripley answered tersely.

'Time will tell,' Fletcher retorted and filled his glass. 'He may be on good behaviour now, but how long will that last?'

'The Colonel can doubtless judge better than you.'

'Well, I wish he wasn't in my company,' Fletcher said in a disgruntled tone. 'And as for giving him a corporal's badge —'

'My decision, I think.' Richard took his place. 'My apologies for being late, gentlemen, despatches from London.' He shook out his napkin as an orderly filled his glass. 'If you can't deal with him, Fletcher, I'll have him moved to another company.'

The Captain flushed angrily. 'Oh, I can tolerate him, I suppose. He'll not get the better of me if I find him playing the same game again.'

'You won't,' Richard said tersely, 'but if there's any trouble I want it reported to me at once.'

Sinclair however contrived not to annoy his captain though Fletcher rode him hard. Richard watched and kept his own counsel. But he did recount the incident to Lord Tarbat who appeared highly amused.

'Some fellows will sell their souls to the de'il for a dram,' he said cheerfully.

'Not in my regiment they won't,' Richard retorted with equal humour.

'Well, it seems you know how to deal with them,' the Viscount agreed. 'I'm glad the work goes well. When do you plan to try recruiting to the west? Do you mean to go to Fort William?'

'Aye, in a few weeks,' Richard answered and was aware of a reluctance to leave Edinburgh. The reason stared him in the face. He did not want to give up his morning rides with Marged Stewart, or the Sunday night suppers. She and Alison Skinner had taken a liking to each other and she called frequently in Lady Gray's Close, always it seemed with a little gift, something unobtrusive for the baby that could not be construed as charity, and Richard was grateful to her for her tact.

Once or twice she sent a carriage for the Skinners and they joined the Sunday evenings. It was all very pleasant and Richard sat in a chair that seemed to have become his and watched Mistress Stewart as she dispensed coffee, watched her mobile face, her lovely dark eyes alight with pleasure. He watched when she held Alison's young Richard and wondered if she regretted having had no child by her marriage to Alexander Stewart. What did it matter if she was a Jacobite and a Catholic when she was the most fascinating woman he had ever met? He tried to put these things from his mind, telling himself it was no more than a friendship made in a strange town and as such of brief duration. But he thrust that thought aside too. Best of all were the times when Miss Robertson had gone to her bed and they sat alone together and she told him more of her people and of places rich in ancient tales and customs. He asked her about the plundering and fighting that seemed to be part of Highland life and she had looked at him, half grave, half amused.

'Oh, 'tis true enough. I am thinking you have heard only the worst of us.'

He was recalling this now as he sat at Tarbat's table. He was also remembering Livingstone's remark, that his regiment might be needed here before ever he took it to Flanders – and he would not want to turn it against Mistress Stewart's people.

The meal was all but finished when there was a loud banging on the door and a moment later, barely waiting to be announced, the Earl of Breadalbane strode into the room. He was fair and wore a great fair periwig, his body thick set and strong; watchful eyes looked out above a jutting nose and his lips were thin. He was forty-eight years old.

'My lord,' he began, 'I came at once to apprise you – ' he broke off as he became aware of a stranger at the table. 'I beg your pardon. I didn't know you had a visitor,' but he said it as if it was a personal affront that Tarbat should not be alone and free to see him.

The Viscount made the introductions, as a Highlander himself giving the Earl his full Highland titles. Called Iain Glas – Grey John – by his people, he was MacCailein 'ic Dhonnachaidh, Laird of Glenorchy and Earl of Breadalbane. Lord Tarbat also asked if he had dined and learning he had not ordered another cover to be set and fresh food to be brought at once. He poured wine for the Earl himself and after the newcomer was served and the lackey had withdrawn he enquired what had brought his lordship in such haste.

Breadalbane, stuffing roast beef into his mouth, cast a glance at Richard and said, ' 'Twill wait. 'Twill wait.'

Richard half rose but the Viscount laid a hand on his arm. 'You can say what you like in front of Colonel Lincourt, Iain Glas. He is in the King's confidence.' And he explained the reason for Richard's presence in Edinburgh.

Breadalbane gave him a rather sour look. 'You'll no be persuading clansmen to join you, Colonel. They're mostly obstinate, stubborn, bloody-minded thieves and many of the chiefs are as bad as the least in their clan.'

Tarbat refilled his glass. 'Suppose you tell us what happened at Achallader. After all, it was at my suggestion that the chiefs were called in and I'd like to know it was not for naught but talk.'

Breadalbane drank off the wine in one thirsty gulp and pushed his plate aside. 'I think I may say I achieved more than talk, though what they expected when they came, God knows! They could see the black ruins of my castle that they burned two years since. Oh yes, they came, Stewarts and MacKenzies, Camerons and the MacDonalds – Glengarry and Keppoch and Glencoe – with 'tails' of tacksmen and pipers and a score of gillies to eat their heads off at my expense. Glengarry even brought General Thomas Buchan, who commands the forces of King James in Scotland, or so he says, though where they are and if he has any at all, no one divulged. We spent the week talking and they eased their sore throats with my best whisky. We gambled and feasted as if we were all the best of friends and they'd never so much as raided my lands. And I'll have no recruiting among my folk, Colonel Lincourt, nor I think would they leave my service for an Englishman.'

'Maybe not,' Richard said quietly, refusing to be browbeaten by this truculent earl. 'If you don't wish it, I'll not step on to your property. I'm aware I'll need the chiefs' permission for my venture.'

'Well, well,' Breadalbane seemed to relax. 'I've no wish to be overharsh.'

'And I might tell you,' Lord Tarbat put in, 'that Colonel Lincourt has raised several companies already and has them drilling smartly down by Leith.'

'Is that so?' The Earl gave Richard a more interested stare. 'Then good fortune to you, sir.' But he did not invite him on to Campbell land and seemed to lose all interest in his doings, turning back to Tarbat.

'To go on with my tale, I proposed a truce to them, a bond between us all, no hostilities for three months while a better treaty is arranged and the indemnity money paid to the chiefs. Young Coll of Keppoch was the first to sign, but Glengarry had a fit of the sulks and only put a scrawl to the paper at the last. He's angry because he's not getting more than a thousand pounds and he'd looked for fifteen hundred. Ewen Cameron, who's the best of them, pulled the others in including young Robert Stewart of Appin who'd have liked to be thought on the same terms as those with more years and sense. As for MacIain, he was cold as ice on the Tay and had no wish to do business with me. Clan Iain Abrach were always intransigent, curse their thieving hides. There's been bad blood between us and a matter of some of my cows that his men filched. He wouldn't admit to it and I'll not deny there were hard words between us.'

'But you got your agreement?' Tarbat asked.

'Oh aye, they listened to me in the end and they signed under pressure from Ewen Cameron. He sees the patrol boats on Loch Linnhe and Colonel Hill's foot patrols in the glens and he knows Sir Thomas Livingstone has an army ready to march if the King orders it. They saw – as I pointed out – that King William on the throne is a fact. 'Tis their honour they're jealous for and they consider themselves bound to King James, but if he released them – well, I intend to put that point to the King when I see him.'

'Then you did all that was needed,' Tarbat said.

'I did.' The Earl seemed very pleased with himself. ' 'Tis

the best hope for peace that we've had. Even MacIain signed in the end, after his sons John and Alasdair Og, and I've sent out messengers to tell all my people what's been done. They'll keep clear of trouble.' He gave a laugh and rubbed his hands together. 'I tell you this, after Achallader 'tis MacCailein 'ic Dhonnachaidh who leads the Campbells, not MacCailein Mor.'

'My lord of Argyll will no doubt envy you your success,' Tarbat murmured politely, but his lips were twitching.

'Well, I'm away to my house.' Breadalbane threw down his napkin. 'Thank you for a good dinner, my lord. I was as empty as a pea pod. Tomorrow I'm for London to tell the Queen and my lord of Nottingham what I've obtained, and then I'll sail for Flanders to see the King.' Whereupon, his haste being so great, to Richard's amusement he leaned back in his chair and recounted all over again his self-considered triumph at Achallader.

When he had finally taken himself off Richard turned to his host. 'Well, sir, what do you make of the treaty?'

Tarbat shrugged. 'Like all such pieces of paper the proof of it will have to be shown in deeds.'

And shown it was, for a group of Glencoe and Stewart men with a young firebrand kinsman of Glengarry's raided a provision boat on the coast of Lorn, seized its cargo and went back to Glencoe in triumph. Colonel Hill was angry and with good reason, for the much-tried garrison at Fort William were in sore need of meal and meat, and he acted promptly by sending a detachment of soldiers with such alacrity to arrest the culprits that they were taken entirely by surprise. They found themselves in the Tolbooth at Inverary where they were forced to sit through the long hot summer days.

Livingstone gave this news to Richard one evening. 'You see!' he said in barely disguised satisfaction. 'For all Lord Breadalbane's talk all he got was fair words. Colonel Hill has striven for years to bring the clans to quiet and was beginning to succeed, but my lord of Breadalbane thinks to win all in a week. You'd best keep your men in readiness, Colonel. I may need them if there is further trouble.'

Richard said shortly, 'I regret, sir, that they are not yet ready for active service.'

Livingstone was angry, not so much at this refusal, as at the flaunting of the truce, but he turned his annoyance on the nearest person who happened to be Richard. 'Need I remind you that while you are here you come under my orders as Commander-in-Chief?'

'With respect, sir,' Richard retorted, 'I do not. I think if you will consult with the Master of Stair you'll find mine is an independent command, though naturally yours is superior.'

'If I need men to keep the country's peace do you mean to say you refuse?' Sir Thomas's face was a fiery hue.

'The situation seems hardly likely to require such extreme measures. The only unrest at the moment appears to have come from a bunch of hotheads and from what I hear Colonel Hill seems to be more than competent to deal with that.'

Livingstone, who had in his temper said more than he intended, blustered a little, but eventually tried to mend matters by saying he was sure the colonel would understand that he was impressed by his men.

Richard inclined his head and said no more.

It seemed, however, that most of the chiefs did not want trouble. There were no further incidents and Queen Mary insisted that the excitable young men in prison at Inverary should be set free, but not before Colonel Hill had sternly reminded them of the promises made at Achallader.

Richard felt he was beginning to understand something of the conflict between Highland and Lowland, and he forebore to mention the raid at Newsteads, though he surmised from something David let slip that they knew of it. And not long afterwards something happened here in Edinburgh that distracted him from speculation about the distant Highlands, something that showed him the fires smouldering beneath the surface.

He was riding back from Leith one evening in late August when the weather was still hot and sultry. The air in the High Street was particularly noisome, apprentices shutting up shops, housewives chatting on their doorsteps, children running about getting in the way of horsemen passing up and down. A crowd seemed to be gathering by the Fountain Well where a young man had climbed up on a ledge and was shouting to the crowd. A companion was calling to people to come and listen. The young man on the well was waving a paper which he proceeded to fix where everyone could see it. He gave an exclamation and edged his horse nearer.

'Good folk of Edinburgh,' David was calling out, his face flushed with excitement. 'never think the cause of our lawful King, King James the Seventh of Scotland, is lost. The French fleet is coming to the west, the clans will rise and we'll have Jamie back. Don't listen to the blether of truces and the like – what's a truce to a man with a loose dirk in his belt and the true cause in his heart?'

There was some muffled laughter in the crowd, but some uneasy muttering. The other young man pointed to the paper David had nailed up and yelled at the crowd to look at it.

'Aye,' David added, 'look well, my friends. God save King James, it says, and when he comes there'll be a pardon even for Willie's men if they join him. God save King James, and so should say all Scots. I tell you – '

Richard had had enough. Authoritatively he pushed his horse up to the well, knocking one man off his feet. 'Make way there! Move, I say!' At the Fountain he leaned forward and tore down the proclamation, crumpled it in his hand and flung it beneath his horse's hooves. David's companion took one look at the red coat and fled, but David stayed where he was as Richard said in a low voice, 'You young fool, get you down from there and go home. Do you want to be clapped in the Tolbooth?'

David, his face scarlet with excitement and mortification, cried out, 'Aye, 'tis your day now but ours will come.' For a moment he glared rebelliously at Richard and then he jumped down, pushed his way through the hastily dispersing crowd and disappeared into a close.

Richard, seeing the incident safely over, was about to ride on, thinking of what he would have to say to the foolish young man later, when he became aware of a carriage at a stand-still and a man at the window of it, watching. He called out, 'You, sir, one moment if you please.'

Seeing a crest on the door of the carriage Richard dismounted and went over to it. The man looking out was pale in colouring with prominent blue eyes and an air of hauteur.

'You wished to speak with me?' Richard asked rather abruptly.

'I do, sir.' The occupant of the coach looked closely at him. 'I don't think you are one of the castle officers, so if I am not mistaken you must be Colonel Lincourt. I'd heard you were here in our town.'

'You have the advantage of me, sir. I fear your crest is unknown to me.'

'I am Argyll. What was that young ruffian doing?'

'Shouting a great deal of nonsense,' Richard said. 'As you no doubt saw, I tore his paper down.'

'And its message?'

'A Jacobite slogan.' Richard objected to being questioned in the street and gathered up his reins.

'One moment.' The Earl held up a hand. He was MacCailein Mor, the largest landowner in Scotland and the head of Clan Campbell, vying with the MacDonalds for the leadership of Gaeldom, and as such entitled to immediate attention.

'You seem to be making light of this, Colonel, but we can't have young firebrands putting up seditious papers in the city. He should be behind bars to learn a lesson.'

'I think I frightened him off. He'll probably cool down and behave himself.'

Argyll looked curiously at him. 'You are over-sanguine. Do you know him?'

'I know the family slightly,' Richard said. 'I'm sure if I speak to them they'll see he does nothing so foolish again.'

The Earl drummed his fingers on the door of the coach. 'And his name. And direction?'

Richard had not wanted to give this information but he felt obliged to answer and Argyll raised his sandy brows.

'A Highlander, eh?'

'By family, sir, but his father was a respected lawyer here. I'll see the boy is duly chastened.'

Argyll gave him a further penetrating look and then leaned back in his carriage. 'Well, that may be enough – or it may not. Good day, Colonel.' And he drummed his cane on the roof of the coach to signify that he wished the coachman to drive on.

The coach trundled away and Richard rode on up the hill, uneasy in his mind. He slept on the matter and the next afternoon he left Leith early and rode to the Grassmarket. Leaving Juno in charge of an urchin, he knocked on the door. There seemed to be a considerable pause before it was opened by Iain Dubh who gave him a stare that could only be described as openly hostile.

'What iss it you will be wanting?' he demanded.

'To see Mistress Stewart, what else?' Richard retorted and prepared to step inside, but the Highlander barred his way.

'I'll see if the Mistress will wish to see you.'

Astounded, Richard said, 'Then at least have the goodness to allow me to wait inside and not here on the step.'

Reluctantly Iain Dubh let him in. He saw Somerled at the back of the hall and said sourly, ' 'Tis the *sasunnach*.'

By this time Richard was growing justifiably annoyed, but before he could protest the parlour door opened and Marged Stewart came out. At the sight of her expression Richard stood rigid. What could have made her look so?'

'You'd better be coming in,' she said and in silence he followed her into the parlour. When the door was closed she turned on him, the tone of her voice unlike anything he had ever heard from her.

'I wonder that you should be coming here, indeed I do, after what you have done!'

'What have I done?' he asked. He had never seen her so overwrought. The dark eyes were alight with anger and contempt, and something more – desperate dis- appointment.

She gave a scornful laugh. 'Don't pretend ignorance, Colonel. You saw David yesterday in the High Street, oh yes, he told me about it and I know he was behaving with the utmost folly, but if you had come to me first – '

He broke in sharply. 'Of what are you accusing me? I did not more than tear down what you must know was a seditious paper and might have landed him in serious trouble. As it was – '

'Might have? Don't pretend you don't know what has happened when you must have been the instigator of it.'

'Upon my honour I don't know,' he said. 'Let me talk to David and find out what it is I am supposed to have done.'

She had turned towards the empty hearth but now she swung back to look at him intently and he returned her gaze with complete openness. If she was blaming him for stopping David's dangerous behaviour he could only tell her he had done it for the boy's own sake. But he was more hurt than he would admit that she could have thought him capable of any treachery towards David or towards her.

'Do you mean to say you don't know what happened this morning?' she asked incredulously.

'I have been at Leith all day. Tell me.'

She was standing very still. 'David was arrested. He's in the Tolbooth.'

'Good God!' he exclaimed. 'I had no notion of it.'

'Did you not report the matter to the authorities?'

'I did not, I swear it.'

Almost appealingly she said, 'I thought it must be you, because you were there and no one else thought to stop him.'

'How could you think I should do such a thing?' he demanded. 'You must believe I had nothing to do with his arrest.'

She was silent and he saw to his surprise that as relief swept over her face she was near to tears.

'Forgive me,' she said in a low voice, 'forgive me for doubting you. I thought – I thought you might have considered it your duty.'

'Certainly not.' In an endeavour to lighten the moment he added with a faint smile, 'I would have read him the sternest lecture he's ever had in his life. And I would have been, I am, angry with him for distressing you, but he's really done little except act with extreme folly. Coffee-house sentiments are best kept off the streets.'

'Someone obviously thought so,' she said and he had a sudden picture of the Earl of Argyll and his cold voice enquiring David's name and where he might be found. But he said nothing. It would not benefit her to know who had done so, and in any case he could not be totally sure.

'What can we do?' she was asking. 'Colonel, will you be after helping us? Perhaps you could make enquiries – you seem to have some influence. Perhaps your friend Lord Tarbat might interest himself? If you could get David freed, oh I would be seeing that he is not so stupid again. Whatever we may believe that was no way to be helping our cause.'

She was looking at him with a mingling of pleading, acute anxiety and restored trust and in that one moment he knew himself to be utterly lost. He came to her and took her hands in his, putting first one and then the other to his lips.

'I would do anything for you,' he said in a shaken voice, *'anything,'* and turning, he left the house.

Chapter 6

He went first to Argyll's lodging only to learn that the Earl had left for London that morning. Then he called on Viscount Stair but Sir James was in bed with a bad cold and a bad temper and would see no one. Finally he mounted the steps of Lord Tarbat's house where he was thankful to find his lordship supping alone with his lady. When Richard explained his business was urgent Lady Tarbat assured him she had finished and left them together.

'What can I do for you?' Tarbat asked. 'Take a glass of wine, Lincourt.'

Richard accepted and briefly recounted what had happened. 'He's young, my lord, and carried away by misplaced zeal, but I think there's no harm in him. He may have learned his lesson.'

Tarbat did not seem disturbed by David's misdeeds, but he asked Richard why he was putting himself about for an obvious Jacobite sympathiser.

'His family have shown me great kindness since I came here,' Richard said, 'and I feel some interest in the lad.'

'Well, I'll give you a note for Bailie Jameson, that's the best I can do. In the meantime you may not have heard of a more serious matter.' The Viscount refilled Richard's glass. 'An order has come from his Majesty, a proclamation to be posted tomorrow at the Mercat Cross.'

'No, I've heard nothing of it, my lord. What will it have to say?'

'It seems William's patience has at last run out, for it will require every man who has borne arms against him and Queen Mary to swear the oath of allegiance. They are to do this in front of the sheriffs of their own shires before the first day of January. If they don't – ' Tarbat paused, 'they are to be subject to the utmost extremity of the law.'

Richard sat for a moment in silence. Then he asked, 'What do you think it will mean? Will it bring the chiefs and their men in?'

'I do believe so, all but the most truculent anyway. Even the MacDonalds may see that this is the only way other than outright war and that I'm sure none of them want. They've no leader of Dundee's standing and the French are too concerned with their own war against the King in Flanders to do more than send an occasional ship up the west coast of Scotland. The chiefs have a few months to think it over and my lord of Breadalbane's truce should keep the Highlands quiet.'

'And those that refuse to come in?'

Tarbat shrugged. 'The utmost extremity of the law, and that can be interpreted in any way the authorities see fit. The trouble must be stopped and stopped by the end of the year. I'm a MacKenzie and Highland myself, but the days of the fighting tribes must be numbered. Now I'll write you your note.'

Richard left soon after with the letter in his pocket. It was dark now and he and John Robb rode up to the castle in a tearing wind. Rain clouds were gathering in the west but regardless of this Richard sent Robb to bed and went out onto the battery that overlooked the town. Here the wind was a gale and it caught his plumed hat, tossing it high in the air, sending it far away down below where in the morning two urchins would fight over the possession of it.

He was hardly aware of the annoyance of losing it. The events of the day crowded too closely – David's arrest, his efforts for the boy, the news of the proclamation, and all these faded before the importance of those few moments alone with Marged Stewart. He knew now that he was deeply in love with her, that he loved her as he had not loved since his father died and that childish love was lost. He knew that this love had brought him to life in a way that was totally new. His loneliness, the reserve and coldness that had stemmed from it, were gone; he was alive, throbbing with life, his body tingling with it, even the breath he drew bringing new energy. Standing here in the high wind, his hair blown wildly about his face, suited his mood, exhilarated him. That such a thing could happen to him was something he had never expected, never thought of. Life had been a sober business and marriage, if he contracted it with Judith, a sober if comfortable affair. Now all thought of that was gone. There was only Marged – a Jacobite, a Catholic, a Highland woman! Good God, he must be mad! How could he contemplate such a union? Yet there could, there must be, no other end. He could not think, now, of life without her. He wanted her for his wife, to spend the waking and sleeping hours with her for the rest of their days.

Rain clouds scudded across the moon, obliterating its light and the first spatter of drops fell. Richard took a deep breath and unaware that he had had no supper went inside to his bed but not to sleep.

Characteristically, he restrained himself from speaking openly to her at the moment, though he was sure she felt some response to him, and he had a great longing to know how much. She had indeed turned to him for help though she must have other friends in Edinburgh, including David's employer, and when he arrived at Newsteads, armed with Tarbat's letter to Bailie Jameson, he found Mr Kirkaldy already there.

'He must have been quite moon-mad,' Mr Kirkaldy was saying fussily. 'I can't think what can have possessed him. Well, I will see what I can do, but I must say, Mistress Stewart, that try as I will, I cannot think he will ever apply himself sufficiently to make a lawyer. As for this last business, I am at a loss for words.'

Privately Richard agreed with him, but he produced his letter and said tactfully that if Mr Kirkaldy agreed he would seek out Bailie Jameson immediately. Marged turned to him gratefully and the lawyer answered in a huffy tone that he supposed as Colonel Lincourt had interested himself in the matter that would be the best course.

He took himself off and Richard said, 'I'm afraid I've

offended him. I'm sure he thinks it his business to get David out of this trouble, which perhaps it is.'

'I'm only thankful for your help,' Marged told him. 'Will you be after going now?'

He nodded. 'I've sent a note to my captain-lieutenant to tell him I'm delayed today. As soon as I've seen the Bailie I'll come back.'

The Bailie proved to be a difficult nut to crack, having no time for tiresome young men who disturbed the peace of his town, but he agreed to bear David's youth in mind when he appeared before him, and he gave permission for David's step-mother to visit him. Armed with this order Richard returned to Marged. She was very grateful and asked him to forgive her if she immediately set about preparing a basket of food to take with her.

'I don't believe he will get anything but porridge in the Tolbooth,' she said with a faint smile.

'It won't hurt him to cool that for a while,' Richard said. 'I'm angry with him for upsetting you.'

'Oh, 'tis David I'm concerned about,' she answered swiftly. 'For his father's sake and for his own I am wanting him clear of this trouble. I really don't know what's to be done if he doesn't use his head. He's so young and gets carried away by those other wild young men at the Club – and I only hope he will see now 'tis not the right way to go about anything.'

Richard was standing by the door, looking across at her. 'To go about what? Furthering the Jacobite cause?'

Marged sat down suddenly, her hands twisted together in her lap. ' 'Tis no use to be hiding the facts, Colonel. I've explained to you that David is on fire to do something to prove his loyalty and one must allow for the enthusiasm of youth.'

'He will destroy himself and do no good anywhere if he's not more careful.' Weighing his words carefully he told her of yesterday's proclamation. 'Don't you see?' he asked, 'it's a way out for the chiefs, for all Highlanders? The King is determined to put an end to dissension once and for all and if they don't avail themselves of this amnesty there will be harsh measures against all who refuse it. If David's brother were alive he'd have to take the oath with the rest.'

'Or take to the hills,' she said sadly. 'I understand, Colonel.' She sat silent for a moment, assimilating what he had told her. 'This makes everything look very different. If the chiefs don't come in – '

' – there will be war,' he finished. 'And God knows none of us want that. And if some come in and some don't, those who don't will be severely punished. I know the King well enough to know that if his orders are flouted he is a hard man. David, I imagine, would be all for fighting, but I'm sure you don't want him to risk his brother's fate.'

'No,' she said in a low voice. 'I couldn't bear to lose both of them.'

She looked suddenly so bereft as if that tragedy had already happened that he longed to go to her, to take her in his arms, but he stayed where he was. This was not the moment and he said merely, 'Please God all Jacobites will see sense and swear before the New Year. Now, if you will permit me, I'll accompany you to the Tolbooth.'

She rose. 'It's kind in you, sir, but not necessary. I've taken up too much of your time already.'

He felt dashed by the dismissal but he stood his ground. 'It is necessary,' he said. 'It's not fitting that you should go alone to that place.'

She inclined her head, accepting his offer, but when he would have gone out to hail a carriage, she said she was used to walking about the town and could certainly go that short distance. They went together, her hand on his arm, Iain Dubh behind carrying the basket.

The crowds were out as usual, busy round the Luckenbooths as they made they way towards the entrance to the prison. Inside the gloomy place the goaler looked for the usual payment for the privilege of a visit and Marged paid him, quietly refusing Richard's instant gesture of reaching for his purse.

'This is a family matter,' she said, and taking the basket from Iain Dubh followed the goaler, leaving her two escorts to wait in stony silence in the dingy passage. Richard stood with his arms folded, leaning against a wall while the gillie remained by the locked and barred door, a look of loathing for the place in his face, and Richard made sure he was included in that black resentment.

It was half an hour before she returned and the goaler unlocked the door to let them out.

'Well,' Richard asked as they made their way back to the West Bow. 'Did you find him chastened?'

With a glimmer of a smile she said, 'Hardly that, I'm afraid. But it's a miserable dark cell and I do pray he won't be there too long.'

He was in fact there for two weeks, waiting to appear before the Bailie and seeing Marged's anxiety Richard said nothing of a personal nature, but he visited her more often and she seemed always glad to see him. He put down that moment when she tried to reject his company to Highland pride, and his love grew with his longing to ease her anxiety. One morning he went himself to the Tolbooth.

David's cell was indeed a wretched little room about six feet by eight and he was sitting disconsolately on a stool, his bed no more than a straw pallet on the stone floor. Despite the summer day outside he was wrapped in a black cloak for it struck chill in here.

As Richard entered he looked up in a far from welcoming manner. 'You? Are you come to gloat or to read me a lecture?'

'I don't think you need it.' Richard ignored the first question. 'I should have thought this place enough of a lesson.'

David had the grace to get up off the stool and offer it to his visitor, sitting cross-legged on the bed himself. On the floor were the remains of a chicken Marged had brought and an empty bottle of wine. 'My step-mother says it wasn't you who had me arrested,' he said rather grudgingly, almost as if he would have liked to blame the Englishman, 'but I'm not sure I believe her. It seemed so obvious.'

'It may well have done so,' Richard retorted, 'but I had no hand in it. Do you think I'd repay her so ill as to have you put in here?'

'Maybe not,' David muttered. He had a week's growth of

beard and he rubbed at it, aware of how unkempt he looked, 'but I can't think who else – '

'The street was full of people. Did you really imagine no one there would see it as stirring up dangerous sedition? You got no more than you deserved. I hope you've had time to reflect on that.'

'Oh aye,' David said bitterly. 'I've had naught to do but think, and I tell you this – I'm not going to be a lawyer. I hate it and I'm not going to waste my time on it, even for the sake of my father's wishes.'

'Your stepmother will be distressed if you give it up,' Richard answered, but in this he sympathized with David. To be chained to a dusty law office when one was young and energetic was hardly desirable except for those with a positive bent for it.

'I'm sorry,' David added, 'but she must make the best of it.'

'What do you want to do?' Richard asked. 'I'm not here to indulge in recriminations but to see what I can do to help you.'

David shifted uncomfortably, the truculent look back on his face. 'I don't know yet, but – '

'Listen to me,' Richard said. 'My offer is still open – a place in my regiment and a chance to fight in Flanders. Would that not be adventure enough for you? Think on it,' he added earnestly. 'Don't throw your life away on a lost cause. You may be Highland by descent but you've lived all your life in Edinburgh and know Lowland ways. King William and Queen Mary are here to stay so try to put aside old memories and grudges – you are young enough for them not to be yours.' He told David of the proclamation and then went on, 'I believe most of the important chiefs will submit – they can do nothing else except to run on our swords. David, I want to help you. Surely you understand that?'

'I don't know why you should,' David retorted ungraciously. 'I've said I'm grateful for what you did but that doesn't make you into a friend – not while you wear that uniform. And I think that compromises my stepmother among our acquaintances. You are too often at our house.'

'And you are an extremely impertinent young man.' Richard rose to his feet. 'I shall begin to repent me of having persuaded Lord Tarbat to put in a word for you.'

David got up off the makeshift bed. 'Oh – did you? Perhaps I should not have said that – about Marged.'

'You should not.'

'But I can only stand by the rightness of my cause and that without help from any Whig lord,' David said with a touch of pride, 'especially one who is Highland born.' And then recollecting himself he added, 'I suppose it was good of you to approach him – I'm not insensible of that – but I can't take a place under your command. I'd rather serve in the King of France's Scots regiment.'

Richard went to the door and banged on it for the gaoler to release him. 'Then I can do nothing further for you. But think of your stepmother.'

'I'm very fond of her,' David said. 'She's been very good to me and to Alan when he was alive, but she isn't my mother and I can't spend the rest of my life attached to a woman's petticoats. Anyway how we get on together is naught to do with you.'

Richard suppressed the desire to box his ears. 'It is to do with anyone who considers himself her friend. Behave yourself in court and keep a guard on your tongue. You may not want my advice but I must give it.'

'Oh,' David said, 'I'm well aware that one can't serve any cause in prison.'

On this defiant note Richard left him, the gaoler having unlocked the door. He went straight to Newsteads where he told the two women of his visit. 'I'm only sorry,' he ended, 'that what I had to say appears to have had little effect.'

Miss Robertson said, 'I wish his father was alive to make him see a wee bit of sense,' and Marged added, 'I wish I knew what to do with him when he comes home.'

Richard was tempted to say it might be better to ship David off to France and let him join the Scots regiment, but he didn't say so and walked back to the castle simmering with annoyance. His nerves were jangling that all this business should have come between him and a declaration of his love, for that he was determined to do as soon as he could. He wished to God he knew whether she cared for him. Or was she only grateful? He was restless, tense when he was out at Leith, irritable with John Robb.

And then an incident occurred that caught him on the raw. He had come back to the castle to find that a chest of money had arrived from London but without its letter of instructions, apparently having been parted from it on the journey. Richard heard of its arrival and went straight to the Commander-in-Chief. Sir Thomas Livingstone was in his office and Lieutenant-Colonel Hamilton was, to Richard's annoyance, there with him.

Without any preamble he said that the chest must be destined for him to pay his men as he had been expecting it for weeks.

'You presume too much,' Hamilton said before Livingstone could open his mouth. 'It is undoubtedly for Fort William and as I am going there soon I shall see that it reaches its destination.'

'I think the presumption is on your part,' Richard answered haughtily. 'Sir Thomas is well aware that I have as yet received no pay for my soldiers.'

'And that the men at Fort William have had no pay for months nor enough supplies to feed them adequately.'

'Gentlemen,' Sir Thomas put in, 'we really can't decide this argument when we have no instructions. I shall write immediately to London and have the matter decided.'

'That will take time,' Richard said, 'and it seems to me to be obvious that the chest is meant for my new regiment. Surely supplies for Fort William go by sea from Glasgow? You have told me so yourself, Sir Thomas.'

'Aye, I did,' the Commander agreed, 'but they sometimes come by ship from London and then overland from Edinburgh to Glasgow. There's nothing to say for what this chest is intended.'

'Except that it is more likely that my instructions, being new, may have gone astray.'

Hamilton said, as if weighing his words. 'I find it exceedingly tiresome that you are here at all. We do not need Englishmen appropriating our young men and the sooner you take yourself off to Flanders the better.'

Sir Thomas made a deprecatory gesture at this astonishing speech, but before he could say anything Richard broke in, 'And I find you insulting, Hamilton.'

To which Hamilton replied, 'As I intended that you should. Furthermore you are interfering in the affairs of this town. I hear you are interesting yourself in a young cub of a Jacobite who needs nothing so much as hanging.'

How the devil did he know about David, Richard wondered angrily? But the town, he supposed, was small enough for news to travel in the way that gossip always did. 'That,' he retorted, 'is none of your business, Hamilton – nor are my affairs. You know by whose commission I am here.'

'And I'm sure your orders didn't include helping imprisoned Jacobites.'

'What is all this?' Sir Thomas demanded. 'Lincourt, to what is Hamilton referring?'

'A youth, sir, not much above eighteen, whose family have shown me hospitality. I merely put a word in for him because he's no more than an excitable lad that I hope to induce to see sense.'

'That sounds reasonable,' Sir Thomas agreed. 'I think, Hamilton, our cause is better served by bringing young men to obedience rather than by hanging them.'

'Sometimes sterner measures are necessary to deter others and quite justifiable,' Hamilton retorted. 'You yourself are ready to take an army into the Highlands if necessary.'

Sir Thomas was beginning to get a trifle hot himself. 'That's a different matter, as well you know. And anyway it seems now as if it may be unnecessary. Nor are we discussing that. We must settle the business of this money. I'm aware that it's needed at Fort William, but you, Lincourt, also have a claim on it. All I can do is to divide it until such time as we hear further or another such delivery is made.'

'Your pardon, sir,' Richard said, 'but am I to begin by putting my soldiers in arrears of pay? That's hardly likely to encourage them. In fact so far I've been paying them at my own cost, and that I can't continue to do. I need every penny in that chest.'

'Good God,' Hamilton exploded, 'is the Commander-in-Chief to be dictated to by a – '

'Be careful, sir,' Richard's temper was rapidly fraying, 'I don't know what you were about to say but I'm sure it's better left unsaid.'

'Certainly,' Sir Thomas agreed. 'Hamilton, pray watch your tongue. Colonel Lincourt is a guest in our country. In any case I've made my decision and that's the end of the matter.'

With that Richard had to be content. His dislike of Hamilton increased and coloured the prospect of his own journey to Fort William as he would doubtless find Hamilton in residence at the end of it.

Passing Hamilton later in the passage he barred his way and said, 'Why you choose to resent my presence, I have no idea but I tell you this, sir, I will not stomach the kind of thing you said to me today.'

'And what will you do?' Hamilton mocked. 'Call me out?'

Richard looked him over in disgust. 'Senior officers do not duel and may I remind you that in rank you are subordinate to me.'

'But not under your command. Complain of me to Sir Thomas if you will.'

'I was not thinking of Sir Thomas,' Richard said and Hamilton flushed.

'I wondered whether you would throw that in my face. But you see I too am under orders, from the Master of Stair, the Secretary of State for Scotland, and so from his Majesty myself.'

'Then you should know better than to behave as you have towards me,' Richard retorted. 'We are unfortunately colleagues.'

'Do you say so?' Hamilton raised his eyebrows. 'I trust you will be gone before my span of duty at the Fort is done.'

'Indeed? I am myself going there to see Colonel Hill.'

Hamilton was startled. Obviously he had not known this but he gave a harsh laugh. 'Is there no end to your vanity?

What in God's name do you hope to achieve there? Colonel Hill has trouble keeping his own men up to strength, and I doubt he'll spare any for you.'

Richard was so angry now he began to wish he could face Hamilton with a sword in his hand. 'Colonel Hamilton,' he said icily. 'you choose to be obstructive and hostile – God knows why – but it won't go unrecorded.' And with that he strode off to make arrangements for a cart and escort to bring his share of the money to Leith. At least he had the satisfaction of paying his men on the following Saturday, but the quarrel with Hamilton, which Sir Thomas amiably thought concluded, nevertheless simmered below the surface. It was not long before it occurred to him that it was odd that Hamilton, a serving officer, should claim to be under orders from the Master of Stair.

*

David was eventually released on a fine of twenty pounds Scots and a threat of further imprisonment if he made a disturbance again. He gave, reluctantly, a promise of good behaviour and came home, dishevelled and dirty and apparently unrepentant. His stepmother told Richard that she hoped, after his good offices, that David would keep his word, but he seemed immediately to go back to his old habit of disappearing in the evenings and it did not take much intelligence to guess where he had gone.

'I am thinking he will not listen to anyone,' Marged said in despair one evening a week after his release. 'I understand only too well what is running in his head – '

' – and chasing after fanatics will bring him nothing but trouble,' Richard finished. 'I wish I could help him but he won't listen to me – there's no reason why he should.'

Marged said nothing but she looked so troubled that he came to where she was sitting on the cushioned window seat and sitting beside her took her hands in his.

'Sometimes I think I am an embarrassment to you,' he said in a low voice. 'I'm not of your persuasion in any way. I can't advise you or help you and I wish I could. Is there no older man or friend whom David might listen to?'

'There's Mr Kirkaldy but he doesn't pay any attention to him, and perhaps our doctor friend whom I think you've met, but you see I would rather not involve them in this. You've done more for us than anyone else could.' She paused and then added, 'If it hadn't been for you David might still be in the Tolbooth and – and your strength has helped me during this very difficult time.'

'Has it?' He could not keep the urgency from his voice. 'Has it? I told you I would do anything for you and it's true. Don't you know? Don't you know I'm so in love with you that I'd give my life if it would serve you.'

She had been staring down at her hands enfolded in his and she thought how strong and square they were, how indicative of his whole personality. Slowly she raised her head. 'Oh yes, I know – as I know my own heart.'

He sat very still, his grasp tightening. 'Am I to believe – do you mean that? Can you really care for me?'

She gave him a little smile that turned his stomach over. 'Yes, I mean it. I think I have known it for some time.'

'And I.' He thought of the nights when dreams of holding her, kissing her, had disturbed his sleep. Releasing her hands, he put his arms round her and bending his head he took the kiss he had imagined so many times, raised his head, looked down at her and then, seeing the expression on her face, kissed her again. And it was far more than those imagined moments.

At last he let her go and putting both hands about her face, he found himself gazing intently at every beautiful feature, all his love in his own face.

She drew in her breath sharply. 'My dear, my dear, I don't know how this came about, but oh, I'm glad it did.'

'I don't know either,' he said, 'nor when it began. Perhaps for me it was when I expected a grey-haired mother for David and you came down the stairs.' He gave a low laugh. 'I was so reluctant to come to Scotland, never guessing the command would bring me to you.'

'Fate is very strange,' she agreed. 'If you had not walked by the close when David was in trouble we might never have met. Yet I think we were destined to meet and to love.'

'I've never believed in fate. I always thought we were masters of our own destinies but now – now I think too we were meant to come together. Chance is too casual an explanation for what has happened.'

She smiled up at him. 'We Highlanders believe there is a pattern to our lives, that certain things are meant to be.'

'There is so much I have to learn about you.' He lifted one hand and touched the dark hair. 'I want to know everything about you. Marged, my love – for I claim the right now to call you mine – there will I know be much to think of, to decide, and no doubt many obstacles, but I want you for my wife. Will you marry me, even though I am perhaps the last man you should take?'

She gave him a long look. 'I would be after taking you if the whole world was against us, but don't let's be thinking of difficulties today. They'll bear waiting for another.'

'I've waited so long to love,' he said, 'so many barren years.'

'Has there never been anyone?' she asked tremulously.

'No, never. I thought eventually to marry for the sake of my mother and my line, perhaps someone I've known all my life, but it would have been a very quiet business, whereas now – my God!' He caught her to him and his kissing deepened, searching her mouth, every nerve leaping as she responded.

At last she leaned against him, her head on his chest, and said softly. 'You may be thinking that because I've been wed before that I've known love like this, but it isn't so – Richard my dearest, it isn't so. Alexander was kind and considerate always, but no more than that, and I never knew what I feel in myself now. And I'm glad, I'm glad!'

'Thank God,' he said in a low shaken voice. 'I'd no right to expect that, but thank God it is so.'

Eventually, hearing the voice of Miss Robertson in the hall, they draw apart and she came into the room. As always she had her wits about her and seeing the two of them together on the window seat, something in their attitude made her pause and say, 'Oh!'

'Yes,' Marged rose. 'Aunt Marie, Colonel Lincourt has done me the honour to ask me to be his wife.'

'And there's no need to spier if you've accepted him,' she added drily. She came across the room as Richard too rose, taking Marged's hand and drawing her to him. 'My dears, I can see you are both very happy and you know you have my good wishes but I think you have a long weary road to travel before you may be wed.'

Richard smiled down at his love. 'We feel today that nothing will be too hard for us.'

Miss Robertson gave him a warm smile. 'And you don't want to talk of difficulties. A glass of wine to toast you both would be more appropriate.'

But when Richard had reluctantly dragged himself away and back to his duties, she surveyed her niece and said, 'Dear Marged, I can see what Colonel Lincourt has come to mean to you but have you thought, have you considered? He is English and Protestant and a friend of King William.'

'I am knowing all that,' Marged said, 'but I love him. It doesn't matter how much may lie between us.'

'But I doubt you've thought what it will mean – leaving Scotland, everything you've known, your parents, David – '

'David is near a man now and I've come to see over the last few weeks that he doesn't need me as he did. If you will stay on here – '

'You needn't ask it, of course I will. It's David's house and we shall managed well together if he gets into no more trouble. But the greatest difficulty is that you are Catholic and Colonel Lincourt is not. You will have to wait until we have a priest in Edinburgh again and then there will be difficulties. You know how matters stand.'

'I am knowing that to. It is in my mind to be marrying him without waiting on anyone.'

Miss Robertson said slowly, 'I think you are too swept away to know what you are saying. Our feelings are not always the judge of what is right and there is much to be considered first.'

Marged sank down in a chair. 'I will never be anything but a Catholic and loyal to my faith, but I don't think, just now, that I'll allow that to keep me from him.' She turned her head away to look out into the sunlit garden. 'I am no green girl, Aunt Marged, to be swept away, as you put it, by a uniform and a handsome face.' She turned back, laughing. 'Is he handsome? I don't know. Perhaps not, but he is to me. Aunt Marie, don't misunderstand me. I cared greatly for Alexander, indeed I did, but in a different way. Don't be hurt if I say it was never like this.'

'Do you think I don't know that?' The older woman came to sit beside her on the window seat. 'My dear, I've not lived in this house with you these many years without coming to know you very well. I know you cared for Alexander, you made him a good wife and you were a mother to the boys, but he was after all no longer in his youth. I often thought, even though he was my nephew, that your youth and beauty were in a sense wasted on an older man. And I was prepared for this to happen one day. I just wish it had been one of our own people. Have you thought that if there was a rising he would be fighting against them?'

Marged pressed her hands together. 'I know – I know – but please God the clans won't rise. Oh, I want our own King back as much as anyone or – ' she paused painfully, 'I thought I did. But now, knowing a rising would bring nought but bloodshed and enmity, I'm no longer sure. Love doesn't always choose wisely, Aunt, and I'm after loving him so much that I can't bear the thought of his regiment marching on our men.'

'We will pray it won't ever come to that.' Miss Robertson touched her cheek lightly. 'My child, I don't want to spoil today for you. No doubt some way can be found for you to be together.'

'I believe that, I must believe it.' Marged's face grew shadowed, her dark eyes not seeing the bright prospect outside. 'But, years, ago, when I was little more than a child, a spaewife in Glencoe told me I should love once and very greatly but that my time of joy would be short. And oh, that makes me afraid.'

'Whisht!' Miss Robertson said briskly. 'Surely you can't set store by such nonsense? I've never believed in soothsayers or diviners or witches or the like being able to tell the future.'

'But you are a Lowland, dear aunt. You're not Highland born and we do set store by prophecies from the folk who have the "seeing". And they're often right.'

'More by chance than otherwise, I'm sure,' her aunt retorted. 'If the Good God had meant for us to know what was in store for us He would surely have arranged things otherwise.'

'I suppose so.'

'It is better that we don't know. Trust in Him that you will be able to be happy with your colonel.'

'I do, I do.' Marged turned a glowing face towards Miss Robertson and leaned forward to kiss her lightly. 'Aunt Marie, you have always been so good to me.'

Miss Robertson smiled and got to her feet. 'That has never been difficult. Bless me, 'tis past three and the bell hasn't been rung for dinner.' She bustled out, leaving Marged to gaze round the room. It still seemed full of Richard's presence and the mutterings of a spaewife long ago faded into insignificance.

David's reaction was explosive and perhaps predictable.

'No, no! It's not possible! Oh, I know you like him and I'm in his debt, but you can't – you *can't* want to marry him. A *sasunnach*! He – he represents all that we hate.'

Marged was shaken by his vehemence but she managed to answer quietly, 'He is not as we have always thought of English soldiers. He had become a friend to us all.'

'On the surface, maybe,' he retorted, 'but he's still an enemy when it comes to it. You're a Jacobite, you're Highland and a Catholic too – it's – it's disloyal, it's a betrayal of everything we believe in.'

'Don't be saying such things.' She felt her calm disintegrating, not only angry at his accusations, but that he should be adding his voice to Aunt Marie's, bringing a disturbing note into this day of joy, but one that in her own heart she knew to be at least part justified. She thrust the thought from her. 'We don't choose where we love,' she said. 'Perhaps you may come to find that out one day. I can keep my loyalties, though indeed I think 'tis a very tenuous hope we Jacobites have now. And whatever happens Colonel Lincourt and I will find a way, a compromise, for we are determined to be wed.'

'Oh?' His eyes were dark with resentment. 'Will you turn your back on us all, on everything you've believed in and become an English lady curtseying to King William. And the Colonel's a cursed heretic – will you turn heretic too?'

'David!'

'Well, I can see it all,' he said. 'My God, if my father could see from *Tir nan Og* what you are doing now!'

'Be quiet,' Miss Robertston said sharply. 'David, you don't know what you are saying. Your father, God rest him, has been gone these two years and more, but do you think he wouldn't want Marged to be happy again?'

'To take a Scots husband, a Jacobite perhaps, not a – '

It was Marged who was angry now. 'Be careful, David. I'll not hear Colonel Lincourt insulted.'

He flung himself away from the hearth and began to walk about the room. 'The whole idea is impossible. What will Dr Beaton and your mother be thinking when you tell them? And your chief, MacIain? You think so much of him.'

'Do you imagine I haven't sat all afternoon and thought about this?' Marged said reproachfully. 'You are being very hard, David. It's not what I would have chosen, of course, but we can't be ordering the way things happen.'

'Well, I think you should tell him it's impossible,' David threw the words at her. 'I don't want him in the family, reading me lectures and trying to tell me what to do.'

'He wouldn't – '

'Oh yes, he would. He'd want to get me into his cursed regiment and I'd die before I put on a scarlet uniform.' Suddenly he seemed near to tears. 'We've been so content together, the three of us, why did you have to ruin everything? It's been bad enough having him always here, although I admit he came to my rescue that night – as he said, anyone would have done so – but I can't and won't live in the same house with a *sasunnach*.'

Marged said, 'There's no question of that. Nothing has been discussed yet, but I don't imagine he will stay very long on Scotland and wherever he goes I'll go with him.'

'You're betraying your birthright,' he cried out, 'everything we've always held dear. It's – it's intolerable.'

Miss Robertson, judging that the conversation had gone on long enough, said quietly, 'David, you are not to speak so. I only pardon you because you're too young to know better. If Marged marries Colonel Lincourt of course she will go with him, and you and I can be very snug together until you get you a wife."

'And practise law?' he queried. 'By God, I can't think of a worse fate and I won't bear it!' And with that he stormed out of the room.

Marged sat still, her hands clasped tightly in her lap. 'I didn't think he'd take it quite so badly.'

'He's only a boy at heart and knows nothing yet of how a man and a woman may feel. The young are very intolerant.'

'But what did he mean by what he said about not bearing it? Have I made a terrible mistake in putting him in Mr Kirkaldy's office? I only did what Alexander wished.'

'I know,' Miss Robertston agreed, 'and if there is blame it is mine too. Now, my hinny, don't be upsetting yourself. He's just an excitable laddie who doesn't know what he wants. David need not be a problem and you've enough to worry about without including him.'

Marged got up and kissed her aunt. 'You could have said to me all the things that David said, but you didn't. Only they are all true.'

'But not in the least helpful,' Miss Robertson patted her hand.

'You – you don't think I should – '

'Give up the Colonel because he doesn't worship in our way? No, my dear, I'm unconventional enough to believe you should follow your own heart – which I know is not the common view. But I've seen too many loveless marriages made for seemingly sensible reasons to want that for you. But what your father will say I don't know.'

'He is wise enough to know I'm a widow and will go my own way.' Marged's spirits recovered from the brief moment of doubt. 'Dear father is the most practical of men. It's mother who will be more difficult about the fact that he's a Protestant, more than that he's English. But you are right in that I must be telling them. It's time and more that I went to Maryburgh again. I'll arrange to go soon, though,' she added wistfully, 'I don't wish to be leaving Richard.'

'No doubt you'll both survive a short parting,' Miss Robertston said and smiled at her niece, seeing the beautiful features alight afresh with the morning's joy after the last rather grim half hour. She had always known it would not be long before Marged married again and although not blind to the difficulties, she happened to like Richard Lincourt. She felt he was a man of judgement and was quite inclined to trust him. He would put no pressure on Marged to change her loyalties, of that she was sure, but nevertheless she went upstairs and spent some time with her rosary in her hand, praying for them both.

Chapter 7

Richard was finding it extremely hard to concentrate on his letter to Mynheer Huygens. In his room at the castle he had already lit his candle although it was only five o'clock, for heavy summer rain was falling outside and the room was very dark. This news he had to impart would no doubt find its way to Flanders to William's camp but he had to send his own report.

> I was at Holyroodhouse, [he had begun] being about to dine with the Commander-in-Chief, when Major John Forbes gave a letter into Sir Thomas's hand. Sir Thomas seemed mighty disturbed about it and showed me the letter, which was from Colonel Hill.

He paused. He had liked Forbes at once, an ambitious but straightforward sort of man, brother to Duncan Forbes of Culloden and Major to Colonel Hill at Fort William. He had ridden hard to deliver the letter.

Richard went on:

> It conveyed the suspicion that there are secret articles in the treaty of truce my lord Breadalbane made with the Chiefs, that the treaty is to be null if King James does not approve it, or if he should return, that a passport be granted to two men to acquaint King James of it with all haste, and that if the clans rise my lord of Breadalbane will join them with his clansmen. I can say little of the truth of all this, for my lord of Breadalbane had no witnesses of our persuasion at Achallader in June, but Major Forbes suspects that the news of the secret articles

might well have come from MacDonald of Glengarry who has no cause to love his lordship. The matter is to go before the Council tomorrow and I have little doubt they will send a report by the same bag as my own to you. My judgement is that the Earl is slippery enough to have buttered his bread on both sides, but I would add that I do not feel qualified to make any certain statement concerning the affair.

Richard paused. He was also of the opinion that the Jacobites should be allowed to go to James at St Germain for he was sure that the campaign and defeat in Ireland had sapped the last of James's energy and that the old man, scratching away with his pen at his pious writings and eaten up with guilt over his sexual appetites past and present, was not likely to stir again. This view of James had come from his knowledge of the man in the old Whitehall days and in a letter from a brother officer who had relatives in Paris. However that was not to say that the exiled King's most fanatical followers would not rise for him, and Richard frowned over his letter, wishing that he had not to write it at all. He added a thumb-nail sketch of those members of the Council whom he had met and then signed his name at the end of it.

The next morning the Council discussed the letter from Colonel Hill and immediately sent it on to the Master of Stair in Flanders for the King's perusal, but my lord of Breadalbane, hearing by a devious method of the business, vigorously denied what it said. He was on Loch Tayside and sent a message to Edinburgh informing the Council it was all gossip by enemies – any great man, he added pompously, who sought his country's good must be prepared for calumny from people who wished to belittle his achievements.

There the matter rested. Richard had a shrewd idea that William would be inclined to trust Breadalbane, for he understood better than most that agreements needed a sprinkling of fair words. Richard had heard him say this and privately thought that William would wait to see if Breadalbane's truce held.

What engaged him more was an affair that blew up a day or two later. He was driving out with Lord Tarbat to play golf when the Viscount told him that a certain Major Menzies, a Jacobite serving under Sir Thomas Buchan, the Jacobite Commander-in-Chief, had managed to gain a passport for himself and his man to go into England and thence to France. The postmaster at Holyroodhouse, who had issued it, was in the Tolbooth for his temerity in doing so without permission. It seemed he owed a favour to Menzies and didn't consider it any great crime.

'There can be no doubt where the Major and his companion have gone,' Tarbat said.

'To St Germain?'

'Aye, it would seem so. The chiefs will be wanting a clear directive from James, but my guess is he'll not stir again.'

Richard said, 'In that case it seems better that the exiled King is consulted. If he allows the Chiefs to make their peace with the Government surely that's a good thing? I would think the postmaster, poor fellow, may have done us all a service and should not be in the Tolbooth.'

Tarbat laughed. They had reached the links now and were dismounting from the carriage while John Robb and Tarbat's man unloaded their clubs. 'You may well be right, Lincourt. My guess is that everything hangs upon King James's answer. You must understand that the Highlander's view of honour is very high-toned and it must be satisfied before they will move either way.'

'I should have thought most men rate their honour above all else,' Richard said rather stiffly.

'Oh, quite so, but I am Highland, Lincourt, and I know how they think. They can be very prickly. I'm glad you are going to Fort William. I beg you to visit Lochiel who is the best of Highland gentlemen.'

'I'll endeavour to do so,' Richard said. 'You think I am going on a fool's errand?'

Tarbat took a club in his hand, weighing it thoughtfully. 'As to that you know best what you are about, but if it's only recruiting, I shall be surprised if you come back with so many as half a dozen clansmen. But be guided by Colonel Hill. He's a sensible man whom I'm happy to count among my friends.'

Richard swung his club and the ball went high, arching against the blue of the sky. Tarbat was no fool, he thought, and wondered if his lordship guessed there was more than one angle to his stay here. Nothing more was said, both of them concentrating on the game, but Richard went back to his headquarters in a thoughtful mood. So much seemed to depend on the Highlanders during the next months. If there really was a new rising he would view it now in a different light for it would threaten his relationship with Marged Stewart. And her loyalties would be put to the test, particularly if David went out with the clans. Where then would he stand with her? But he was so deep in love that he could tolerate no hindrance. There could be no other outcome but marriage and if he could have married her out of hand tomorrow he would have done so.

He pondered this extraordinary change in himself and after supper with his officers sat down to write to his mother. He must write to Judith too and this would be more difficult.

He had almost finished the letter to Lady Standen when there was a knock on the door and John Robb came in with a note. At first he had no idea who it was from as he didn't recognize the thin neat writing. Then, as he glanced at the signature he saw it was from Marged and he had a moment's delight in seeing her hand. He read the note, gave an exclamation and seized the new hat that had replaced the one blown away on the night he realized his love for her. In ten minutes he was at Newsteads and being shown into the parlour. As soon as the door was shut he went to her and took her hands.

'My dear, what is it? What's happened that you should need me so urgently?'

'I'm sorry to ask you to come so late,' she said, 'but I was not knowing what was best to do.'

'And you turned to me.' He put up one hand to touch her cheek. 'As it is right now that you should. Tell me, is it that boy again?'

'Yes,' she admitted. 'He was out all day yesterday and

didn't come in last night. We thought he might be staying at a friend's house, though he usually lets us know if he is doing that. We waited for him to come home today, but when it was past ten o'clock, I began to get worried.'

'He sometimes stays very late with the Killiecrankies, doesn't he?'

'Yes, but Iain Dubh went down there at my request and he wasn't there. I went up to his room and found there's a valise missing and most of his clothes. He had some money always locked in a box on his table and that's gone too. Then I sent for you.'

'Rightly,' he agreed. He led her to a chair and made her sit down, drawing up a stool beside her. 'Have you any inkling where he might have gone?'

'None. He was in such an odd excitable mood two days ago when I last saw him, as if he had some secret he was not telling me. Aunt Marie thinks I am being too anxious and she has gone off to bed certain David will be back tomorrow, but I'm not so sanguine.'

'She may well be right. The young are always getting into scrapes.'

'I know, but – you see he was in such an angry state when I told him about us. He reacted so – so violently and he resents you, Richard, which is what upsets me so much. He threw every argument he could think of in my face.'

'Young puppy!' Richard said. 'I wish I could teach him some manners.'

'I know he feels restricted here and at his work. Perhaps I've made a mistake with that.'

'It's he who's made the mistake if he troubles you,' Richard retorted grimly, 'for he'll have me to deal with now. Do you think he could have been so misguided as to join one of the Jacobite leaders who I'm told are still in hiding in the hills? And if he did, to what end? There's no fighting now and if all goes well there won't be.'

'I don't know,' she said wretchedly. 'Oh Richard, what shall I do, what can I do? Wherever he's gone it's my fault, I'm sure, for putting him to the law when he hated it. But I did think he'd outgrow that and learn to like it as his father did.'

'You mustn't blame yourself for anything. I'm positive David isn't so insensitive as to leave you without a word. Maybe you'll hear something tomorrow. I would go out and look for him if I thought it would help but if he's taken a valise he's hardly likely to be still in Edinburgh.' He put his arms about her. 'My darling, try not to worry. We talk of David as a boy, but he isn't – he's a man grown and must make his own decisions, whatever they are. I won't have you blaming yourself.' He bent to kiss her gently. 'Come, my Marged, take that worried frown from your face. I'll set about some enquiries in the morning. In the meantime, it's very late, do you have a spare bedroom I can use? Then if there should have been an accident or any such trouble I shall be on hand.'

'Of course,' she said at once. 'It will be such a comfort to have you here. Where can he have gone?' She laid her cheek against his. 'With Alan dead and David gone goodness knows where it seems as if all the hopes Alexander had for his boys are spoiled. He would have been so distressed.'

'No one can say what their children will do,' Richard answered. 'I'm afraid I'm a great disappointment to my mother.'

She gave a shaky laugh. 'Oh Richard, why? I should have thought that as a colonel and in your King's confidence – '

'She wanted me to be a courtier, a statesman in high office with undoubtedly a peerage, and to be married long before this. But at least I'm preparing to remedy that last objection. I've been writing tonight to tell her about you.'

'I hope she will like me,' Marged said. 'I can't be what she had in mind for you. A Catholic – '

'She will love you,' Richard broke in. 'As to the difference in our faiths, surely that's not impossible to live with. Others have done, it, men that I know.'

'But very few, I suspect.'

'Perhaps,' he admitted. 'I suppose your Church will consider me a heretic? Do you?'

Painfully she said, 'I must. But, my love, even that isn't a barrier, we can't let it be a barrier.'

'You're not thinking to convert me?' He said it in a light tone but there was an edge in his voice that she detected.

'No, indeed,' she answered at once. 'I wouldn't be after treading on such delicate ground. I'm sure your faith is as much to you as mine is to me.'

It seemed to him suddenly imperative that he should know exactly where he stood. 'This is not perhaps the best moment to raise the suject,' he began, 'but Marged, I see no reason for us to wait longer than necessary, only I don't know what the situation is here in Scotland between Catholic and Protestant who want to wed. Have you known anyone who has arranged it?'

'Oh yes,' she said at once, 'one of the Hamiltons and Lady Mary Hay. But the law is not easy, even when I married Alexander who was also a Catholic we had to find a priest first to marry us according to our Church and we travelled to South Uist to find one. Then we came back to Edinburgh and were married in St Giles Kirk.'

'You would want us to do the same?'

'Yes, for you see although through a Catholic ceremony the marriage would be valid it wouldn't be legal, and we had to be married legally in the kirk because of the matter of property and wills and other legal affairs. Alexander arranged all that.' She paused and took his hand. 'In our case of course you would want a Kirk wedding and that I understand.'

'But I thought your priests were proscribed.'

'They are, my dearest, but there are those who go bravely about ministering to our people wherever they can and I wouldn't consider myself truly wed without the blessing of my Church. Would you mind that so much?'

'No,' he said slowly, 'but I see it may be difficult to arrange. I suppose that was what your aunt meant when she said we would have problems to face. It is a question of finding a priest.'

'Yes,' she nodded. 'It's the only way my parents, and MacIain would accept it. Do you understand that too, my heart?'

His grasp on her hand tightened. 'If it must be, it must. I respect your adherence to your Church and I honour you for it. It can't be easy. But how long will it be before we can find a priest? I would travel anywhere – '

'I know. We rarely have the comfort of one to say Mass for us in Blackfriars Wynd. I'll ask Lady Mary. In the meantime,' she stole a quick glance at him, 'I have been thinking – I wonder if you will think me very forward if – '

'If what, my adventurous love?'

'If we could be legally betrothed in front of a notary. It is often done here and – would you like that?'

He let go of her hand and put both his about her face. 'Like it! My darling, to have you promised to me before all the world would be the first step. What should I do?'

'Mr Kirkaldy, David's employer, would arrange it for us. If I give you his direction you could call on him.'

He leaned over to touch her lips with his. 'I'll do it tomorrow.'

Later, when he lay in the spare bed next to David's room he was so conscious of Marged sleeping on the floor below that he found it hard to rest and it was dawn before he closed his eyes. They were taking an early breakfast together, he and she and Miss Robertson, who was far more annoyed with than worried about David, when there was a knock on the outer door.

Marged started. 'I wonder if – '

But it was not David, it was a letter brought to her at once by Iain Dubh. She looked at it and her colour rose. 'It's from David,' she said and broke the wafer to read the letter aloud:

Dear Marged,
   I fear you will be very Displeased at my Conduct, but I cannot stay in Edinburgh because I cannot keep the Promise I made to the Bailie. I am Gone into France. I hope to join the Company of Scots fighting for the King of France. Don't fear, we shall be Back with King James one Day. Pray God very Soon. I will Write from Paris. My love to Aunt Marie and my respects and love to you, Dear Marged.
                                        David Alexander Stewart.

Marged laid down the letter and looked from one to the

other. 'But how can he have gone? He's got no passport.'

Miss Robertson had given a shocked exclamation. 'Foolish laddie, what's he about? He's little enough siller and forbye will find himself starving in Paris.'

'I should have understood,' Marged agreed. 'But I suppose there's ways of going over the border into England and finding his way to France.'

Richard looked up sharply. 'Of course! I think I may have the solution to what has happened!' And he told them of Major Menzies' flight with a manservant. 'That may well have been David with him,' he said, 'and if so then he will have a legitimate passport. Menzies is bound to have been in touch with the Killiekrankies and fired David with his fanatical ideas.' He caught himself up. 'I'm sorry, but it's my guess that is what has happened. And if it is, they'll be too far into England by now for anyone to stop them.'

Marged put down the letter. She was near to tears. 'It is all my fault. I didn't understand. If I had only – '

'My dear,' Miss Robertson said, 'there's nae words more useless than "if only". The thing's done and there's naught we can do to mend it. Davie's a man and must gang his ain way.'

'And I must be about my day's business,' Richard put in regretfully. He laid his hand over Marged's. 'I'm sorry to leave you, but I'll come back this evening. And don't fret. I'm certain David will not be careless of your feelings and you'll hear from Paris. If he is with Menzies, at least the Major will look after him on the journey, and maybe help him to a place in the Scots company. Though I could have wished – ' He broke off. 'I don't want to be on opposing sides to him, but it may come to that. It seems we can neither of us change the way we are.'

Marged leaned her head on her hand in a weary gesture. 'I can't bear to think of that.'

'My dearest, he may well find that nothing is quite as he imagined it and come to think Scotland not so bad a place after all.'

She gave him a wan look. It was obvious that she too had not slept much. 'I want only what is best for him.'

He rode down to Leith, consigning David's nonsense to

the devil, but he had become fond of the boy. If he had had him under his command he thought he could have made something of him, but David was wayward and excitable and would as Miss Robertson said go his own way – though it seemed to Richard it was a vain and hopeless cause he had embraced. Thinking over the conversation at the breakfast table he realized how far apart were his loyalties and those of the family at Newsteads. It was not easy to prevent himself making the odd remark from his point of view that could not but offend. He had to remember that Celtic blood flowed in David's veins only to a slightly less degree than in Marged's and he began to see that his love was a woman of deep emotions, that she held firmly to the Highland way of life, a way that as yet he had hardly begun to glimpse. Was their love strong enough to overcome all these differences or would they wear it down like water on a stone? He braced his shoulders – neither he nor she, he believed, would allow that. They would overcome the obstacles and out of that striving would come an even stronger love, he was sure of it. He thought tenderly of her, longing to protect her from the harshness of reality, to make it his life's object to care for her. He would even leave the army and take her to Heronslea if that would remove one of the difficulties. But as he came down to Leith and began to occupy himself with the training of his men he knew it would be a hard decision to make. In the afternoon he saw the lawyer and arranged the betrothal with no fuss and then took his dinner with Otwell, for here in a strange exile, only to Otwell could he speak of the anxieties that lay closest to him. But first he told him of his betrothal.

'My dear Richard,' Otwell's reaction was one of straightforward approval, 'I'm more glad than I can say. I see that she is just the wife for you. She'll stir you out of your prosaic ways and no doubt you will add a note of sobriety to her Highland fire. Alison, my love,' as his wife came into the room, 'here's Richard to tell us he's going to wed Mistress Stewart.'

Alison Skinner was as pleased as her husband and they both wished him well, pressing him to bring his promised bride to a celebration supper as soon as he could.

'You've wasted no time,' Otwell added with a grin. 'When you make up your mind you move fast, I'll give you that. How long have you been here – three months?'

'Time didn't seem to enter into it,' Richard said. 'We are both free and not in our first youth but there may be considerable delay before we can wed.'

'Oh? Why should that be?'

'She's a Catholic.'

Otwell was silent for a moment. 'I didn't know. Richard, that's going to make difficulties for you.'

'None that I care about.'

'There won't be conflict between you over it? You've enough in that she's a Jacobite.'

'We won't allow anything to part us,' Richard said confidently. It was not that he wore his own faith lightly. It was a firmly Protestant faith, preferring the plainest form of worship, but he also had, unusually for his day, a tolerance that his father had practised and which would not allow him to impose his own way on others. He abhorred the idea of a Catholic King but felt equally that Catholics should be free to worship in their own way as long as in their turn they did not seek to impose that way on anyone else.

He saw no conceivable reason why he and Marged should not live together, each worshipping in his and her own way – he had seen one brother officer achieve that successfully – and if he was blinded by love he was shrewd enough to know that that was what would carry them through.

If Otwell privately had reservations he did not voice them. The fact that Mistress Stewart had Jacobite sympathies seemed less important to him. She was a woman and a few romantic dreams of the lost Stuarts were not likely to deter Richard who could well overcome any problems there. And when, later, he saw his friend and Marged Stewart side by side at his dinner table he thought he had never seen Richard look happy before. Then he tossed the word aside. What they had seemed to him to be beyond mere happiness.

In the carriage, on the way back to Newsteads, Marged

said suddenly, 'Richard, I have been thinking – didn't you say you were planning to go soon to Fort William to see Colonel Hill?'

'I suppose I must,' he said reluctantly. 'I hate leaving you but I was ordered to go, at my convenience of course, and it can't be until Ripley is back. I've sent him recruiting in Fife.'

'I was wondering,' she went on, holding his hand tightly, 'if we might not go together? I must see my parents to tell them about our plans and if you are at Fort William you could be meeting them. I know you will be going with an escort, but couldn't I avail myself of your protection for the journey?'

He was staring at her in the darkness of the carriage. 'Why didn't I think of it? Of course, it would be the perfect arrangement and not an unusual one for travellers to attach themselves to a detachment of soldiers on the march. There are no doubt unruly men in the hills, looking for folk to molest and rob.'

Her eyes were dancing. 'As to that, I must admit I've done the journey many times with only my maid and Iain Dubh, and as for the broken men in the hills I've never yet been robbed. But I can be useful to you for I know all the places to lodge overnight.'

'I never thought of you as my guide,' he said and laughed. 'Dear heart, it would be all I could wish for, and especially having you at Maryburgh when I'm there.'

'Then it's settled,' she said. 'I would like to go while the weather is clement. And I can stay with my parents until you are ready to ride back.'

He put his arm about her and turning his head touched her mouth with his. 'I think I'm inclined to bless David for setting you free to come with me.'

'I wish we could go tomorrow.'

'So do I,' he said regretfully, 'but I must wait for my major to come back. He should not delay long now.' He thought of the long days of riding with her, seeing in them one of those odd unexpected pleasures that come occasionally and he thanked God for it. He saw her face, as he set her down at her door, bright with love and hope and he caught his breath – that this should be for him!

Two days later they stood before Mr Kirkaldy with Miss Robertson and Otwell Skinner for witnesses and exchanged vows of intent to marry. It was a simple affair over in five minutes but for Richard it changed everything, for now he looked on Marged as bindingly his in a manner that nothing and no one could sever.

Chapter 8

Sir Thomas Livingstone unwittingly took a hand in their plans and long afterwards Richard thought that if he had not there might have been a very different outcome of that journey so eagerly anticipated. The Commander-in-Chief sent a message that he wished to see him and upon his arrival told him that a certain Colonel Armstrong was disbanding his regiment of Foot which had long been serving on the Highland line. Armstrong was ill and his regiment had become depleted by sickness. Colonel Hill who was also under strength was to take some of the remaining troops, but with the truce and the prospect of peace in the Highlands Sir Thomas was of the opinion that the rest could be best used by Colonel Lincourt. There were apparently some four hundred men who wished to re-enlist, half of which had already left for Fort William.

'The other one hundred and ninety-six will bring you near your number,' Sir Thomas said. 'You'll accept them, Lincourt?'

'Willingly,' Richard agreed. 'Are there officers among them?'

'Aye, two captains for sure, three lieutenants with several non-commissioned as well as two ensigns. I'll send the order for them to report to you. You'll no doubt have them in a week or so.' Sir Thomas paused and gave him a thoughtful glance. 'You'll maybe not need to go looking among the clans. In any case you would be wise to wait until we know if the chiefs come in to take the oath. If they do then they might release some of their more hot-blooded fellows to the King's service?'

'Release? Do their men have no free choice?'

'You've much to ken about the Highlands, Lincourt. No clansman would think of joining you without his chief's permission.'

Richard went back to Leith pondering on this conversation. Men he surely needed and experienced troops would be a boon but it meant postponing his journey to Fort William. Major Ripley had returned this very morning with over ninety men from his foraging and Richard had thought he would be able to leave Ripley in charge and be away in a couple of days, but now it meant waiting to oversee the integrating of the new troops with all the attendant paperwork. Much he could delegate but certainly not all and there would doubtless be decisions that only he could make. Furthermore he must write another report to the King.

He told Marged at supper that night and if she was disappointed she did not show it but said, 'Of course the care of your regiment must come first.'

'I'm sorry,' he said frankly. 'I wanted to be away before the end of the week, but it's impossible now.'

She laid a hand over his where it rested on the table. 'It will be all the more to be enjoyed when we can go.'

'You're very understanding,' he said. 'I do care about my regiment. I've looked forward for a long time to having my own command and I must admit I find it very satisfying. I'm growing proud of my boys and hopeful they may eventually acquit themselves well. But we must face the fact that I'll have to take them to Flanders as soon as they're ready. That was my direct order from the King, even if Sir Thomas may have nurtured other plans for me – though I think them unlikely to be necessary now. Still, as he told me today, I've a lot to learn about the ways of the Highlands.'

She laughed. 'Did he say that? Perhaps you have, but I'll be your teacher.'

'I want to learn,' he said. 'But, Marged, when I do go to Flanders, will you come with me? You could be lodged comfortably in the Hague, in fact my Colonel and his lady would, I'm sure, make you very welcome in their house.'

'Of course I would come,' she agreed without hesitation, 'but oh, I wish it could be as your wife.'

'I know,' he said and his grip on her hand tightened.
'The waiting gets harder every day. But I'll write to
Colonel van Wyngarde tomorrow.'

As September progressed the evenings grew chilly and
Marged had a fire lit in the parlour. Miss Robertson
generally went to bed early and the two of them sat over
the hearth, learning more about each other in the
contented manner of lovers.

One evening she asked him about his childhood, if it was
happy.

'Very until I was nine years old.'

'And then?'

'Then my father died and everything changed.' And
suddenly he wanted to tell her of the thing that had set the
pattern of his life until he had met her. It had happened
on the night his father died. Robert Lincourt had been ill
for some time and the young Richard went often to his
bedside to sit and listen to him telling of his military days
in the army of the Commonwealth, remembering in the
way of a man who knows his life is at an end, recalling old
battles and great leaders, talking of General Fairfax and
General Cromwell. Richard, however, was blithely certain
his father would recover. Though he was so young there
was a great understanding between them and it was taken
for granted that Richard would be a soldier.

And then came the evening when his tutor came up to
his room where he was about to get into bed and told him
that all was over, that it was God's will. He told him to try
to go to sleep and not to disturb his mother. Richard
crawled into his cold bed to lie there huddled and
shivering as much with shock as with the cold. He could
not even close his eyes and about one o'clock being thirsty
he got up and padded down the stairs in the dark on his
way to the kitchen. He had to pass through the great hall
and there a totally unknown and horrifying sight met his
eyes. A bier had been set up with a tall funeral candle at
each corner and standing at one end, keeping watch, was
their steward, Harrison, whom he had known all his life.
On the bier Robert Lincourt lay covered with the standard
that had been borne at his side when he commanded a

regiment during his Civil War battles. His hands were folded over his breast, his face still in the repose of death, austere yet peaceful. The boy had never seen a dead man before and he crept forward, reached out to touch his father's hand. It was icy cold and the further shock of this was something that seared itself into his mind. It was then that he realized what death was, that his father was really dead and would never speak to him nor smile at him again. He let out one scream and then collapsed on the floor, sobbing in wild grief.

The steward came to him and gathering him up, spoke to him in a hushed, kindly voice. 'Come now, Master Richard, you must be a man and bear it better or you'll upset your mother.'

Somehow the boy had suppressed his sobs and Harrison carried him back to bed, to be left shivering and crying silently for the rest of the night until he fell into an exhausted sleep. It was the beginning of a withdrawal, a burying of personal feelings. His sister Dorothy wept most of the next day, but she was a girl. He was expected to be the man of the house and he repressed his grief. His mother took his hand and held it during the funeral obsequies, but she offered him little comfort. And she had recovered quickly and gone off to London, eventually to marry Sir Walter Standen.

Richard grew lonelier. He realized, he told Marged, that the night of his father's death had ended his childhood and changed his nature. The shock and lack of any understanding from his mother was a wound from which he had never recovered. She, locked in her own rather shallow grief, could not help him and his little sister was too young to comprehend the bond there had been between him and his father. And so began a covering up of his feelings, a hiding of what was deepest in him, and a building up of that intense reserve until all emotion was decently buried, and this in an age when men laughed and wept freely. It was this that gave him the reputation of being a cold man and perhaps only Judith and Otwell Skinner knew something of the man beneath. His natural warmth, so long suppressed, had been in waiting for the

time when Marged Stewart would strip away the layers
and bring it forth.

'Until now,' he said in a low voice. 'I've never told
anyone about that night. Only old Harrison knew and he
said nothing.'

Marged had tears in her eyes. She could see the dark
hall, the dead man on the bier, the funeral candles and the
young Richard sobbing inconsolably on the floor,
needing love that never came in the form he needed it.
She laid her head on his shoulder. 'I think often we don't
realize how children can be hurt. My poor Richard.'

'Oh,' he braced himself. They were sitting on a settle by
the fire which made a secluded place. 'The years since I
was seventeen have been too busy to allow for much time
to ponder things concerning myself, but the time between
that night and my joining the army wasn't happy. I had my
sister Dorothy, of course, but she was younger and a girl
and couldn't join in my occupations. It's all so long ago
now, but it'll never be quite forgotten, nor my dear father.
I don't know why I spoke of it, except that I don't want to
have anything hidden from you.'

'I'm glad you told me,' she said. 'It helps me to
understand you all the better. To grow up constantly
repressing one's feelings must be very bad. It's not the
Highland way.'

Richard turned to her and to his own astonishment felt
for the first time since that night moisture in his own eyes.
'I don't know what I've done to deserve you,' he said. 'It's as
if the years since my father died have been barren until the
day I met you. I think I was but half a man.'

She put her arms about him, kissed his cheeks and then
the unshed tears from his eyes. She began to understand
now how that incident in his childhood had made him the
self-contained reticent, strong-willed man that he was and
that underneath that strength lay a need for warmer
feelings, for the love he had been denied, though perhaps
even he had not realized the depth of that need.

'God has been good to us,' she said softly. 'I think
neither of us knew we could be so happy.'

He held her close and they stayed thus for a long while,

her head on his shoulder, while the fire slowly died. Towards the end of these long firelit talks their love-making grew deep and Richard went back to the Castle in the dark, aware of aching, unfilfilled desire in him. He wanted her and the prospect of a long and weary wait began to chafe him; he was sure it was the same for her too.

He worked hard, which occupied the days, played golf with a Scots gentleman whom he had met at Lord Melville's house, for Viscount Tarbat had gone to London. And one Saturday he took Marged to dine with his officers. He was in the habit on this day of inviting the wives to join them and it had become something of an occasion, the cook rising to it as far as he was able, serving a side of Scotch beef with a piquant sauce which was generally but not always free from lumps. Young Jock MacPhail opened the meal by marching round the table, piping in the cook's efforts, a ceremony which Richard was becoming used to since dining so often at the Castle. The table was set with plain but good pewter dishes and mugs and in the long low room looked very well. Today as he saw his officers putting themselves out to be pleasant to their colonel's lady he in turn studied them, in particular the new company captains from Armstrong's regiment.

There was one nearing middle age who had obviously missed promotion and he would need watching; the other two were younger, one a Lowlander, the other a man from Aberdeen red-haired and somewhat self-assertive but he seemed to be keen enough and asked his new commanding officer a number of questions about the fighting in Holland. Two young lieutenants listened respectfully to the talk and Ensign Fuller had taken the young ensigns in hand. On the whole a satisfactory addition to his compliment, Richard thought.

Mrs Fletcher was sitting opposite Marged and kept looking shyly at her as if envying both her bearing and her beauty, having neither in any great measure herself. Richard had introduced Marged as his betrothed and several of the officers looked at her with open admiration. The talk turned on the series of reverses suffered by the King this summer in his war against France.

'All the more need for us,' Richard said. 'I fear we're too late for this year's campaigning but we should be ready for action in the spring.'

Ripley looked up to ask, 'Do you plan to winter us here or in Flanders, sir?'

'In Flanders. If I'm not delayed by my visit to Fort William we should be there by Christmas or soon after.'

'The Hague will be a comfortable place for our ladies who wish to come,' a Captain Smith put in. He had come up from England with a bold black-eyed girl for wife. Glancing at her he added, 'That will suit you, eh, Mary?'

She flashed him a quick smile and said, 'One advantage of being an officer's wife is that one is able to travel to new places. Shall we like the Hague, Colonel?'

'I'm sure you will,' he answered. 'It's the cleanest, neatest city I've ever seen and I'm sure none of you Scots will be offended if I say it's more than can be said of Edinburgh.'

There was some general laughter and Marged said across the table to Mistress Fletcher, 'We ladies shall have to company each other there, for I hope to be going too, to stay with Colonel Lincourt's former colonel and his lady.'

'Oh, I shall enjoy that,' Mistress Fletcher agreed shyly, but her husband, who as usual had been drinking freely, said, 'You know nothing about it, Cecily. I'm only on loan to Colonel Lincourt and now that he has more officers it's unlikely that the Commander-in-Chief will release me to go into Holland.'

She flushed with embarrassment and Marged interposed quickly, 'If you cannot come with us, Mistress Fletcher, perhaps you will let me write to you and give you a description of the place and what we do.'

'Oh, would you be so kind?' Cecily Fletcher said breathlessly. 'Thank you very much.'

'In any case,' Richard said, 'nothing is settled yet. I'm surprised, Fletcher, that you should think it is.'

The captain shrugged his shoulders in obvious annoyance but he said nothing more. The exchange however made Richard determined to get rid of him as soon as possible. He was a trouble-maker and though Major Ripley had only been back such a short time they had already had one exchange of words, over the quality of the new men allotted to Fletcher's company. He called them country oafs incapable of learning musket drill and Ripley told him sharply that anything might be made of them if the officer was diligent. Fletcher took this as a personal insult and thereafter the two spoke to each other only when necessary.

Ripley who happened to be sitting next to Cecily Fletcher on the other side made a point of passing her a dish and filling her glass, talking to her of Holland, telling her of the dykes and the windmills so peculiar to the place in a manner most unusual for so taciturn a man, and which caused her husband to glower even more.

Afterwards Richard said to Marged, 'I'm grateful for your kindness to Fletcher's wife. She's a poor, shy little thing and he is unnecessarily harsh with her.'

'If you'll give me her direction I'll call on her. I felt very sorry for her.'

'That would be good of you, Marged. I doubt she has many friends.'

They were in the hired carriage driving back to Newsteads when Marged added suddenly, 'Did you know that Major Ripley is looking at her with more than mere politeness?'

Richard was taken by surprise. 'I've seen nothing to indicate that.'

She smiled. 'Dear Richard, I'm thinking you would not. But a woman is more likely to see these things. Today was not the first time they had met, was it?'

'No, but – ' He pondered for a moment. 'I know very well that Ripley dislikes Fletcher, in fact it's mutual as you no doubt observed, and maybe Ripley is kind to Mistress Fletcher to annoy her husband.'

'Oh, I am thinking it's more than that. When the Captain was rude to her I happened to glance at Major Ripley. And I observed his expression again when he served her. Perhaps it began because he wanted to take her side against her husband, but I think it's more than that now.'

'Then it had better stop and at once,' Richard said

promptly. 'I can't have that sort of thing going on among my officers. But I'm astonished. Ripley has never been a man for the ladies.'

Marged laughed. 'Were you, before you met me?'

'No,' he agreed, 'but thank God you were free. If Ripley really does care for Mistress Fletcher then it's the worse for him because she is not. Poor fellow, I like him far too well to have him suffer over another man's wife. I'll get rid of Fletcher as soon as possible and then there'll be no cause for Ripley to see her. When we go to Holland he'll have to put her out of his mind.'

But Sir Thomas Livingstone was not inclined to have Captain Fletcher back. 'I've no place for him at the moment,' he said firmly, 'and if you are going shortly to Fort William you'll need all the officers you have to remain with your troops. What do you intend them to be doing while you're away?'

'Field exercises,' Richard said. 'Major Ripley is first hand at that. I can entrust it to him.'

'Then you'll need Fletcher. He has an intimate knowledge of the countryside around here and will know the best places for training your men.'

'He and Ripley don't work well together.' Richard was aware of sounding terse, but Sir Thomas continued to look blandly at him.

'Och, I'm sure they'll do well enough. I'll ride out and watch your fellows at their business one day and see that all is well. You'll oblige me by carrying letters to Colonel Hill?'

Richard could do no more than leave the matter there, but it was into October before he felt the regiment in sufficient order, the new men settled and the officers and companies ready for the field exercises. He went to Marged one evening and told her that he was now ready to ride west.

'I've been waiting for you to say so,' she said eagerly. 'I can be ready the day after tomorrow.'

'Then Wednesday it is,' he agreed. 'I never dreamed when I was ordered to visit Fort William that it would be with my future wife by my side.'

'You are sure you don't mind the being alone?' Marged asked her aunt an hour later.

'Whisht!' Miss Robertson retorted, 'I've never been so poor a female that I couldna bear ma ain company. I shall do very well and as you know I've friends enough in the toon. I'm only glad you have your colonel for company. I'm thinking it will be a very happy journey for you.'

'I think so too,' Marged bent to kiss her cheek. 'Perhaps by the time I return there will be a letter from David. If one comes do be opening it and reading it for I know you're as anxious as I am.'

'That laddie can take care of himself,' Miss Robertson said cheerfully and refused to admit to any anxiety.

Viscount Tarbat was back in Edinburgh the day before they were to leave and Richard called on him, being immediately pressed to stay to dinner.

'I don't quite know what your journey will achieve,' Tarbat said lazily as they sat over their claret. 'It seems you have the numbers you need now that Armstrong's has been disbanded.'

'Yes,' Richard agreed, 'but it was his Majesty's wish that I should try to enrol some Highlanders and I must make the attempt.'

'My lord of Argyll has taken what he can of the men of his own lands and I can't see any of the other chiefs receiving the suggestion very well, with the exception of Lochiel, who is a gentleman of sense. I suppose however, if they do make peace with the King they may permit some of their wilder clansmen to satisfy the urge to fight under your banner.'

Richard said nothing for a moment. Then he added, 'I do wish very much to meet Colonel Hill in any case for I believe he may have known my father during the war between King and Parliament.'

'He's a good man and it's time and more that he had recognition of his services, as I've said more than once in London. He knows the Highlands and the chiefs as well as any man south of the border and he's much respected. In fact,' Tarbat paused, 'left alone he might have brought peace a great deal sooner. Too many directives have come from men who don't understand the situation. But you'll no doubt sum it up for yourself when you get there.'

'I hope to,' Richard said. 'Then when I return I'll be away with my companies to Flanders.'

'I shall miss our conversations and our golf.' Tarbat gave him a swift smile. 'I never had so apt a pupil. Perhaps we'll meet in London.'

'I sincerely hope so, my lord. Your hospitality has made my time here pass pleasantly indeed,' Richard said. He had written little but good of the Viscount to Mynheer Huygens, for though he guessed Tarbat to be something of a cynic who served his own needs first, nevertheless he owed him a great deal, not least his always pleasant company, and he said goodbye with some regret. Regret was there too when he took leave of Otwell and Alison Skinner. He took a silver cup for little Richard and thanked them for their kindness to Marged.

' 'Twas never anything but a pleasure,' Otwell said. 'But we shall surely see you when you come back to Edinburgh?'

'Very briefly,' Richard said. 'I mean to take my men to Hull as soon as possible and take ship there for Flanders before the worst of the winter.'

The last thing he did before leaving was to have a private interview with his major. He had left everything in order on his table and only had to bring Ripley up to date with the latest lists and orders to suppliers. He then asked if he had anything further to ask or say.

'No, sir.' The Major appeared to be his usual monosyllabic self.

'Sit down,' Richard said. 'I want to talk to you.' For a while he discussed the regiment's officers who would all be under Ripley's command in his absence. 'Keep an eye on Coleman,' he suggested, 'and see if you can induce Grant to be more alert. I've had my doubts about how he will show in the field but I'm inclined to think that if he stirs himself he might make a good company leader.'

Ripley agreed, adding, 'You may trust me, sir, to do all as you wish.'

'I know that,' Richard agreed, 'and I'm very content to

leave my own company in Johnstone's hands. He is
turning into the first class officer I thought he would. Now
there's another matter – Captain Fletcher.'

'Yes, sir?' Ripley's face was totally expressionless.

'Come, George, we've known each other long enough to
be frank. I'm well aware you don't like the man.'

'No, sir, I don't.'

'Well, you will have to deal with him while I'm away and
I don't suppose he will make anything easy for you.
Obviously you know he's overfond of his drink.'

'I do.'

'I'll not, as you know, tolerate drunkenness. If you see
any sign of him going too far you must deal with him in
your own way, and if it gets out of hand you will have to
take the matter to Sir Thomas Livingstone. After all,
Fletcher was one of his officers. But you are the senior
officer here and I'd rather it didn't come to that. I'm only
concerned lest the quarrel between you becomes too
personal.' He saw a muscle twitch at the corner of Ripley's
mouth but no other change of expression. He had
watched the Major since Marged's observation and though
nothing of any moment occurred he surprised a glance
between Ripley and Cecily Fletcher at the next officers'
dinner. It was brief but it told him what he wanted to
know.

'I've no intention of letting anything of a personal
nature interfere with my duty,' Ripley said in answer to his
last remark, sitting rigidly on the edge of his chair.

Richard nodded towards a table. 'I've a bottle of good
brandy there that I brought from England. Pour us two
drams, as the Scots would say.'

Ripley took two silver cups from Richard's travelling
case and as they settled with their drinks, Ripley taking the
chair opposite, Richard went on, 'I have no wish to pry but
I must be open with you and say I have come to believe
that your interest in Fletcher's wife is more than one would
expect. Am I right?'

Major Ripley flushed scarlet and sat fingering his glass,
the first time Richard had ever seen him so out of
countenance. 'I see I am,' Richard went on. 'This makes

for a very awkward situation and one I don't like leaving
behind me.'

Stiffly Ripley said, 'I repeat, sir, nothing shall be
allowed to interfere with my duty while you are away.'

'I'm glad to hear it. I've complete confidence in you, but
you have not, I think, had to face such a situation before.
You disliked Fletcher from the beginning and as far as
that goes I understand your feelings, but now – '

Suddenly Ripley burst out, 'He treats her so damnably,
sir. Once when her sleeve became caught and showed her
arm I saw a great big bruise there and I know he caused it.'

'It could have happened some other way,' Richard
suggested. 'You can't be sure.'

'I'm sure,' George Ripley said and Richard wondered if
he had managed a private talk with the girl.

'Well, I've tried to get Fletcher transferred back to the
castle but Sir Thomas won't have him, more's the pity. I
don't know what to say to you, George, but for God's sake
keep the matter to yourself. It's a useless business to
meddle with another man's wife. It may be thought a
subject for free amusement at court, but not in the army
and not, by God, in my regiment.'

Ripley sat very still in his chair. 'I know, sir, and I know
it's hopeless. It's only that – she's so unhappy.'

'I'm sorry for you and for her, and I feel for you both
now in my own changed status more than I would've done
before, but there's naught to be done, is there? Try to put
the business out of your head.' But even as he said it,
Richard thought of Marged. Could he, if ordered, put her
out of his head? He knew he could not. 'I can't add
anything further,' he went on. 'You will know all I'd say in
any case. Only I trust you to put the care of the regiment
above all else while I'm away. And that means working
with Captain Fletcher.'

The Major gave him a straight look. 'I can at least
promise you that, sir.'

And there Richard let the conversation end. He and
Ripley understood each other very well.

Early on Wednesday morning he reviewed his troops and
gave them a harangue on behaviour while he was gone.

His eyes wandered over them as he spoke, especially over his own company with young Johnstone at its head – he had no worries there. In order to take the invaluable Morrison with him he had put one of Armstrong's sergeants in his place and he knew he could trust Johnstone to work with him and the new recruits. They all listened to him respectfully and when he finally rode off on Juno with John Robb leading his spare horse and a packhorse with his baggage and Sergeant Morrison at the head of his small detachment of men he felt he had done all he could to leave his regiment in order. Only as he passed Captain Fletcher, seeing the man's face, slightly puffy, the little red veins pronounced, was there a moment of unease. But as he took the road to the city and the meeting with Marged even that anxiety faded. Ripley was a good man, a sound man, and he could only hope Cecily Fletcher had not completely turned his head. Ripley was capable, he thought, of stern stuff and would surely not allow that pale slip of a girl to deflect him from his duty.

It was only when he and Marged were riding out of the West Port that he put the matter from him. There was after all nothing he could do about it and he had ahead of him a week of journeying with his love.

Chapter 9

Falkirk was behind them and Stirling on its high rock and on the third evening they were approaching Loch Lomond and its wooded surroundings. As the pattern had settled itself Richard and Marged rode always a little ahead followed by Iain Dubh with Marged's maid Jeanie up behind him, with Robb and the led horses. Ensign Fuller rode in front of the marching sergeant and the detachment of men, increased on Sir Thomas's recommendation to a full dozen, with Jock MacPhail who seemed to have enough breath to march and play his pipes at the same time for what seemed to Richard an unconscionable part of the day.

The weather was pleasant, mild October sunshine lighting up the bronzed leaves, rowan berries great clumps of scarlet. Marged sat her horse easily, wearing a brown jacket with an orange skirt and a large brown hat decorated with an orange ostrich feather on her head, and Richard rode beside her, looking with pride every now and again at this woman who had promised to be his.

At Luss they stayed at the home of a hospitable laird who, seeing them looking for an inn, offered them shelter in his own large house. He and his lady made them welcome and the men were cared for in the kitchen quarters. The next day, passing beyond Callander, they left the mellow countryside and began to enter wilder scenery, the horses moving at a comfortable pace, Sergeant Morrison and the men tramping along behind. Richard had brought five of the soldiers who had originally come from Flanders and seven of the new recruits so that they might learn something of a march and occasionally he heard Sergeant Morrison ordering them. They were young and eager lads, two of them irrepressibly untidy but he hoped the sergeant would mend that. Another watched him with a sort of dogged devotion which amused him and was always first to unload his saddlebags at night. For him the journey was the pleasure he had hoped it would be because of the woman at his side. They talked of various subjects in the desultory manner that being on horseback decreed and Marged told him many things about the history of her country and the places they were passing through. The roads were little more than rutted well-worn tracks and she said it would become wilder yet.

By Strathyre they slept in a change house, Marged and Jeanie taking the only bedroom. Richard in his cloak and with a saddlebag for a pillow slept on the floor by the fire with his men and here for the first time he beheld the performance of donning the kilted plaid. The night before Iain Dubh had simply unbuckled his belt and wrapped the loosened plaid about him for sleep, but this morning he laid the large piece of tartan cloth over his belt stretched out on the floor, pulled the material into pleats and then lay down on it. With a deft movement he wrapped the ends about his body and fastened the belt and then rose to pull the remainder of the plaid up his back and over his shoulders to fasten it with a brooch. His sporan he tied in place with leather thongs and slung his dirk through his belt.

Richard thought with some amusement of the mirth the whole thing would cause among some of the more ribald of the officers he knew, but it seemed to him an extraordinarily practical form of dress. Once he had asked Marged if Iain Dubh could not find some better shoes, his being full of holes, at which she had laughed and said his brogues were made thus to let the bog water run out. Richard decided he had as yet a great deal to learn and it occurred to him that the top of a red stocking was not a bad place to keep one's knife.

The landlord gave them a porridge of meal and whisky for their breakfast and then they were on their way again.

Marged guided them through the braes of Balquidder with Ben More towering on their left and on towards Glen Dochart. It was a shorter day's journey than their usual twelve to fifteen miles, but it was slower for the terrain was more difficult, but she said it cut off many miles. They saw no one but a solitary crofter, driving a few cattle down from the higher ground, and Richard was occupied with the wild scenery, with the snow-topped grandeur of Ben Mor, the little river tumbling over its stones, the narrow way over a rocky surface. The heather was nearly all brown by now but an occasional purple clump remained and when they stopped at a shieling to eat bread and cheese Marged picked a sprig to fasten in her hat.

'The MacDonald badge,' she said smiling.

As they came to Glen Dochart, Richard remarked upon the grandeur of the mountains.

'Some people call them gloomy and overpowering, and they can be threatening. We couldn't come this way in winter,' she told him. 'But I'm thinking there's a great beauty to them at any time. Look, there's an eagle,' as a great bird soared overhead.

The days of travelling were, for Richard, increasing in fascination for the spectacular scenery coupled with the joy of sharing the journey with her and he wished he could lengthen the time it would take them to come to Fort William. She pointed out so many things as they went, oyster catchers by the little Loch Lubhair, red deer high on a long narrow path worn by generations of their ancestors, grouse flying high, hoodie crows in black droves. At evening they came to a croft and asked for shelter. The crofter had no English but Marged spoke to him in Gaelic and promised they would pay for anything they had. There were two rabbits in the pot that he had snared that morning, he said, and brought them all in to crowd the small room. His wife looked up, a stained apron about her waist, accepting the visitors without being in the least perturbed and she accepted a gift of meal from their store.

'We must be eating their dinner for several days,' Richard said in a low voice, 'yet they don't seem to resent it.'

'In the Highlands we have strong laws of hospitality,' Marged said proudly. 'We would turn no one away, not even a foe.'

She talked with the crofter who looked uneasily at the red coats, telling him they were bound for Fort William. He remembered her coming this way before, and she told Richard he was a tenant of MacCailein Ic' Dhonnachaidh, the Earl of Breadalbane.

'This is Campbell country,' she added. 'A traveller from the south can hardly reach Fort William without passing through some part of it.'

The food was good and as night fell the crofter offered Marged rest in the box bed he normally shared with his wife, insisting he himself would sleep on the floor.

'I wish you could have seen the falls at Dochart,' Marged said as they rode off the next day, 'but it would have taken us too far east.'

Some fifteen miles brought them to Dalmally for the next night, then on round the head of Loch Awe, deep and still, past the great black keep of Kilchurn castle on the shallows, the Earl of Breadalbane's stronghold where MacIain and the other chiefs had accused him of retaining the gold sent from London to buy their loyalty. They followed the river Awe as it tumbled through the Pass of Brander, pausing to look at the cascading falls of Cruachan. Here the mountains towered over them on either side and the marching men looked askance at the great rugged slopes as if expecting some evil force to come down on them but for a while only eagles soared over their heads. It was indeed an awesome place, the river rushing over polished rocks by the narrow track and on the right Ben Cruachen dominated all, the lower slopes wooded, the top bare and split into two peaks.

'There are sometimes broken men hiding here,' she said, 'but I expect your redcoats are enough to keep them away.'

They had not however gone another mile before, as if she had the 'seeing', they became aware of figures flitting from the trees and clambering over the rocks, kilted men in fawn shirts, the philabeg over their shoulders, blue bonnets on their heads. They held drawn claymores or black knives in their hands and Richard swiftly counted them to about twelve or thirteen in number. He called an order over his shoulder and the sergeant put the men on alert, the bayonets fixed to their muskets.

Richard's first thought was to protect Marged, and he eased Juno between her and the strangers.

'There's no need, I'm thinking,' she said. 'I'll talk to that big man who seems to be the leader.' She called out in Gaelic and the bearded Highlander came to stand on a rock a few feet above the track. He answered her and they spoke for a few moments.

'What's he saying?' Richard asked.

'He is a MacGregor,' she explained. 'He wants to know if you are here to rout out broken men, but I told him you were not.'

'Then promise him no harm will come to him or his men from my soldiers if he does not attack us.'

Marged repeated the words and the man looked suspiciously at Richard. Then, surprisingly, in good English, he said, 'Why then are you coming this way? What for do you bring redcoats through the pass?'

''Tis the shortest way to Bonawe and so to Glencoe.'

He glanced at the spring of heather in her hat. 'Then you're after being a MacDonald and no friend of mine.'

'No enemy either,' she retorted, as his men came closer gathering in a knot behind him, all of them silent and staring. The soldiers shifted their feet and stood equally silent, watching, Ensign Fuller and Sergeant Morrison in front of them. John Robb took from a capacious pocket the pistol his master had given him and without which he never travelled. He knew how to use it. Iain Dubh slid down from his horse and drawing his dirk placed himself beside Marged's stirrup.

'I'm going home from Edinburgh,' she retorted, 'and as this officer was coming to Fort William I availed myself of his escort. But I wonder that you flaunt your name to him.'

'Proscribed my name may be but I'll live and die with it,' the MacGregor retorted. He eyed the points of steel facing his men. 'We're fairly numbered, I'm thinking.'

'Do you want a fight?' Richard asked. 'If so, I'll give you one, but why shed blood for no reason? I've no orders regarding broken men, if you are such.'

The MacGregor considered this. 'I could throw my *sgian dubh* into your heart before your men could move.'

Calmly Richard withdrew his pistol, which he always carried loaded, and cocked it with a slow deliberate movement. 'You are welcome to try. But I believe I can match you for speed.'

The man laughed. 'I like your spirit. I was a gentleman – once!'

For a moment their glances met and held. Then he said something to Marged in Gaelic and turning his back scrambled off with his men over the rocks and into the shelter of the fir trees.

'What did he say?' Richard asked.

Marged smiled. 'That it was not a day for killing.' Behind her she heard a gasp of relief from Jeanie and she nodded to Iain Dubh to mount up again.

'Thank God for that,' Richard said. 'I abhor useless blood-letting and I didn't want any near you.' He called to the men to resume the march, at the same time thinking that Marged had taken it all without appearing in the least perturbed, and he began to see that all she had told him about the turbulence of the Highland spirit had its place in her too.

As the light faded they came to gentler Bonawe where they spent the night at a passable change-house. Marged and Richard sat in the taproom eating good venison stew, both relaxed after the hazardous day's ride. Fuller and the sergeant were in another corner while at the far end of the room the men were gathered about a long table, mugs in their hands, a leather black-jack of ale between them, several of them complaining of the quality of its contents.

'Tomorrow's ride will be easier, through Barcaldine Forest,' Marged said.

'I'm glad,' he answered. 'I hope there are no broken men skulking there. I don't want to see you in danger again as you were today.'

'I wasn't afraid,' she said without any sign of bravado,

'except for you. I could never trust a MacGregor and I know how swiftly a *sgian dhu* can kill. But if I'm to be a soldier's wife I must be knowing that you will sometimes be in danger, and I must match your courage.'

'You will, you do,' he said and suppressed a desire to reach for her hand. Instead he drank some of the poor wine which was all the inn could provide. 'Your mountains are more impressive than I'd imagined. I think the men felt uneasy in that pass. How do the MacGregors live there?'

'They thieve cattle,' she said simply, 'and anything else they can lay their hands on. They'll sell a stolen cow for meal and whisky sometimes.'

'We owe our safe passage to you,' he smiled across at her and she answered, 'More likely 'twas to your muskets.'

'When I came north,' Richard said slowly, 'I realized I knew nothing of Scotland, let alone the Highlands and the clans and I'm only beginning to understand. Why do the MacDonalds hate the Campbells?'

She told him the long history of the feuding between Clan Donald and Clan Diamaid, tales of constant quarrelling, fighting over cattle, raids and killing. 'There's bad blood between us, but Argyll himself is our overlord in Glencoe, to our sorrow. I brought you through the mountains because of it. We could have taken the southern route by Inverary, but that is the Campbell town and the seat of the Earl of Argyll himself. 'Tis not wise to walk about the streets there with a sprig of heather in one's bonnet, but 'tis a fair size with a Tolbooth and a Court house and many shops, and there is great herring fishing in the Loch. Oh, you can see the Campbell power in Inverary and I am not liking it at all.'

'Then I'm glad we didn't take that route.'

A little smile lifted her lips. 'They don't have things always their own way,' she went on. 'Lord Breadalbane and his cousin, Campbell of Glenlyon, were the poorer for our men passing through Glenorchy and Tayside when they came home from Dalcomera near two years ago. Many of our houses in the glen are the richer for the expedition.'

She spoke of it with complete unconcern and Richard was silent for a moment. It was a side of her he hadn't reckoned on. It seemed to him a primitive, lawless society that she came from, though she herself, the product of it, appeared far removed from it in Edinburgh. Yet here, in the wild scenery they had passed through today, he could see she had come home, that she knew it, understood it, was part of it as he could never be. The mountains, the poor crofts, the broken men were a world away from the gentle countryside and educated society in which he had grown up. He could see her in his surroundings, but he could not see himself in hers, and the matter troubled him and kept sleep from him for a long while that night.

In the morning they took the ferry at Connel over Loch Etive and Richard stood beside Marged, Juno's reins in his hand, looking out over the stretch of water. Iain Dubh held her mount quiet. On this journey the Highlander had spoken little and Richard sensed his hostility becoming even more overt both towards himself as his relationship with Marged deepened and towards the marching soldiers behind him.

By evening the rain was spattering down and as they approached Invercreran at the head of the loch, Marged said, 'The creel house here is a poor sort of place but two miles further on is the house of the Laird of Craigieduir. I've known him all my life and he will give us better hospitality.'

'We'll be guided by you,' Richard said. 'It will be a relief to get out of the rain.'

They came up to the house as dusk fell, a low two-storey building of stone, quite spacious, with outbuildings and a large barn. A barking dog announced their arrival and the door was opened by a manservant who peered out at them, startled by the sight of a contingent of redcoats.

'Good evening to you, Rory,' Marged said cheerfully. 'Will the Laird be offering us shelter, do you think?'

He exclaimed, '*Dhé*, is that you, Mistress Stewart? Come you in-bye this minute, but how is it you are coming with redcoats?'

She had dismounted and went up the steps, followed by

Richard. 'They're bound for Fort William, and this is Colonel Lincourt who is escorting me. If you would tell the Laird – '

'He and his lady are away to Inverary to stay with Sir Colin Ardkinglas,' the man Rory explained, 'but come away into the parlour. I'll be having a fire lit for you at once.'

'We'd as soon as not go back to the creel house tonight,' Marged began and he added, 'No, that you will not, mistress. That Duncan keeps a poor place for travellers. I know the laird would want you to be sleeping the night here. 'Tis dark outside now and the rain enough to drown a body.'

He showed them into a pleasant room and in a short time had a fire blazing in the hearth and was setting mulled wine on the table. Another servant took Sergeant Morrison and the men round to the rear quarters and a maidservant took Marged's Jeanie under her wing. John Robb saw to the unloading of baggage and then went off to the kitchen quarters where a steely-eyed cook kept a watch over the giggling maid-servants, excited by the presence of so many redcoats.

'Mistress Mackay will be cooking you a bite of supper,' Rory said. 'and I'll have rooms prepared for you as soon as maybe.'

Richard and Marged went to stand by the fire, cups of the warmed wine in their hands, Marged holding her damp skirts to the blaze of dry logs.

'I think we shall be better served here than anywhere,' Richard said. 'I hope your laird will not mind entertaining us in his absence.'

'He and his wife are very kind,' Marged assured him. 'They would want us to make free with their house.'

Rory appeared some fifteen minutes later, suggesting they might like to see their rooms and change their wet clothes. A corridor ran the length of the house and he opened a far door for Marged, showing Richard to the one next to it. Here a fire was also burning and Robb unpacking his travelling trunk to lay out a dry shirt and stockings and his buff coat. Richard changed, glad to get

out of his wet clothes and washed his hands in the warm
water Robb poured into the basin. The room was small,
the bed almost filling it and the fire soon took away the
evening chill. When he was ready he sent Robb off to the
kitchen for his supper and went down to the parlour.
Marged joined him a few minutes later and supper was
brought in, an excellent meal of beef, partridge pie,
fresh-baked bannocks and cheese. As they ate they became
aware this was the first time they had been alone since the
journey began. Rory had withdrawn, and Richard laid his
hand over Marged's, blessing young Fuller's tact in taking
his supper elsewhere.

'I think I am very glad the owner of this house is away,'
he said. 'I've wanted all these days of riding to have you to
myself.'

'We rode ahead together,' Marged pointed out, but her
dark eyes were dancing with amusement.

'With a dozen soldiers marching at our backs, to say
nothing of John Robb, your maid and Iain Dubh!'

'Yes, we were hardly alone,' she agreed. She had
changed her riding clothes for a gown of simple green
cloth with a tartan shawl about her shoulders. She added,
'I never guessed Donald Stewart and Mary would be from
home but I can't help being glad too.' She gave a little
laugh. 'Richard, tomorrow we shall be in Glencoe and I'm
glad you are agreeing to spending a day, maybe two, there
for I want you to be meeting with MacIain and his sons.'

'I'm curious to meet your chief,' Richard said. 'I've
heard much about him. And Glencoe too. What I've seen
so far on this journey is all so very different from what I
had expected. You must remember I'm seeing it all
through English eyes.'

She smiled across at him. 'That's what makes it all so
enchanting to me. The travelling days with you have been
– ' She broke off, glancing round the room, 'all leading us
here. It is as if this is our own house and we home from a
ride. Perhaps we've been to Maryburgh and we're glad to
be back in the shelter of our own walls.' She began to walk
about the room, touching the objects in it. 'This cupboard,
yes, we brought it back from Holland when you'd been

compaigning there, and the table and chairs we had sent from London. Now those two stools and the book shelves, they were made by George MacDonald, the carpenter at Maryburgh.'

He laughed, enjoying her child-like fantasy, yet sensing the longing beneath it. 'I'm beginning to think anything possible after our journey. I suppose we are quite an old married couple?'

'Oh yes, we've lived here many years and we are very comfortable together.'

He rose and going to her took her into his arms. 'Please God it will come true before too long. You will like Heronslea. It's larger than this, of course, and there is plenty of parkland for your rides as well as the countryside, gentler than it is here, but very pleasing in its way.'

'But we shall come back some time? I love the mountains so much, and I don't imagine there are any in your country.'

He laughed. 'None, but I promise you we will journey back one day, when it can be arranged.'

She rested her head against his shoulder. 'Sometimes I think there is only one moment to be loved, the one that is now – that's the only one we're sure of. Oh Richard, don't you see? It is a gift – this place, this house without a host, you and I alone together, and tonight – tonight is part of the gift.'

'Marged,' he lifted her face so that he might look into it, 'what is it? You sound almost afraid.'

'No, no, I'm not afraid – we'll be having years together if God wills it, but – Richard, hold me. Don't let me be alone tonight.'

He stood very still. 'Marged, do you know what you are saying?'

'Yes,' she whispered. 'It is part of the gift. The fates have been kind to us and we mustn't refuse it.'

She seemed in so strange a mood and he was trying to grasp it, understand, but it was his own desire that answered. 'Beloved, do you truly mean it?' His grasp on her tightened. He could find no other words and stood there, looking down at her.

She returned that look, her eyes holding his, clear and

honest. 'We aren't green young things, Richard my love, and I would think it no shame to be mistress before I am wife.'

'My God!' he said and bending his head, kissed her long and hard and they stayed together thus for some time, only going to seats by the fire when Rory and a maid came to clear away the dishes.

'Are my troopers settled for the night?' Richard asked and Rory nodded.

'Aye, sir, and I've offered your man a share in my bed, foreby he thinks to sleep by your fire.'

'There's no need for that,' Richard said. 'I'll send him down to you with my thanks for your hospitality.'

When he had gone Marged said, 'I'll tell Jeanie to sleep with the maids.'

Their eyes met, Richard aware of a leaping excitement such as he had never known in his rare sexual encounters. It seemed impossible that he was about to take something which he had schooled himself to think might be months or even years away. That she should want to give herself to him was overwhelming and he sensed some thread underneath, bound up with her fantasy, her awareness of things beyond his knowledge, that he had never so much as thought of; he longed for her to lead him into that world, out of the prosaic one in which he had always lived. He reached out his hand to her and she clasped it across the hearth and the leaping flames between them.

Rory came back shortly after with candles and in silence they followed him up the stair. He showed Richard to his door and then Marged to hers at the farther end of the corridor.

John Robb was busy laying out his master's night gear and as he began to undress said, 'I'll be taking my rest on the floor here, sir.'

'I think not,' Richard said. 'There's little room and the man Rory was kind enough to offer you comfortable quarters. I think you should take them. I understand the Highlanders are very touchy about hospitality.'

'Very well, sir.' Robb never commented on his master's orders and when he had seen everything ready, the fire banked up and the bed turned down he wished him a good night and left the room.

Richard sat by the fire, his hands clasped between his knees. In a state of waiting so that the minutes seemed endless he thought of the journey that had brought them to this point, the days of riding through the incredibly beautiful scenery that assaulted his senses, the enchantment he had felt day by day – he, a seasoned, down-to-earth soldier – and it now seemed inevitable that it should end in this present miracle. The obstacles to their marriage faded into insignificance before this present night; they would have to be faced but only in due time and he put them to the back of his mind. There was nothing but the firelight and his love awaiting him.

At last he heard her door open and shut as Jeanie left her for the night. Rising, he put his long black cloak over his nightrail and opened the door to go quietly along the dark passage. A light tap, and he heard her low voice, bidding him enter. It was a larger room than his, comfortably furnished, a fire burning, the bed with red damask curtains and a post at each corner, a single candle burning on the table to give a soft light. Marged's travelling trunk lay on the floor, her skirt spread over it to finish drying. She herself was standing by the window in a long white nightgown, the curtains drawn back. Silently he came to her and opening his cloak drew her into the warm circle of it.

'You'll take cold standing here without a shawl,' he said.

She was still looking out of the window. 'It's raining so hard I can't even see the loch, and it's such a lovely view from this window.'

He put up a hand to draw the curtain, shutting out the outside world and holding her inside the cloak bent to put his mouth to hers, feeling the control of years slipping away. Words began to tumble from him who had always been so reticent. 'My darling, my love, never has there been a woman like you. You've changed the world for me. My heart's treasure, I'll never let you go again. I want you with me always, always – '

'Come,' she said and led him to the bed, sliding in between the sheets. He followed, blowing out the candle and drawing the bed curtains, enclosing them both in a small dark world.

The weather had indeed broken and in the morning when they met for breakfast the rain was streaming down the window panes.

'Do you think,' Richard said, 'we could stretch our absent host's hospitality for another day? There's no point in going on in this weather and it would benefit the men to rest for a day. After all, we're not on a campaign march! And as for us,' his hand went out involuntarily for hers, 'what would it not give us?'

She rose at once, a soft smile on her face. 'I'll speak to Rory. I'm sure there'll be no objection.'

It was easily arranged and the soldiers settled happily for a day in dry quarters with plentiful food and the maids to ogle. Richard and Marged stayed in the parlour, sometimes talking by the fire, sometimes strolling up and down looking at the pictures on the walls for the Laird was a man of taste and had travelled widely. She found a book of Gaelic verse translated into English and she read to Richard, singing one particular one for him in the original language before telling him its meaning.

Strong is the love that binds us all,
Strong is the love that holds me in thrall.
Strong is the love that death cannot stall,
And strong is my heart that leaps to the call.

'My heart is *mo cridhe* in my tongue,' she said, 'and that is what you are to me, my very heart.'

To him there seemed to be a glow about her today, an indefinable difference, and having seldom had time to read much, he found himself listening, enthralled, to the soft lilt in her voice as she sang to him, and he thought the haunting lines of the love poem would stay in his memory.

Towards evening the rain stopped and the sky cleared to give a golden sunset. Rory brought Richard his dram in the silver quaich belonging to the master of the house, and if he had been suspicious of the redcoats Mistress Stewart's presence had dispelled any anxiety and he seemed only too pleased that they had stayed in out of the rain.

'I must write to the Laird,' Marged said, 'and thank him for his hospitality. If we stay here on the way back I can do it again.'

'I'd like to return to Edinburgh before the turn of the year,' Richard said. 'If we get snow your glens will be hard to travel.'

'Impassable,' Marged smiled at him. 'We'll have to take the coast road and go by Inverary to Dumbarton and Glasgow. The way we'll go tomorrow by Gleann an Fiodh is too bad once the snow has come.'

'Shall we be in Glencoe by nightfall?'

'Easily,' she said and gave a little sigh. 'I'll be glad to see them all again, John and Eiblin and Sandy and Sarah, but oh, it's sad I am to leave this house.'

She went out of the room to give Jeanie orders to be ready to leave in the morning and came back almost at once, a shawl about her shoulders. 'Richard, come with me, I want to show you something.'

He took her outstretched hand and she led him out of the house to the dark drive where a bare slope led down to the tiny loch. Only a few pine trees clustered there, the breeze stirring through them, but it was at the sky she was pointing and Richard stopped, amazed at what he saw.

It was alight with flashing colour, red and green, yellow and pink and orange, the shades mingling and blending, ever moving, ever changing.

'What is it?' he asked. 'I've never seen anything like it.'

'We call them the northern lights,' she said. 'You only see them here in the north and mostly in the autumn.'

He stared at the spectacle as the colours shot across the dark sky and they stood together in silence, his arm about her, absorbed in so dramatic a sight. At last the lights began to fade and slowly they walked back to the house.

'I'm glad you've seen them,' Marged said. 'They're part of our Highlands.'

'And I'd never have imagined them from a description,'

he answered. 'What I was told about your country never led me to expect what I've been seeing and learning ever since we left Edinburgh.'

She gave a low laugh. 'I'm not making light of the black side of us, it's there, but I think no one has ever told you of what I am wanting to show you.'

'You turn my head,' he said. 'How can I think about the reason I'm here when you look at me like that?'

'Dear Richard, I mustn't distract you. You have your work to do, and I'll be staying with my mother and my father just near enough for you to visit me when you wish.'

'When I wish?' he echoed. 'That would be every day, but it can't surely be as it has been here.'

'No,' she agreed in a low voice as he opened the door for her.

Later as they lay together in her bed he said, 'When will it be like this again? Not in your chief's house, nor most certainly in Fort William.'

'I know,' she whispered. 'If only we could be wed, so that we might be honestly together before the world.'

His arms tightened about her. 'After this I want you with me every night of our lives. How can I face weeks without you?'

'Once we are back in Edinburgh it will be different. I may do as I please in my own house.'

'I know, but it's hole in corner and I want you as my wife. Marged – would you consider marrying me without waiting for the priest?'

She hesitated for a long time. Then she said, 'It's odd – I should think that a sin, yet, I don't think of being together like this as wrong, though it is, it must be. It seems a sin to wed against my Church's laws, yet none to be your mistress and God Himself knows how many do it.'

'You haven't answered me.'

'Oh Richard, I don't know. I must try to think rationally about it. Only when we are together like this, I can't begin to think about it. All I care about is to be with you always.'

'And I,' he said and began to kiss her, his hands moving over her in a manner calculated to banish all their anxieties to oblivion. Time for them by day, he thought, and not in this warm bed with Marged in his arms. His lips close to hers he murmured, 'Nothing, *nothing*, can undo what we have done here. You are mine.'

Later when he stirred from a short but deep sleep it was to hear her catch a sobbing breath and when he put out a hand to touch her face he felt moisture there.

'What is it?' he asked. 'Why are you crying, beloved?'

She was struggling to suppress the tears. 'It's so foolish of me – Aunt Marie said it was all nonsense – but oh, I've just dreamed that it was true, that I was in the heather, running, and you couldn't reach me, and I knew – I knew I'd never see you again.'

He held her close, smoothing back her hair. 'Tell me all of it.'

She spoke stumblingly of the spaewife of long ago. 'And now I've known the joy she prophesied these last two nights, such joy, Richard, that I'm feared the rest will come true – the time of it will be short and I can't bear it – hold me, hold me – '

'What does it matter what an old crone said years ago,' he said soothingly. 'Someone with such beauty as yours was bound to be loved greatly, don't you see? There's nothing to fear, and if you are looking for omens don't you think the lights we saw tonight were part of the whole miracle of this place, auguring well for us? I won't have you unhappy on this night of all nights.'

'I'm not, dearest, dearest Richard, but my dream was so vivid and we Highlanders set such store by them.'

'Dreams are to be forgotten when we wake. And I've a way of making you forget, my heart.' His kissing grew more intense and as he folded her to him his love-making was such that he knew by the response of her body that he had succeeded for a while at any rate in driving out the unnameable fear. At least he heard her give a long happy sigh and rolling over lay on his back beside her, both of them deeply content. They slept again and when Richard woke and drew the curtain the grey light had come. As he leaned over her she awoke too and he said, 'It's dawn, I must go.'

She put her arms about his neck. 'Oh, so soon? Stay a little longer.'

'Long enough,' he answered and gave a low laugh.

At last, reluctantly, he left her and gathering up his cloak went quietly back to his room. The unslept-in bed was cold and he lay there thinking of the warmth of the night in the other bed. Happiness he had looked for, hoped for, but it seemed to him they had found ecstasy.

The morning was grey but dry. After breakfast Richard pulled his purse from his pocket and asked Marged if he could leave payment for all he and his soldiers had received.

She shook her head, smiling across at him. 'Oh no, it would offend greatly. We have a saying: "Never shall my house be closed against anyone, lest Christ close His House against me". '

Chapter 10

It was late afternoon when they came to Laroch. The waters of Loch Leven were shimmering in the last of the sunset and down by the shore trees clustered thickly by the road from Ballachulish. The ride had been more silent than usual, Richard having a sense of leaving something hallowed behind and Marged sitting her horse quietly content, her eyes on the distance, though occasionally she glanced at Richard and a smile passed between them. John Robb, who had happened to come up to his master's room very early, had rightly guessed at the truth. He had always thought his master lived too harsh and repressed a life and as far as he was concerned if Mistress Stewart had put that new and gentler expression on the Colonel's face he was glad of it.

Now as they entered the place she loved so much Marged began to point out landmarks, among them the little island of Saint Munda where the MacDonalds were traditionally laid to rest.

'I would like my bones to lie there,' she said, half laughing, 'but no doubt when we are old we shall be far from here.'

To their surprise suddenly Iain Dubh spoke up behind them in Gaelic. Marged answered him rather sharply and Richard asked her what he had said.

'Oh, nothing of importance. Really, sometimes his attention to me is almost too much.'

'But what did he say,' Richard persisted. 'I would like to know.'

She looked across to the island and then gave a shrug. 'Only that if he is alive he is wishing to be the one to carry me there.'

A curious revulsion swept through Richard, a retreat from the passionate intensity, the preoccupation with dreams and death of the Highland people, but it was only momentary and quickly thrust aside. 'Curse his impudence,' he said. 'Marged, when we are wed there'll be no need of him in our house.'

'I had thought of that,' she said. 'He has been with me since I was a child. He was my father's groom and he lifted me on to my first shelty. I'm very fond of him, but I am thinking that England, and Flanders too, will not be places that would suit him at all. I'll ask MacIain to find him a wife and then perhaps he'll be content to stay in the glen.'

They had spoken in low tones so that the Highlander should not hear but he kept his eyes fixed on Marged's back, a fierce resentment in them.

Marged raised her whip and pointed along the shore to the mountains rising on either side of an opening. 'There, that is the beginning of the glen. That peaked mountain is the Pap of Glencoe. MacIain has his winter house in the trees below it. And away to the right there is the mountain I love, Meall Mor. Round its far slopes is Gleann Leac where he lives in the summer. Tis very pleasing to be there on warm days.'

Richard looked at the rugged slopes of her mountain, the lower part green with trees, the heights brown and grey, the peaks stark in the distance as the glen ran east. They turned away from the loch, riding beside the little river Coe and so came to the bridge across it where it rushed over its stones, full after the recent rain.

There the Chief's eldest son, John MacDonald, who had evidently seen them coming, came out with four gillies at his back to greet them. 'Travellers, you are welcome – ' he began the formal speech and then broke off. 'Why, it's our little Marged! Now you are welcome indeed. We weren't expecting you.'

She leaned over to receive his kiss. As he was a tall man he reached her easily and she explained how they came to be there for he was looking with some surprise at her companions. She presented Richard to him and he said easily, 'You are welcome, Colonel Lincourt, and your men with you. You'll bide the night? I suppose you are bound for Fort William.'

Richard dismounted and bowed to this courteous man who spoke perfect English. He thought him fine looking with long dark hair and a neat moustache, dark eyes deepset in a bronzed face. John MacDonald wore tartan trews rather than the kilted plaid of his gillies, a brown leather coat with silver buttons, silver buckled shoes on his feet and a blue bonnet on his head, an eagle's feather kept in place by the silver badge of the MacDonald's, a crown, a mailed fist and a cross. His men stood behind him, the full folds of the philabeg over their shirts, bonnets on their heads, rough brogues on their feet, and they stared suspiciously at the *saighdearan dearg*.

'I thank you for your welcome,' Richard said. 'Yes, I'm on my way to the Fort, but I was anxious to see the place Mistress Stewart had spoken of with such affection.'

If John MacDonald was as curious of their being together as his quick glance betrayed he said nothing, but invited the guests to come to his father's house. The Chief's home at Carnoch was built of dry stone and wood, a white-washed, two-storied building roofed with blue Ballachulish slate and facing to the south to catch the warmth of the sun. To one side lay stables and to the other various outhouses for the baking and brewing, an avenue of trees leading to the main door. The gillies came behind the soldiers mostly in silence for only one had a smattering of English.

'We'll lodge your men in some of the cottages at Inverrigan,' John said, 'if that is pleasing to you.'

'I wondered,' Richard said, 'if your people would wish for that. Would they not be better at the change house we passed half a mile back?'

'We would welcome the Devil himself if he needed shelter,' John returned cheerfully and Richard laughed, appreciating the finer point of the man's humour. He began to like John MacDonald.

'You of course,' the Chief's son went on, 'will be lodged either in my father's house or mine which is less than two miles up the Valley of the Dogs.'

Richard thanked him and as they came up to the Chief's home turned to lift Marged down from her saddle before either her cousin or Iain Dubh could perform that office. A little colour in her cheeks she tucked her arm into John's and walked between him and Richard to the house.

The door opened and there Richard made the acquaintance of MacIain, Alasdair MacDonald, twelfth Chief of Clan Iain Abrach. He had never seen such a giant of a man, above six and a half feet tall and broad with it, wearing tartan trews and a doublet of bull's hide which, Richard was to learn later he had filched from a Campbell enemy. He had a mass of white hair reaching to his shoulders, and great white moustachios the end of which were twisted into fearsome points to fall each side of a strong full-lipped mouth. He looked, Richard thought, like a Viking and carried himself proudly and erect for all he was near seventy years old. On being presented he put out a huge paw in greeting and bade Richard welcome in English spoke with the light lilt of his people. Then he bent down to kiss Marged on the cheek.

Her face was glowing as she said, 'It's so good to see you again, MacIain. I have longed for this day.'

'And you are as welcome as the blue harebells in summer,' he said, smiling. 'Come you into my house.'

He led them inside into a long room where candles were already lit. Lady Glencoe, his wife, gave Marged a kiss and a warm embrace and for a while there was the usual bustle of arrival, the travellers gear unloaded and brought in and Richard had a moment to take in his surroundings. Here was no wild rebel's hovel but a well appointed place with panelled walls. MacIain had been to Paris in his youth and brought back quite a few luxuries. On the central table were silver and glassware, fine pewter plates and goblets even though no guests were expected and Richard knew many gentlemen who lived no better. There was a high-backed chair by the hearth and another at the head of the table, several stools and a finely carved cupboard in one corner. The two windows overlooking the avenue and the river actually had glass in them stolen, he was to find out later, on a raid into Campbell country.

He was shown to a guest room on the ground floor where Robb was laying out his saddlebags and travelling chest, a maidservant pouring water into a basin and setting out a clean towel. He washed his face and hands, asked Robb if he was comfortably settled and receiving an affirmative answer went back to the main room. Marged came down the stair at the far corner and gave a little crow of laughter.

'I know what you are thinking,' she said as she saw him glance at the table. 'You were no doubt told the MacIains were savages and now you see they are not!'

He smiled at her. 'I admit you read my thoughts. It's not as I expected.'

They said no more for Lady Glencoe followed Marged down. She was in her sixties, her hair white as her husband's, but neatly dressed under a white kerchief, her white plaid belted, her sleeves of scarlet cloth. There was a look of health in her warm colouring and a similar pride in her bearing for she was of the Keppoch MacDonalds and entertained in this remote house as if she were in Edinburgh society. MacIain came in followed by his two tall sons whom he had summoned to share the meal, bringing their wives with them. The second son, Alasdair Og whom everyone addressed as Sandy, was the most extrovert of the family, but his talk to Richard was stilted as he enquired after their journey. It was John who suggested that Marged should take their guest up the glen that he might see the whole of the Valley of the Dogs.

'I would like to see it,' Richard said, 'but I'm expected at Fort William and my men will be a burden to you.'

'That they will not,' MacIain answered from the head of the table. 'Be after staying at least a few days, Colonel. If this is your first visit to the Highlands you must be seeing something of the snuggest glen there is.'

Richard accepted, thinking a day or two well spared, for he saw the pleasure on Marged's face and as he ate he studied the people at the table, the two younger wives in dresses of homespun tartan cloth with larger checks than the tartan of trews and philabeg. Eiblin, red-haired and with fine hazel eyes, was the stronger personality, the smaller Sarah flaxen-haired unlike most people of the glen. She seemed a quiet girl and overawed by her husband. Of the two sons it was he who kept up the flow of talk, though it was John who interested Richard the most.

The food was good and while they ate a piper entertained them from outside, Big Henderson of the Chanters, MacIain informed Richard, who made the sweetest music in all Appin. A servant named Duncan had the charge of serving the guests and several dishes were brought in, kippered salmon and herring from the loch, fresh beef for they had not yet to resort to the brine tub, bannocks and butter and cheese. To drink there was whisky but also a good claret and Richard caught himself wondering if that too might have been diverted from its proper course. But he caught himself up, for these were not surely 'the gallows herd' the Master of Stair had spoken of, but a courteous hospitable folk who were making him welcome whatever they might feel about the colour of his coat. He was questioned politely about his reason for being there and he explained his wish to take back some stout fellows to make into soldiers to fight in King William's war, thereby bringing about a momentary silence.

Richard paused, wondering whether to elaborate, before deciding honesty would best serve his host. 'But I am advised,' he went on, 'that it would be wiser to wait until you and the other chiefs have taken the oath.'

MacIain looked at him beneath thick lowered brows. 'That is a matter we are considering for it touches upon our honour,' he said at last in his deep resonant voice. 'No decision need be made before the end of the year and you would certainly be wise to bide your time until it is resolved. The outcome is by no means certain.'

Richard said stiffly, 'I beg your pardon, though on my honour I am not sure what for.'

A shadow of a smile crossed MacIain's face. 'At the moment I would not give a groat for your chance of gaining a man more than a few malcontents who would be of little use to you.' His eyes strayed to Marged and then back to Richard, as if wondering to find her in such company. 'It may be,' he added slowly, 'that we will be needing all our men.'

This was not lost on Richard, but he answered, 'Nevertheless, sir, I am ordered to make the endeavour. But I will take your advice as far as I am able.'

MacIain shrugged. 'I fear you have a thankless task.' Dismissing the matter, he asked how the Colonel had met his god-daughter and it was Marged who broke in to tell the story, explaining how helpful Colonel Lincourt had been when David was in trouble.'

'He must be a braw laddie now,' Sandy put in, 'if he's gone off to fight for the French. He'll come back with a sword for our cause.' He stared boldly at Richard out of dark brown eyes, as if throwing out a challenge.

John interposed to say, 'If swords are needed. It seems as if we may have to learn to live quiet.' It was not long since he had gone to Colonel Hill at the Fort and made his own submission, and he saw no use in high sentiments that had no backbone of reality. He gave his brother a warning glance, but Sandy would not meet it and sat fingering his knife and staring at the cheese on his pewter platter. Richard sensed an animosity towards himself that was not present in John's attitude.

Another odd little silence fell. The Chief poured more wine into his visitor's cup and then roused himself to ask Richard how he liked the mountains and glens he had travelled so far. The talk turned into less dangerous channels and Marged asked MacIain if he had seen her father.

'I'm looking forward to greeting him and my mother again,' she said, 'for I've news to tell them.' She glanced at Richard and it was he who said, 'I think I should tell you, Glencoe, that Mistress Stewart wishes them to know that she has done me the honour to accept me as her future husband.'

This caused a ripple to run round the table, differing reactions from members of the family. MacIain subjected Richard to a long stare, John looked thoughtfully at him while Sandy's expression was one of amazement hardening into a scarcely concealed hostility. The two younger wives looked equally surprised, gazing incredulously at Marged. It was Lady Glencoe who came to the rescue of the awkward moment.

'You have surprised us, dear Marged, but I'm sure we all wish you well.'

Thus encouraged Sarah said shyly, 'And if my dear Sandy can be content with a MacGregor who has a Campbell for an uncle, why shouldn't you be with a *saighdear dearg*.'

She then realized what she had said and blushed scarlet. The fact that both Richard and Marged laughed eased the moment but as Lady Glencoe asked about their plans, Richard was aware of a restraint in the conversation that followed, to which her younger son made no further contribution.

Marged was looking at the Chief, waiting for a word from him and at last he reached out to where she sat beside him and enveloped her small hand in his. '*Mo caileag*, it is for you to know your own mind in this, but I think we must speak together of it later. Colonel Lincourt,' his piercing dark eyes fixed themselves on the guest, 'if you are Marged's choice then you must be doubly welcome. I can't be saying you have either of you chosen an easy road, but doubtless you have thought of that.'

'We have,' Richard answered, 'and I know it would mean much to Marged and to myself to have her Chief's approval, though,' he added, 'I'm bound to say we are determined.'

'That's honest at least.' MacIain gave a laugh that shook his big frame. 'Come, Duncan, fill the cups and we will drink a toast to them both.'

He called for his bard, Iain MacRaonuill Og, who sang to them in their own language, a song Richard did not understand but which Marged whispered was a song of betrothal and of the joy of bairns to come. Instinctively he put out a hand towards hers but immediately withdrew it at which MacIain laughed again.

'Take the lassie's hand, Colonel, we don't frown on such things here. But I think we'll not tell you the rest of the words.' There was more laughter, rather to Richard's embarrassment and Marged said spiritedly, 'I'll be after telling him when our wedding day comes.'

The evening ended convivially for John told their guest that no bottle should be left half empty when the food was gone. As Richard undressed in the guest room he could not help wondering what the family were making of the prospect of a *sasunnach* and a redcoat to boot marrying their cousin of whom they were obviously very fond.

Outside the wind soughed in the fir trees, but apart from that a great silence held the place and Richard felt the peace of it, but as he lay in the darkness he could only think of the night before and long for Marged to be beside him as she had been in the house of the Laird of Craigieduir. The night was cold and so was his bed.

In the morning the Chief suggested that Marged might like to take their guest riding along the seven miles of the glen and called for their horses to be saddled. They mounted and rode out, for once succeeding in dispensing with both Iain Dubh and John Robb. The bright autumn weather showed the Valley of the Dogs at its best, the air crisp and fresh. Here at the beginning of the glen the ground was open, the meadows bare after the harvest, the last of the cut hay safely in. Small ragged sheep wandered on the slopes of the crags above dry stone walls. Here beneath Meall Mor was the farm of Inverrigan, the man himself a tacksman of MacIain. Crofts and huts were dotted about and by the clachan of Achnacon was a fine grove of oak trees.

Achnacon himself was outside his house of stone and thatch with a tally stick in his hand while some of his men herded cattle into a pen. 'For the winter slaughter,' he said when Marged had greeted him. 'I've over many for the keeping through the bad days and my brine tubs are empty. While my lord of Breadalbane may have a few less,' he added with a twinkle in his eyes, ' 'tis not my fault if they are straying across the moor, and the Campbell beasts taste as sweet as any.'

So he was a cattle thief and not afraid to own it, Richard thought with some amusement.

Kilted men with their plaids tucked around their waists

for ease in work, blue bonnets on their heads, were busy everywhere, some tending the livestock, a few parties of younger ones setting off with dogs and guns for the hunting of the red deer and duck by the loch, ptarmigan in the mountains, while some of the women had tables outside and were kneading bread, baking bannocks over their fires. Some were spinning wool into thread to be woven into tartan cloth, dyed red and blue and green with heather, juniper and lichen, and they sang as they worked while children played, the sound of their voices carrying on the light breeze. Dogs roamed everywhere, barking and nosing for scraps and outside each house were piles of peat blocks for the winter burning. There were two rather better houses, about a quarter of a mile apart, and Marged said they belonged to John and his brother.

The beginning of the valley seemed to Richard a fertile place, sheltered and gentle below the mountain called the Pap but as they rode eastward the glen grew more rugged, the great jagged ridge of Aonach Eagach on their left and the mountains called the Three Sisters on the right with the majestic bulk of Bidean nam Bian dwarfing all. He found Sergeant Morrison and his men out on a piece of flat ground with a group of clansmen, being introduced to the game of shinty while his piper sat on a rock with Big Henderson, both with their pipes, Henderson teaching the lad a pibroch of the MacDonalds.

Ensign Fuller came up to Richard at once. 'I hope you'll not be displeased, sir. I thought it would do the men good to be at the sport this morning after their march. My host, MacDonald of Inverrigan, suggested it. He's made us very welcome.'

'They seem to be taking to the game,' Richard said, watching the scarlet coats mingling with the kilts and brown shirts, one of his men hopping about from a crack on the shin. 'A little drilling this afternoon perhaps. I think we'll be staying here until Wednesday or Thursday.'

'Very well, sir.' The young ensign gave Marged a shy smile for on the journey he had quite lost his heart, at an appropriate distance, to his colonel's lady.

Two miles further down the glen the river ran into little

Loch Achtriochtan and half a dozen streams fell down the mountain side. Marged pointed to a cleft high in the rock. 'That's Ossian's cave,' she said. 'He was the son of the great Fingal, our ancestor. He was a poet who left us fine songs for our heritage.'

Achtriochtan himself had seen them and came out of his house to stand by Marged's stirrup and welcome her back. He was a big man in his forties and both the father of Eiblin and the brother of Achnacon. He pressed them to come in for a dram. His house was long and low, divided into three rooms, a wicker division separating off what Richard guessed to be a stable, and all built under a cruck they called a roof-tree. Peat smoke seemed to fill the low room and escape unevenly from the hole in the thatch, and by the fire Achtriochtan's old father, Ranald of the Shield, sat on a wooden hearth seat, half blind and stiff with rheumatism. He had been a great fighting man in his day, Marged whispered to Richard as the old man greeted them in Gaelic.

Achtriochtan introduced his wife, another daughter and his son to Richard. Then he said, 'This is the village of poets, Colonel, and this,' he brought forward a man with a ragged red beard and startlingly bright brown eyes that never seemed to be still, 'is Aonghus MacAlasdair Ruaidh. He fought at Killiecrankie, as most of us did, and has written a mighty fine poem about it.' Without any hesitation he added, 'Were you against us on that day, Colonel?'

'No,' Richard said and was glad for some reason that he could make that answer. 'I was not in Scotland then, nor, from what I hear of your prowess, do I think I might be alive to be here today if I had.'

Achtriochtan laughed, enjoying the compliment. 'That's a fair thing you are saying.' He nodded to his man, Kennedy, who produced cups and whisky. The house might be primitive with no more than a beaten earth floor, but the hospitality was warm and Richard found his interest in these people growing. There was nothing primitive about Achtriochtan's bearing and speech and he pressed Marged and Richard to take a fresh bannock and butter with him before they left.

Afterwards as they rode on the glen grew more stark, the mountains rearing above them. There were a few stone crofts here, the doors barely the height of a short man with roofs thatched with bracken and heather and held down by netting weighted with stones. Mere huts, Richard thought them, such as would not be tolerated in England. Even the meanest of his tenants at Heronslea had better than that, but the people that emerged from them, the children who came to stare seemed no less content, strong and rosy after the summer. There were black cattle everywhere and he judged there must be a thousand head or more.

'Winter is not a good time in the glen,' Marged said. 'The snow stays on the mountains and fills the braes and the corries while the wind whistles down the gullies, but in the valley bottom it clears quickly because it's near the sea. If there's not been a good harvest there is hunger with the cold. The men there are digging peat and there's plenty up on the moor for the fires. And in the evenings there are songs and stories to be told, and shutters are put up to keep out the wind.'

'You've been here in the winter?'

'Not often, but the year before I married I came to spend Hogmanay with MacIain and his house. 'Twas a good time,' she added wistfully, 'but my mother doesn't travel anywhere now. She has poor health and must bide at home. You will be meeting her and my father in a day or two, Richard and oh, I am wanting you to like each other.'

He said, 'I fear I am hardly the second son-in-law they would have chosen.'

Marged smiled across at him. 'I know what you are thinking, but when they know you they will understand why I love you.'

He responded to that look but he said, 'My dearest, I doubt whether that is at all certain!'

All the way along streams cascaded down the mountain and at the Meeting of the Waters, wild foam rushed to meet the Coe. The clefts of the Coire Gabhaill and the Lairig Etive thrust up on either side of Buachaille Etive Beag. They could be climbed, Marged said, but they ended in high jutting rocks and wreaths of mist. Here too was the end of the Pass of Glencoe, a steep outlet leading to Rannoch moor.

'There's Appin land to the north and south of us,' Marged said, 'and for the most part they are our kin and friends, but the Earl of Argyll bought the superiority from them and now he is our feudal lord which we are not liking at all.'

Richard drew rein and sat Juno, looking at the rocks and tumbling water. 'An easy place to defend,' he said. 'Glencoe is its own world.'

'The only way in is across the moor which is a dreary place, except for the Devil's staircase which is part of the road leading to Fort William but it's little more than a track and no easy ride even in summer.'

'A few men could hold this pass if they were well prepared,' he said, and then added, 'equally it could act as a trap to hold the people in the glen.'

'I suppose so,' she agreed, 'but no enemy comes at us this way. Only those who make their way in as friends could hurt us.'

It seemed an odd thing to say and though he didn't comment it was a phrase he was to remember.

They were returning down the glen past Achtriochtan and its loch, and were between the clachans of Achnacon and Leacantium when the accident happened. They had taken the track that led to John MacDonald's house, meaning to call in on him, and had just crossed the river that came down from the glen when a plover rose screaming into the air. At the same time a hovering eagle swooped at it almost under Juno's feet. Marged's horse was more placid, but Juno, terrified, reared up. Richard struggled to hold her, to calm her, but she came down heavily, put her foot in a hole and fell forward on her neck, pitching Richard clean over her head. He was thrown violently against some rocks by the river, coming down hard on his right side across a large boulder and hitting his head against another, to lie half in and half out of the tumbling water.

Marged uttered one startled cry and unhooking her leg

slid from the saddle to plunge over to him. Two crofters working nearby began to hurry towards them. Flinging herself down beside him Marged called his name and lifted his head clear of the water. He had only briefly lost consciousness and he tried to struggle up, but sick and dizzy he became aware of appalling pain in his right thigh.

'My leg,' he said faintly, 'I think it's broken.'

Marged held his hand in hers. 'Then lie still, my love. I'll get help.' She called to the crofters and they ran off in the direction of John MacDonald's house. Richard turned his head and tried to raise himself on to his elbow but his head swam so much that he sank back against her.

'My horse – is she hurt?'

Marged glanced back to where the mare lay, struggling in vain to get up. 'I think she must be, she can't seem to get to her feet. Oh, Richard my dear, how do you feel now? Is it very painful?'

'Very,' he said, but he managed to give her a brief smile. 'And I hit my head when I came down. It's aching damnably.'

'I've sent for help,' she said and shifted her position to half sit in the cold water so that his head might rest in her lap. He lay with his eyes shut, still feeling very faint and a few minutes later John himself came up with four of his men and a large blanket. He knelt down by them.

'Colonel Lincourt, can you hear me? I've brought gillies to carry you to my house. It's the nearest,' he added as Richard opened his eyes, 'and will pain you less than to bear you back to Carnoch.'

'Thank you,' Richard said. 'My apologies, Mr Mac-Donald. I thought I could manage my horse better.'

John glanced at Marged. 'How did it happen?'

She explained and Richard looked up to say, 'My poor Juno, I think she's ruined. Despatch her if you think it's necessary.'

John nodded and got to his feet to inspect the mare. She was terrified, her eyes rolling wildly, every effort to get to her feet rendered useless by her own broken leg. The gillies unrolled the blanket and with care managed to get the injured man on to it, though he gasped with pain during the operation, and as they carried him off the rocks to the track the nausea and dizziness returned.

Marged walked beside him in great anxiety but sensibly she let the gillies get on with their task. A moment later there was the sound of a shot, and Richard realized John must have used his own pistol to put Juno out of her misery.

Chapter 11

There then began for Richard what he thought were the strangest and in some ways most enriching weeks of his life. He was carried into the main room of the house, stone-flagged as was the Chief's, and Eiblin came hurrying to him in great concern as John explained what had happened.

'You'll not be trying to take him up the stair,' she said to the gillies. 'Lay him on the bed in the little room.'

'I'm sorry,' he managed to say on a gasp and at once she broke in. 'Don't be worrying at all, Colonel. We will be caring for you.'

The little room was to the left of the main one and at the opposite end to the stair. It was small, holding only a narrow bed, a table and stool, but the bed itself was comfortable. Richard himself would not have cared at that moment if they had laid him on bare boards as long as they set him down for the pain of every movement was excruciating.

'I'll send for John Robb,' Marged said and went out to give the order to one of the gillies. He was back with Robb in a very short time, both having run all the way, Robb's face creased with anxiety.

'I've lost poor Juno,' Richard said. 'Take that look off your face, Robb. I'm not like to die of a broken leg.'

'We must be getting the clothes off you,' John MacDonald said and sent the gillies out. Marged went with them while he and John Robb began the operation. 'I'm afraid we'll have to cut off your boot,' he added. 'If we try to pull it off it will be paining you too much and maybe doing damage to the break.'

'They cost me a deal of money in the Luckenbooths,' Richard said ruefully, 'but I can see it must be done.'

John took the knife from his belt and slit the seam. He was very careful but even so every action caused pain. Then he and Robb eased off Richard's coat and cut away his breeches until at last he lay exhausted in his shirt under the blankets. A hastily summoned man of the glen who was accustomed to dealing with injuries and ailments came in.

'I am Ailean Mor,' he said. 'I will be after setting your leg.' He had two pieces of wood under his arm and some strips of linen. Carefully he examined the injured leg and shook his head. ' 'Tis a bad break, high by the thigh and not easy to heal. I am fearing this will hurt you.' He worked slowly with gentle fingers but even so it was ten minutes of agony for Richard and he was sweating when it was done, but he managed to thank Ailein Mor. Then they left him quiet and Marged came to sit beside him.

'Dearest,' she said and took his hand. 'Is it very bad?'

'I can't deny it.' His fingers tightened on hers. 'But when you sit here I can think of something better.'

'Eiblin is preparing a draught for you that will deaden the pain a little and help you to sleep. John Robb has gone for your baggage. Oh, I am so sorry that this should be happening to you.' Privately she was very concerned for he was white-faced with a thin line between his brows and his mouth drawn in, and she was sure he was suffering a great deal. She knew from being a doctor's daughter that the break was in the most difficult place to heal.

'It couldn't have come at a worse moment,' he said. 'I must think – make some arrangements – '

'Not now,' she said swiftly. 'Just rest and leave other things until tomorrow. Ailein Mor knows what he is after but I've sent Iain Dubh for my father.' She had had words with her gillie. Iain Dubh had come at her summons from Carnoch but at his own pace, once he knew she was not hurt, and when she said the Colonel had broken a leg muttered that he wished the eagle and the plover had made a better business of it.

She had been very angry. 'How dare you? I am thinking

I shall be sending you from me, Iain Dubh, for there will
be no peace between you and my husband when we are
wed.'

Stubbornly confident that she did not mean this he
merely asked what it was she was wishing him to do.

'You will go at once to Maryburgh and fetch my father.
Go by the ferry and don't be idling on the way.' Iain Dubh
gave the injured man one glance and then departed
without comment.

'My father has great skill,' she went on to Richard, 'I
shan't rest until he's seen you.'

'Hardly the introduction I had expected,' Richard
murmured.

'No.' She smiled lovingly down at him and when Eiblin
came in with a cup, she helped him lift his head to drink.

'I ask your pardon for being an uninvited guest,' he said
to his hostess. 'I must apologize for the trouble I'm causing
you, Mistress MacDonald.'

'Don't be thinking of it,' she said in her low musical
voice. 'You are welcome until you are well again, and your
man to bide with you.'

A little boy, something over two years old, had followed
her in and was standing staring wide-eyed at the
newcomer, a finger in his mouth. She said, 'Come you
away, Alasdair,' and taking him by the hand left the room.

Richard lay back against the pillow. It was dusk now and
Marged took the candle in its holder to the fire in the
living room and lit it, to set it on the table in the guest
chamber, closing the wooden shutter over the window.

'This is damnable,' Richard said weakly. 'Marged, will
you see that my ensign and Sergeant Morrison are
informed?'

'That's already done,' she answered. 'They wanted to be
coming at once to see you, but I told them to wait until
tomorrow. Eiblin is seeing after the "great meal". Will you
be eating something?'

He shook his head and then wished he hadn't for it still
ached intolerably. 'No food,' he said, 'but a cup of
MacDonald's whisky wouldn't go amiss.'

She fetched it for him and he drank, glad of its fieriness

in his stomach. Then she said, 'It's getting dark and I must go back to MacIain's house, but I will be here as soon as it is morning. Try to sleep, my love.'

He was indeed growing drowsy. She bent to kiss him and with that benison he slipped, despite the pain, into unconsciousness.

He woke in the night to the deep silence of the glen. Robb was asleep on a pallet of heather and bracken on the floor. Richard asked for a drink and he got up at once to fetch water from the jug left on the table by the thoughtful Eiblin, but after he had gone to sleep again, Richard lay wakeful. The pain was too penetrating to allow further sleep and he lay wishing he could shift his position but any movement increased the discomfort and he cursed the eagle and the plover and mourned the loss of Juno.

Dawn came greyly through the chinks in the shutters and the first sound he heard was of rutting stags high on the mountain behind the house, fighting their seasonal battles, antlers crashing together and bucks howling. The house began to stir and John was his first visitor.

'*Beannachd leat*,' were his first words, as they were to be every morning, and he immediately translated them to, 'Blessing be with you. May the Holy God ease your pain. Did you sleep, Colonel? I'm fearing you can't have rested very comfortably.'

'No,' Richard agreed, 'but thanks to your wife's potion I had a few hours' rest.'

'She is wise with the herbs,' John nodded. He had come in holding his small son by the hand. 'The pride of my house,' he said, smiling. 'He will be the fourteenth chief after MacIain and myself.'

'He looks a fine healthy boy,' Richard said, and for a moment thought of Heronslea and Marged there and a son to bring life to the place.

'He thinks the *Sitheachan* brought you – cunning fairies,' John explained, 'who play tricks on us, eh Alasdair? Your man is bringing your breakfast, Colonel.'

'The "little meal" as they called it consisted of porridge made of oats, fresh milk, hot bannocks and butter and Richard found he was quite hungry. His headache had subsided and the pain of his broken leg was bearable if he lay still. His next visitors were Ensign Fuller and the sergeant.

He cut short their proffered sympathy by saying, 'Yes, it is the most damnable thing, but we must be practical. The men will do no good playing games here for the weeks it seems it will take my leg to heal. You'd better march them on to Inverlochy. Our host will give you directions and I'll write a note to Colonel Hill and ask him to lodge you at the Fort. He can use the men as he wishes until I come. A patrol or two will be good for them.'

'Very well, sir,' Fuller agreed, 'but I don't like leaving you here like this.'

'There's naught you can do for me and I'm in good hands. Robb will of course stay with me. It's cursed ill luck, but I must make the best of it. I can tell you I don't relish weeks of lying here doing nothing.'

'No, sir, I'm mighty sure of that. When do you want the men to leave?'

'Tomorrow morning will be time enough. I'll have a letter ready for you to take to Colonel Hill.' Richard said and after they had gone lay and thought of the disastrous collapse of all his plans. His work in the Highlands would be set back for weeks, delaying his return and that meant that his regiment was left marking time instead of getting to Flanders where it was needed and he almost groaned aloud at the thought of his raw recruits. This accident also meant leaving Ripley in charge for possibly another month and while he didn't doubt the major's competence it was not good for the regiment to be without its colonel for so long. He had better write to Sir Thomas Livingstone and ask him either to give Ripley his lieutenant-colonelcy and appoint a new major, or send someone down from the castle as a temporary measure. Either way it was unsatisfactory – he only hoped Ripley had got over his infatuation for Mistress Fletcher and was having no further trouble with her husband. But the whole situation was irritating and it did nothing for his condition that he lay there fretting over it.

His next visitor was MacIain himself, his huge frame

darkening the whole doorway. He expressed his sorrow for his guest's accident, apologized for the eagle and the plover and regretted the loss of Juno.

'I would offer you a horse from my stable but your man tells me you have a spare mount lodged there. However if you would like it I have a fine stallion you are welcome to be having when you can sit a horse again.'

'No, indeed, though I thank you,' Richard said, rather overwhelmed by this generosity. 'The accident was no one's fault except perhaps my own.'

'Sometimes the spirits of the glen have a mischievous way of teaching us things we would not be knowing otherwise,' MacIain said seriously. 'Rest you, Colonel. If anything is needed for your comfort you have only to be saying it.'

'Nothing,' Richard answered, privately dismissing the laughable idea of 'spirits'.

Marged had come with MacIain and, when he left, stayed beside the bed; John Robb tactfully withdrew, and Richard said, 'Take pity on a poor fellow who can't possibly make love to you and come and kiss me.'

She complied, sitting carefully on the bed so as not to touch his leg and Richard kissed her for the first time since leaving the Laird of Craigieduir's house. Then he lay back for a little while, content just to look at her, their hands locked.

At noon Doctor Beaton rode in, followed by Iain Dubh who looked surlier than ever. The doctor was still an exceptionally handsome man, even in middle age, and Richard could see at once where Marged got her beauty. He came in out of a dank day and shook the rain from his cloak.

'It is sorry I am to see you so,' were his first words, 'especially as Marged has been telling me you and she plan to be wed.'

'Yes,' Richard said, 'I'm aware, sir, it must be something of a shock to you. We had hoped to break the news in a more seemly manner.'

'To her mother it may have been, for Iain Dubh is not the best of messengers, but to my mind Marged is a woman full grown and a widow and it is for her to choose for herself, though,' he added with an honest smile, 'I'm not denying it was a surprise.'

For a moment he and Richard exchanged glances and then Richard said, 'It will be my life's task to make her happy.'

Doctor Beaton nodded. 'I can see that you mean it. Now let me look at this leg.' He removed the covers, Richard wincing a little as he began his examination. He was careful, moving the splints as little as possible and commending Ailein Mor's work. 'But it's a bad break,' he said, 'and I fear it will take a long while to heal, Colonel Lincourt.'

Richard lay still, thankful the inspection was over. 'I feel very bad about this. I am imposing on John MacDonald and his wife. I suppose it's out of the question to move me to Fort William?'

'Certainly it is, unless you wish to impose an agonizing journey on yourself and probably damage your leg for life.'

'I see,' Richard said. 'In that case I fear I must remain an univited guest, but it must be a great nuisance for the MacDonalds.'

'They will not be looking at it like that,' Dr Beaton assured him. 'I have been knowing John all his life and there never was a more open-handed man. Mind you,' he added, his lips twitching, 'that's not to say he's not a handy man at the rieving and the fighting; they all are in this valley, but hospitality is a sacred trust and no one comes to harm under a MacDonald roof. I am knowing them well, you see, for Beatons have been physicians here for a long time and sad I am that I've no son to follow me. But I've a nephew training at St Andrews so there'll be another Beaton after me to doctor in Appin and Lochaber.'

'I still feel uneasy at accepting so much,' Richard said, 'and I've discovered one does not pay for what one receives in the Highlands. How long do you think my leg will take to heal?'

'Two months, maybe more, maybe a little less.'

'Two months?' Richard was aghast.

'I'm afraid so,' the doctor said. 'In any case don't try to hurry the business, or you will leave yourself with a bad limp. I'm afraid that may happen anyway. You must be patient, Colonel. Are you a patient man?'

'I fear not,' Richard admitted. 'Marged will tell you that.'

The doctor laughed and opened the door, calling for his daughter who was waiting in the main room, talking to Eiblin and with little Alasdair on her knee. 'Come in, my dear. Here's your colonel telling me he is not a patient man, but I fear he must reconcile himself to a good many weeks on this bed.'

'I am sorry,' Marged came to stand beside him. 'You will have to watch his progress, Father, and so you will both get to know each other.'

'You would think I have no other patients,' he said teasingly. 'but yes, I will come when I may, though there's little I can do. All it needs is time. I came over the military road to the Devil's Staircase today but that won't be open to any respectable traveller when the snow falls and coming by the ferry is a slow business. All I can do, Colonel, is to urge you to be still and let the good God be healing you in His own time, which may not be yours.'

Richard grimaced. 'I will heed your words, sir.'

'And now I'm afraid I must be taking this girl of mine away from you from a while. Her mother is so anxious to see her, and she is far from well just now.' He paused for a moment, giving Richard a straight look from under his thick dark brows. 'I don't know you as yet, Colonel, but if my Marged has chosen you, then I am wishing to amend that. When you are well again and at Fort William, will you be after calling on us?'

'With pleasure, sir. I've no idea exactly how long I shall be at the Fort, but I may have to cut my work short because of being here so much longer than I intended.'

'And carry my daughter away with you, eh? But we are reconciled to being parted from her,' the doctor said with a sigh. 'Well, well, a woman must be after going where her husband goes, 'tis in the nature of things.'

'It will mean Flanders,' Richard said, 'but I can't say how long the war there will last. It's no way to being won or lost

yet. But one day we'll come back.' He glanced at Marged.
'It's a journey that will mean a lot to us.'

'Well, I'll be leaving you in Eiblin's hands and see you
again in a week or so.' The doctor held out his hand and
took Richard's in a firm grasp. 'I wish you well, sir.
Naturally I think you are the one to be gaining with my
Marged for wife, but no doubt from what I see in her face
she's thinking herself equally fortunate.'

'Thank you,' Richard said. 'She will always be my first
care.'

'And I'll send her back to you soon. All I can wish you
now is patience.'

With that thought Doctor Beaton went, leaving Marged
to say her farewell. 'I'm so sorry to leave you, Richard, but
I must be going with my father. My poor mother will be
waiting so anxiously and I am not liking what he says of
her health. But it won't be for long.'

'I feel so helpless,' he said restlessly. 'I never dreamt of
such a thing happening. I've not fallen off a horse since I
was a boy.'

'Perhaps as MacIain says some good will come of it.'

'I doubt it. It keeps me from my work and soon the
worst of the winter will be on us and my regiment lying
idle at Leith. It hardly bears thinking about.'

'My poor Richard.' She couldn't keep back a smile. 'As
you rightly admitted to my father, you aren't the most
patient of men, but it's a virtue you'll have to be cultivating
while you are lying here. And I'll come back to be with
you. Perhaps I'll be teaching you the Gaelic, and read you
Ossian's poems in his own language.'

'When you are here,' he said, 'I'll not fret for the
fruitless hours.'

But when she had gone the little room seemed dark and
cheerless. Richard lay and cursed silently and when John
Robb was disposed to talk about the glen and the folk he'd
met told him roundly to take himself off for a while. Robb,
used to his master's sometimes peremptory manner,
understood the reason for it on this occasion and went
down the track to the house of the smith who had dealt
with Juno's carcase. The smith had finished work for the

day and they took a friendly mug of strong-ale together, neither understanding the other's language but managing to communicate well enough by signs.

Shortly after Marged had gone John MacDonald came in with an armful of books. 'The thought is on me,' he said, 'that you will want something to beguile the time, Colonel. I've brought you a few books, though whether they're to your taste I am not knowing. There's a history by Turk and the works of Josephus and a Bible if you are minded to be reading the scriptures. Eiblin shall find you some more cushions so that you may be better able to hold a book.'

'I'm grateful,' Richard said. 'I can't express how I feel about being such an encumbrance to you, but though I asked him the doctor will not hear of my being moved to Fort William.'

'Indeed not,' John agreed and added cheerfully, 'Don't be thinking of it at all. Do you play at cards? Or at backgammon?'

'Both,' Richard answered and John promptly promised him a game that evening. He placed the table by the bed and laid down the books where Richard could reach them and then left him alone. Richard turned over the leather-bound volumes and began with Josephus, finding the military annals interesting enough, but half his thoughts were with Marged, riding away from the glen.

Not only did John MacDonald come himself after the five o'clock 'great-meal' but he brought his brother Sandy and the three of them played cards for modest stakes until near midnight when Eiblin appeared with her long hair unbound and scolded them, saying that the injured man needed rest.

'Whisht, woman,' John said, 'Good it is to be taking his mind off his injury.'

The days seemed to settle into a pattern. In the morning Robb brought him a bowl of fresh mountain water to wash in and during this operation he could hear Eiblin singing as she prepared the porridge and whey for breakfast. He had no idea whey whipped up could taste so good. During the morning while she was about her household tasks with her servants and Alasdair's nurse, Moir, and her husband was out about his, Richard read or sometimes talked with Eiblin through the door. It was left constantly open, thoughtfully, so that he might feel part of the household.

Actually he felt far from cut off because there was another door in his room, opening into the back of the house and this he discovered led to a storeroom where sacks of meal stood, brine tubs with the winter's supply of meat, cheeses, butter and milk. They ate well, John said, until the summer's stores ran out and then it was the hungry time until there were new young deer on the mountains and the fields began to yield again, the earliest beans welcome in their stewpots. Also in the storeroom were targes, round studded shields of leather on wood, some of them spiked with steel, hunting guns and knives and one or two muskets. There seemed to Richard to be a constant coming and going to the storeroom despite there was a door at the back which didn't seem to be used, and though there was always an apology if the person had the English, it distracted him and broke up the day. Blue peat smoke drifted in from the main hearth where he could see salmon and herring hung up to smoke and when they were served to him he enjoyed them very much indeed.

Eiblin tended to his needs, leaving those of a more personal nature to John Robb, and Richard thought her a most sensible and likable woman. He liked listening to her singing as she worked. The boy Alasdair ventured at first as far as the door but when Richard called his name he ran away; then gradually he ventured more often until at last he came, still with his finger in his mouth, right up to the bed.

'Man hurt,' he said in English somewhat to Richard's surprise for he had heard him talking in Gaelic to his mother.

'Yes, but man getting better,' Richard returned gravely and thereafter Alasdair wandered in and out, mostly chattering in his native language, but sometimes with a word or two of careful English. Eiblin told the injured man to send Alasdair away if he was a nuisance, but Richard never did. Instead he watched the little fellow, thinking what it might be like if he and Marged had a son, and he took pleasure in the first day when Alasdair actually sat upon his bed, legs swinging.

The evenings became very convivial. Often Eiblin's father, the tacksman of Achtriochtan and his brother of Achnacon came down and they all played cards, the amiable Achnacon puffing tobacco smoke into the small room which combined with the smoke from the peat fire made Richard deplore the habit, but not for anything would he have said a word, though sometimes it was as if the room was wreathed in fog.

Even MacIain came occasionally and he questioned Richard about his military experiences, probing into his past, his family, his attachment to King William whom he unhesitatingly referred to as 'the Dutchman', a term which Richard thought wiser to ignore. He liked the old man and listened in turn to tales of his wilder days. Sometimes he thought of his interview with the Master of Stair before he left London and remembered Dalrymple's words – 'a sept of thieves, a gallows herd'. What did Dalrymple know of these people, of the Highland way of life? Nothing, Richard thought, and certainly nothing of their better side, their friendship, their high sense of honour, their hospitality. Thieves they undoubtedly were, but it seemed to be an accepted part of their lives.

Sandy came occasionally, bringing his abrasive personality like a strong wind into the little room. At first he merely formally enquired after the invalid but gradually, as he joined in the games of cards in the evening, his animosity began to fade. Sometimes he brought Sarah who shyly gave Richard some biscuits she had made, and every now and again there was what they called a *ceilidh*. Eiblin played her harp and sang some of the old songs of the clan, which Richard didn't understand, but he recognized one tune, 'Coll of the Cows', which Marged had sung to him at the house of Donald Stewart.

MacIain's bard, Iain Dall, sang or told tales of their ancestors, of Fingal and his son Ossian, of the Feinn, his wild warrior band, of Angus Og who fought with the Bruce at Bannockburn, and of his bastard son, Iain nan

Fraoch, John of the heather, to whom he gave the land in Glencoe. It was from Iain, John told Richard, that the clan chief was given the name of MacIain and the heather badge.

Richard had hardly realized until now how few clansmen had the English, nor how they derided the 'English-speakers' with the exception of their Chief and his family for whom it was, they thought, a tiresome necessity.

The main room was crowded on these evenings with folk from the nearby clachans who loved to hear the old tales again and again. There was dancing to the pipes of Big Henderson, old women chattered by the fire and the old men puffed their tobacco smoke into the air as the younger folk danced. Those who had a few words of English came to speak to the injured *saighdear dearg*, plying 'the red soldier' with more drams than he really wanted.

The evenings usually ended with uproarious choruses roared out with the vitality of a people who had known them from the cradles, one in particular.

Hi rim horo ho ro ha,
The MacDonalds won the day

the refrain so catchy that Richard found himself humming it.

All this made the time pass and though he longed for Marged to come back the days drifted by. Iain Dubh brought a letter from her in which she said that her mother was very poorly and she didn't feel able to leave just at the moment, thus causing Richard's spirits to sink. She also said that Aunt Marie had sent on a letter from David in which he wrote that he had entered the Scots regiment serving under King Louis and was liking the life very much. Richard wished, for Marged's sake, that the lad had entered his own service. With an eye for picking good material he had been sure that soldiering would answer for David.

Robb brought him his little case containing pens and a silver ink bottle and he wrote both to Sir Thomas

Livingstone and to Major Ripley explaining what had happened and asking the Commander-in-Chief to do as he thought best regarding the temporary leadership of his regiment, adding that he would prefer promotion for George Ripley. There was nothing he could do to hurry the healing and he must leave its welfare to others. They would simply be wintering in Scotland instead of in Flanders but a newly formed regiment needed a strong hand, as he knew. He wrote also to his mother and sisters and to Otwell Skinner. His mother might or might not have passed on the news of his betrothal, and knowing Lady Standen's obstinate way of shutting her eyes to what she didn't want to see it was possible that she was hoping his attachment to a Scottish lady might not be permanent. She wanted Judith for a daughter-in-law. Consequently he thought it encumbent on him to write to Judith and make clear the whole situation. In the end he thought the letter looked formal and stilted but he saw no way to amend it. He also wrote to Mynheer Hygens and impressed on him his changed opinion of the Highlands and the Mac-Donalds in particular.

He then gave Robb his letters to take to Ballachulish where, John said, the carrier passed through on his way to and from Glasgow, and he lay back in the confident hope that the King, reading what he had tried to convey, might learn something in their favour of his more distant subjects. He was not naive enough to think this would persuade William or his councillors to think the Highlands subdued, but that a meeting place might be achieved with sweet reasonableness on both sides.

His leg was less painful now and he was getting very weary of lying in bed. His back ached a great deal and he would have given anything to be able to turn over, but Ailein Mor urged him to keep as still as possible. However, despite the inactivity, the disarray of his plans, he was not unhappy. The days, beginning as they always did with John's words of blessing, always contained some hours when he was alone and he found himself taking stock of his life as it had been. It now seemed to have been sterile in many ways. Of course he had his work, his soldiering for which he cared more than he had ever shown, but apart from Otwell Skinner he had had no friend like John MacDonald whose open warmth drew a wholly new response from him. His friendship with William, he saw now, had been a cold one and Richard, deeming himself to be of the same nature and shying from expressions of personal feeling, had once been glad of it. He had wanted no intrusion into his privacy. Now in this little house there was no such thing as privacy but instead of resenting it he found himself part of this close-knit community and drawn into it in a manner that totally defeated his old reserve.

He would lie looking out of his window at the cold wintry scene, sometimes bright and frosty, at other times thick with mist or dreary with a downpour of rain, and he was oddly content. He felt for all his imprisonment on this bed and in this tiny room, a warmth and freedom for the first time in his life, a process that had begun, he thought, in a tearing wind when he had stood on the battery at Edinburgh Castle and lost his hat, and discovered that he was in love. Now he waited, but without count of days, for Marged's return, thinking for long hours of her and the love she had given him. No man he thought could ask for more than he had now.

One afternoon Sandy came in and told them all a tale he thought highly amusing. 'Rob Roy MacGregor has been busy again,' he said. 'Have you heard tell of the lad, Colonel?' And when Richard said he had not, went on, 'He's a bonny man with the cattle. You'll not have the understanding of our ways on you, sir, but cattle are our business in the Highlands. We drive them south in the autumn, in fact some of our men are not long back from the tryst at Stirling where we sold our summer stock very profitably.'

His eyes twinkled and he added, 'You must not be thinking we are thieves because we rieve a cow or two from our enemies like the Campbells or the MacPhersons for they take a few of ours, if they can find them, and stray cattle are any man's for the taking, but we do legitimate business the while. Well,' he warmed to his tale, 'the

Livingstones were taking two hundred head to Stirling and Rob is not after liking the Livingstones who are Government men and there's bad blood between them. He waited for them by a village called Kippen and there was some sort of affray with the villagers which Rob regretted for it was all a mistake, but he took Livingstone's cattle, sending the drovers running, and drove the beasts home to his own territory north of Loch Katrine. No doubt he'll present a few to my lord Breadalbane for bands of MacGregors find shelter by Tayside and his lordship employs some of them as a watch over his own beasts.'

Richard was scandalized. 'But I thought the Earl was a Government man, a Whig.'

'Oh we all know Iain Glas up here; he may be Willie's man in Edinburgh but King Jamie's in the Highlands!'

Richard digested this with some surprise. 'We saw a party of MacGregors on our way up here, I forget just where. They were suspicious of my redcoat soldiers but Marged talked to their leader and no harm came.'

'I doubt if it was Rob,' Sandy said. 'He's after living respectably most of the time. And for all he's not yet twenty he's a mighty strong fellow with such long arms he can tie his garters without bending. I've met him at cattle trysts and he knows as much about moving cattle as any man in the Highlands and with a head for a good trade.'

'To the Government's loss, no doubt,' Richard said drily and both brothers shrugged as if that was not a matter to be concerned over. The King's writ ran weakly here, Richard thought but he said no more and Sandy was soon off on another and less provocative tale.

He began to think of these people as friends. After all, they were Marged's kin and the time was moving towards the deadline of the first day of January by which they must take the oath of allegiance. Would MacIain do it on their behalf and his own? If he failed to do so they would be punished – what was it Sir Thomas Livingstone had said? 'To the utmost extremity of the law'. Something in him revolted against that. Whatever their past of stealing and killing and wild forays he wanted a new peace, a better life for them now. And John seemed to wish for them to live quiet in their glen. But he had said no word of his father swearing and Richard eventually brooched the subject one evening at the end of their game of backgammon.

John was gathering up the pieces. 'No,' he said at last, 'MacIain has not been after swearing yet. But there are four weeks left. No one, I'm thinking will do it until the last minute – a sop to Highland pride, if you like. I've made my peace with Colonel Hill and Achtriochtan has in his sporan a letter of protection from the Colonel, though I don't know whether these are enough. Perhaps – if MacIain swears.'

'And if he doesn't? I like you all too well to wish any harm to come to you.'

John's face was shadowed. 'You will not be understanding that it is against all we are loyal to.'

'Tell me,' Richard said. 'I would like to understand your position. I know a little from Marged of course of the Jacobite loyalties, but tell me more.'

John pondered for a moment. Unlike the impulsive Sandy he took time to voice his thoughts. He pulled at his moustache and then said, 'You must know that King James has our allegiance because he is a Stuart and we are bound to the Stuart Kings. I've never seen him, but you must have been to court. Be after telling me what kind of man he is.'

'I've not seen him these twelve years to have any kind of conversation with him. I was in the late Duke of Monmouth's Life Guards and I was at Bothwell Bridge in '79 when we beat the Covenanters, but not long after Monmouth fell from favour and lost his command. I never quite forgave King Charles for that because I thought it unjust. I liked Monmouth especially for his mercy to a beaten enemy and to take away his command made me, a lad of twenty, unwilling to serve under his successor. So I took my sword to the Prince of Orange and even less could I forgive James for executing Monmouth. I've been with William ever since and though I have returned to England occasionally it was only to see my family.'

'But you did know King James? And his brother King Charles.'

'Oh aye,' Richard agreed. 'No one could help liking Charles for his wit and his way of saying the right thing to the right person. Unfortunately his brother hadn't got that gift. But you want to know about him. James is tall with a long face and a heavy manner with none of his brother's graciousness. He foolishly made religion an issue, Mr MacDonald. If he had kept his own within the confines of his palace chapel and left the English people to theirs he might not have lost his throne.'

'But we Catholics prayed he might ease some of the laws against us. We've not seen a priest here for two years and more.'

Richard said nothing for there seemed to be no immediate answer to this whole vexed question and as a soldier he wanted to have as little as possible to do with politics and the wrangling over religion. He wished each man free to obey his conscience without going to war over it. He added honestly, 'But I'm not denying James had qualities, he was a fine sailor by all accounts. That was where his talents lay and where I believe he would have been the most content. Better a royal duke at sea than a king in exile, but fate chose otherwise.'

'Let me explain something to you,' John said. 'We of the Highlands resent very deeply the harrying of King James the seventh, the second to you, the turning of him from his throne, for it was not only the English one he occupied. Since King James the sixth came to rule over you nearly ninety years ago Stuarts have ruled both countries, but they were our royal house first and you can't be surprised if we stay loyal to them.'

'But many Scots have accepted King William,' Richard said. 'I met a good many gentlemen in Edinburgh who have done so and are content enough that it should be so. Viscount Tarbat, whom I consider my friend and who tells me he too is a Highlander, is one. The Earl of Breadalbane too, though you say his loyalty is divided, and my lord of Argyll but I've seen him only once.'

'Once is too often, Campbell dog!' John's response to this was swift enough. 'He is in league with Covenanters and Presbyterians, men who care for their trade and their pockets above their honour as Scots. I have been in

Edinburgh myself when I was at St Andrews University.'
He saw the surprise on Richard's face and laughed. 'Oh
aye, I've attended there. Chief's sons are not ill-educated,
Colonel, for they have to deal with more than their own
folk. If you go to see Lochiel, as you say you plan to, you
will find him a travelled and cultured man. But I didn't
care for the city, a place of merchants and trade, a city of
money. I'm sure you can see that life is very different here.
To us the honour of our name is what matters and a man's
given word.'

Richard lay silent for a moment. 'Yet you raid each
other's cattle and goods. You tell me these very books I'm
reading are stolen.'

'Some of them,' John admitted readily enough. 'I took a
few from Campbell of Ardentinnie who owed us for a raid
or two himself. It was after a bloody battle at Perth. We'd
won at Killiecrankie though we lost our Bonny Dundee,
may his share of Paradise be his, and we set out to take the
city. It was a murderous fight and we failed to take the
place, mainly because the Cameronians burned it rather
than yield it, Psalm-singing sons of swine that they are. We
lost many a clansmen in that fight. We came home by Glen
Lyon and Achallader and the men had to have their pay in
some form – you know that, Colonel – and we'd little
enough siller, so we took from our enemies.' He laughed
harshly at the memory of it. 'We left Robert Campbell of
Glenlyon so little he had to take a commission in the army
to feed his family and he near sixty. We took horses, a fine
stallion my father rides, cows and sheep and goats for our
men. 'Tis the way of things up here and the Campbells
have done as much ill to us in their time.'

'It's a lawless way to live,' Richard said, wondering at the
contradictions in this man he had come to like so much.
'As a soldier I live by order and discipline. Don't you see
that lawlessness must stop?'

John pondered again. 'Aye, I'm after thinking that
myself and Colonel Hill is the man to bring it about if only
the ignorant men in London would be leaving him to do it
in peace. But Sandy is not agreeing with me.'

'I find such a way of living hard to understand.'

'Yet the thought is on me that you understand us better than you did.'

'That's true enough,' Richard agreed. 'Your hospitality is beyond what we English could expect. But there's another aspect I find difficult to comprehend. You say you are Jacobites yet you fight each other, clan against clan.'

John clasped his hands about his knees and began to recount to Richard the long history of the Gael, how the struggle for the leadership of Gaeldom had begun, how the MacDonalds of Sleat led now by Sir Alexander MacDonald, together with those of Glengarry, Keppoch and Glencoe, were the greatest clan in the west and how gradually the Campbells fought them for that leadership. The Campbells had become Whigs, more and more Government men, John said scornfully, 'Trimmers, all of them, and the Earl of Argyll thinks he is the head of all Gaels but none of us would own it, nor Locheil, nor the Mackenzies nor the MacLeans and Macphersons nor the Mackintoshes.' John closed his lips suddenly on this impassioned speech and getting up poured them both a glass of French brandy.

Richard said suddenly, 'Do you think there is too much difference in every way between Marged and myself?'

'I did,' John said straightly, 'but now that I know you, Colonel, it is becoming plain to me that you have a great love for her, and she for you, and that is a gift of the Most Holy Being and not to be denied.'

'Thank you,' Richard said. 'I care for your approval.'

John smiled across at him. He had an attractive smile. 'We shall be kin when you marry, so I would like to dispense with formality. Your given name is *Ruiseart* in my language, may I use it?'

'I would like that,' Richard said. 'And I am glad that we shall be kin.' Cattle thief, Highland rebel, these John MacDonald might be, but Richard meant the words without any reservation for he perceived in him paradoxically a man of high concepts of honour and loyalty.

Chapter 12

Marged came back to the glen on a dreary day in December when the snow lay on the top of Aonach Eagach and the Bidean and Meall Mor and deep in the high gullies though it had not yet lain in the glen itself. A bitter wind tore at Richard's shutter and whipped through the cracks and Eiblin brought extra covers to his bed. This morning he was beginning to feel time slipping away with no sight of her when he heard hooves outside, her voice in the doorway, and then she was beside him. He threw his arms about her and kissed her hungrily before either spoke.

'Are you still in much pain?' Marged asked. 'It must be so very tiresome for you.'

'The pain is much easier,' he said, 'as long as I don't move the leg which gets very frustrating, but Ailein Mor thinks it is healing well.'

'My father's down with MacIain,' she told him. 'He will be coming shortly to see you. I'm afraid the weeks must be dragging by for you.'

'In one way yes, because I'm not used to inactivity and I lie here and think of the work I should be doing and my idle regiment at Leith, but in another way,' he paused, 'Marged, I am learning so much about your people and liking what I see. My much imposed-upon host has become my friend.'

She smiled. 'I was thinking you and John would like each other if you had the chance to become acquainted, but I never thought it would be from so drastic a cause.'

'And all thanks to that eagle and the plover.' He told her of some of the subjects they had discussed and then it

occurred to him that her eyes were exceptionally bright
and that she was caught up with some great news.

'What is it?' he asked. 'Has something happened?'

'Yes, oh yes, my dearest.' She seized both his hands. 'Last
week a priest, Father MacHale, came through Maryburgh
and I talked with him. He said he was on his way to visit
the Catholics in the Isles, Skye and Mull and the Uists, but
he hopes to be back here by the middle of February. Then
if we wed at the little kirk in Maryburgh he will give the
blessing of my church on our marriage.'

'Marged!' His hands returned her grasp. 'Is it really
possible? It's all I could want, but – ' he hesitated, not
wanting to throw cold water on the plan, 'but I ought to be
gone back to Edinburgh long before that.'

'Surely you'll not be finishing your work here too soon,'
she said in a disappointed voice. 'It's into December we are
already and you not yet walking.'

'I sit on the side of the bed now as you see with this leg
on the stool most of the day, and Ailein Mor is making me
a pair of crutches. If your father thinks it is time I'll try
them out as soon as I can. I should be able to sit a horse
soon after that and when I can I must go to the Fort. My
men have already been on Colonel Hill's hands for too
long.'

'I understand that, but I think you will have to be
finding out first how you feel when you are trying to walk,'
she pointed out. 'After so many weeks it will take time to
get the strength back into your legs. And when you can
ride you want to be after seeing Lochiel and Coll of
Keppoch and some others, don't you?'

'That's true,' he admitted. 'If I can't get started until
January – '

' – When the weather may be against you – '

'I see it will probably be into February before I shall be
free to go back,' he finished. 'Beloved,' he put both hands
about her face, 'I don't want to make objections to what I
desire most in the world. It's only the thought of how long
I've been away from my regiment that's haunting me. I
have a duty to try to persuade the chiefs to encourage
some men to join me and then to return as soon as I can.'

'No chief will give you any answer,' she said. 'until we have heard from King James, whether he will give them leave to swear the oath. Oh,' she gave a sudden little shiver, 'I'm as loyal to our King as anyone, but I'm thinking he is not after helping us now and we can't be carrying on the fight alone.'

'I have tried to persuade John of that and begged him to get his father to take the oath. I think he does see it is necessary but Sandy is a different matter.'

'MacIain will wait to hear from Paris first,' she said, 'I know that is the truth. It's on his mind he will be hearing before the end of the month. There are still fourteen days.'

'King William and Queen Mary are in London,' Richard pointed out, 'and St Germain is far away. I want peace for these people, Marged. And I want to marry you – my God, how I want that!'

'The thought is on me that it will so please my father if we can be wed here and even if my mother can't be quite reconciled we can ask the priest to bless us in my father's house and that will make it well for her.'

'Two months,' he said, 'two short months and you'll be mine.'

'You understand, dear Richard, that I want the blessing of my church. It is how Lady Hay, my friend in Edinburgh, arranged it for her cousin who married a Protestant.'

'I will agree to anything you wish,' he said, 'to have you as my wife.'

It was noticeable to John MacDonald that the invalid appeared suddenly to shake off the depression of a slow recovery and expressed his pleasure when Marged told him of their plans. Doctor Beaton came to the house and pronounced himself satisfied with Richard's progress. They talked for a while and the doctor told his daughter afterwards that he considered Colonel Lincourt an extremely sensible man. 'Though,' he added with a twinkle in his eyes. 'I'm sure that was not the reason you accepted him.'

Marged laughed and kissed him. 'Now I wonder why I did? A William's man and a redcoat!'

A week later the crutches were produced but when Richard tried for the first time with their help to stand he was appalled at how dizzy he was. It took him some time to get any sense of balance back, even his good leg felt weak, and just getting into his clothes exhausted him. More time was spent getting used to being up again and to using his crutches, but the first evening he sat down at the family table for the evening meal it was treated as a cause for celebration. John produced a couple of bottles of claret and sent a gillie to bring Sandy and Sarah to join them.

Marged sat beside Richard and he felt that these people had really accepted him as the man she would be marrying, though he wondered if MacIain had ever said anything to try to dissuade her. The Chief was courteous when he came but he was a dignified rather unbending man and their conversation was sometimes a little stilted. He thought he knew the reason, for as December progressed he felt a tension growing in the house. There were low-voiced conferences in the main room. John was clearly anxious, Eiblin's songs sometimes broke off half sung, and Sandy when he came was restless. Once Richard heard him say, though they rarely spoke alone together in English, 'It's more than we are after bearing. Where's the pride of Clan Iain Abrach?'

Another day when MacIain was in the house, ostensibly calling on the injured man, afterwards he went back to John and Eiblin. At first they spoke quietly but something John said caused MacIain to bang his fist on the table and shout, 'Have I been loyal to my King since I became a man to abandon him now without his word to release me? All we are asking is the right to be loyal to our ancient line of kings and I'll not be turning my back on that in my heart even if I have to submit to the Dutchman. I'm an old man and no good for the fighting any more maybe, but by the great God I'll go out if I must.'

John said in a vibrating voice, 'Do you think I'd be holding back if the clans rose? But we've not enough strength. I was in Maryburgh yesterday and I was told there's four hundred more men of Argyll's arrived at the fort.'

'Curse all redcoats that come into our glens,' MacIain said furiously.

'Father!'

MacIain lowered his voice. 'Oh aye, I'm knowing what you mean, but he's a single Englishman, and they are Argyll's men and Highlanders who've put on the redcoat. May the spirits of our ancestors rise against us if we give in to them!'

No such appeal could fail to move a Gael and John said slowly, 'May my soul be cursed if I should shame my fathers, but we have to see the truth and the truth is you are faced with a decision that must be made, and made soon. There's little time left, MacIain. If you don't swear, letters of fire and sword will be issued against us and God forbid that should happen to our people.'

'Oh.' There was an anguished whisper from Eiblin. 'To have our men killed and women and bairns turned into the snow, our homes burned – no, 'tis not to be borne.'

Marged, who had been silent up until now, added, 'No, that must not be risked. I have lived long enough in Edinburgh to know the temper of the men that rule Scotland, Argyll, the Master of Stair, Lord Breadalbane – '

'I fear mischief from no man more than Iain Glas,' MacIain said. 'He's not forgiven us for our raid on Tayside, though it's near two years since.'

'Then take the oath,' John begged.

'Is it my own son who is speaking, the next MacIain? Am I hearing what I am hearing?'

'It's reality we must be facing.' There was both force and despair in John's voice. 'How many fighting men can we bring out? Seventy, maybe a hundred? It's no good without all the clans together and help from France. You know that, MacIain. We are too small a people to act alone. For all our sakes, if there's no news from Paris by the end of the month, take the oath.'

'To a Campbell?'

'If it must be, it must be.'

MacIain let out a great curse and stamped out of the house.

A few moments later Marged came in to Richard and shut the door. 'You heard? MacIain was using the English so that the servants and men about the place should not be knowing what we said.'

'I'm sorry for you all.' Richard had been listening with growing concern. 'But if MacIain doesn't swear there'll be a deal of trouble.'

'I know,' she said, 'but he's adamant he'll not break his allegiance to the King without word from him, and I can't tell how it will end. If only we could hear something from St Germain.'

'I wish you might,' Richard said. 'And I've been thinking that my presence here must be an embarrassment at this crucial time for them all. But please God I'll be able to leave soon and relieve John and Eiblin of an uninvited guest.'

'How can you say that?' Marged's retort was swift. 'You've said yourself they are now your friends. They've cared for you, nursed you –'

'I didn't mean to sound ungrateful,' Richard broke in. 'Indeed, I'm not. I'll never forget what they've done for me, but the fact remains that I'm an English redcoat and I'm sure they'd all rather be rid of me.'

And though, later, when John came in he behaved as though nothing untoward had happened Richard sensed the tension in him as the time began inexorably to run out.

The snow came in a sudden storm and a week of bad weather gave Richard no chance of trying his crutches outside, but now he had Marged's company and they talked a great deal of their plans. John said that if the weather permitted he would bring his wife to see them wed, but there was a permanent crease of anxiety between his brows and Richard knew the cause well enough.

'I don't understand what your king is about,' he said in some exasperation to Marged one morning. 'He has left you all in suspense though he has had months to decide what he wishes you to do. He must know there will be severe punishment for those who don't take the oath.'

'St Germain is so far away.' Marged gave an unhappy sigh. 'We don't know what he is told or what he thinks. MacIain says nothing about the business but it hangs heavily on him. It's all very well for the chiefs of large people, like Glengarry and Keppoch and Lochiel, but we are small and vulnerable and MacIain feels that. I too saw more soldiers arriving before I left.'

'I wonder by whose order they've been sent,' Richard said, and the thought was on his mind that he wanted to get Marged as far away from this trouble spot as he could and as soon as possible.

'I heard nothing of that, but they are of Argyll's Foot, and the word is in the town that they are there for no good purpose. The rumour is that they are to take Glengarry's castle but I don't know how true it is.'

Richard stirred uneasily. 'I don't like it. I wish the Highlands could be settled peacably.'

'So does Colonel Hill. He came to dine with us one evening and I could see how anxious he was. He doesn't get on with his second-in-command.'

'I'm not surprised,' Richard said. 'I met Lieutenant-Colonel Hamilton in Edinburgh and had a run in with him myself. Sir Thomas Livingstone thinks him a competent officer and so he may be for all I know, but the man has a harsh nature and I disliked him intensely. I'd not trust him to show any clemency if this business is not resolved soon.'

But to his intense relief and who knew he thought but to MacIain's also, at dusk on the twenty-ninth of December, when hope of hearing from the exiled King had all but gone, an exhausted messenger arrived in driving snow and went straight to MacIain's house. Then a gillie was despatched to John's house and relayed the news that five days ago Major Menzies, the same man who had taken David Stewart to Paris in August, had returned to Edinburgh. He had made the journey from Paris in nine days. The King was pleased to inform the clans that much as he appreciated their loyalty, they might do what they deemed best for their own safety.

Permission had come, 'but almost too late,' Marged told Richard. 'MacIain says he will go to to the fort tomorrow to swear the oath.'

'Thank God,' Richard said and when John came in from a conference with his father, expressed his relief.

John was still frowning. 'I am thinking the oath ought to be sworn before a sheriff, but MacIain is of the opinion that Colonel Hill can take it as Governor of Lochaber. I wish this blizzard would ease, it will delay the chiefs travelling to the swearing, if Glengarry comes at all. But at least the messenger said Lochiel is already away to Inverary. He got the news before we did and if he's gone Keppoch will go too.'

'Once King William's peace runs in the Highlands,' Richard said with a confidence he was not entirely feeling, 'you will see it's for the good of the people here.'

'I hope you're right, my friend,' John said but there was enough doubt in his voice doubly to disturb his guest.

A cold day passed, the snow thick everywhere, drifting against walls and peat stacks. Richard and Marged sat by the fire, the boy Alasdair playing on the floor nearby. Richard discarded his crutches and tried walking up and down the room with the aid of a stick.

'As soon as this snow clears I must go to Fort William,' he told Marged. 'I'm sure I could sit a horse now.'

'We will be going together when you feel ready,' Marged agreed. 'I'll stay with my parents while you are about your work. With the swearing done you may bring back a few lads who want the activity they can't be getting when the clans are at peace.'

Eiblin looked up from her spinning, bright strands in her hands. 'We will be after missing you, Colonel, when you are gone.'

Little Alasdair, leaning against Richard's good knee, looked up to say, 'Not go.'

He smiled and ruffled the boy's dark hair. 'I must, my wee man.'

While it was still dark the next morning a gillie came loping through the snow, bare knees blue, banging on the door of the house and bringing John down from his bed. He gabbled out his news in his own tongue, Richard heard Eiblin's voice as she came down and a few minutes later John came in.

'Are you awake, *Ruiseart*? I'm afraid you can't help but be so with all that noise.'

'Aye, I'm awake,' Richard roused himself to lean on one elbow. 'What's happened?'

'It was one of my father's gillies bringing me disturbing news. MacIain went to the fort but Colonel Hill would not be taking his oath.'

'Oh? I thought he was your father's friend.'

'So he was from years gone by, so he is, but he was saying he can't be taking the swearing from him; it must be before a sheriff. I suspected as much and told my father so. He didn't even come home last night but was after going straight on to Inverary and in the worst snow of this winter. God knows if he will get there in time.'

Richard opened his shutter and looked out into the grey driving snow as first light came up. 'How long will it take?'

'In this, two days, maybe less, maybe more. I can't be telling in such a storm. But he's an old man to be making the journey in this weather.'

Richard pulled the shutter close as a flurry blew snow into his face. 'In God's name why did he have to leave it so late to find out where to swear. It's the last day of the old year.'

'I am knowing that,' John said and in those words seemed to hang fear and menace and an ominous foreboding.

That night the clan celebrated Hogmanay but, Eiblin said, it seemed half-hearted with MacIain away to the swearing and no one in the mood for the usual singing and dancing and drinking. The clan waited, some not understanding the full implication of what was being done down in Inverary but the Chief's family and tacksmen under no illusions. Achtriochtan said gloomily he was glad his eldest son was away serving in the French army and his eyes rested unhappily on Alasdair, his grandson. The big man, Achnacon, kept to his house and told his wife to bring his pistols to him so that he might clean them.

It was a week into the new year before MacIain returned. Richard had felt unable to leave before he learned the outcome, for he was more than aware of the importance of the oath to all these people and to the Chief's heir in particular.

The weary MacIain, buffeted by the weather, sent out a summons for the whole clan to assemble by the Chief's stone where all pronouncements of general importance were made. John prepared to take his household along the glen and Richard asked tentatively if he might accompany them. 'You'll not be understanding the Gaelic,' John said, 'but if you wish to come, I'll have one of my shelties made ready for you. Marged will be coming, I'm sure, and she can tell you what is being said.'

So for the first time in two months Richard sat on a sheepskin astride the sturdy little Highland mount and found it enjoyable, causing only a momentary twinge in his leg. He had not worn his red coat during all that time and he was not wearing it now.

The clan was assembling by the stone, coming from up and down the glen, warmly wrapped against the sharp wind. The snow had ceased and they stood patiently in the cold awaiting the arrival of their chief, the tacksmen and their families in the nearest places. MacIain came at last, riding a garron, the three eagle feathers of a chief in his bonnet, his plaid about his shoulders and followed by his 'tail' – his bard, his piper, his hanchmen, and half a dozen gillies. He dismounted and climbed on to the stone, looking down at his people, at Achtriochtan and Achnacon and their sons, at the tacksmen of Inverrigan and Leacantium with their families, wind fluttering the tartan as they stood waiting. It was apparent that every man had come prepared for what the Chief might ask of him, for they were all armed, dirks hanging from their belts, swords at their sides, pistols for those who had them, targes on their backs. If MacIain said they were to fight they would fight and Richard saw them today in a sterner guise, every blue bonnet carrying the heather badge and set over determined faces.

MacIain stood for a moment until there was absolute silence. He looked old and worn and haggard. 'My children,' he addressed them at last, 'I will be telling you what has happened since I left this place. I went to Colonel Hill at Inverlochy but he was telling me he could not take my oath and he was angry with me for not knowing it, but there, he is Governor of Lochaber and who'd have thought he'd not be able to do it!'

He did not look at John as he said it, for only stubborn pride had made him seek any way to avoid going to Inverary and humbling himself before a Campbell. 'So I went into the storm,' he continued, 'and as I passed on the Ardgour side of the loch I was seeing a light from my own house and there was no time to seek its warmth. No man can say I lingered on the way.'

He paused again and Marged whispered to Richard what he had been telling them so that Richard had a picture of that proud and valiant old man on his garron, his half-frozen gillies beside him, driving through the storm of sleet and the biting wind to the ferry and then on down the coast of Loch Linnhe.

'We came to Barcaldine,' the Chief took up the tale, 'and there a captain, Drummond was his ill-begotten name, chose to ignore Colonel Hill's letter to the Sheriff of Inverary which was in my pocket. He locked me in a cursed garderobe for the whole day and my gillies in a cellar before he would allow us to go on. May his carcase rot in hell for his spite; 'twas nothing else, for Colonel Hill wrote plainly enough that I had come in time, and he craved the kindness of Sir Colin Ardkinglas to be after swearing me. 'Twas almost beyond men's strength to be going that night through the Pass of Brandar in snow as deep as we found there, but we sheltered in a shieling for an hour or two to get strength back in us and so we came to Inverary.'

Every eye was fixed on the speaker, the men and women standing in silence, listening to the humiliating tale, a slow anger growing that their Chief had had to submit to their old enemies.

'Ardkinglas is a decent man and an honest sheriff from all I hear,' MacIain went on, 'but he was away across Loch Fyne spending Hogmanay with kin and not expected back for a few days.' MacIain paused, his eyes shadowed as he remembered the waiting in a small change-house in the Campbell capital. 'Inverary is no place for a man with the heather badge in his bonnet and we waited there for four days for Ardkinglas to return. Then when I showed him the Colonel's letter he was not knowing what he should be doing. He made us wait again while he thought on the matter but in the end, and I with tears on my face to my shame, he gave me the oath.'

A sound like a growl seemed to go round the listening clansmen. John said, 'Thank God,' and Sandy, with one glance at Richard added, 'May every devil's curse be on the Campbells and the redcoats and the Whigs and the Dutchman for the evil they've brought on us,' which speech Marged did not translate.

There was a lot of discussion which Richard did not understand, some of the tacksmen looking relieved, others disgruntled and some actively rebellious. Achtriochtan's younger son asked boldy where the spirits of Fingal and Coll and the old giants of the glen had fled to? He was told by his father to hold his tongue but it was clear many of the men felt the same, shifting their feet awkwardly, angry that their Chief should have been so shamed. But MacIain's word was law and gradually the muttering subsided. He dismissed them with a blessing and a few final words about living quiet now until spring brought a fresh activity back to the glen.

'I have done what I have done with King James's permission,' he finished. 'I would not have moved without it but it is for your welfare. We are after being safe now in our glen and the redcoats won't harm us. We are indeed a small people and it's not for us just now to be causing trouble. Go you to your homes and bide quiet.'

He climbed down from the stone, mounted his garron and rode away towards Carnoch. Slowly the clan dispersed, the men for the most part silent, some of the women whispering, the children jumping and running, released from the necessity of standing still and quiet. John's small son had run to him and he lifted the boy into his arms.

'We are all behaving,' he said in a low voice to Richard, 'as if all is well. But my father took the oath late, whatever the reason.'

'Owing to a mistake,' Richard protested, 'and Colonel Hill vouched for his arrival in time at the Fort.'

'Would you vouch for the English Government

honouring that?' John asked and Richard did not answer.
'MacIain knew it was a mistake even when honour kept
him at home.' John went on with sudden passion. 'But he
would not be yielding in time. He waited too long, by all
the holy saints!' His voice shook with the intensity of his
feeling and little Alasdair, sensing something was wrong
put his arms about his father's neck and buried his face
there.

'I'm sure his intention will be taken into account,'
Richard said and tried to keep the doubt from his voice.
He remembered the Master of Stair at their interview and
his hatred of the MacDonalds, undisguised and coldly
vindictive.

'And the weather,' Marged added. 'It was noble of him
to make that journey in such a storm.'

'And the spite of Captain Drummond,' Eiblin put in, as
she walked beside her husband. 'Sure and Sir Colin is not
that sort of man from all accounts, for all he is a Campbell.'

'It is in the hands of the Good Being,' John set his son
down as they approached the house. 'Eiblin, we've not
eaten yet this morning.'

The next day the sun shone and Richard prepared to
leave the glen, once more as a redcoat, with John Robb
and his baggage pony, Marged and Iain Dubh and Jeanie
accompanying him. With deep regret he said goodbye to
his hosts.

'I owe you more than I can ever repay,' he told them. 'If
you'd not taken me in, if I'd had to go to the fort I might
not be on two good legs now.'

'And how should we not be sheltering you and you
Marged's betrothed?' Eiblin asked in smiling
astonishment, and her husband held out his hand.

'*Beannachd leat, laochain,*' were his parting words. 'That
means friend in our language. Come back to visit us soon.'

Richard took the outstretched hand and smiled down at
the boy Alasdair. 'God keep you all. We'll return when we
can and in kinder weather.'

He left them standing in the doorway and rode away
past Sandy's house and Inverrigan's farm, by the oak trees
of Achnacon and across the bridge where he paused

briefly to collect Marged and say farewell to MacIain. The Chief shook his hand heartily and kissed Marged. He seemed more himself this morning.

Then they set off down the road to Ballachulish and Richard turned back once to look at the mountains, Meall Mor white and wreathed in mist which the sun was only slowly dispersing. He remembered MacIain saying to him when he first broke his leg that such events sometimes happened to teach a man things he would not be otherwise knowing. And it had been true. He was taking away with him not only a knowledge of a people he hadn't known before, but a new knowledge of himself and he left the glen with part of that self wishing contrarily that he was back in his room with Eiblin singing at her work.

Sir Colin Ardkinglas was indeed an honest man. He had had to search his own conscience before administering the oath to MacIain and was now convinced he had done what was right. Better forget the few days' lapse of time and think of the people saved from the Government's punishment. He wrote to Colonel Hill:

> I have received the Chief of Glencoe, great lost sheep that he was, and am assured by him and will take his word that he will keep his people in obedience. Please ensure that none of his suffer. The Privy Council and the King must make their will known in this matter but I hope and pray they will accept his reason for not coming to me first and welcome him and his followers into the King's peace.'

Hill immediately and with relief wrote to MacIain that he now lived under the protection of the garrison at Fort William, while Sir Colin sent Hill's letter to himself together with his own list of those received to the Sheriff-Clerk of Argyll in Edinburgh. The man was also a Campbell and he consulted other Campbells, as well as Viscount Stair, the Master's father. The clerks to the Council were also approached and they too gave it as their opinion that MacIain had sworn too late, being well after the first day of January. He had had, Lord Stair commented drily, four months to decide the matter. Accordingly the Sheriff-Clerk took his pen and scored the name of Alasdair MacDonald, Chief of the MacDonalds of Glencoe, from the list, without troubling himself to set it before the Council.

In London when the amended list reached him, the Master of Stair drew a deep satisfied breath. He invited the Earl of Argyll and the Earl of Breadalbane to dinner where he told them they might now be about the scheme, Breadalbane's in conception, that was nearest their hearts.

Chapter 13

Colonel John Hill was an old man nearing seventy. He was tired and he had been ill this autumn, an illness from which he had thought he might not recover, but somehow determination to keep his command, to see his work done, had kept him alive. An old Cromwellian officer, his concept of duty was high. He also had a great deal of commonsense and saw only too clearly how to handle the Highland problem if left alone. But he was hampered now by too many directives from London and Edinburgh, too little money, a dearth of supplies and a lieutenant-colonel whom he could not stomach at any price. Lieutenant-Colonel Hamilton had been foisted on him when he wanted his own major, John Forbes, son of his old friend Duncan Forbes of Culloden, to be promoted to the place. On top of that they had sent him a colonel, albeit delayed by a broken leg, who was supposed to be recruiting here, of all the foolish ideas, when he had enough trouble keeping his own garrison up to strength. Now Colonel Hill was waiting for him in a mood of weary resignation.

Richard came in, shaking the damp of an early evening shower from his cloak and the two men shook hands. 'I believe I am greatly in your debt,' Richard said. 'You've had the kindness to feed and house my men these two months. I hope they've been of some use to you.'

'They've worked with my own troops improving the defences of this place, and in patrolling the glens,' Hill said. 'Pray sit down, Colonel, and take a glass of brandy to warm you.' He poured it out and handed it to the new arrival. 'I'm afraid the misfortune was all on your side. Is your leg healed?'

'Tolerably, sir,' Richard said, though he had found sitting in the saddle tiring and had not yet discarded his stick. This room seemed cheerless to him, a north-westerly wind sending the smoke of the peat fire out into the room instead of up the chimney and the fire itself gave out little heat. He thought the thin tired-looking man at the table should have been retired long ago with a comfortable pension instead of doing duty in this out of the way place. 'Your fortifications seem strong,' he said by way of conversation. 'I noticed the works as I came in.'

'Oh aye,' Hill agreed, 'but it's not been easy. There's no wood to be had round here but useless birch, or fir which takes too long to mature, and my frigates from the Clyde bring me nothing better, though God knows I've written often enough. I've set aside quarters for you, Colonel. As you'll have seen we're very crowded, some of the men still under canvas but I hope to have the new barracks completed in a week or so.' He gave Richard a penetrating look from rather bloodshot blue eyes. 'You've seen much service, sir?'

'Under the late Duke of Monmouth when I was a very young man and these last twelve years with his Majesty in Holland.' Richard emptied his glass, glad of the warming brandy. 'I believe, Colonel, you may have known my father, for I understand you once served in Fitch's regiment.'

'In Fitch's? Aye, so I did.' Hill was surprised. This man before him had certainly taken trouble to find that out. 'I have it now! Never tell me you are related to the Robert Lincourt who served with me under Colonel Fitch?'

'His son,' Richard said and was aware of a glow of pleasure. 'It's rare for me to meet with anyone who remembers him.'

'I recall him well,' Hill said warmly. 'As brave a man in a fight as I ever saw. You must dine with me tomorrow, Colonel, and I'll tell you of him for I was in several fights with him. Ah, we were young then and eager. We were the russet-coated captains that General Cromwell said knew what they fought for and loved what they knew. Is your father still living?'

'No, he died back in '67.'

'I'm sorry to hear it. It was an honour to have served with him and for his sake I welcome you here, Colonel, though you've come at an ill season for recruiting.'

'You mean because of the weather? I'm afraid my broken leg put all my plans out. Or do you perhaps mean the oath-taking?' Richard asked.

'Both – and other things.' Hill was wearing his great-coat over his scarlet coat for the room was cold and he rubbed his gnarled hands together to warm them. 'It's a bad time to be riding round the glens and I tell you plainly, Lincourt, that those who sent you have no knowledge of the Highlands or the people. Now I was serving here fifty years ago and I began to understand them then. They're like children and with proper handling may come to peacable living. But as for serving King William – ' He shook his head.

'I hear Lochiel has taken the oath,' Richard put in.

'Aye, and MacDonald of Keppoch is come in and asking for a commission in King William's army for his brother.'

'Then I must see him.'

'Do so,' Hill agreed, 'and if you ride out soon you may well see Lochiel before he leaves for London to see the King in person, which he tells me is his intention. I've also had news of the outer islands, where MacDonald of Sleat says he will submit in his father's name for the old man is dying and I've every hope that when the weather eases young Clanranald will come over from South Uist.' The old man gave a deep contented sigh. 'It has been my work these two years to bring peace to the Highlands, Colonel, and if that is a legacy I leave behind me I'll count myself well content.'

'It seems as if all the situation needed was a man who had proper understanding of the folk here, and I'm afraid this isn't fully appreciated in London,' Richard said soberly.

'That is true, sir. It was better understood in General Monck's day. Ah,' Hill's faded blue eyes took on a look of reminiscence, 'the General used to say he had brought such quiet that a man might travel across Scotland with a hundred pounds in his pocket and no more than a switch in his hand. George Monck was a great man. I never saw him lose either his temper or one jot of his authority and the chiefs respected him. Those days sadly are gone and all the work undone.'

'I can appreciate why my father was a Parliament man at the time,' Richard said, 'though I hope it's not treason to say so now.'

Hill laughed out loud. 'You are an honest man, Colonel, and, as Sir Thomas told me in the letter he wrote about you, a sound William's man having the privilege of the King's friendship.'

'I am so honoured. His Majesty holds to the principles for which Parliament fought.'

'It is those principles I try to instil up here,' Hill said, 'but the people hold fast to their Jacobite beliefs. 'Tis only now, I think, that they are beginning to face reality; the oath has seen to that. Glengarry, contumaceous fellow that he is, still holds out, with some others. Sir Thomas orders me to set out to take his castle from him but I'm afraid the Commander-in-Chief asks an impossibility. Glen Garry is hard to come at, the castle newly fortified and I've neither cannon nor bombards for the business.' The Governor paused and refilled their glasses, his hand stiff with rheumatism.

'Would you advise me then to keep clear of Glengarry when I ride out to meet the chiefs?' Richard asked.

'I would indeed. See Lochiel and Keppoch too, and then if you'll take my advice you'll ride on to Inverness and try your fortune there, but frankly, Colonel, I think you've been sent on a fool's errand.'

Considering the whole scheme had been the King's Richard said nothing to this, for if William knew nothing of the Highlands Governor Hill was far from Whitehall.

'There's the language difficulty for one thing,' Hill went on. 'You probably don't realize how few of the ordinary clansmen speak English and even if you could get them what use are recruits who can't understand a plain order?'

'I suppose they can learn,' Richard said. 'In any case, I have to try. Perhaps some of the better educated may come in.'

'Orders have to be obeyed,' Hill agreed, 'but for men of our rank, Colonel, tempered by local knowledge.' He himself had no intention of implementing the order to move against Glengarry, and he proposed to ignore what he considered to be Sir Thomas's fatuous suggestion. 'However you must do as you think fit.'

There was the briefest knock on the door and without waiting for permission to enter Lieutenant-Colonel James Hamilton came in. He took one look at Richard and said without preamble, 'So you've arrived. If you will listen to advice, Colonel, you'll take your men away again and do your business in the Lowlands.'

'I believe I did not ask for it,' Richard answered curtly. 'If I need guidance in my affairs I'll seek it from Colonel Hill.'

Hamilton shrugged. 'It seems the Secretary of State must have had some purpose in sending you, though it eludes me. However, as things are he has other plans for the gentry up here.'

Now why, Richard wondered, did Hamilton mention Stair in particular, not the King from whom all orders stemmed, nor Sir Thomas Livingstone who was Commander-in-Chief for Scotland. Stair held no military rank. Choosing to ignore him Richard rose and set down his glass. 'If you will pardon me, Colonel Hill, I'll seek my quarters and see my men.'

'Of course,' Hill said at once. He had been considerably perturbed by this exchange between his Lieutenant-Governor and the new arrival. He called for an orderly and as Richard went out he heard Hamilton say, 'We could have done without – ' and then the door closed.

The Fort was a cheerless place. Set like a five-pointed star on the ground near the inlet called Nevis water stemming from Loch Linnhe and beneath the dominating presence of Ben Nevis, it was nevertheless from a military point of view set in a commanding position, well placed for men to patrol Lochaber and the glens west towards the Isles, with access by water along the loch to the sea and thence to the Firth of Clyde and Glasgow. It should have been well supplied but a niggardly government filed the Governor's letters of request and little was done.

Richard spent the next few hours familiarizing himself with the place. There was a chapel and a smithy, barracks and stables and weapon stores, but the lack of money showed everywhere. He had been given lodgings near the Governor's and he thought the whole place cold and damp, the peat fires giving only a sluggish warmth. The men sat about trying to keep warm, smoking their clay pipes and getting drunk when there was sufficient ale. Now and then apparently there were desertions. Despite Hill's efforts his regiment was still badly clad, some of the men in little better than rags. The new uniforms he had chosen had been too few in the last assignment from Glasgow and it seemed to Richard the mood of the men was sullen and slow. He was experienced enough to be a fair judge at assessing morale. He was in truth appalled at the conditions in which they were expected to live. The ration of meal was insufficient, there was little meat and only an occasional issue of eau-de-vie, and the rebellious spirit in them was understandable. In contrast the newly arrived men of Argyll's regiment were in far better case with good scarlet coats, breeks, white stockings and strong shoes, green plaids over their shoulders and the boar's head badge in their bonnets.

He said as much to Ensign Fuller and Sergeant Morrison when they appeared in his room in response to his summons. Fuller had kept a careful list of their activities and this he presented to his commanding officer.

'We've done the best we could,' Morrison agreed, 'but the men here are a poor lot, sir. I'd like to have them three months under your command, though I must say fair words of the Governor here who works as hard as any officer. Lieutenant-Colonel Hamilton is freer with the lash than Governor Hill, and the Argylls don't help matters for they think they're better men than the fellows here.' He spoke with the freedom of years in the same service as his commander.

'And our men?' Richard asked. 'How have they fitted in?'

'Well enough, sir, but the vitals is poor, and not enough for men to work on in the winter. Still and all they're in good heart and better since they heard you was come.'

There had been some slight trouble between them and

the Argylls over quarters and the Argyll sergeant, a man named Barber, had, so Morrison said, presumed to tell him what to do with the little company of Lincourt's. He was a rough hard man, Morrison added, who said openly in the sergeant's quarters that there'd not been enough killing for men under arms since Cromdale and that it would do the new men good to have their swords bloodied. 'Are we to move on, sir?' he asked hopefully. 'That is, if your leg is healed?'

'Well enough,' Richard said. 'I'll come down now and see our men.'

He talked to them, encouraging them with a promise of more activity than they'd had while he was laid up.

'We'll be out of here in a day or two,' he assured the little group and saw the immediate response in their fresh alertness. It seemed to him however that Fuller and Morrison had done a good job in keeping up their spirits.

He found a letter waiting for him from Sir Thomas, regretting the wasted time due to his accident but suggesting that when the weather permitted he might return to Edinburgh as his regiment would be the better for his presence, which cryptic remark filled Richard with unease. He must get the work done here as soon as possible but – he pulled himself up short – he wanted to stay until his marriage could be arranged and he could take Marged back as his wife. Also his orders included seeing as many of the important men up here as he could and that would take time. He sat down to write to Mynheer Huygens his first impression of the Fort.

From the first it was plain Hamilton resented his presence. At supper that night he said in what could only be described as a provocative manner, 'I imagine it is agreeable for you to be taking supper with gentlemen again.'

Richard gave him a wintry look. 'Colonel Hamilton, I owe the MacDonalds a great deal for their care of me, and if one may judge a gentleman by his manners then there are as many in Glencoe as seated round this table.'

Hamilton's colour rose. 'Among that tribe of thieving tinkers? Your judgement seems warped, sir. But perhaps you were out of your head some of the time?'

Hill stirred in his chair at this piece of rudery and it roused Richard's anger. 'Your remark is in very bad tone,' he said, 'seeing you can know nothing of the Chief or his sons but what you have assumed.'

'Well,' Hamilton retorted, 'one can only say that your experience is based upon a short spell in bed by which to judge them. You did not, I imagine, see them coming back from a lawless raid with stolen cattle and God knows what else filched from a neighbour?'

'I did not, and I believe their intention is to live peacably from now on.' Richard turned to the Colonel at the head of the table. 'Don't you agree, sir?'

'I do,' the Governor nodded. 'I have MacIain's word.'

'The word of a thief and a murderer?' Hamilton queried cynically. 'He may have been frightened into wanting peace now but he's a blackguard at heart and no doubt his sons are as evil as he is.'

Richard was really angry now. 'You talk of my inexperience,' he said, 'but tell me, do you know them? Have you spoken to MacIain or to John MacDonald or his brother?' And when Hamilton merely shrugged the question off he went on, 'Well, I have lived two months under John MacDonald's roof and I know him. I'm not so simple as to deny their past but believe they mean it to be the past.'

The younger officers at the table were listening fascinated to this exchange and they turned to see what Hamilton would say to this, while the Governor sat frowning and staring down at his empty plate.

'I may not know them personally,' Hamilton retorted, 'but ask Captain Campbell here what he thinks of them and what they did to his home in Glen Lyon.'

Robert Campbell of Glenlyon was a tall man who had once been good-looking, but at sixty his face had the little red veins, the puffiness, the slighty bleary eyes of the habitual drinker. 'Oh aye,' he agreed in a slurred voice, 'I owe them much and one day please God I'll repay the devils in good measure. My best stallion is in MacIain's stables and my house was near stripped of goods, my glen of cattle and sheep. Aye, despite my niece being wed to Sandy MacDonald, I've scores to settle in plenty.'

Hill said sharply, 'Glenlyon, we'll forget such talk of revenge, if you please. The army is no place to indulge it. I've worked hard for this peace and I'll not have it broken by the settling of old quarrels.'

Robert Campbell as always took refuge in his glass, only muttering something about the Highland way of doings things, and Richard dismissed him as an officer not to be depended upon. Two young officers, Captain Farquhar and Lieutenant Kennedy, had exchanged glances and in the silence that followed Farquhar eventually said tenatively that he was glad there was no further need of punitive expeditions into Appin or Glencoe.

'You know nothing about it,' Hamilton said in a crushing tone. 'I doubt if the Government will be satisfied with things as they are. The Highlander's second nature seems to be to rob and kill and to my mind we need more forts and more men to put them down once and for all.'

'That is not my way,' the Governor said quietly, 'and certainly not General Monck's and he reduced the Highlands to quiet in a moderate and fair manner, leaving them their pride which is all important to them.'

'Aye, forty years and more ago,' Hamilton said with the contempt of one who was not even alive at the time.

'I think you forget,' Hill sat upright, 'that there are Highland officers at this table.'

Hamilton shrugged and inclined his head in a manner that was hardly propitiatory towards Glenlyon and Lieutenant Lindsay of the Argylls. None of the officers said anything but busied themselves passing round the claret which had arrived that day on one of Hill's frigates from Glasgow. Richard's anger simmered and when the uncomfortable meal ended went away to his room, wishing Hamilton anywhere but here. He liked Colonel Hill and Hamilton had set out to belittle the man and his command.

The next morning he had an interview alone with the Governor, ostensibly to enquire for courtesy's sake if Hill had any further advice or instructions for him before he set out for Loch Arkaig and Locheil's house of Achnacarry.

'None,' Hill said, 'but to beg you to give my kind wishes to Locheil. When do you propose to set off?'

'Tomorrow morning,' Richard said. 'I have a call to make in Maryburgh before I go.' The Governor looked surprised that he should know anyone in the little town and Richard felt obliged to explain, asking if the Governor knew Dr Beaton.

'Very well,' Hill told him. 'He assists my regimental surgeon from time to time.'

'Then I should tell you, sir, I am betrothed to his daughter and we propose to wed here when I come back from my journey.'

'Oh?' Hill bent a stare on him. 'Then you are fortunate. I dined with the Beatons when I first came here and met Mistress Stewart then.'

'I think myself so,' Richard agreed. 'You'll understand, sir, that I wish to see her before I leave.'

'Of course.' The Governor reached out an arm towards several papers set out on the table. 'By the way, two letters came for you by the last packet which reached us yesterday.' His large cuff caught on a pile and spread them out, one falling to the ground.

Richard picked it up and saw that it was addressed to Lieutenant-Colonel Hamilton and was in handwriting he recognized, having had letters of introduction himself from the same hand. It was that of the Master of Stair and for the second time Richard wondered at the connection between Stair and Hamilton. And why should the Master be writing to the Deputy-Governor instead of the Governor? But the affairs of the Fort were none of his, thank God, and he merely put the letter back on the table.

He spent the rest of the day with Fuller, planning their march, and with Morrison and his men, watching drill, commending the young recruits he had brought with him on their progress. Then in the late afternoon, to the beat of Tap-to in the Fort he set off into Maryburgh. He had left Marged at her door last night so he knew where the house was, but passing the Mercat Cross in daylight it seemed to him a town of squalid little houses. There were a few shops, a smithy and an inn, and a kirk that he looked at with a sudden alertness, but as he left these behind there were one or two better houses with small gardens.

At the entrance to one of these he dismounted, tied his horse to a post and knocked on the door. It was opened by a maidservant and as he entered he saw Iain Dubh observe who the caller was, then deliberately turn his back and disappear towards the rear of the house. Really, the man was insufferable!

But Iain Dubh was thrust from his mind by Marged's entrance into the well furnished room. However as he took a stride towards her he saw that she had another lady with her and assumed it was her mother, but Marged immediately presented him to Mistress Marsali Beaton, her father's cousin. Richard kissed her hand and announced himself happy to make her acquaintance but he wished she would go away.

Eventually, after some general talk, she did go and as soon as the door was shut, Marged said, 'She is such a good soul, she cares for my mother and looks after the house now that mother is not able. She is too ill to leave her bed just now.'

'I am sorry,' he said. 'Am I not then to have the pleasure of meeting her?'

'Not yet,' Marged said and looked so troubled that regardless of who might enter he came to her and took her into his arms. 'My darling, I can see how anxious you are. Is she very bad?'

'I'm afraid so.' Marged leaned her head against his chest. 'She was ill when I came home with my father after you'd broken your leg and perhaps I should have stayed then, but I was – upset, and the wish was on me to be with you, especially after I met Father MacHale.'

'I understand that, but why were you upset?'

'My mother was after taking the news of our marriage so badly. I didn't want to worry you with it then and I thought she'd grow accustomed to the idea. But it seems she can't support the idea of my marrying a Protestant, let alone one in that uniform.'

He stood very still. 'And? What of our plans?'

'They're not changed, my dear one. I'm not wanting to

lose the chance of Father MacHale being here. I told my mother that she and my father arranged my first marriage and that I was about to have the ordering of my second, but she is very weak from her illness and she can't be thinking as she might. She weeps and is so unwell that my father who, God bless him, is very understanding, thinks it better that you should not be meeting her yet.'

'I'm sorry,' he said again. 'I wanted all to be well with your family. I can see how she might feel about me but I thought that if we met I might persuade her I am not such a bad fellow to be marrying her daughter.'

Marged raised her face and reached up to kiss him. 'You would, I know you would. Perhaps when you get back from seeing Lochiel and the others she will be better. And my father will talk to her. He likes you, Richard.'

'And I like him very well,' he said, 'apart from owing him and Ailein Mor two good legs to stand on when I thought I might only have one sound one. Where is he? I should like to talk this over with him before I go.'

'He's away over into Keppoch's country to see a man who fell off his roof-tree when he was repairing it,' she told him and taking his hand led him to the settle by the fire. 'Supper will be served soon and Marsali comes down for that. You'll stay?'

'Thank you, yes.' He sat down beside her. 'I'm sorry not to be seeing your father. What does he think about our marrying under the present circumstances?'

'He thinks there is no objection,' she said. 'Being a doctor he understands my mother's condition and he feels that if he brings Father MacHale here to see her she will be at least partly reconciled.'

'I respect his decision,' Richard said 'and I'm thankful for it.'

'He'll arrange the ceremony at the kirk and have our banns called while you are gone and then – Richard, Marsali has a little house near here which she is not living in at the moment because of caring for my mother and she has offered it to us for the short while before we leave for Edinburgh.' She paused, her eyes alight, and added, 'It will be our first house, Richard even if it's only for a few days.'

He bent and kissed her, gazing down almost in awe at the light in her face. 'I can't believe it, that you'll be mine so soon. The mere thought of it turns my head.'

'And mine too. A little house to ourselves! It will be like it was at Craigieduir, only better.'

For a while they were silent, close in each other's arms. Then at last he said, 'But you understand I do have to go back to Edinburgh almost immediately? As soon as possible after we're wed?'

'I know,' she answered and gazed away from him into the fire. 'Only I may not be able to come. While my mother is so ill – '

'Marged! I can't leave you behind. You will be my wife.'

'But I feel I have neglected her, distressed her by what I am going to do. My marriage to you is giving her so much sorrow. I am praying Father MacHale may help her, but I must see her better in every way before I can leave her.'

Such a possibility had not entered his head and the thought of the journey back to Edinburgh without her so soon after making her his wife was intolerable. But he could not stay. It was obvious from Sir Thomas's letter he was urgently needed in Leith. 'I'm sorry about your mother,' he said in a low voice. 'Perhaps when I come back I can see her, persuade her that I will make you happy, but after all she is used to you being absent. I won't leave you behind, Marged. God knows for how long it might be and I've waited long enough to find my wife whom I love.' He raised her face to his. 'I shall be your husband, I *am* your husband in all but words in a church.'

She gazed up at him, tears in her eyes. 'I know, oh I know. Do you think I am not wanting to be with you more than anything.'

'Then that is settled,' he said firmly. 'If your father will arrange matters for us while I'm gone there need be no delays.'

'But my mother – she is so weak – '

'You think I'm being brutal?' he asked. 'Try to see it plainly. She may be ill for a long time, months even. Would you stay here and away from me for so long? I know I sound selfish but I think your father would understand what I am saying. He will be her best care. Would you have me journey to Flanders without you?'

Two tears rolled down her face and mutely she shook her head. Then suddenly she put both arms about his neck. 'Ah, don't be misjudging me, my heart. Don't think I'm not loving you more than all the world. I would go anywhere with you. It's just that my poor mother is looking so ill and unhappy. But we'll talk to her while you're away, prepare her, and then when you come back – whatever the situation I'll go with you.'

'I wish I'd not to go off on what everyone at the Fort tells me is a fool's errand, but I must get the business done and then – Marged, my love, my darling!' He sanks his mouth on hers and kissed her with a hunger that grew every moment as she responded, and only the sound of a bell and a step outside parted them.

When he left she came to the door, resolute now, 'You lie first on my heart,' she said, 'never doubt that, my Richard.'

He caught at the reins and then on a sudden impulse came back to her. 'I never in my life found it so hard to be about my duty,' he said and held both her hands in his. 'I'll get the business done as soon as I may, two weeks at the most, ten days perhaps.'

'And then!' she said and as he mounted up he thought he would remember the look on her face as long as he could remember anything.

Chapter 14

In the early days of February when a mild spell had settled on the land Mistress Beaton died and both Dr Beaton and his daughter, grieve as they did, were glad her suffering was over.

Wiping away a few tears the next morning Marged said, 'Sorrow is on me that she never met Richard. If she had but seen him – '

'I know,' her father said. 'It is very hard for you, my lass. But I think she would have accepted him in the end, I talked to her of it only yesterday and I told her that from what I knew of Colonel Lincourt he was a man to whom I could willingly entrust you.'

'Dear father, you liked him from the start, didn't you?'

'I did,' he agreed, 'and I believe I had half persuaded your mother that he was very well for a Protestant, but you have to remember she had never left the Highlands and knew nothing of the world outside.'

Marged was silent, pondering over the last weeks when her mother had begun to sink. There had been long days and nights of watching, shared by herself, her father and cousin Marsali and yesterday, when it was plain the end was coming her mother could no longer speak and could manage only a slight pressure of the hand Marged held. She had been a gentle person, inclined to be afraid of what she didn't understand and Marged wondered if her planned marriage had been too great a blow to the sick woman. She said as much to her father and he gave a deep sigh.

'I wish I could say it was otherwise, but she did seem yesterday to have become at least a little reconciled.'

'Or perhaps too weary to care,' Marged said sadly. 'I wish, oh how I am wishing she had been after seeing Richard even once.'

'I wish it too but it is of no use to blame yourself for what has happened.' Her father took her hand in his. 'My dear child, I have known for months how ill she was, she would not have recovered. And you are young and have to make your own decisions. If you are to live your life with an English soldier you must not feel any recriminations on that score.'

'I love him so much,' she said and wiped away her tears with the other hand.

Her father kissed her forehead. 'Then you are very blessed.'

'I feel sad to be leaving you and going so far away.'

'My child, you have to go where your husband goes, and I shall do very well with Marsali to look after my needs and my patients to care for. We shall be looking forward to your letters.' Never a man to indulge too long in emotion he got up and stood with his back to the fire. 'Now we must be practical. Your mother wished to be buried on St Munda's Isle with the dead of her own people and I must accede to that wish. I'll ride down tomorrow and arrange it with MacIain. At least when Father MacHale comes we can have the benefit of a Catholic priest to say the words over her according to our faith.'

She stirred and said, 'It can't be right for Richard and I to be getting wed so soon afterwards, but we may not see another priest for a long time.'

'I think you can't miss the chance,' her father reassured her. 'It can be done very quietly.'

On the following evening, after dark, there was a knock on the door and the maidservant admitted a small tired-looking man in an ordinary brown coat, a black hat on his head and a black cloak over his arm. He was Father MacHale, used to riding about the country in disguise, ministering to his people where he could, one of only four priests in the whole of the north-west. When he was told there was both a funeral and a wedding for him to conduct he said in his gentle voice, 'That is what I am about.'

He talked with Marged, learned the circumstances, and told her she need have no compunction about accepting the offices of a priest when one was to hand. Word passed quietly around the Catholics in Maryburgh and the surrounding crofts and the next morning, while it was still dark, he celebrated Mass in Dr Beaton's parlour. People slipped in unobtrusively, under the very eye of the Fort, the darkness hiding them. Every one was aware that they were breaking the penal law against them but matching their courage with that of the itinerant priest. For Marged it was the first Mass she had been able to attend for more than two years. Prayers were said for the soul of her mother and she wondered how long it would be before these faithful people receiving the Host would taste that Bread again. It was of immense comfort to her.

Three days later a little funeral procession left Maryburgh and wound its way along the shore of Loch Linnhe, the coffin drawn in a cart by a black working horse. Marged rode beside her father and thought of her childhood when her mother was well and happy.

MacIain greeted them at the landing stage at Ballachulish with his 'tail' and his sons and their families. 'Sad we are at this passing of my cousin,' he said to Dr Beaton, 'but she's away to *Tir Nan Og*, the Island of the Blessed Ones. Come you down to our shore and the boats.'

The little island was a place of graves, a few fir trees and a little stone chapel, and there Marged saw her mother laid to rest in the grave prepared for her. A sad depression hung over Marged on this quiet day, the air still, a wreath of mist over the Pap of Glencoe, the water scarcely moving. She wanted Richard, his strength and his love that could, she thought, bear her through anything.

When it was over Father MacHale expressed his wish to accompany the Chief back to the glen and minister to the people there, but MacIain said, 'Grieved as I am to be saying so but it would not be safe for you. We have soldiers in the Valley of the Dogs.'

'Soldiers?' Dr Beaton queried. 'How does that come about, MacIain?'

'They rode in some days ago,' the Chief told him.

'Campbell of Glenlyon and a hundred and twenty of them asking for billets. He said the Fort was full and they need quarters until some of the troops had been moved on. We are not liking it at all, but what can we do? Glenlyon himself is quartered on Inverrigan where he can keep an eye to his men, but he dines with me sometimes and we take a hand at the cards together.'

'And I was going to ask you to keep my girl here for a while,' the doctor said. 'It would do her good after the anxious weeks we've had, but I see you'll not be having room.'

'That I will,' MacIain set his great arm about Marged, 'if she'll not be minding a mattress in my business room among the account books and tally sticks.'

'But I can't be leaving you just now, father,' Marged was beginning when he interrupted. 'My dearest, I insist. I have a great deal to do and many patients I've neglected while we've been nursing your mother, and you are needing a change.'

'Aye,' MacIain said and smiled down at her. 'Come you home with me, child, and the air of the glen will be putting warmth into your cheeks that are the colour of a gull's wing.'

'I'll send Jeanie and Iain Dubh and your baggage over to you,' her father assured her. 'Bide you here, my dear.'

Marged accepted thankfully. The thought of a few days in the glen was like balm after the days and nights of watching a dying woman. She said goodbye to her father as he turned for the ferry, only begging him to send for her if Richard came back before she did.

He smiled. 'And do you think I'd not be doing that? Forbye I don't doubt he'd come for you himself. Now that Mr Ramsay has called your banns there's naught to prevent you being wed.' He saw a moment's struggle on her face and added, 'Oh, I know we are in a time of mourning, but you must be journeying back to Edinburgh with him and 'tis best for you to go as his wife.'

'If you are not thinking it wrong,' she murmured.

'I am not,' he answered firmly. 'If you were seventeen and this your first wedding it would be a very different matter, but not as things are. Am I not in the right of it, MacIain?'

Aye,' the old Chief agreed. 'And if your husband will be after spending a night here as you set off no one could be more welcome under our roof.'

Marged reached up to kiss his leathery cheek. If the two men she most deferred to were in agreement, then she could argue no more against what, in truth, she wanted more than anything.

She settled into the Chief's house, having to tolerate as they all did, the Lowlanders who were billeted there. Wanting solitude to mourn a little she went out one morning a few days later to have a shelty made ready for her. Some soldiers were hanging about the stables and one of them with more about him than the others came forward and asked if he might not do it for her, MacIain's groom being elsewhere. She accepted, Iain Dubh not yet out of the house and in a few moments took the soldier's hand to mount. Iain Dubh came hurrying out and almost snatched the bridle from him, and there was a ripple of laughter from the other soldiers that put a black frown on his face.

Marged rode up the glen with him loping behind her, which was as good as being alone for he seldom spoke unless she addressed him first. In the townships some of the soldiers were playing shinty, others doing pike drill, clansmen seeing to the morning feeding of beasts, but presently these were left behind and she reached the easternmost end of the glen. There she dismounted and sat on a rock by the meeting of the Waters. An eagle soared overhead against the grey sky and she wondered if it was the same one that had caused Richard to be thrown from his frightened mare. How strange that had been! It had given Richard all those weeks when he came to know her people as he might never have done otherwise, and being intensely Highland and finding deeper meaning in the twists and turns of every day happenings she saw one in this. And she perceived what it had done for Richard. The cold and formal soldier she had first known had long gone, because of her, she knew that, but the transformation had been completed by weeks under John MacDonald's roof. She had fallen in love back in Edinburgh, she thought, with the man an instinct had seen underneath the severe outer facade and now that love had blossomed into something beyond what even she had hoped for. She remembered those two nights at the house of Donald Stewart. Soon there would be more and she had a great longing to be lying in his arms in the darkness. Would they have a lifetime of such nights? Hope said yes, but glancing back down the valley she could see the little low thatched cottage where once the old spaewife had lived. She thought of the words spoken over a fire, the shoulder-blade of a sheep twisted and turned in the old hands as the woman muttered, 'Great joy but its time will be short.'

Marged gave a little shiver and dragged her gaze from the house. Richard had laughed at the tale, thought it nonsense, and surely his robust commonsense was more to be trusted than an old woman's havering. But was it nonsense? She wished she knew. Everyone in the glen listened to those they considered prophets and seers and there were always one or two. She thought of the song she had sung to Richard on the second of those two nights at Craigieduir: 'Strong is the love death cannot stall.'

Then she braced herself. She was thinking of death only because of the recent burial on St Munda's isle and on this Friday afternoon in February, with the spring not far away she must think of life and all that lay ahead. Glancing about her at the mountains she loved, though forbidding perhaps to strangers, to her they were familiar and dear, balm for a troubled or saddened spirit: the great Bidean with its snow-covered peaks, Aonach Eagach sheltering the northern side of the glen, the Three Sisters great outthrusts of rock, and she sat there, wrapped warmly in her plaid, letting the peace of them seep into her heart.

It was then that she saw It. Looking across to the falls she saw a woman washing something in the rushing water. It seemed to be a shroud and she was washing it again and again as if trying to get rid of some stain that would never be cleansed and there was something about the woman that was not human. She knew what It was, though she had never seen It before. It was the *Bean Nighe* whose presence signified death. Marged put both hands before her face, shuddering, her whole body rigid with fear. She cried out to Iain Dubh, 'Do you see? Do you see her?'

'I see,' he said, his ruddy colour faded a little, and he came to stand between her and It. 'Mistress Marged, let's be going. It is not good for us to be here. Come – '

She rose and instinctively they both turned once more towards the falls, but there was no one there now, only the water tumbling in its eternal torrent over the polished rocks, spraying up in a white froth.

Marged whispered, 'But she was there – or were we after the "seeing"?'

'She was there,' he said and brought up the gently grazing shelty. 'Look to the west, there are storm clouds coming up.'

The wind had risen and now as they turned back down the glen it grew colder, the clouds yellowish and heavy with snow. Around the crofts people were beginning to clear up the day's tasks, the soldiers seeking their billets. Everything seemed as usual, but Iain Dubh said under his breath, 'I am wishing the cursed redcoats gone from the Valley of the Dogs. They bring unease to the spirits of our ancestors.'

'I expect they will move off soon,' Marged said in as normal a voice as she could muster and to try to take their minds off what they had seen she added, 'I am leaving you here when I wed, Iain Dubh. You and a redcoat will never live in peace in the same house and I cannot be having your black looks at my husband. Be after marrying the daughter of Achnacon's daughter. Mary Kennedy is a bright soul and will bring joy into your life.'

He was silent for a moment. 'To serve you is all the joy I was ever asking of the Good Being.'

'Your home is here,' Marged said and added with a faint smile, 'Don't be after telling me you ever liked Edinburgh, and London you would hate even more.'

He sunk his chin on his chest, his black beard dark against the tartan, his eyes black with a bitter look. 'Oh aye, 'tis mebbe so, but I'd even be bearing with the *sasunnach*, the *saighdear dearg* who's taking you from us if I might stay near you and serve you as I've always done.'

'My sorrow!' she said sharply. 'And I wonder if he'd be after bearing with you! I was never a possession of yours. I am thinking you are forgetting yourself, Iain Dubh.'

He glowered at the ground, not looking at her. Then he muttered, 'We have seen death this morning. I pray the great God it is mine not yours.'

'And I pray it will be neither of us. Marry Mary and I'll stand godmother to your first ween. Perhaps she will be the taking of that black look from your face.'

The snow had begun to fall now but nevertheless she turned the sheltie away from the path under the oak trees that led to Carnoch and went first to John MacDonald's house. She found him with Eiblin by the fire, the nurse Moir in the act of carrying Alasdair up the stairs. Marged greeted them but waited until Moir had gone before she said abruptly, 'I have seen the *Bean Nighe.*'

Eiblin cried out, 'Holy Mary, save us!' and crossed herself, but John said:

'Are you sure? The water there can spray up like a white ghost.'

'Yes. Iain Dubh saw it too.'

For a moment John said nothing. He led her to a stool and made her sit down. Then he said reluctantly, 'She was seen yesterday by Robert MacEwen who was up the glen visiting his father.'

The three of them sat silent, not wishing to believe, yet sure enough for three sightings could hardly be contradicted. At last John said, 'Sandy was here a while ago. He came with an odd tale. One of his servants said a bairn was watching the shinty with a soldier and the redcoat spoke to a rock and told it it would be better out in the heather.' He paused and said, 'I am not at ease in my mind.'

Eiblin came to him and he put his arm about her as she asked, 'Is there danger from these Argyll men? Is Alasdair – '

John said, 'Trust me to care for my own. But there's nothing here to cause us to be more than a little watchful. I talked to Glenlyon an hour since and asked him plainly if any harm was intended to us and he laughed very heartily and was asking me in turn if I thought he would harm his own niece and her kin by the marriage tie.' He paused, a frown drawing his brows together. He had not liked Glenlyon's over-effusive manner. There had been a letter stuck in the Campbell's cuff and John had seen it delivered by Captain Drummond, the man who had locked up and delayed MacIain on that desperate journey to Inverary and the swearing. He summed Drummond up as a petty and vindictive tyrant and he liked him not at all. The letter was probably no more than orders to move on, though Glenlyon had not said so, and John thought it wiser not to mention it to the women. He merely said Glenlyon had invited himself and Sandy to a game of cards that evening at Inverrigan's farmhouse.

Marged rose. 'Since I have been betrothed to Richard I have been trying to think differently of English soldiers. But the redcoats here are Campbells and our enemies, guests though they are at the moment. Indeed,' she forced a smile, 'when we were at dinner the other night I wondered if Glenlyon noticed a pair of silver candlesticks that were from his own house.'

John laughed. 'Aye, when we raided his glen on our way home two years ago. The man's an improvident drunken fool. If we had not been taking some of his goods he'd have lost them at the card table. What a *gòrach* he is! The sooner we're rid of him the better. I must admit to being weary of the Lowlanders who are living here. Their manners are such as I would not tolerate among any of my people.'

'They are foreign to us,' Eiblin said, 'and though I would share my bread with any guest I am wondering if gall is not mixed in with the dough I baked this morning.'

Marged said, 'I must go back to Carnoch. Lady Glencoe will be expecting me. John, are you truly thinking something is amiss?'

'I don't know,' he said. 'I will be keeping my eyes open, but you know our people, always full of tales. They hate having the redcoats and are imagining all sorts of evil, but I have Glenlyon's word.'

On that note of confidence she left. As she entered the

avenue that led to the Chief's house the snow was falling heavily, blown almost horizontal in gusts and she drew her plaid closer about her head and shoulders. When she reached the stables a soldier dodged out as if he had been watching for her and fondling the shelty's nose he said in a low voice so that Marged could barely hear the words, 'You are in need of a good ride, little beast. If I were you I would trot on until you are away to the ferry and back to Maryburgh.' He gave the animal a pat and then, red in the face, hurried away. It was the soldier who had helped her saddle up this morning, and she gazed after him. Surely it was a warning, the same warning another had given the child by the rock?'

At the house she dismounted and gave her reins to Iain Dubh. Inside she looked for MacIain and found him in the little room that served her and Jeanie for a bedroom, a pile of papers in front of him, the top one covered with figures.

He looked up and smiled at her, ' 'Tis always the same, more sums we have to pay than those that are coming in. 'Tis a pity if our raiding days are over. A few of Breadalbane's fat cattle would swell my herd.'

Marged came to lean against his shoulder. 'MacIain, I am so uneasy.'

'Why?' he asked.

'I have seen the *Bean Nighe*.'

He pondered for a moment, too much the Chief of Glencoe to ignore such a statement, yet wishing he had not heard it. 'That's strange enough, but perhaps it was just one death she was telling of, an old man perhaps, maybe myself, eh?'

He gave a laugh and she cried out, 'MacIain, don't jest!'

And she told him of what John had said, of the soldier outside this house.

The laugh died then, but after a moment he said, 'I'll not believe ill of the Campbell soldiers which is what you are all thinking. These men are our guests. What's more they are Highland men who've been eating our bread under our roof-trees for near two weeks. How can they possibly be thinking harm to us under that trust?'

Marged straightened. 'No, of course you are right. I am imagining too much. But I did see the *Bean Nighe*.'

She sat in her place at the big table, listening to the talk but saying little. MacIain was the genial host as always and he had for a guest today Murdoch Mathieson, a young poet and composer of songs employed by the Earl of Seaforth. Returning from Inverary he came by Glencoe and was welcomed at MacIain's table. His witty talk and charm of manner contrasted with the uncouth behaviour of Lieutenant Lindsay and another Lowland officer at the table. As soon as the food was done, without having the courtesy to wait for the convivial winecup to end the meal they excused themselves and left.

'Sons of dogs,' MacIain said. 'I would not be a guest in their house.'

Marged sat sewing by the fire with Lady Glencoe and they talked of the future, of her forthcoming marriage and other cheerful topics, but when they parted for the night Marged lay down on her makeshift bed too wide awake for sleep. The disturbing events of the day would not be dismissed from her mind and she went over and over them, dwelling finally on the remark of the soldier to her shelty. She longed for Richard and she tried to settle her mind for sleep by thinking of him, seeing every feature of his face, remembering his broad shoulders in which she thought lay an indication of his whole strength as a man, and she recalled too the strength of his hands that could yet be so gentle with her. She tried to hear the familiar tones of his voice as he spoke of his love, and she made up her mind to ride back to Maryburgh tomorrow, to be on hand for his return.

The wind was howling outside now, shaking the wooden shutters for there was no glass in this little window, and the noise of it kept her wakeful, the blizzard sweeping round the house. But at last she fell asleep and seemed to have barely closed her eyes when about five o'clock in the morning there was a fierce banging on the outer door. She heard a servant hurry to open it. There was the tramp of feet on the stairs and overhead in MacIain's bedroom and she wondered what could be amiss at this hour.

Suddenly, exploding into the night were two pistol shots, one after the other, a wild screaming from the Chief's wife and another shot, this time downstairs as Duncan Rankin who had opened the door ran out in terror.

Marged leapt up. There was no mistaking the evil content of those sounds that wrecked the night's sleep and one movement had her shaking Jeanie by the shoulder though the girl was already awake and terrified.

Instinct drove Marged to the window. 'Quick!' she whispered, 'Help me – the shutter –'

Jeanie to her credit didn't scream but with ashen face and eyes wide with fear scrambled up to help her mistress. Somehow they got it open. Marged seized a plaid and her slippers and they climbed out, dropping silently into the snow. The blinding blizzard struck them and in the darkness they heard more shots and more screams. Terrified horses neighed and kicked their stalls and disturbed cattle lowed. Flaring torches of pine-knots broke the darkness and a nearby croft began to burn.

'Oh God, run!' Marged cried out. 'Jeanie, run!' She seized the girl's hand and together they stumbled away towards the trees. In shock and terror and fierce cold they ran and Marged's mind threw up the seeing of the *Bean Nighe* that afternoon and the memory of the kindly soldier's words to her horse – why hadn't she heeded, why hadn't they all heeded warnings that were plain enough now?

She lost one slipper and cut her foot on a stone so that her blood marked the snow as she ran from the fear that had been on her all day and was now grim truth. Somewhere along the path she realized she had lost touch with Jeanie's hand and she called her name, but there was only the wind and the blinding snow and she could see nothing. One thought was in her head now – to reach the mountain. Numbed by shock and the cold, shaking with terror, she stumbled forward, praying she was going towards Meall Mor where the wooded slopes and rocks could provide hiding places. She heard the tumbling river on her left and ran on towards Inverrigan. Once Richard's name broke from her lips on a sobbing breath.

Some soldiers were coming down from the farmhouse,

their lips blackened from biting open their cartridges, their bayonets red with blood for they had just killed Inverrigan and eight of his men. One of them, seeing a white wraith come out of the driving snow, cried out and raised his musket.

Chapter 15

Richard had come down the Great Glen as the snow clouds gathered and by the time he reached the Fort it was falling steadily, the bitter wind rising. He was tempted to see Marged before he went to the Fort but his sense of duty would not allow it, the men must be returned to barracks before he thought of his own concerns. As he turned in at the gate the snow was falling and he turned up the collar of his greatcoat.

He had not had a very productive two weeks but they had been extremely interesting. The several days he had spent with Sir Ewen Cameron of Lochiel had been pleasant for the Chief of Clan Cameron had been very hospitable. Richard had found him an educated and intelligent man who had been to the English court in his youth. After submitting to General Monck he had accompanied him to London to join in the triumphal return of King Charles II and some twenty years later Charles had knighted him. He and Richard found many topics in common and went hunting together on the mild February mornings. But as far as any of his people taking service in King William's army was concerned Lochiel was both distant and doubtful; however he took Richard riding round the clachans and the son of one tacksman with tolerable English and a desire to see the world had volunteered, seeing that his chief approved. Richard had already learned that a chief's word was all that counted to a Highlander and that he would do nothing without it, but it seemed to him that Lochiel ruled his considerable domain like a small king.

After a few days the Chief said reluctantly he must be on

his way. 'I'm going to London to make my peace with the King in person,' he said in a manner of one conferring a favour, and Richard wondered how easily Lochiel wore that loyalty. Lochaber was remote enough from England, let alone London, yet this man was not the isolationist that Glengarry was.

They parted at the eastern end of Loch Arkaig and Richard pursued his way north. He spent several days in Inverness but all Sergeant Morrison's blandishments produced no more than three recruits, two of them idlers with no apparent means of supprt and Richard thought they had ridden a long way for men the Sergeant would have difficulty in turning into soldiers. The third man was of a better cut, the younger son of a lawyer whom Richard immediately destined for the rank of ensign.

On the way back he turned into Keppoch country and visited the Chief, Coll of the Cows, who apparently boasted that he never robbed a poor man, the inference being obvious. He was young, handsome, arrogant, but amiable enough playing host in his own country, deeming the position of chief of such a large branch of Clan Donald one to be envied by any man. He said he had already applied through Colonel Hill for a commission for his young brother and would be very happy if it should be in Lincourt's regiment. Richard accepted the fresh-faced youth, promising to speak to Colonel Hill about the matter, and thinking himself lucky to have recruited any, returned to the Fort with his new men.

As soon as he entered the gates he knew with a soldier's instinct that something was afoot, some action in the planning. The men were alert, weapons being polished, their 'twelve apostles' that carried powder being prepared, the doors of the armoury open, pikes in neat stacks. He wondered if Hill had changed his mind about tackling Glengarry in his fastness, but it seemed unlikely in this driving snow.

He went up the stone stair to his quarters and changed his muddied and wet clothes before going to Colonel Hill's room where he must report before seeing Marged. He went in to find a number of officers there. Hill sat at his table in the act of signing an order, and as Richard entered he set his scrawling hand to it. It seemed as if Lieutenant-Colonel Hamilton, standing by the table, almost snatched it up. Major Forbes, recently returned from Edinburgh was looking distinctly uneasy and several young officers were waiting to be given their orders, among them Captain Farquhar and Lieutenant Kennedy.

And odd hush greeted his entrance. 'Good evening, Colonel Hill,' he said, 'we are glad to be back in shelter on so wretched a night.'

Hill muttered a greeting and Richard thought he looked very grey in the face, his eyes sunken and deeply troubled. He glanced from him to Hamilton, and then to Forbes. 'Well, gentlemen, it's obvious you are about some action. May I know of it.'

'Certainly,' James Hamilton answered before his senior officer could speak. 'I have my orders and you and your men may accompany me if you wish.' A flicker of a mirthless smile was on his lips as he passed Richard the order in his hand and stood with folded arms while Richard read.

You are with four hundred of my regiment and four hundred of my lord of Argyll's under the command of Major Duncanson of Ballachulish, to march straight to Glencoe and there put into execution the order you have received from the Commander-in-Chief.

Given under my hand this 12th day of February. John Hill, Governor of Fort William.

Richard read it in some bewilderment. 'I don't understand. What is this order that Sir Thomas has sent? And how does it concern Glencoe?'

'No, of course you don't understand, or don't wish to,' Hamilton retorted. 'You've made friends of the thieving tribe that live there. But there's to be an end of them, thank God.'

Richard stood still. There was no mistaking Hamilton's tone. He turned to the Governor. 'Sir, what's to be done?'

Hill sat huddled in his greatcoat, his hands twisted

together. 'I have my orders,' he said, 'whether I like them or not, and now Colonel Hamilton has his.'

'But what – '

Hamilton interrupted sharply. 'Surely you are not so simple as not to realize what must be done? Glencoe himself has brought this trouble on his clan. He was too late when he chose to submit, having had four months to come in, and then he was six days late. It was right that his name should be struck off the list.'

'Who struck it off?' Richard demanded. 'And on whose authority?' He had a sense of something fearful building up and had been a soldier long enough to get the whiff of a punitive expedition.

'It was done in Edinburgh,' Major Forbes said with evident regret. 'By whom I'm not sure, but it was done before ever the matter reached the Privy Council.'

'And was His Majesty informed of this?'

'I don't know,' Forbes said honestly. 'Certainly the amended list went to London and orders came from the Master of Stair, both superscribed and subscribed by the King. I saw the paper myself in Sir Thomas Livingstone's hand and he's acted upon it in writing to the Governor.'

A deep fear was growing in Richard's mind. He looked straight at Hamilton for it seemed obvious that he was in command, not the diminished man at the desk. 'I want to know,' he reiterated. 'You offered me a part in it so tell me if you please what you purpose in Glencoe.'

'An example must be made,' Hamilton answered. He seemed to be relishing the explanation. 'Once and for all the people up here must learn a lesson. One clan must be made to pay for the rest and they've not all submitted yet. A swift, secret and sudden stroke will do, and the Glencoe tribe is perfect for the business.'

'What business?' Richard repeated, though the answer was growing plain enough. 'What do you purpose for this clan that is too small to threaten you?'

'They're not too small to have been threatening and robbing and killing for a good many years,' Hamilton said shortly. 'Now is the time to put an end to it, and the plan is simple. Major Duncanson is to march from Ballachulish where he is at the moment with four hundred men while I myself will go over the military road and down by the Devil's Staircase to block the eastern end of the glen, the Laird of Weem is to cut off the Perthshire road and my lord of Breadalbane the Glenorchy passes. Neat, isn't it? The place is perfect for it. And of course you won't know that Captain Campbell of Glenlyon with one hundred and twenty men has been quartered there these two weeks ready to play his part. He has been informed of the details this afternoon by Captain Drummond.'

'Good God!' Richard drew in his breath sharply. 'You mean he is to turn on a people who've sheltered him and his men for two weeks. Are they to be taken prisoner or driven out?'

'Oh no.' Hamilton shook his head. 'The Government does not wish to be troubled with prisoners. Glenlyon has his orders – to put all to the sword under seventy and to have especial care that the old fox and his cubs don't escape.' He was watching Richard through half-closed eyes. 'It's to be done early tomorrow morning when all are in their beds and unsuspecting. That way none will escape the retribution they've been earning for years. They'll be cut off root and branch. And it's no more than a public service to be ridding the country of them.'

It was clear that none of the younger officers had yet been told what they were to do, for several now bore looks of consternation and Captain Farquhar let out a gasp, hastily suppressed. As for Richard, the room rocked beneath his feet.

'You can't – you cannot meant it. You have ordered them to be murdered as they sleep? Women? Children?'

'Oh,' Hamilton was watching the satisfying effect his words were having. 'Only the men are to be slain, their women and children may be driven into the hills, though to my mind 'twere best if the clan were cut off completely. But it will be the end of the Glencoe MacDonalds.'

Richard turned to Colonel Hill and said hoarsely, 'Sir, I thought you a fair man. You can't be about to order this?'

'I've already done so,' Hill said and added in a strained voice, 'I've had no choice, Lincourt. I am a soldier as you are and we obey orders. Here under my hand are mine from Sir Thomas Livingstone.'

Into Richard's mind came a picture of that great giant, MacIain, with his courtesy and hospitality, of John and Eiblin who had sheltered him and cared for him. He thought of John slain in his bed, of Eiblin driven out into the winter's night with little Alasdair, of Sandy and his family, of Achnacon and Achtriochtan and their wives and children, of Inverrigan and his enjoyment of their cards together; he thought of all the kindness and care he had received, of the convivial evenings, the songs and the ceilidhs. And he remembered how Marged had said when they rode up the glen that only those who came as friends into their secure home could work a mischief on them, and how he himself had answered that what seemed so secure could become a trap. And now that trap was about to be sprung, and in what a manner!

In drowning horror, he said, 'It – it's butchery, it's "murder under trust". They've sheltered and fed Glenlyon and his men; it's beyond what a soldier should be ordered to do!'

'If you are so lily-livered, pray do not trouble yourself to accompany us,' Hamilton said coolly in answer to this outburst. 'I merely thought you might relish a fight.'

Richard turned to him. 'Great God, I've been a soldier these sixteen years, a great deal longer than you, Colonel Hamilton, and I have never been asked to do such a thing. I'll fight any enemy but honourably. I've had nothing but generosity from the MacDonalds and I'll have no part in this. What you're proposing is the worst sort of treachery. Colonel,' he turned to Hill, 'can't you wait? Query Sir Thomas's meaning? Let me to go Edinburgh, talk to him, find out what the King intended.'

'It's too late,' Hill said wearily, 'and even if – '

'Of course it is,' Hamilton brushed the suggestion aside. 'The orders are gone out. I'm surprised, Lincourt, that you are so sensitive over such a pack of lawless vagabonds.'

'At least,' Richard said desperately, 'let it be done decently, make a clean fight of it, though eight or nine hundred against that little clan could hardly be that.

There's not above a hundred fighting men there, if that many. And as for the women and children – God in heaven, man, look out of the window!'

Hamilton barely glanced at the driving snow outside, nor listened to the rising wind. 'The weather is unfortunate, for our soldiers, but it will no doubt finish our work for us. Any that escape will not get far in this.'

Richard looked at him with loathing and disgust, aware of uneasiness among the other officers at this exchange, but too distraught to care. 'It's the most damnable bloody scheme I ever heard of and you, sir, are a butcher if you go upon it. There are some orders no man of honour is required to carry out if his conscience forbids it.' And at the back of his mind was the thought – Thank God, Marged is safe in Maryburgh.

There was a sudden movement and Captain Farquhar stepped forward. He was a fair young man with a naturally pale skin but now it was ashen. He drew his sword from its sheath and said, 'Colonel Lincourt is in the right of it. I'll not go to murder in their beds men who've housed and fed our own soldiers, nor will I be a party in driving out women and children to die in the snow.'

'Traitor!' Hamilton shouted. 'How dare you? You will do your duty, sir.'

But the captain, holding his sword in his right hand, took the tip in his left, lifted one knee and with a swift movement snapped it in two. 'That is my answer, sir. I'll not go, whatever the consequences.'

'Nor I.' Lieutenant Kennedy came forward to stand beside his friend. He drew his own sword and laid it on Colonel Hill's table. Hill looked unhappily at this unwanted gift, but before he could speak Hamilton swore, 'By God, you're a pair of damned insolent cubs. You're under arrest, both of you.' He strode to the door, bellowed for the guards on duty and without deferring to the Governor had them both sent away to be confined to their quarters. Both went unrepentant and Captain Farquhar glanced at Richard as he passed, clearly sorry for the predicament so senior an officer found himself facing.

'At least there's some honour left,' Richard said.

He was casting about in his mind for some way of sending a warning. If he could get Robb out with a message for John, or go himself on the pretext of visiting Marged and then ride on to the glen. But no, he couldn't do that, he couldn't explain his presence there for one thing and for another his soldier's oath forbade it. Yet there was the thought of John, his friend, of that little household and all the others, warm and snug on this bitter night, without an inkling of what was planned for them. How could he let that happen? Yet how prevent it?

Acutely, as if reading the agony of indecision on Richard's face, Hamilton said sharply, 'I see you are infected by your stay with those rebels. If you are planning to warn them – ' he turned to the Governor, 'I suggest, sir, that Colonel Lincourt is also placed under arrest until all this is done.'

'Damn you, you go too far! It's not for you to order that.' Richard turned to Hill in one last plea. 'Colonel, can't you see how this business will stink? When it is known, God knows what a stir it will make. All your names will be sullied and if, as I suspect, the orders came from the Master of Stair, his too.'

'And the King's?' Hamilton queried in a mocking voice.

Richard swung round, seeing no hope to be got from Hill whom, in truth, he pitied for the terrible position in which the Governor was placed. In an icy voice he said, 'Permit me to tell you, Hamilton, that I know the King and if he signed the original order, and I suppose I must believe that, I don't believe he knew what interpretation would be put upon it.' He remembered his meeting with Stair and the man's hatred for the 'gallows herd'. Oh yes, he could believe it of the Master of Stair, yet the actual plan must have been finalized here in this fort and he could only lay that at one door. 'The scheme is one which no officer of principle can be willing to carry out,' he added emphatically, 'and if I can do anything to prevent it – '

It was a rash thing to say and he regretted the words the moment they were out for Hamilton leapt on them.

'You see, sir?' He turned to Hill. 'This man threatens to

aid the enemy. It's no affair of his, yet he speaks of trying to foil it.' He gave a harsh laugh. 'It seems that a few weeks of eating their disgusting porridge and drinking their whisky has addled his head.'

'You impertinent dog,' Richard snapped. 'May I remind you that I am senior to you in rank.'

'But not in standing here.' Hamilton was undaunted. 'Colonel Hill, Lincourt should be placed under arrest immediately.'

The Governor seemed to rouse himself from his paralysis. He got to his feet, and said, 'You are not in command here, Hamilton. Get about your business and leave Colonel Lincourt to me.'

He sounded suddenly so determined that Hamilton, after one moment's hesitation and a quick look at his watch, had no answer but to leave the room, followed by Major Forbes who looked wretched but had not thought it became him to enter the controversy. The younger officers who had listened in silence, left after him, none of them relishing the affair but not prepared to risk their careers as Farquhar and Kennedy had done. Only one hard-faced young man hurried eagerly after Hamilton.

The room seemed silent and empty after they had gone. With a deep sigh Colonel Hill sank down in his chair again. Regretfully he said, 'I'll not have you arrested, Lincourt – Hamilton exceeded himself to suggest it – but I must confine you to your quarters until the business is done, much as I dislike it.'

Richard opened his mouth to speak and closed it again, and Hill went on, 'This is none of our choosing. In fact I will tell you that I've had the order under my hand for two weeks and not until today have I brought myself to sign it, though I knew that I must.' He sat slumped in his chair. 'I'm an old man and I want only to see peace here before I return to London, but I can't risk my half-pay on a protest, a gesture that will do nothing to alter the course of things and only bring me into trouble with my seniors. You may think that is weak, but I'm nearing seventy and I can't do it.'

Richard too had sunk into a chair and had his head in

his hands. 'But to order such treachery, such a breach of honour! To allow Glenlyon and his men to eat the MacDonalds' bread and then put them all to the sword – my God, it doesn't bear thinking of!'

'Well,' Hill said wearily, 'I had no part in planning that. It was arranged by others. You must have observed that Colonel Hamilton is in the confidence of higher powers, a confidence I apparently do not share.' He regarded Richard for a moment and then said, 'Tell me, sir, what would you have done in my place? Ignored an order from the Commander-in-Chief?'

Richard was silent, staring between his knees at the floor, engulfed in horror. What would he have done? God alone knew. He was a soldier, trained to obey orders, and if such an order were refused there would always be another, a James Hamilton perhaps, to carry it out. What good would a gesture however gallant, like that of the two young officers, do to help matters? But his rage, his loathing was directed at Breadalbane who was watching to cut off any escaping MacDonalds, at Argyll whose men were already in the glen preparing to commit the ultimate betrayal, at the Master of Stair whose hand was behind it all whether or not he had personally devised the exact scheme. The Campbells – Argyll, Breadalbane, Glenlyon – had cause to hate Clan Donald and tonight was to be the time of their vengeance, to be carried out in the most despicable manner, abhorrent to an Englishman and even worse, he knew now, to a Highlander with codes he regarded as sacred. It made him feel sick with loathing. And this old man was only a pawn, ordered by Sir Thomas, manipulated by the contemptible Hamilton. What indeed would he have done if he had been Governor of Inverlochy, sitting behind that littered table?

Slowly he got to his feet. There seemed to be nothing more to say. 'I'll go to my quarters, sir.'

Hill looked up at him. 'I'll not put you to the shame of having a guard at your door if you will give me your word that you will not leave the Fort nor contrive to send any message to Glencoe.'

'And if I refuse?'

The Governor sighed. 'Then I shall have to place you under detention, though I've no wish to do so.'

Heavily, Richard said, 'You have my word.'

Hill nodded and he turned to leave the room. As he reached the door Hill said sadly, 'I always liked MacIain, old rogue that he's been. And John was a worthy son of such a gallant old man.'

'You say "was". Has the killing already begun?'

Hill sat upright. 'No, 'twas a slip of the tongue. The hour is not yet. Seven o'clock is the time, so I require you to remain in your quarters until I give you leave to go out, should you so wish.'

Richard inclined his head and without another word left the room. His quarters faced on to the courtyard and below he saw Hamilton's men assembling in the driving snow. In a curiously detached way he thought, they will have the devil of a march in this weather in the dark, and it occurred to him to wish Hamilton might fall into a gulley and break his neck. But even that would not save the MacDonalds now.

He sent John Robb for a bottle of whisky and though normally never one to drink too much he sat by his table watching the candle burn down as the bottle emptied. He sent for another and drank until he could no longer think of John and Eiblin in their bed and red-coated Campbells bursting in to shoot or bayonet them. He thought of the boy Alasdair – would they kill him too? And he realized he had come to love the child. They were supposed to spare the women and children and maybe he and Eiblin would only be driven out on this appalling night. Could they survive on the bitter mountain? He thought of all in the glen that he now called his friends and seemed to see them lying dead, dying the snow with their blood, their houses burning. And MacIain himself? What was planned for him? What had Hamilton said? That Glenlyon was to be sure neither the old fox nor his sons escaped.

He reached for the bottle and drank again. And tomorrow when it was all over he would have to go into Maryburgh and tell Marged what had been done to her kin whom she loved in the place which she loved. How could he tell her? How could be break such ghastly news to her? Would she ever want to see him again? Would she ever want to see any man that wore the redcoat. In any case after this horror there could hardly be a wedding in a few days' time in the little kirk; nor any happy hours in Marsali Beaton's little house. He could not ask that of her, even if she didn't turn from him in loathing. The hideous deed being done this night had even if he had no part in it, wrecked his own plans and hopes.

Oh God, what a coil, what a set of unforeseen and treacherous circumstances to drive them apart! The blood of the slain MacDonalds would for ever lie between them. Perhaps there had been too much from the start. With a groan he beat his fist on the table with such ferocity that the whisky spilled from his silver cup. He was tormented, the night alive with gruesome pictures leaping in his mind. And he saw the face of Marged, his beloved, looking at him with hatred and disgust, all the love gone. If only he could have got Robb away to the glen, so that at least he could tell her he had done what he could. But his word as a soldier was given, he was impotent, helpless.

In such rage and misery as he had ever known, slowly the hours passed. As the night faded he found himself thinking about the vile plot. If the punishment of Glencoe, planned for an example and approved by the King had included the killing of the Glencoe men he still could not believe that the ultimate betrayal, the 'murder under trust' had been planned at Whitehall. From what Hamilton had said it had devolved on him to carry it out in any way he could – and all Richard's animosity extended to the man who would give the final order, Campbell of Glenlyon, in a burning hatred. It was almost a relief to have such a door at which to lay the blame, a focal point for the emotion that was devastating him.

He staggered to his bed sometime around dawn and flung himself down fully clothed, hardly aware of the devoted Robb who had heard him move and slipped into the room to pull off his boots.

'Sir,' he said in a low voice, 'sir, what's amiss?'

'Everything,' Richard answered in a slurred voice,

'everything is in ruin,' and he turned his face away.

Robb sat down on the floor, leaning against the wall, remained there until first light. Now his master, after hours of tossing, lay heavily asleep, the whisky having done its work and Robb drew a blanket over him. Then he put more peat on the fire and sat down again. At nine he fetched some hot coffee.

Richard stirred as he came in. Astonished at first that he had slept in his clothes he sat up. Then memory came back and he seized his watch. Dear God, it would all be over by now! He took the coffee mug with a shaking hand and drank.

The hours passed slowly. No word came from Hill and the Fort was quiet. The snow had ceased and a wintry sun came out on a white world. Richard paced the little room with restless jerky movements until he felt he was going out of his mind. The longing to go to Marged overwhelmed him, even if it meant facing rejection. Robb brought him his dinner but he could eat nothing. Ensign Fuller came for orders, but Robb intercepted him and told him the Colonel was unwell, and Fuller went away again.

At last in the late afternoon the gates of the Fort opened and Hamilton rode in with Major Duncanson and Major Forbes followed by Captains Campbell and Drummond. After them came the long files of men and there was not one soldier who did not have plunder hanging from his belt or his musket – cups and plates, plaids and buckles and brooches, anything that could be carried. Glenlyon was leading his own stallion that MacIain had taken from him two years ago and from his saddle bow dangled a pair of silver candlesticks. Below the Fort men were driving hundreds of Glencoe cattle and sheep to the recreation ground to be penned in.

Richard felt nauseated and turned away. He had seen men with plunder often enough but this had a different taste to it. The short winter daylight was fading now and the thing was over, his friends butchered, everything they had taken away from the Valley of the Dogs and he had done nothing, could do nothing but pray that some had escaped the carnage. And pray he did, in unhappy broken phrases for the people who had sheltered him.

After another hour there was a knock on the door and to Richard's surprise Colonel Hill himself walked in. He seemed to be in an odd state, wretched and yet half relieved. Richard dismissed Robb and offered the old man a chair.

Hill sank down. 'Well,' he said at last, 'the business is done. Glencoe is ruined, everything burned, but – ' he paused and didn't look at Richard, 'it has been bungled. Major Duncanson was late, leaving the setting on to Glenlyon who failed to arrange proper watches on the routes to the south through the mountains, thinking them impassable under the snow perhaps – which they are not to men of the mountains. Colonel Hamilton was later still, delayed by the weather. It was all done when he got there some hours later and the only satisfaction his men had was in killing one old man.'

'And MacIain?' Richard asked hoarsely.

'He is dead, his lady fled. In fact many of the clan escaped. It seemed some of them sensed something was afoot and got away before it began and I'm told the snow was driving so fast that the troopers could scarcely see an arm's length ahead at times. There's no doubt Glenlyon bungled it. His head is always full of the fumes of the drink.' Hill raised his head and added, 'There appear to be no more than about thirty-eight slaughtered and the Chief's sons were not among the bodies counted.'

Richard let out his breath. 'Thank God, thank God.' And he walked away to the window.

'I think,' Hill said slowly, 'you would be wise to keep such sentiments to yourself, though I – I share them. And so I suspect did some of our soldiers. The Argylls are Highlanders themselves and maybe some of them liked the business as little as we did and contrived now and then to look the other way.' He got up and went to the door. 'You are free to go where you will, Lincourt. By the way Doctor Beaton's wife died a few days ago.'

He went out and Richard stood where he was, shaking with the force of his relief. Thank God John and Sandy had somehow got away, the blackness was not total, they had escaped the barbarous slaughter. He had no idea where they could have gone except into the mountains and he could not imagine how Eiblin and little Alasdair would fare in the ice and snow of the high passes but at least they were away and free and he found his vision blurred with sudden tears. Hastily he brushed them away, called for Robb and some hot water and made himself respectable again.

Then he went out, taking Robb with him, and they rode out of the gate and towards Maryburgh. He saw none of the officers returned from the massacre and he was thankful for it. At Dr Beaton's house he dismounted and leaving Robb to hold the horses knocked on the door. The doctor himself opened it. He had obviously heard nothing.

'Ah, Colonel Lincourt, come in. I'm glad to see you back. Pray take a dram with me.'

'Thank you,' Richard paused in the doorway, 'but before I do I must see Marged and tell you both something that may make you wish to withdraw that invitation.'

Dr Beaton was still holding the door wide. 'I can't imagine what that could be but come in out of the cold. You'll not have heard that my wife went to her rest a week ago.'

'Colonel Hill told me. I'm very sorry, believe me, but what I have to say can't wait, despite your mourning, nor –' He did not finish the sentence. 'Would you be kind enough to fetch Marged, sir?'

'But she isn't here,' her father said. 'No doubt she'll come back though, the moment she knows you're returned.'

'Come back?' Richard echoed in a stupefied voice, 'Where – where is she?'

'Why, she's in Glencoe, staying with MacIain. I thought after all the care of her mother – Colonel Lincourt!'

He broke off for Richard, with one anguished gasp, had flung himself back into the saddle and was gone, riding headlong down the road towards the ferry to Ballachulish. John Robb, without a word to the startled doctor, mounted up and rode after him.

*

It was quite dark when they reached Ballachulish. The sky had clouded up again, the wind rising. It was bitterly cold and a sharp frost set the snow glistening on the trees as they rode into Carnoch. No word had been spoken on the ferry except by the ferryman who grumbled at being dragged out again, claiming he had done naught for hours but ferry redcoats across the water. He looked warily at Richard and made no comment on the thing that had happened.

Richard stood on the boat, hardly able to bear the slowness of its progress across the black water, the cold night wind in his face. His head was throbbing. He could neither think clearly nor accept the horrifying fact that she had been there this morning while the inhuman business was being done. Had she fled into the hills? Was she hiding somewhere, driven out of her warm bed and into the bitter cold of a February night? Would she, would any of the women and children survive it? And how could he look for her, where could he look for her?

He drove one fist into the other in an agony of not knowing. What ill-fate had left her in Glencoe when he thought her safe in her father's house? If he had known last night, he thought he would have broken his word, got out of the Fort somehow, reached her in time to bring her out. Neither Glenlyon nor any of his Argyll men could have stopped him.

But he had not known, had never guessed she had gone back, and all the miserable night while she was in such terrible danger he had paced his room and drunk himself into a stupor. He didn't know how to contain this knowledge and waited in an agony of impatience for the ferry to come into the landing stage. Finding a coin he paid the man and Robb led their horses off. Then he was away down the road at a furious gallop. He had no idea if sentries had been left in the glen but they were not going to prevent his search.

When he reached Carnoch, however, it was plain there was no need of sentries. The Chief's house was still burning and as they arrived the last part of the roof crashed in, sending a shower of sparks upwards. Apart from that there was no sound, the glen black and still, only the little stream running unconcernedly over its stones. A body lay half in the water, and everywhere the snow was trampled by the feet of many soldiers.

Richard dismounted and went round to the front of the house. There he saw MacIain. The old man lay where the soldiers had left him when they dragged his dead body out to lie ignominiously in the snow. His great limbs were sprawled, his only clothing a night shirt. He had been shot in the back and in the back of the head, his face bloodied and wrecked where the ball had come out. Richard stood looking down at him in pity and in rage. He had fought many battles, killed men, but no corpse had ever given him fury against man's bestiality in killing that this one did.

He turned away. If Marged had heard the soldiers coming, if she'd escaped, or even if she'd been driven out perhaps with Lady Glencoe which way would she have gone? To the river, to the loch? But there was nothing there but the long track round by Kinlochleven or the road back to the ferry and both would be guarded by soldiers. Down the glen to the east, perhaps, to one of the long corries that led into the mountains, but the slaughter would have been going on all along past Achnacon and Achtriochtan and Hamilton himself was at the eastern end. God, what had happened there to those men who had come to cheer his evenings when he lay helpless in John MacDonald's house?

He braced himself. No, she'd not have gone that way. The only possibility lay towards Inverrigan's farm and the tree-filled lower slopes of the mountain there. There, he thought, hiding places could be found though undoubtedly Glenlyon would have had men at Inverrigan and not spared its inhabitants. He turned towards the mountain, darkly silhouetted against the sky, only the snow lightening the gloom.

'Bring the horses, Robb,' he said. 'Search to the left towards the mountain. I'll go this way.'

He moved forward, drawing his sword for there might be survivors who would sell their own lives if they could take a *saighdear dearg* with them. He found a man lying spread-eagled, his blood turning the snow scarlet and he thought it was one of MacIain's gilies. He called once to Robb, and Robb answered, 'Nothing yet, sir.'

They had covered more than half a mile and now Richard could see smoke rising where Inverrigan must be and sudden spurts of flame from cottages that had belonged to some of his men. Another roof collapsed and in bitter rage he remembered the place as it had been, activity everwhere, children playing. Now there was no life left, nothing but snow and burning buildings. Once he thought he heard a dog howl somewhere in the distance.

And then he found her. She lay in the snow, where she had fallen, her arms flung out, in her white nightdress, her plaid fallen aside, one foot still in its slipper, the other bare with encrusted blood from the stone cut.

'Oh Christ!' He flung down his sword and fell on his knees beside her. 'Robb! Robb!'

Gathering her up, he wrenched off his cloak to wrap it round her ice-cold body and as Robb ran up he said, 'Her feet – try to warm them.'

Robb squatted down, drawing them on to his knees and chafing them one by one. 'Is she alive, sir?'

Richard put his hand against her breast. 'I think so.'

Bending over he detected a faint breath against his cheek and opening his coat he held her close to the warmth of his chest, kissing her ice-cold face in a frantic endeavour to bring some life back into her. He could see her wound now, a bullet hole below the region of the heart, the snow red where she had lain, blood clotted by the cold, and he crushed her to him. He had seen wounds often enough to know that nothing could be done.

But she was not quite gone and she stirred; her head moved against Richard's shirt and a faint sigh escaped her.

'So cold … so cold … ' The words were so faint he only just heard them.

'Marged, my love, my darling, I'm here. I'll make you warm. All will be well now.' Strange that one could say such things, knowing them to be an impossibility, yet longing to make them the truth.

She seemed to grasp his presence, that it really was his

arms holding her. 'Richard? Oh, how I was praying ... you would come. I wanted to live ... until you came.'

'If only I had known,' he groaned, 'if only I had guessed you were here, but I didn't know – I didn't know any of it until it was too late. Oh God, Marged, you must live, you must!'

He had his small brandy flask in his pocket and opening it he held it to her lips. She swallowed awkwardly and then gave another little sigh. 'I am thinking ... the spaewife was right ... but now you are here ... I am only remembering the happy things ... all worth the pain ... and one day ... you will be coming after me.'

He bowed his head over hers. 'I thought you might hate me for what's been done here.'

'Hate you? It wasn't your hand ... that did it. Dearest Richard,' she drew another difficult breath, 'I loved you from ... the beginning ... nothing will ever change that.'

She was so weak he could scarcely hear the words but he clung to them as he held her close trying to pour some of his life and his warmth into her, knowing it was no use.

She moved one hand a little as if trying to hold him and then it fell away and he sensed that the fragile breathing had ceased.

Crouched in the snow, crushing her body against his, a terrible shuddering seized him.

At last, after a long while, Robb, in tears himself, said, 'Come, sir, oh come. What shall we do? Where shall we take her?'

Very slowly Richard raised his head. In a dazed voice he repeated. 'Take her? I don't know.' And then after a moment he said, 'To where she would want to lie, on that island in the loch.'

'But if there's no boat, sir?'

'We'll find one,' Richard said and knew it would be so.

Somehow with Robb's aid he got to his feet, still holding her pressed against him, and together they turned back towards Carnoch, Robb leading the horses. The half mile they had come seemed like two as they went past the Chief's burning house. The flames were dying down now, only a sullen smoke curling upwards in the rising wind.

At the edge of the loch where the fishing boats always lay the soldiers had piled them together and set fire to them. John Robb left the horses and began to pull the still hot blackened wood apart and in the centre found a small boat the flames had not destroyed.

'Here's one, sir,' he called out and struggled to pull it free, scarcely noticing the blistering of his skin. Searching for oars that were not broken and fed to the fire he found one lying some distance away and another broken in half. He pulled the boat right side up and floated it on the edge of the water, then helped his master step in with his burden. Holding Marged's body across his knees, his arms wrapped about her, Richard sat on the little seat in the stern as Robb endeavoured to row them across with inadequate oars. He could no longer think clearly.

As the boat grounded on the pebbly shore Robb sprang out and pulled it up. Then he held it steady for Richard to step out.

'Where shall we lay her, sir? We've naught to dig with.'

Richard gazed round. He could see the outline of the little chapel, the knot of trees, the old graves. 'There,' he said, and without needing to be told more John Robb went to a patch of loose rock washed clear of snow. Kneeling down he pulled away the stones until there was a hollow. Richard knelt too but for a moment he could not relinquish her. He was so numb that he was incapable of movement. Robb put out his arms to take her but at that Richard shook his head. Gently he laid her down, still encased in his cloak. He kissed her cold face and then taking off his coat wrapped it about her head so that it might lie protected from the stones. Then they covered her, raising a mound of them above her.

When it was done Richard got to his feet and stood there. Robb said. 'Oughtn't we to say a prayer, sir?'

Richard turned to him. It seemed the end of life, nothing left, an empty void, but he murmured, 'Yes – yes, if you will.'

But he scarcely heard Robb's low voice as he recited the Lord's prayer until he came to 'Forgive us our trespasses as we forgive … ' Then suddenly Richard shook once more with that engulfing rage, the loathing that had seized him during the night.

'Never! Never! I'll not forgive as long as I live.'

Blindly he turned and strode away to the boat.

Robb followed him and as he climbed in said, 'Sir, you'll be so cold without your coat and cloak. Take mine.' He put it about his master's shoulders and slowly rowed them back to the shingly beach. Then as he stepped out he said, 'I'll get the horses, sir,' and wished he might say something, anything, to take that dreadful look from the Colonel's face.

Richard stood by the shore, wondering if this was reality, or some horrific nightmare from which he would surely awake. But he could still feel the precious weight of Marged's body in his arms and he thought of the nights at the house of Donald Stewart and her song – 'Strong is the love that death cannot stall'. Oh, it was a fine sentiment to sing of but the reality of having her torn from him was more he thought than he could endure without losing his sanity. How was he to go back, to the Fort, to his life as a soldier, as it had been before she came? He stood facing the prospect, sick and cold. Would it not be better to climb into the mountains, her mountains, lose himself, go on until he dropped in the snow, to lie there until he too was dead from the icy cold, as so many must be up on those cruel jagged ridges? He was still standing there when the decision was taken from him.

Suddenly, out of the darkness, a figure launched itself at him, eyes and hair wild, screaming, 'Son of a swine, bloody murderer, where is she? What have you done with her, *sasunnach* dog.'

Still dazed Richard said involuntarily, 'She's there on the island, where she would want – '

'Devil! Devil! I was coming to bear her there – it was my right. May the Evil one curse you – '

It was Iain Dubh hysterical with rage. He had a murderous dirk in his hand and he flung himself at the man he hated.

Richard reached for his sword only to find an empty scabbard for he had left the weapon where he had dropped it when he found Marged. He flung up both hands to shield himself but Iain Dubh was on him. The dirk flashed and went high into his shoulder. It was wrenched free and he gasped with pain, trying blindly to catch at the weapon. He felt the man's breath on his face as Iain Dubh struck again and this time the knife went deep into his abdomen. The agony of it drew a groan from him and at that moment there was a shot. The Highlander collapsed forward as Richard's knees gave way and they fell together, Iain Dubh sprawled on top of his victim, the dirk plunging once more into Richard's defenceless body.

John Robb dropped the smoking pistol and running to them heaved the figure in the plaid off his master, saw the blood and the wounds. Wrenching the dirk free and stripping off his shirt he tried to stem the flow of blood, but almost at once he realized they were beyond his skill. He pressed the shirt over the stomach wound and tied it down with Richard's scarf and then ran headlong for his horse, galloping for Ballachulish and help.

But Iain Dubh was not quite dead. He stirred and crawled over to the unconscious Richard, groping for the dirk. But his strength was gone and he fell over Richard's inert body, dying there on top of him, and he would have been horrified to know that in doing so he saved his enemy's life.

Chapter 16

It was one of those days that seem to occur towards the end of March when there is a promise of spring, when mild sunshine warms the earth and brings the first buds to bursting. On such a day for the first time Richard was allowed out of bed to sit by his window and let the warmth shine on his face. Below in the courtyard it was quiet: Drummond, Glenlyon and Duncanson with their companies of Argylls had gone to Leith to await transport for Flanders, and only Hill's own regiment, sadly depleted by winter deaths, was left.

He sat looking out at the great hump of Ben Nevis, snow still glistening on the summit, the sky above that pale blue of the early part of the year. He was not thinking of anything in particular, the weakness of his healing body requiring only that he should stay quiet. The very act of dressing had tired him.

But presently there was a tap on the door and Governor Hill came in. 'Ah, Lincourt, you are up. This is good news indeed. How are you feeling now that you are out of bed?'

'Wondering where my old strength has gone,' Richard answered. 'though Doctor Beaton assures me I am making good progress.'

'I'm glad to hear it. He's been most careful of you.'

Richard nodded. It had taken him a long time to lose the wish to be left alone to die. He remembered little of those early days, but he did recall waking once to see Dr Beaton's haggard and grief-stricken face bent over him. He had muttered, 'How can you bear to touch me?' And the Doctor had answered, as his daughter had, 'You had no part in that vileness. Your man has told me it all. And Marged loved you.'

Richard remembered no more for some time after that because of the high fever that gripped him. He had a faint memory of one night and being very near death. There was candlelight and brandy being forced down his throat, and he thought he had tried to push the spoon away, wanting only to be allowed to die. But Dr Beaton had said something to him, something he thought about living for Marged's sake, but the recollection was all jumbled in his head. When the fever broke it left him too weak to do more than lie and let others care for him. It seemed that whether he wanted to or not he was going to live.

Gradually other memories came back in snatches, of the weight of Iain Dubh's body on top of him, strangely keeping him from the worst of the cold and stemming the blood from his wounds while John Robb made frantic efforts to get help; of being in a cart and in acute pain, mercifully lost in bouts of unconsciousness. But it was all very hazy, the details told to him afterwards by Robb.

The shoulder wound healed easily but it was the one to the stomach that had put him in danger of death, and perhaps as he began slowly to heal the long illness had been a kind of blessing, for it drained his strength so that the murderous hatred, the grief, the desire for revenge were deadened, leaving him in a state of mental and physical exhaustion. Sometimes when he woke from sleep it was to think that all was as usual and it was only slowly that the horror of it all washed over him once more, and he wished Robb had let him die there by the loch.

His only visitors were the doctor and Colonel Hill, though Ensign Fuller came occasionally to stand awkwardly by the end of the bed and ask if there were any orders. The first time he came he tried to say he was sorry, that they all were, to hear – Mistress Stewart – it was wicked – and then lost himself and his eyes filled with tears so that he stood there fighting them, ashamed to have brought that twitching together of the brows and look of deeper suffering to the face on the pillow. He excused himself and didn't come again until he was sure he could master himself, his grief for the Colonel's lady going very deep.

Now Richard was in the listless state of early

convalescence and wished the Colonel had not come. But John Hill drew up a stool to sit beside him.

'I'm afraid I've had no reply I like from my betters in London,' Hill began, 'only an inhuman suggestion that the MacDonalds left in hiding in the mountains should be rounded up and transported to the American plantations. It is not, thank God, an order so I shall ignore it, even if it were possible to accomplish, which it is not.'

Richard drew a deep breath. 'There are bloody-minded men in the south who know nothing.'

'Aye, that there are.'

'And here,' Richard added. 'Is Colonel Hamilton still in the Fort?'

'Officially yes, but he's away to Glasgow on regimental business and I have my major acting as my deputy.'

The two men were on better terms now, Hill full of sympathy for what the sick man had suffered and Richard understanding better what crisis of conscience Hill had endured before he had signed that paper. And he understood too that the cruel refinement of the plan born in London had been Hamilton's. It was he who had been ordered by Livingstone to be secret and sudden and it was he who had devised the 'murder under trust'. It was Hill, however, who told Richard that my lord of Breadalbane was panic-stricken over the whole business, never dreaming the original idea of getting rid of tiresome neighbours would turn out as it had, and when the Glencoe cattle were sold he said that if any of his people bought them they should be returned to the survivors – a statement which scarcely rang true. He believed far more in Colonel Hill's open horror when he learned on questioning John Robb why Richard had gone to the glen that night and what he had found there. Hill said little but showed his outraged sympathy in concern for the wounded man. Robb also told Richard of the anger among his own little troop, those who had ridden with him from Edinburgh, at the killing of the Colonel's lady, and apparently there were black looks and loosened swords between them and the Argyll men. Fortunately the Ensign and Sergeant Morrison between them kept the men busy and as far as possible from the Campbells, thankful when the latter were sent off to Leith.

As he convalesced, Richard went over and over in his mind every detail of the terrible twenty-four hours and the worst torment came one morning when he suddenly realized that if he had not gone on that futile recruiting to Inverness, if he had been at the Fort, she would never have gone back to Glencoe after her mother's burial. So in a sense he was responsible for her being there. He recoiled from the thought, and commonsense tried to tell him he had merely gone about his duty, that there was not the remotest chance he could have known what was going to happen, but it preyed on his mind, would do so, he thought, as long as he lived.

The real perpetrators, thank God, had gone long before he was likely to be about again, and as for Hamilton he could only pray their paths might never cross again.

He let out another sigh. 'Thank God he's gone. If I'd seen him when I had my strength back he wouldn't have lived another day.'

'And what would that achieve?' Hill asked quietly. 'A court martial, and a firing squad for you? I'd not have wanted that. And now that this whole business is known everywhere, with, I understand, great disquiet in London, people shocked as well they might be, the Jacobites are making the most of the scandal to further their cause. An account of the massacre, as it is being called, is published in a pamphlet that is in every coffee house in Edinburgh and, I don't doubt, in London as well. So is Major Duncanson's order.' He broke off, an unhappy man whose honest Christian faith had fought a bitter battle against his own orders. 'But there's some good news. Now that the weather is better MacDonald of Sleat has come in, and Clanranald too and other smaller chieftains. Young Robert Stewart of Appin swore at the end of February, and though I know his people are trying to aid the Glencoe survivors I shall say nothing of it.'

Richard leaned his head on his hand. It seemed to him Hill was trying to purge his mind by relating every scrap of gossip and information, every tale going the rounds of the coffee houses. He felt tired and in no mood to listen. Nothing less than the court martial of those who laid the plan would satisfy him. Yet she was gone and nothing could bring her back. As soon as he was strong enough he would leave here, go back to Leith and collect his men and then leave Scotland for good, never to return to the land that had brought him so much joy and then unbearable grief.

He didn't know what he would do with the rest of his life. In disgust and loathing of what the army had done his first reaction was to resign his commission at once, make it known why he did so, but that he couldn't do for he had a duty to his men at Leith. When he had delivered them to the King then would be the time for decision, and part of him clung to the way of life he had known for so many years as a way in which to sink his private feelings. But at the moment he was really incapable of thinking further ahead than the return to Edinburgh.

All of his mind was taken up with going back, not forward, and he sat for long hours living over and over again every detail of every moment with Marged right from the beginning when he saw her coming down the stairs at Newsteads. He dwelt in precious memory on the time at Craigieduir. It brought consciousness of the joy of being loved by her that was at the same time racking inconsolable sorrow that she would never lie in his arms again. And part of him wished he had never set foot in this remote and beautiful country, while the other half knew that it had given him far more than it had taken away. And there was one thing he planned to do before he left.

It was three more weary weeks until at last Dr Beaton pronounced him fit to travel. 'I wish you well on your journey,' the doctor said, 'and wherever you may go in the future. I've lost wife and daughter but you have lost the bright hopes, the future you and my Marged would have shared.'

'You've been generous in your care of me,' Richard said, 'and I'm grateful for it, though at one time I wished – '

'I know,' the Doctor agreed, 'your state of mind was understandable. But you have your life and your best tribute to Marged's memory is to make the best use of it you can.'

They parted with a handshake that said what neither of them could put into words, and Richard began to make his preparations for leaving. During this last week he had forced himself to write to his mother, telling her there would be no marriage and that when he came home he wanted no discussion of it. The letter sounded cold and formal but it was the best he could do.

He sent John Robb on an expedition into Maryburgh with orders to be extremely discreet and then, with his packhorse more than usually laden, he took his leave of the Colonel and Major Forbes and rode out of the Fort at the head of his small contingent of men, swollen by only six recruits, one other having come in from the island of Sleat.

At Ballachulish they crossed on the ferry. Spring was coming now, the first green leaves on the branches and from this boat one could not see the lonely desolation of the Valley of the Dogs. Only the little burial isle with its dark fir trees held his gaze. It was quiet there, the water gently lapping on the stones, and he thought that all his heart, all that was best in him lay buried there with her. He must go back to the old sterile life, the empty lodgings in London, the even emptier great house at Heronslea and he wondered how he was to endure it. But he was stronger now, and he had never been a coward. He only hoped that his mother would take his words to heart, and warn his sisters and Judith too that sympathy from people who could in no way understand what had happened up here was the last thing he wanted.

Once on shore again they took the road south, but several miles short of Barcaldine Castle he produced a letter he had written and called Ensign Fuller to him. He gave him orders to take it to the commander of the garrison there, not knowing whether it would still be Captain Drummond, asking for accommodation for his men for a few days while he conducted some private business in the area. They went, a small red line, and he turned inland towards Craigieduir, taking only Robb with him. It was going to be scarcely bearable to go there again

but he must steel himself to enter that place of sacred
memory for she would approve what he was doing and he
only prayed the Laird was at home.

Riding along the track to the house, above the slope to
the loch and the little copse of pine trees he thought of the
night when he and she had stood watching the northern
lights and how confident their hopes had been then. Even
Marged's revelation during the night of the saying of an
old woman in the glen had not been able to cloud his
happiness. And he had been happy, happier than he had
ever dreamed possible, so much so that he believed he had
driven all foreboding from Marged's mind. But the old
crone's words had been fulfilled and broken their lives
apart, robbing them of their love when its fulfilment had
scarcely begun.

Donald Stewart fortunately was at home and when
Richard explained who he was bade him enter. 'You were
welcome to my hospitality then and you're welcome now,'
he said, 'though I must tell you feelings are running very
high hereabouts concerning the late massacre, for I can
give it no other word.'

'I know that, sir,' Richard agreed, 'but I must tell you
that what I am about to do could order me the severest
reprimand if I am discovered, if not instant dismissal, but
for Marged's sake I must do it.'

'I understand,' Craigieduir nodded. He was a small man
in middle age with a leathery face and deepset grey eyes
which regarded his visitor thoughtfully. 'Dr Beaton wrote
to tell me what had happened. I'm very sorry for you
personally, but my regard for your kind is hardly what you
would wish to hear so I think it better not to speak of it.'
He saw the lines of grief in the pale face opposite him and
added perceptively, 'But come you away in and tell me
why you are after coming at all. I doubt if you would've
done it without a good reason.'

'You are right,' Richard said and followed him into the
parlour. There for a few moments he could not speak,
only aware of that first supper here and Marged's delight
in her game of pretence, that it was their home. There
were all the familiar objects she had pointed out to him,

and the pain of being here without her was scarcely bearable, but he forced himself to speak.

'I've come, sir, because you are a Stewart, your land is not far from the southern slopes of the Glencoe mountains and easy to reach. I must see John MacDonald before I leave.' He saw the Laird's start of surprise and went on, 'He became my friend while I lay two months in his house with a broken leg and I can't go without an attempt to see him. I've also got an animal outside laden with some bare necessities for his people. They must have had a desperate hungry time since February.'

'They have indeed,' Stewart said, 'though my clan, many of whom are their kin, have done what they could to help.'

'I'm sure of that,' Richard agreed, 'but what I bring will no doubt serve for them a while. I shouldn't be doing it, but 'tis little enough to risk what might happen to me if it was known, in return for what they did for me.'

'I see,' the Laird began to pace the room, deep in thought. Then he said, 'I think I believe you to be sincere.'

'I swear to you I want only to help them. If you can but tell me where John – I suppose we must call him MacIain now – is in hiding I'll go to him with only my man and my pack-horse.'

'And you think I'll help you?'

'I hope so,' Richard said plainly. 'I think the Stewarts are in the best position to reach the Glencoe people and the new Chief. If you know where they are – '

'Aye, I know, but whether to take you there is another matter. But what I can do is send a gillie to find out if MacIain is after wanting to see you.'

With that Richard had to be content and he spent the night in the room that had been his before, only thankful that he had not been shown into the one Marged occupied. If he had, he doubted if he could have slept in that bed. As it was he slept little, reliving every moment of their time here until he could barely support the grief it brought him; his longing for Marged, for one touch of her hand, for one look from those lively dark eyes, keeping him miserably awake for a long time.

He tried not to think of the island of St Munda, of her body that he had loved here through those two nights, lying cold and wrapped in his cloak beneath the stones. But during the night he dreamed of the little isle and it was peopled by men and women in the tartan. The late Chief was there, towering above the others and he had his arm about Marged and was taking her away somewhere. Richard tried to go after them but his legs were like lead and he kept falling on the stones. The last time he got to his feet again it was dark and there was no one there. He wanted to cry out but no sound would come and then he woke up. But the dream was oddly comforting: it was as if he had seen her and knew now that only her mortal body lay under the grey stones where he had laid her.

He breakfasted with the Laird and his wife, a proud woman taller than her husband, and she made Richard feel uncomfortable. He was sure she disapproved of what her husband was doing. The talk at the table was somewhat stilted, the massacre being on all their minds, but not mentioned. All the surrounding clans had been furious, the Camerons even arming themselves and standing to war, and he did not blame them, only hoping that they would not make matters worse by any rash act. But even the temperamental Glengarry had come in now, saying he didn't wish to have his house 'Glencoed'.

At noon the gillie returned, saying MacIain wished to see the *sasunnach* and accordingly Donald Stewart and Richard, with John Robb and the packhorse, set off to the north into the mountains. It was a long ride into difficult country, up narrow corries with high rocky passes where they had to dismount and lead the horses. At last, in the late afternoon, they came to an open space beneath a snow-covered peak, and there met the remains of Clan Iain Abrach, a place so hidden, Richard thought thankfully, that no patrol was likely to find it.

It was John himself, thirteenth chief of this remnant, who came forward to greet them, his hand held out to Richard as he swung himself down from his horse.

'It's good of you to come so far so see us,' were John's first words and Richard answered:

'Good! How can you say that to me after what's been done? I've brought you what I could, meal and salt and whisky and some other things.'

'Then that is good too.' John led him towards one of the low bracken-thatched huts. There was also a cave among the high rocks and at its entrance were gathered men, women and children who had seen him arrive. They all seemed pale and unkempt, the children standing listless, some holding to their mother's skirts, though a few older boys were kicking a ball made of rags. One, about fourteen, stared at him with strange, vacant eyes as if the night of the massacre had removed his reason.

The men looked at the Laird and nodded, but for Richard there were cold unfriendly faces; some of the women held babies in their arms and must have been pregnant when the massacre took place. From inside the cave the smoke from a peat fire billowed out into the clear crisp air of early spring, and though he saw a set of pipes no one played them in greeting.

And then as he followed John a child detached himself from the rest and ran forward to tug at the skirts of Richard's coat, both arms held out. It was Alasdair and Richard lifted him into his arms, almost unmanned by the affection of the child. Alasdair had both arms about his neck and Richard buried his face in the boy's dark hair, struggling to force back the sudden tears.

'Come, my laddie,' he said at last, 'let me set you down and look at you.' He saw the pinched face, the thin arms and legs that had not long ago been solid and healthy and a great anger rose in him. He took Alasdair's hand and together they entered the shieling. Eiblin and Moir were trying to make the little hut more welcoming but there was practically nothing in it; several beds of dried heather on the far side, a table and a couple of stools used by the Stewart crofters when they drove the cattle up here in the summer.

Eiblin said, 'Welcome you are, *Ruiseart*, but I doubt we have songs to greet you now.'

Sarah, Sandy's wife, was also there, she too looked thin and pale and her eyes were haunted, as if the shock of her uncle Glenlyon's treachery, of his lying protestations that he meant no harm to his kin, had been too much for her. She was pregnant too, and after glancing once at Richard she moved away in silence, to busy herself about setting some wooden bowls on the table.

Her husband Alasdair Og, was crouched by the fire. He got to his feet and stood looking at Richard, not speaking, but with a great bitterness in his face.

'Sandy,' Richard nodded to him and thought of their games of cards and how long it had taken him to win Sandy over. It seemed that trust was gone now.

John pulled forward the stools for Richard and Donald Stewart, but before Richard would sit, he said, 'One moment, John. There is something I must tell you.'

MacIain interrupted him at once. 'My dear friend, don't be putting more grief on yourself by telling us about Marged. We know.'

'How do you know? Did Mr Stewart – '

'We knew before that,' John said. 'One of my gillies went down to the Valley of the Dogs in the evening to see if the soldiers had gone, so that we could at least go down and bury our dead decently. He saw you carry Marged away. Where did you take her?'

'To St Munda's.' Richard looked across at Eiblin and saw her eyes fill. 'You will find her grave by the shore.' He paused and his gaze wandered from one face to the other. 'I don't know what to say to you all. I was away until the very evening when the soldiers were given their orders, and when I returned and heard – '

'You were not after warning us,' Sandy said. 'You sent no messenger to us who had sheltered you.'

'God knows I would have done so if I could,' Richard said desperately. 'Colonel Hill had me under restraint, knowing it was what I would have tried to do. I begged him not to let the plan go through, to query the orders, but they had come from far higher sources and the lieutenant-colonel there rules matters. And there was no turning him.'

Sandy shrugged, as if doubting the explanation, and turned away to put another peat on the fire, the smoke drifting upwards through the vent-hole in the roof, and it was John who said, 'We knew you could have had no hand in it and we all grieved for you when we found out that Marged was slain. Apart from her only one other woman was killed in the glen and one child, may God curse the man who did it, but many more died in the hills. 'Twas hard for them and the ones with child as well as the bairns to survive that dreadful night and the bitter cold without shelter. But you, *Ruiseart*, if you see the effects of the sorry business among us I see a change in you too. You have been ill?'

'Yes,' Richard said. 'Iain Dubh found me by the loch after – after we'd laid Marged on the isle. I'd dropped my sword when I found her and he came at me with a dirk. My servant shot him but not before he'd knifed me thrice.'

John gave an exclamation. 'He was always wild, that one, and wild that night with grief, I imagine. Marged was his life.'

And mine, Richard thought, and mine! To turn from the tormenting thought he said, 'I saw your father.'

'Did you so? We buried him where he lay until the day we can take him to the island. My mother we buried up on Meall Mor.'

'I prayed she had escaped.'

'No,' Sandy broke in harshly. 'Do you know what they did to her, your redcoats? They stripped her naked and when they couldn't get her rings off they chewed her fingers until they could wrench them free – then they drove her into the snow.'

'Sandy!' John's voice was sharp with a new authority. 'I doubt if they were *Ruiseart's* redcoats.'

'My men had naught to do with it, nor would I have permitted them under any circumstances to behave in such a manner,' Richard said vehemently. 'I am both ashamed and angry that men wearing the King's uniform should have been allowed to do that they did. If ever I see any of the officers concerned – ' He broke off. What he might say to the men who were in the same service as himself was irrelevant to these desperate people. 'As for your mother,' he went on in a low voice, 'I grieve deeply for her, and for you.'

'We wrapped her in a plaid and bandaged her fingers when we found her,' John said, 'but it was all after being too great a shock for a woman of her age and she died that night. Are you knowing how Marged escaped the house, for my man saw you not far from Inverrigan's farm?' And when Richard shook his head, he added, 'She was sleeping in my father's account room, the house being full. Maybe being on the ground floor she went out by the window when she heard the shots.' He saw the expression on Richard's face. '*Laochain*, I can be giving you little comfort but to say that Marged was a Gael and for her death was only a pathway to the haven of the Blessed Ones prepared for His people by our Lord Christ. She will be knowing that you will follow her.'

There was a silence. Richard found it hard to speak but at last he said, 'I wish I could be as sure. But at least she was still living when I found her and for long enough for me to know she didn't hate me for the evil thing that was done.'

'It was the more vile because of the way it was done,' Sandy muttered, and John added, 'We're used to raids on each other's lands, *Ruiseart*, as I told you once before. I suppose the Campbells of Glenorchy and Glenlyon thought they owed us much for our raiding after Dalcomera, but never, never would we be breaking the laws of hospitality as those Campbells did.'

'How did you both get away?' Richard asked.

It was Sandy who answered. 'I was not after being easy in my mind all afternoon. A captain came with orders and though Glenlyon said nothing to us I was thinking they boded no good to us. There was that in his manner – well, I couldn't be sleeping and went to John. There seemed to be naught wrong but more soldiers were on guard and awake than I liked.'

'I thought 'twas merely the storm,' John took up the tale, 'but I dressed and we went to see my father. He said there was no cause for worrying but when I went home I was laying me down in my clothes.'

'So did I,' Sandy added, 'and then when I was seeing soldiers with fixed bayonets coming to the house I had my people and my family up and away to Glean Leac and up on to Meall Mor.'

'It was the same for me,' John said. 'We thank God for our wakefulness that night for it saved our wives and bairns. I got my household out of the old door at the back of the store-room beyond your bedroom, *Ruiseart*. Sandy and I ran into each other by chance on the same path and tried to see what we could through the blizzard. 'Twas a fierce night but that saved some others, and a good many were warned in time because the soldiers used their muskets instead of plain steel.'

The low entrance darkened as a man came in and Richard saw with real pleasure that it was MacDonald of Achnacon. 'Thank God you escaped,' he said. 'Tell me how.'

Achnacon had no hesitation in shaking his hand. 'Your man has been after telling me you'd naught to do with it, nor did I think you would have done, willingly. Those sons of swine, the Campbells, came into my house firing their muskets at us, and my servant, may his share of Paradise be his, was after throwing himself between me and the bullets and I only got one in the shoulder though I was knocked to the floor. That hard-faced Sergeant Barber asked me if I still lived and when I said I did I begged them at least to be shooting me outside and not under my own roof where he'd eaten my bread for many a day.'

The vivid picture conjured up nauseated Richard. 'What happened then?'

'They set me against the wall, so close that their bayonets were almost touching me and then before they could be at firing their pieces I threw my plaid over their heads and ran for my life into the snow. Never did I thank the Good Being for so much as for that blizzard, but,' Achnacon paused, 'I am not rejoicing when the rest of my people lie dead in the ruins of my house, for the soldiers burned it over them, dead and dying as they were. Indeed we've not much to be rejoicing over here with not enough food for hungry bairns, though our neighbours and Donald Stewart here are doing what they can. But there's not so much as a pipeful of tobacco left for us who are after being used to it.'

'There's tobacco in the pack I brought,' Richard said, 'though I'd no idea if there were any left that would smoke it.'

Achnacon gave him a great grin, as if the spark of his uproarious old self was not entirely put out, and he went off to find John Robb and help him unload the packs. Robb had found his friend the smith had survived and was happily shaking his hand.

'What happened at Achtriochtan's house?' Richard asked and it was Sandy who answered. 'He was shot with several of his men, and he with Colonel Hill's letter of protection, because he had sworn, in his sporan. Their bodies were thrown on the midden. And a dozen more of our people were burned alive in a barn. Kennedy's boy ran shrieking to Glenlyon and clung to him begging for his life, but he was shot in the head by that officer who brought the orders. Achtriochtan's son saw that, but he, praise God, managed to get away to the Black Mount. Oh, we know it all from those who escaped.'

He spoke jerkily, each sentence flung at Richard to taunt him and Richard sat with his hands clasped between his knees, staring at the floor. A few of the more talkative soldiers at the Fort had regaled John Robb with further incidents and Robb had brought them to him, the whole picture becoming horrifyingly clear.

Seeing his distress John said, ' 'Tis no use to be going over that night. You see we are in a poor way here, *Ruiseart*, but some of our friends have shown us great kindness. MacDonald of Grimmish came down from the Isles by boat and left us a cargo of meal and other things we need, and the Stewarts, thanks to Donald here, have given us arms and necessities like blankets and kettles. These shielings are theirs.'

Richard said, 'There aren't many of you here. Are you all who survived?'

John shook his head. 'Some of our people got away to Keppoch country for the end of the glen was unguarded at first and they got help there, others went to Dalness and the Black Mount to our own summer shielings, and those who had kin here came down into Appin. Clan Iain Abrach is sadly scattered, my friend.'

'Great God!' Richard's anger flared. 'It's the most damnable thing. It would be bad enough in a state of war, but – '

'The Lowlanders have a great hatred on them for us,' John said. *'Mi-run more nan Gall*, and to them and to us it is as if peace never existed between us. But for the while we are beaten and must be submitting. Only yesterday one of my gillies took a letter to Colonel Hill telling him of our wish to live in peace and to go home to the Valley of the Dogs in quietness.'

'I pray God he will persuade the authorities to grant you that,' Richard said soberly. 'I promise you that when I am back in London I will ask for an inquiry into the whole affair which might, and should, result in some compensation for you. We English are famous for our love of justice and I can't believe mine will be the only voice saying you have paid too high a price for the past. There will be English folk who will have turned in horror from the news and will see the dreadful injustice of it after your father had sworn. I'll write to you but where can I send the letter?'

'To me,' Donald Stewart said, 'and I will see it reaches MacIain wherever he may be.'

'And I'll be after writing to you,' John put in, 'if you will leave me your direction. Donald here has been kind enough to supply me with paper and pens and ink.'

Richard took out his pocket book and tearing out a page wrote down the address of Heronslea for that would find him wherever he was. There was, to him, something poignant about this exchange between him and a man in hiding in the mountains in a worn and torn plaid with holed stockings and clearly not enough to eat. Somehow John was keeping the remnants of the clan in hope; he was their Chief and even if they were cold and near to starving there was still pride left here.

'You can't be going back in the dark,' John went on. 'You'll have to be sleeping here tonight though we can only offer you a bed of heather and a poor enough supper – yet better than it would have been without your gift.'

'I'll thank you for the bed,' Richard said, 'but I'm not hungry.' Not for anything would he have eaten one mouthful of their food.

But Eiblin and Sarah made a porridge of the meal as the other women were doing in the cave and they ate as if it was a rare feast, adding the butter Richard had brought to their rough bannocks and relishing every mouthful. The boy Alasdair climbed on to Richard's knee with his bowl and wooden spoon and there he fell asleep when he had eaten. Richard laid him down on a pile of heather and Moir covered him with a plaid.

After the meal Richard did take a quaich of whisky with John and then when everyone settled for the night John took his arm and led him outside to walk up and down under the stars.

'I wanted to speak to you alone,' he said. 'Is the order still out for the MacDonald men to be slain? I imagine on that night the command was for every man to be butchered and the Government can only be sorry so many of us escaped.'

'I don't know for certain if there are any fresh orders, but I tell you this,' Richard said. 'Colonel Hill will allow no more killing. He was written to the Duke of Hamilton and Lord Tweedale as well as Sir Thomas Livingstone on your behalf. And though I know patrols are sent through your glen at times they've no orders to kill any more of your people. Colonel Hill has seen to that.'

'We are desperate men,' John said. 'The Stewarts have given us weapons to hunt and to defend ourselves if need be.'

'I imagine you are safe enough in these mountains. No one could find you that you didn't wish to do so and that pass we came in by is easy enough to defend.'

'So I thought,' John agreed. 'Our mountains are our fortress. But you are seeing the plight of our bairns and of the women.'

'I see,' Richard said, 'and it seems to me that you are all bearing it more bravely than I could have imagined. When I think of Alasdair going hungry – '

Suddenly the calm John had shown so far was banished by an explosion of rage. 'Never think,' he said in shaking voice, 'that my blood doesn't cry out to be revenged, to slay Glenlyon with my own hands, to dirk Lindsay for the vicious Lowlander he is, the slayer of my father, to cry out *Dh'ainneoin co theireadh e*, my clan's war-cry! What would I not give to lead the sons of Angus Og to fight against those treacherous Campbells! The souls of my mother and my father call out to me for vengeance against the bloody men who slew them.' He was MacIain in truth now and his dark eyes burned in his pale face and he was trembling. 'The spirits of all the dead on St Munda's rise up to cry out to us who are living to avenge them. Do you know what the filthy Campbell piper played as they left the Valley of the Dogs? A rant called "The Glen is Mine"!' He shook with the force of his rage and Richard had never seen him so stirred.

As suddenly the rage was forced back, and John paused in his pacing, his face lifted to the sky. 'But what is the use to think of it? We have a few pistols, a sword or two, and a dirk for each man, thanks to Donald Stewart, but these are no more than we need to hunt to live. We are beaten just now, but I am Chief and, God willing, one day I'll take my people home and we will rebuild our houses and begin again. Alasdair must have his heritage.' A hard grim smile touched his lips. 'I'll be telling you a thing that may amuse you. A week after that night a man came to me from Campbell of Barcaldine, my lord Breadalbane's chamberlain, and he had the audacity to say that if Sandy and I would swear the Earl innocent of any part in the affair the Earl would be gracious enough to try to procure a pardon for us! You can imagine my answer.'

'It's beyond belief,' Richard said and had no desire to laugh. 'The man is well called a fox but I'd no idea he could be so cowardly.'

'Aye, guilt must lie on him or he'd not have been after sending Barcaldine's man to us.' John agreed.

For a while they walked silently and then Richard took his arm. 'What can I say? My dear friend, you've had a great wrong done you. When I get to Glasgow I'll try to send more necessities to you by Mr Stewart.'

'Thank you,' John said warmly, 'but I brought you out here to be asking what your own plans are now that you've lost our dearest Marged?'

'I don't know,' Richard said. 'I don't know if I can continue to wear the uniform that I'd not have provoked your people by wearing here today. But if I leave the army I doubt if I can face living alone on my estate where I had hoped – ' he could not bring himself to say her name, nor contemplate his dream of taking her to be mistress of

Heronslea, without the tearing grief that devastated him.

It seemed as if John understood for he said, '*Laochain*, my heart is heavy with your sorrow.'

They paced in silence, the night quiet, only a gentle breeze stirring. Tomorrow, Richard thought, he would be leaving these mountains and this crisp cold air that was like nowhere else, and returning to what he once thought civilization, and he thought too of the contrast between the society he had been used to and these desperate homeless hungry people. And it was with great heaviness that he contemplated that future.

Again John seemed to understand for he said, 'I am sorry for your going because I see what it means to you – an end to all you have found here with us and you can't see clearly what lies before you. My little son will be sad because he's grown to love you.'

Richard could only say, 'And I him. Let me have news of him when you can. I would like to know how he goes on.'

In the morning he said goodbye to them all, though Sandy failed to join the group gathering by the shieling, and he was greatly moved by the fact that were was so little animosity towards him. They watched as John held out both arms and embraced him.

'The Most Holy God Himself alone knows if we two will ever meet again,' John said. 'but you will always be after being in my prayers, *Ruiseart*. May He go with you and bring you safely back to your people.'

Richard thought of his mother and his sisters in a curiously detached way. 'I think,' he said, 'I leave whatever is best in me buried here.' He bent and lifted the boy Alasdair to give him a last kiss and then mounted and rode away after Donald Stewart, John's familiar, '*Beannachd leat*', following him as his horse picked her way down the track.

Once he looked back, saw the mountains Marged had loved, the majestic heights of the Bidean nam Bian in the distance, the shifting April sunlight playing on the bare slopes, the little group by the primitive shielings, MacIain standing a little in front of the rest, his son's hand in his.

Chapter 17

Edinburgh was the same, teeming with life, dirty, noisy, thriving, men bargaining over goods, housewives chattering, children running everywhere and getting in the way of sober folk about their business.

To Richard, coming back to this was something he found very hard to bear. He sent Ensign Fuller with the men out to Leith and went himself to report to Sir Thomas Livingstone.

It was a sour interview. 'Your plans went very much awry,' Sir Thomas said touchily. 'Near six months you've been gone and I've had the feeding and paying of your companies without so much as a penny piece from London.'

'I ask your pardon for a fall from my horse and for being dirked by a Highlander out of his mind with grief,' Richard answered sardonically, beyond caring how he spoke to the Commander-in-Chief.

It seemed Sir Thomas was in an irritable mood this morning for he picked up a letter and sat fingering it. 'Well, from what Colonel Hamilton reports I understand that the dirking was your own fault, that you'd gone alone to Glencoe on the evening of the ruining of it. What in heaven's name were you doing there?'

'It was a private matter.'

'There are no private matters when it comes to army discipline as you very well know. You must have been out of your own mind to go back.'

'If I was,' Richard said shortly, 'it was as a direct result of the abominable treachery of Glenlyon and his men, ordered by Colonel Hamilton.'

'I don't want to discuss that,' Sir Thomas retorted and Richard thought, No, I'm very sure you don't, my friend, seeing where the responsibility lies.

Sir Thomas went on, 'If ever an affair was bungled! Apparently Glenlyon began it with shooting, enough to warn the MacDonalds, but there is no point in bewailing the fact that so many got away.'

'The orders to put all to the sword came from you. Do you then think the using of bullets was a mistake?'

Sir Thomas banged his fist on the table at the recognisedly hostile tone. 'It is not for you to criticise, Lincourt. Do I have to remind you that I am Commander-in-Chief for Scotland?'

'No, sir, but do I need to remind you that I am not strictly under that command. I'm answerable only to his Majesty.'

A dark flush filled Sir Thomas's cheeks. 'You are damned impertinent and insubordinate as well. A report on your behaviour will be sent to the Secretary of State and he will doubtless inform the King of your doings up here.'

'Pray don't put yourself to the trouble.' Richard kept his voice cool. 'I shall myself be leaving for Holland as soon as I can arrange transport for my men.'

'Oh, you will, eh? Well, let me tell you you have a matter to sort out first. There has been trouble among your officers.'

Richard's heart sank and he knew instinctively to whom Sir Thomas was referring. He folded both arms and waited.

'It seems your major, Ripley, and Captain Fletcher have been at odds for a long time. Fletcher complained to me that Ripley was pursuing his wife. I told him, and rightly, that such affairs were not the business of the army. Anyway, as I understand it, there was an unseemly quarrel one evening and Fletcher drew his sword on Ripley, his superior officer – a court martial offence, as you know. But it never got that far.'

Richard listened with growing apprehension. 'Perhaps you would be good enough to explain.'

'Oh, there were plenty of witnesses. Fletcher was

undoubtedly drunk at supper and shouted abuse at Major
Ripley. Before anyone could stop him he had his sword
out and was rushing at Major Ripley whose only weapon
was the knife in his hand with which he'd been cutting up
his meat. He tried to defend himself with it.'

'I hope you aren't going to tell me he paid for his
indiscretion with his life.'

'Oh no,' Sir Thomas said, 'it is Fletcher who is dead. He
took the knife in his heart and died at once. Until
yesterday Major Ripley was in one of my cells here.'

'Good God!' Richard said, 'you can't have condemned
him for self defence?'

'No,' Sir Thomas admitted. 'I presided over the court
martial and he was exonerated. He's back at Leith today.
Of course I've had to send another senior officer to take
your place whom you may now return to me. You've been
away too long, Colonel Lincourt, neglecting your main
body for a few possible recruits. How many did you
bring back?'

'Six,' Richard said tartly and endeavoured to keep his
temper. 'But my long absence was none of my choosing, as
I've explained. And as for this affair, may I remind you
that it was you yourself who sent me Fletcher, and before I
left when I asked you to remove him from my regiment,
you refused.'

'As I'd every right to do. Fletcher was my choice.'

'Whom you knew for a troublemaker.'

'The troublemaker seems to have been your major in
this case. He undoubtedly provoked Captain Fletcher.' Sir
Thomas seemed suddenly tired of the argument. 'Well, he
has been cleared. I suggest you go to Leith and put your
regiment back into shape. All this business has brought
about slackness and some desertions. Will you be wanting
your old quarters here?'

'No,' Richard answered and did not care if he sounded
ungracious. He had no desire to be back in that room that
overlooked the very chimneys of Newsteads in the
Grassmarket. Neither did he wish to remain in the
company of Sir Thomas. 'I shall stay at Leith with my men.
Obviously I have work to do there.'

'Very well,' the Commander agreed but he added persistently, 'By the way, Colonel Hamilton reported to me that you were in Glencoe all the time your leg was healing. It would have been better if you had been brought back to the Fort.'

Richard said nothing, refusing an explanation, and Sir Thomas went on, 'Are you going to tell me why you went back that night?'

'No, sir, I am not.' Richard said. 'And I must tell you I am going to press for an inquiry into the whole affair.'

Sir Thomas was furious. 'It's not your place to do such a thing. And I have every intention of having you called to account for consorting with our enemies.'

'As the soldiers did in Glencoe before they butchered them?' Richard queried and went out, not caring what construction Sir Thomas put on his words. He was wise enough to see his good name as an officer was in jeopardy but at the moment it was not his most pressing concern.

He steeled himself to walk down to the Grassmarket where he spent an unhappy hour with Miss Robertson. It was unbelievably hard to be in this house again, where everything reminded him of Marged – the window seat where they had been sitting when he first spoke of love, the settle by the fire where they had kissed and sat enfolded together in the warmth of sheer happiness, the table where they had eaten together. It put such a strain on him that he was afraid he broke the news more brutally than he intended. But Miss Robertson was made of strong stuff. She wept a little and then firmly put away her handkerchief and sat erect in her chair, her hands twisted together in her lap. She promised she would write to David,

'The laddie will be so distressed,' she said, 'he will be reproaching himself for the way of their parting.'

'If there is any reproach it's mine,' Richard said. 'I think I was blind not to see what was coming.'

'But you couldn't have known that Marged would go back to MacIain just at that moment. Take one thought with you when you leave my country, Colonel – that Marged loved you and you gave her, I believe, the greatest happiness she had ever known.'

He left her shortly after, the last words threatening to destroy his self-command, yet immensely comforting. The short ride to Leith brought him back once more to his camp and he could see at once in the attitude of the men, the sullen looks, the slackness, the untidy uniforms, that morale was low, though the man Sinclair whom he had once flogged was drilling his little contingent, all of them smarter than the rest. He saw his Colonel and a look of relief swept over his face as he brought the men to attention.

'Pray continue your drilling, corporal,' Richard said. 'Your men at least look in good heart.'

He found Ripley in his old headquarters striving to put some order back into regimental affairs and after half an hour of questioning came to the conclusion that the court martial had passed a correct verdict.

'I'm only deeply sorry, sir,' the major said, 'to have brought so much trouble on you. I was about to try to mend matters. I'm afraid the affair had a bad effect on the men and the officer Sir Thomas sent while I was absent had no real interest in Lincourt's.'

'We'll soon put matters to rights,' Richard said, 'but as for your trouble I can only say I warned you. However, recriminations are useless and I'm thankful you aren't facing a firing squad. Where is Mistress Fletcher now?'

'Gone home to her parents, but,' Ripley paused and then added, 'I must tell you, sir, that after a decent interval her father will bring her to Flanders or wherever I am so that when I can get leave we may be married. I can't pretend I'm sorry Fletcher is dead, though I swear to you I didn't mean to kill him.'

'I believe you, and I think you may thank God to have come so well out of this. I wish you joy with Mistress Fletcher.'

Ripley smiled, his lean face creased in unusually contented lines. 'Thank you, sir. And are you and Mistress Stewart to wed soon?'

He should have expected the question but so concerned had he been with Ripley's affairs that it struck Richard like a physical blow. He walked to the window, unable to speak.

Suddenly Ripley said, 'Oh God! You took her to Fort William, and you said she had kin in Glencoe – never tell me, sir, she was there when – ' he stopped abruptly.

'Yes,' Richard managed to say. 'She was there, but we will not speak of it, if you please.'

And George Ripley, smitten by the contrast between his own happy conclusion and his senior officer's loss, had the tact to pause for a moment or two before turning to regimental matters. No more was said between them of Glencoe but Ripley put himself out in every way he could to help his colonel.

'It would break your heart to see him,' he told Cecily Fletcher. 'He is hiding a great grief. I spoke to his man and got the whole story, but he will not let any of us give him sympathy. Lieutenant Johnstone and I do what we can but 'tis precious little.'

To Richard the only relief was in work and for the next month he rode himself and his men so hard that at night he fell into an exhausted sleep. Only with Otwell and Alison Skinner did he speak of Marged. Their sorrow was very great. Alison wept and said little Richard was lying under the very cover Mistress Stewart had made for him and Otwell sat with Richard over their whisky, saying little, but relying on long standing friendship to bring some comfort.

Richard did not, rather to his relief, see Lord Tarbat who was on his estates, for he did not think he could bear the inevitable questioning, but he did wonder what Tarbat had made of the whole business. His lordship, Otwell told him, having gleaned the information in his usual way, being Highland was determined that a full inquiry should be held, and Richard wrote him, offering his services as a witness should he be required. He had a very civil letter back in which his lordship thanked him for the offer and hoped to have the pleasure of seeing him before he left for Holland.

As it was it was another meeting that proved more emotive and near disastrous. He with Otwell had gone one evening to the Royal coffee house, Otwell trying to persuade him to do normal things instead of sitting alone at his headquarters working until the small hours, for Otwell guessed, and rightly, that quiet sleep was something Richard had not known since the night of the massacre.

They had barely sat down when Richard became aware of a man seated at the other end of the room. His scarlet coat was unbuttoned, his shirt hanging out, his wig askew and he was banging his pewter cup on the table and calling for more wine. He was alone but he was glancing round the room, looking from face to face in an oddly defiant manner.

'My God!' Richard said, 'That's Campbell of Glenlyon! He's the man who carried out the killing in Glencoe.'

He rose, but Otwell caught at his cuff. 'Richard, don't, don't do anything you'll be sorry for. Leave the man be. He's drunk.'

Richard shook off the restraining hand and strode across the room. Leaning over the table he caught Glenlyon by the edges of his coat and literally shook him. 'Damn you!' he said between clenched teeth, 'damn you, I would like to kill you where you sit. Do you sleep at night? Can you? Or do you see the flames and hear the cries of those you slew?'

Glenlyon, stunned by this sudden onslaught and with his senses blurred, nevertheless put up his hands, trying to free himself. 'Let me go, curse you. Who – who are you? Why the d-devil should you c-care?'

'It's enough that you killed men I called my friends.' Richard shook him again. It was as if he was seeing the man through a red mist of rage. 'You bloody murderer!'

Glenlyon, though his head was fuddled, groped towards some understanding. 'I – I know you. You were at the Fort – but you'd been in Glencoe. Let me go-go, you madman. Soldiers obey orders – and I had orders. I'll show you – ' and he fumbled for his pocket.

Richard shook him with such force that he fell back in his seat. 'Show me then.'

Thoroughly shaken and somewhat sobered Glenlyon pulled out a folded piece of paper. 'There – see!'

Richard took it and spreading it out, read:

You are hereby ordered to fall upon the Rebells, the Macdonalds of Glencoe, and putt all to the sword under seventy. You are to have a speciall care that the old ffox and his sones doe upon no account escape your hands. … This is by the Kings speciall command, for the good and safety of the country, that these miscreants be cutt off root and branch … Expecting you will not faill in the fulfilling hereof …

Ro. Duncanson

When he had finished Glenlyon snatched it back and regarded Richard out of bloodshot eyes. There was fear in them and a haunted look. 'I'd do it again,' he shouted to the curious stares of the rest of the men present. 'I'd dirk any man if King William told me to! So should any loyal subject.'

'Liar! Murderer! What soldier is commanded to butcher men in their beds, and women too?'

'No,' Glenlyon gasped as Richard seized him by the collar. 'No – no women but one who ran at my men with a pitchfork.'

'And another,' Richard said. 'You're coming outside with me where I shall kill you but at least it will be with a sword in your hand.' All the suppressed grief of the last weeks found expression in a blaze of rage as he hauled Glenlyon to his feet and began to propel the stumbling drunken officer towards the door.

Otwell, coming as fast as he could on his crutches, cried out, 'Stop! Stop, Richard, for God's sake! You can't do it.'

But even as Richard reached the door Glenlyon collapsed, his head lolling against Richard's shoulder, mouth slackly open.

'He can't hold a sword,' Otwell said and by this time several other gentlemen had come up to them, protesting at the disturbance, the owner of the coffee house asking Richard to take his quarrel elsewhere.

For a moment Richard held the pitiful man on his feet. Then he let him go. Glenlyon hit the floor and the fall brought him to his senses. There he crawled to his knees, holding the leg of a table to try to pull himself up.

Richard looked down at him. The rage receded and gave way to disgust and contempt. He turned on his heel and walked out into the dark street where he stood shuddering and drawing deep steadying breaths.

'Thank God,' Otwell was beside him. 'Richard, I thought you were going to kill him.'

'I meant to,' Richard said. 'I meant to – at least then I would have done something to avenge her.'

'Do you think Marged would've wanted that? Or the consequences for you? And Glenlyon isn't worth killing.'

Richard stood still. Slowly the heat faded from his face. What indeed would she have said to him? In the dark noisome street he conjured up the sound of her voice and tried to think. 'You're right,' he said at last. 'Glenlyon is worth nothing.'

'And whatever he may say of his orders, which can't be denied, didn't you see the fellow's look?' Otwell asked. 'Can't you see he's haunted? He'll be haunted till the day he dies by Glencoe, and his own thoughts will do the work for you.'

In silence they walked up the street to the close where Otwell lived. 'Come in,' he said. 'Come in and have a dram.'

Richard shook his head. 'No, not now, though I thank you for being with me tonight. But for you I don't know what I might've done.'

'It's over,' Otwell said. 'Hate is poison. Let it go, Richard.'

Poison? Perhaps that was what it was. And what would killing a drunken babbling fool like Glenlyon have achieved? Nothing, but to let it out of his system. And as he rode back to Leith Richard felt it begin to drain away. He would now take the right way, try to get something done for the survivers, try to get the perpetrators brought to justice. That was what Marged would want him to do, and as he went down the hill and towards his quarters, for the first time he felt the pain ease a little, as if Marged herself were smiling at him, glad he had not repaid evil with evil.

At last, on a bright May day, almost a year since the King

had given him his orders for Scotland he stood aboard one of two transports with his regiment in good order safely aboard. A fresh wind was billowing out the sails and blowing in his face as he took his last look at Edinburgh, the castle high on its rock and silhouetted against the blue of an early summer morning. A brief year – yet it had brought him everything he could have hoped for, and if he took nothing away at least he knew now that what he had gained, what he had experienced of great love, despite the bitter grief, had made every moment worth the living of it.

*

He found King William in camp outside Namur which he had been besieging in vain since the beginning of this year's campaign and consequently in a gloomy mood. To Richard's annoyance the Master of Stair was there, in a room in a merchant's house that William was using as his headquarters, writing at a table, two clerks busy at another by the window. William sat by the fire which he had ordered to be lit despite the warmth of the day for he felt cold most of the time. Opposite him Colonel van Wyngarde stood leaning against the mantelshelf.

Richard bent low over William's outstretched hand and then greeted his former commanding officer, giving the Master no more than a silent courtesy bow. He reported on the regiment he had the honour to present for the King's service and hoped no awkward questions would be asked.

He was soon disillusioned however for though William graciously agreed to review the men in person in the morning and though he invited Richard to be seated he didn't waste time on trivialities.

'Lincourt, we hear disturbing things of you,' he began without preamble, 'and we are hoping you may be able to dispel some of what has been written to us.'

Richard sat very still in his chair. So there was to be no way out, and he listened as William, picking up a paper read a letter from Sir Thomas Livingstone based on a report by Lieutenant-Colonel Hamilton.

'Well?' William said at last. 'I'm sure you can explain. I've not known you for all these years without being sure there is some misunderstanding here.'

'I think not,' Richard said. 'If I could speak to your Majesty alone, that is except for Colonel van Wyngarde – ' It was pointed but he didn't see he could do otherwise; however it did not seem as if William was prepared to accede to that for though he flicked his fingers at the two clerks who quietly left the room, he did not dismiss Stair.

'These matters concern the Secretary of State for Scotland,' he said, 'and I think Sir John would be as glad as myself to hear what you have to say.'

'Indeed,' Stair agreed coolly. 'It seems, Colonel Lincourt, that you have misused your commission in my country.'

'That, sir, is for his Majesty to judge,' Richard retorted and turned to the King. 'Sire, I did only what you wished.'

William inclined his head. 'Your letters came regularly to my hand, but from the time you reached Fort William your behaviour appears to have verged on the extra-ordinary.'

'Sir,' Richard said in some desperation. 'I carried out your orders. You have had your reports and I've brought you a regiment, slightly lower in numbers than I could have wished, but serviceable. Can we not leave the matter at that?'

'No, I fear we may not,' the King answered. 'I have heard that you had to be detained in your quarters on the night of the business at Glencoe. I will have an explanation of that if you please.'

Richard felt his shoulders sag, a deep depression settling on him. He saw the Master sitting with narrowed eyes and no very pleasant expression on his face, his friend van Wyngarde anxious, the King waiting in some impatience. So, inevitably, he had to tell the story with the exception that he omitted all reference to Marged. He made it appear that he went to the glen in the dark merely because he felt a great debt of gratitude to the inhabitants and wished to see if any were left alive. It sounded plausible, but it smacked of treason, as did the behaviour that made

Hill confine him to his quarters, and there was no masking that. Of his subsequent visit to the pathetic remnants of Clan Iain Abrach he did not feel impelled to speak.

When he had finished William sat bolt upright. 'Lincourt, you astound me. This is the last thing I would have expected of you, who have been one of my most reliable officers. You knew the MacDonalds were to be rooted out, rebels and thieves that they are.'

'Sir, you don't know them,' Richard said desperately. 'MacIain had come in, although late, and was ready to live in peace.'

'We know nothing of that,' Stair said. 'His name was not on the list that came to my hand.'

'But it was,' Richard broke in, 'so Colonel Hill told me, and I was there when MacIain made it clear to his people that he had sworn to keep the King's peace.'

Stair shrugged. 'If he swore, then it was too late and his own fault for being so.'

'But the circumstances – '

'He had four months to decide,' Stair said coldly. 'I'm only sorry any of the vagabonds got away, especially the Chief's sons.'

Richard swung round on him. 'I'm aware, Sir John, that the Dalrymples have always hated the Highlanders, particularly the MacDonalds. In fact you yourself were kind enough to warn me before I left against the very men who showed me nothing but hospitality and care. Tell me, was it yours? The plan to murder them in their beds?'

'Lincourt!' van Wyngarde broke in hastily. 'Pray watch what you say.'

'I want to know,' Richard said. What use caution now? 'Tell me, Master, did it come from your pen?'

'I do not bother myself with details of how orders are carried out.' Dalrymple's voice was cold and passionless. 'Sir Thomas Livingstone had his and passed them on in whatever form he wished to Colonel Hill.'

'To be "secret and sudden". Yes, I know,' Richard retorted. 'But someone thought of the foul and treacherous method that was used. Did you know, sir,' he turned to the King, 'that the men of Argyll's regiment stayed two weeks as guests of the MacDonalds, eating their bread, and then, abusing every law of hospitality, turned on them in the night and put them to the sword.'

'We have heard the report.' William's tone was equally cold. 'It seems you are in a great heat about a parcel of rogues who have plagued honest folk for too many years. It is unfortunate that you should have been forced to spend some weeks in the place and had your judgement warped by the setting of your leg and a bed to lie on, but that doesn't alter what the MacDonalds have been.'

'I'll not deny they've broken the law many times, but they didn't deserve this – this butchery. For God's sake, sir, tell me you didn't know, though I'm aware you signed the order, exactly how it was going to be done.'

William was growing angry. 'I signed an order for a tribe of rebels to be extirpated, turned out of that glen and put to the sword if they resisted. The interpretation of the order is not my affair. I cannot be called to account for every detail of government in my kingdom.'

'I want to believe, sir, it was not on your direct instructions that murder was carried out in so dreadful a form,' Richard persisted and Stair leaned back in his chair to look at him with cold curiosity.

'You are turning soft, Colonel Lincourt. A harsh lesson had to be administered in the Highlands to bring the rest to heel, and I believe as it turns out the action was justified for the rest of those stubborn Highland chiefs have come in to swear.'

'A harsh lesson has achieved that, I agree,' Colonel van Wyngarde said uneasily, 'but I would also like to know who devised the exact method which seems to me not worthy of men who wear the King's uniform.'

'It is really irrelevant,' the Master said. 'If the orders were exceeded it was no more than the rebels deserved and I'm glad there's an end of them. The details of the matter and the author of the plan are of no interest to his Majesty.'

'There are plenty of candidates,' Richard retorted, 'from Glenlyon, though I think he's too poor a creature to have thought of it, to Colonel Hamilton and upwards – but

I'm ready to believe it was he who exceeded his orders. I can only thank God that at least some of the MacDonalds, including the new chief whom I call my friend, escaped in the blizzard that night. One might be pardoned for thinking, as they do, that God Himself came to their aid with that storm.'

There was a sudden silence in the room. William sat up abruptly and began to cough. Colonel van Wyngarde fetched a glass of his cordial and he managed to drink some of it, the paroxysm subsiding. Stair looked oddly satisfied, as if he had been expecting Richard Lincourt, if given enough rope, to hang himself.

Richard, aware of what he had done, sat silent, unrepentant for now at least the matter was in the open. 'Furthermore,' he added, seeing he had nothing further to lose, 'I wish to ask your Majesty for a full inquiry into the whole matter that blame may be properly apportioned.'

Van Wyngarde gave a gasp and William said in a voice of ice, 'Lincourt, I think you have indeed taken leave of your senses. And if you went to Glencoe to aid the survivors, then you no longer deserve to wear my uniform. That there were none left to aid does not exonerate you.'

Richard rose. This had, he supposed, been inevitable ever since that night in Fort William when he had been confined to his quarters. 'Sir, I have served you for twelve years and regret not one moment of that time, and now I've brought you a fine regiment as you ordered, which I shall leave with regret, but I see I have no alternative but to tender my resignation. I will send it in writing in the correct manner tomorrow.'

'I believe Colonel Lincourt should face a court martial for his behaviour,' Stair said sharply, but William turned on him.

'I had not asked for your opinion. Lincourt, for the sake of the years you've been with me and, I thought, my friend, I'll not take any proceedings against you, treasonable though some of your actions may have been. But I think it is best that you leave my camp tomorrow.'

Richard rose. William did not hold out his hand nor did Richard attempt to kiss it. He bowed and withdrew, his military career in ruins, his regiment that he had raised with such care without a commander, the service he had loved barred to him. Outside he stood leaning against a wall, trying to think what to do next.

A moment later Colonel van Wyngarde came out and seeing him came over to him and said, 'Richard, I'm extremely sorry that everything should end like this for you. But in honesty I can only say you have no one but yourself to blame. Some of your actions have been – quite extraordinary. If you wish however I'll speak to the King later when he's had time to think things over, ask him to reinstate you.'

'Thank you, sir, but I think not.' Richard roused himself. 'It isn't clear to me who is to blame for the tragedy of Glencoe but I can't consider the Master clear of it and the King did sign the original order. Obviously I can't stay as I've been before so I must go.'

'Then I'm sorry,' van Wyngarde said again, 'doubly so as another man will have to take on Lincourt's regiment.'

It was that that hurt most, Richard thought, as he later ordered John Robb to pack their baggage and prepare to return to England.

In the morning he called his officers together and told them that owing to circumstances he could not confide to them he had resigned his commission and would be leaving them at once. He saw blank astonishment on their faces, disbelief and then a variety of reactions. He shook each one by the hand with a warmth he had never shown them before – Ripley first, less inarticulate than he used to be, with no thought for his possible promotion, only a regret for the loss of a commander and a friend he respected; then Johnstone who said, 'I'll never forget what you've taught me, sir,' and his face was pink with the effort to keep his emotion repressed.

Two officers who had come from Holland with Richard had tears in their eyes and young Ensign Fuller, remembering that fateful ride to Glencoe, was weeping openly. He burst out, 'It's a shame. If they only knew the truth,' but he encountered a look from Richard and bit back the dangerous words.

Taken aback by the depth of their feeling for him and even by his own for them, Richard brought the meeting to an end by calling for the men to be assembled. Then he rode out in front of them for the last time. William had sent a message that he would not review the regiment until a new colonel had been appointed, an action Richard could not but regard as a piece of spite, for he had after all done the work and he would not before have thought William capable of such a reaction. But it was all part of the souring of their relationship.

He rode the length of the ranks and saw the upturned faces, Sergeant Morrison's expressing incredulity, Corporal Sinclair's mouth open and his face reddening, all the men showing what they felt when the sergeant raised a cheer for their departing leader. He might have been a hard commander at times, but they had soon learned that he was fair and just and they honoured him for it, cheering lustily.

Richard let his gaze wander over them, looking at the men who had come to him in twos and threes, now smart and efficient soldiers, and he turned away with their voices echoing in his ears, raising his hat to them as he went and knowing that despite all that had happened he did not want to leave the army or the regiment he had raised with such care.

*

London was in the grip of an early heatwave when he returned and he found his lodgings like an oven. For a few days he stayed there, trying to decide what to do with the wreckage of his life. What was there to do but go to Heronslea and try to live like a country squire, to interest himself in the estate, in things like cattle and crops and tenant farmers. But the great house would be empty and it was a bleak prospect.

At last after nearly two weeks of struggling with waves of grief and despair, his longing for Marged so great that he even contemplated using his pistol on himself, he pulled himself together and went out to face his mother and his family.

At her house he was told that she was out with Sir Walter but would be back for dinner, so he wandered into the parlour and there, to his surprise, found Judith. She looked up when he came in, receiving a shock as she saw who it was, a little colour running up under her fair skin at the sheer surprise of it, for she had thought him in Holland. She gave him her hand but the words of welcome died on her lips as she looked up at him. Outwardly perhaps he had little changed, though he was thinner, but she saw so great an inward change, reflected in his eyes, the new lines on his face, that she could not keep back the words she knew he didn't wish to be said.

'Richard! Oh my dear, my dear, I'm so sorry.'

'Don't,' he said. 'Judith for the love of God, don't! I can't bear pity and I don't want to talk of it.'

She took both his hands and drew him down to sit beside her. With sudden sure knowledge of what he needed she said, 'No, not to your mother, nor anyone else in the family, they would ask too much, but to me, Richard – you've always been able to talk to me. Don't you see that it might ease you? You told us so little and I would like to understand. It's not pity, you know.'

He stared out of the window. London was just the same, horsemen passing to and from the city, crowds of walkers all busily hurrying along, beggars and street urchins importuning people, just as life was in Edinburgh and any other city. Nothing had changed. He had been gone a year, lived through heaven and hell, and now back again London was uncaringly about its business. He had not, from that moment when Iain Dubh struck him, said one word of his sufferings, either to the faithful Robb, or even to Otwell. Would it not be a relief to tell Judith the whole story? He looked at her, seeing in her face compassion and more than that and he reached blindly for her hand. Then he told her, in short clipped phrases, the simple bare facts, but once he had begun keeping nothing back.

Judith listened without speaking, without asking him any importunate questions, and at the end he knew she was weeping. For a while they sat in silence. Judith found a handkerchief and wiped away the tears.

At last she said, 'What can I say to you, Richard? It's a terrible story. How wicked, wicked people can be – the Master, Breadalbane, Argyll – even the King. What will you do now?'

He gave a heavy sigh. 'I wish I knew. Soldiering's been my life since I was seventeen. I suppose I'll go to Heronslea.' But as he leaned back to rest his head against the back of the settle on which they were sitting he felt a curious sense of relief. The telling of the story, painful as it had been, stirring all his emotions, his love, his grief, his anger, had somehow relieved him. He said at last, 'What do you think I should do?'

Judith looked down at her hand still in his. 'I think you should go to Heronslea. Old Sir Joseph Harrison won't stand for Parliament again, why don't you take his place? Then you could try to do something for the people in Scotland for whom I can see you care so much.'

He stared at her. 'Judith, you're a wonder! That's what I'll do. At least in Parliament perhaps I can get justice for them. But that house – it's so damnably big and empty.'

Judith thought of Heronslea and had a vision of fair-haired children playing on the deserted lawns, a vision she had repressed so often that it had retreated into the hinterland of dead dreams. Calmly, though inwardly dreading an answer that would finally wreck all those dreams, she said, 'Then I think you should marry me.'

He gave a gasp of utter astonishment and she went on, 'Oh I know, my dear, that you don't love me, but I also know what is at the back of your mind – that you can't abide the thought of the loneliness of the place, of long empty years.'

'It's true,' he murmured. 'You have always been very perceptive, Judith.'

'Of course,' she answered. 'You see I've always loved you. Even when they made us separate and you went away, young as I was that didn't change.'

'But,' he said in amazement, 'you've made it clear, many times, that however much my mother wanted the match that it was no longer to your taste.'

'Oh no.' She shook her head. 'It was just that I was not

going to have you co-erced into it. I refused to let you think I was considering it until the day came when you needed me as I hoped, I believed it might. Only I never thought it would be like this. I'm not saying this out of pity or even sympathy which I know you don't want, but so that you will know there is someone near you who cares enough to help you bear it all.'

He was silent, looking at her helplessly. Then he said, 'But, Judith, I've nothing to offer you. Oh, materially, yes, every comfort you could need, but of myself, nothing. All that was best in me, all that made me alive, died in Glencoe and lies buried there on a small lonely island. What's left is a mere husk of a man.'

'I know you think that now,' she agreed gently. 'but, dearest Richard, time will help you. And if I may venture to say this, I believe she would tell you, as I do, that it will not be good for you to be alone.'

He looked out of the window again for a long time. At last he said, 'I've thought and thought about the solitary years at Heronslea and it's not bearable. I think after a month I might want to blow my brains out.' He managed a faint smile.

'Then we will be married as soon as it is suitable.'

'It – forgive me – seems like a betrayal.'

'No,' she said, 'I don't think it is. It's for your comfort, to make life livable again for you. I don't ask anything of you, Richard, more than you wish to give – until you wish to give; only to be your companion, to be there for the bad moments.'

'You would do that for me?'

'Oh yes,' she said simply.

He gave a long tired sigh and for a moment closed his eyes. Beloved, he thought, and saw Marged's face as it had been when in answer to his declaration she had said that she too knew her own heart. And with that came a flood of other memories – Marged on horseback, the wind blowing the orange plumes in her hat, laughing across at him; the ride to Craigieduir and the ecstasy of those two nights; the moment by the loch, watching the lights in the night sky; arriving in Glencoe and being greeted by John; Marged's pride in her people, incorrigible in many ways yet producing men of the calibre of MacIain and John himself; and the last and most tender memory of Marged lying white and still in his arms, the laying of her in his cloak in her grave of stones.

Glencoe was far away now from this London room yet it would be with him till he died, haunting him, as it would haunt Robert Campbell of Glenlyon, yet in a way for which perhaps he would one day thank God. But could he live with the best and the worst of these memories if he had only his own solitary company, for in a moment of enlightenment he saw that he was now vulnerable in a way he had never been before Marged came into his life, pouring into it her own vibrant life and love?

And then, unbidden, out of the memories came one, stronger than the rest: John's words as he rode away, '*Beannachd leat.*' They seemed to lie on him once again, holding out that familiar blessing and with it a promise of peace.

He opened his eyes and looked at Judith. Was she to be the bearer of it? Would it be wrong to take this shred of hope, to accept what she offered? Her very qualities of kindess and tact and a natural restfulness in her very attitude at this moment drew him. It hardly seemed fair to her, but it was, miraculously, her choice.

Slowly he lifted her hand and put it to his lips. 'You deserve better, but if you will take what is left of me – '

He would never, Judith suspected, love again as he had loved the Highland woman, but her own love, surely, would suffice for them both to make a future together after all that he had endured?

Calm though she appeared at this moment, judging rightly it was the only attitude he could accept, Judith longed inwardly to take him in her arms, to kiss the sorrow from his face, to draw his head down on to her shoulder, but being a wise person she did none of these things but sat quietly beside him. His hand remained in hers and with that she was content.

Historical Note

It was not until August that Colonel Hill finally succeeded in gaining permission for John MacDonald to take the remnants of Clan Iain Abrach back to Glencoe to rebuild their homes and their broken lives. An inquiry into the massacre was eventually held by public demand in 1695, at which John and Sandy and other MacDonalds gave evidence, but none of the perpetrators was there. Colonel Hamilton had fled to Ireland and refused to return. Glenlyon, Drummond, Lindsay and Barber were to be summoned home but as the Argyll regiment had ignominiously surrendered to the French none of them appeared. It was agreed that a great injustice had been done, but though John claimed compensation for the loss of their homes, money, goods and livestock, none was ever paid to him or his people. That they managed to survive and flourish again was a tribute to their courage and perseverence. The little boy, Alasdair, carried from the scene of the massacre by his nurse, lived to lead his clan on the battlefield of Culloden in 1745. As late as 1777 he was still alive and living in Glencoe.